Kelly, Piet and Company

Bubbles and ballast

A description of life in Paris during the brilliant days of the empire.

Kelly, Piet and Company

Bubbles and ballast
A description of life in Paris during the brilliant days of the empire.

ISBN/EAN: 9783741176258

Manufactured in Europe, USA, Canada, Australia, Japa

Cover: Foto ©Andreas Hilbeck / pixelio.de

Manufactured and distributed by brebook publishing software
(www.brebook.com)

Kelly, Piet and Company

Bubbles and ballast

BUBBLES AND BALLAST.

BEING A DESCRIPTION OF

Life in Paris during the Brilliant Days of Empire;

A TOUR THROUGH

BELGIUM AND HOLLAND,

and a *Sojourn in London.*

By A LADY.

BALTIMORE:

KELLY, PIET AND COMPANY,

174 and 176 Baltimore Street.

1871.

CONTENTS.

CHAPTER IV.

CHAPTER V.

CHAPTER VI.

CHAPTER VII.

CHAPTER VIII.

CHAPTER IX.

CHAPTER X.

CHAPTER XI.

CHAPTER XII.

CHAPTER XIII.

CHAPTER XVII.

CHAPTER XVIII.

CHAPTER XIX.

CHAPTER XX.

CHAPTER XXI.

PREFACE.

----o----

These pages, dedicated in love and gratitude to my mother, and originally destined for her eye alone, are—at the solicitation of friends—offered to the public with no other ambition than that they may serve to while away a dull hour or two. As life is half made up of baubles, I have mingled some of them with things of solid worth. Does not the sea-weed dwell with the pearl?

M. E. P. B.

Washington City, May 1, 1871.

BUBBLES AND BALLAST.

CHAPTER I.

ROYAL MAIL STEAMSHIP JAVA.

October 9, 1867.

THIS morning I left the Tremont House, Boston, to embark for Europe, with heart pulsating to the emotions of hope and fear; but amid the confusion and excitement on board the *Java*, bore up bravely when the time arrived for taking leave of my family escort. The English flag was given to the breeze, anchors were weighed, guns fired, and down the harbor we steamed to the bar, where there was a detention of several hours. Precisely at meridian the ship was finally off, and our strained eyes following the receding tugboat caught the last waving of handkerchiefs. As we stood upon the deck with what were our hearts most burdened, and who would have laid bare for perusal the thousand emotions that filled them? Were there not visions prospective and retrospective of home—of the peaceful green land about to be exchanged for the dark, troubled sea? and did there not come from the depths of those

B

hearts the murmuring undertone ? We are going—we are coming. God be with you and with us ! Sad indeed are the feelings of the traveler on his first voyage, as a city's greatness fades away and the last streak of land disappears; and among the many partings that occur in life, and answering to every description, from the simple every-day farewell to the one heavily fraught with danger, none is more impressive than the embarkment of a beloved object upon that vast eternity—the ocean—which stretches far away beyond the limits of sight, and with strange and unequaled power holds its own dominion, making earth seem a mere atom at its mercy. Thus, to that uncertain power friends are given up, and the *good-bye* uttered in sadness lingers on the fitful breeze, mingles in the music of the wave, follows the ship in its trackless course, sounding the echo of something sweet from the distant land—the last words of loved ones ! The early morning mist that had hung over Boston and spangled her shores (perhaps in sympathy with bedewed eyes) had risen like a vail and gone to meet the sun, whose glorious rays were beginning to flush sky and water. Out of that *embrace* came cheerful light, and as *ours* with friends was ended, smiles took the place of tears. Thanks for the bright sunbeam that penetrates the mist and gloom of nature, and forces its way into darkened hearts ! Thanks also for man's ingenuity, that fashions such ships as this to resist the storms of ocean ! A fine breeze set in with our sailing, and our company at once indulged with zest in a promenade on the hurricane deck. Fellow-passengers should

fraternize at the start, forming, as they do, a little world
of themselves, in which dependence is ever strongly felt.
So I thought on finding that a perfect stranger was to
share my stateroom, and the conviction is fast strengthened upon discovering the intelligence and amiable qualities of Miss Tracy, of New York. I crave at the out-
set some special indulgence in the mention of names, and
should I at any time endeavor to throw a web of interest
around them, I hope for pardon, at least from those who
yield gracefully to Mother Eve's weakness. On ship-
board it seems that every one has individuality, and a
name that has never known fame, or has worn a stain, is
washed by sea-brine into some notoriety, if for no other
reason than that all are travelers on the *high* sea, and
may never be tossed so *high* again. Mr. Valentine
cannot elude a distinguished mention, presiding over
bank treasures in the great London, and serving as United States Commissioner to the Paris Exposition. The
jovial face of Captain Moodie gives an air of cheerfulness to the ship, and his officers are handsome men of
the English type, wearing the naval uniform. It is indeed refreshing to see the ruddy hue of health that glows
on their cheeks, and we do not wonder that many
enthusiastically exclaim, "The life of the sailor for me!"
There must be something glorious in the bounding wave,
the showering spray, and the pranks of old Boreas!
The stewardess, not an unimportant character to those
who succumb to *mal de mer*, already engages my regard,
for in counting the days to be passed aboard ship, coming
evils suggest themselves, and I therefore appreciate the

necessity of providing a friend for adversity. ⸳ Our dinner-meal to-day gathered together all the passengers.

It is said that the first day out affords the Captain, perhaps, his only opportunity to inspect all the human freight; for often the vessel that leaves a dock teeming with life and good health, presents a few hours later the appearance of a hospital, whose yellow flag might well supersede the pennon at the mast-head.

Thus far we have not become wretched beings deploring existence, but are respectable in looks, having stomachs worthy of insurance. All are in a mood to enjoy seats on the upper deck, and to watch the sun go down to his evening rest. I shall go to mine with prayer upon my lips, God forgive me, if more earnest than it should be always!

October 10.—"Bright and beautiful,—how favored!" was the exclamation upon nearly every lip to-day. Several timid women, however, commented upon the freshness of the wind and the rise of the waves, wondering if the ocean could hold still greater terrors in reserve; but their fears were laughed at by a mischievous old tar, who said, "Wait, ladies, until you get into the trough of the sea, and then you will see something to be frightened at." A friend handed me the latest New York *Herald* with its interesting items, social and political, all of which were eagerly perused to the exclusion of maritime intelligence. Then came a peep at the pictures of my family album! Should we not bless that wonderful art, which preserves to us the images of cherished ones; for although the heart may hold its revel of memory, and delight in the love it bears for the absent, the eye finds greater joy in tracing in the silent and inanimate counterfeit, features familiar and well-beloved? We watched from time to time a little bird that had followed us from Boston, hovering about the bow of the ship, and chirping and trilling as if it momentarily expected the man on the lookout to announce green fields, trees and flowers.

As the first streak of land (Halifax) appeared on the horizon, it stretched its pinions for flight, bestowing a few farewell notes, and we were not long in following the little wanderer to shore. The light-house signals were responded to at the distance of three miles, by the hoisting of four streamers that spelled our name. Before reaching the harbor the saloon filled up rapidly with passengers bearing writing implements, all anxious to send off letters to family and friends. In my instance, either the hurried and close application to paper or the downward inclination of head occasioned a sudden qualm, the prolongation of which might have resulted in a calamity unworthy of a passenger within sight of land; and I therefore sought the deck, to enjoy not only the air and sunshine, but a view of the town. Watches were drawn from many a snug vest-pocket and tiny waist, to note the happy hour which would grant a short respite; and it was half-past two, P. M., when the boom of a gun announced the arrival of the *Java*. The *coup d'œil* gave a nautical world in the hundreds of mast-heads that crowded the shore, and in the numerous

B*

schooners, sloops and brigs anchored out, all of which lay, as it were, in quiet submission to a black, frowning *monitor*, said to have been purchased of the United States by the French Government for the sum of one million of dollars. The mention of so much money pleased our ears far more than did the *iron-clad* our eyes; for, nearly hidden by the water, it appeared truly insignificant. However, in our late war-service this may have been "stooping to conquer," and if it crosses the turbulent Atlantic in safety, France will have made a good bargain, whilst her navy will be a match for that of any of her hostile neighbors. What a bustling interest the arrival of our steamer occasioned! The greeting of citizens and soldiers to us strangers awakened the feeling that we are all brethren making the voyage of life—toiling together, and hoping to reach at last the strand of the "spirit-land."

Having found a substantial footing on shore, our party, to avoid the fatiguing ascent of the high hill, secured a carriage. It may have been done on the selfish "double-quick," as vehicles were few and persons many; but this consideration for self and comfort enabled us to see more of the town, which wore an aspect decidedly foreign, its garrisons bearing evidence of Britannia's rule. The attractions were few, yet some boast could be made of several massive buildings, and a superb height, crowned by a fort—the towering glory of the place, with its sloping sides in emerald green. One sad spectacle met our gaze—the funeral of a British soldier. The hearse, with its heavy black drapery and mournful plumes, was followed by comrades clad in gray, whose slow measured steps accorded perfectly with the solemn music. The notes of the funeral march died upon our ears as we returned to the ship, which seemed more of a resting-place or more like home than the land, for the reason that we were destined to belong to it for some time.

Our dinner, as we lay at dock, was gotten up in good style, with an abundance of fine fruits and other delicacies, that were happily enjoyed, there being no jostling of elbows from "sudden swells" and "shipping seas." How trying must be those moments when mermaids and sea-nymphs raise aloft their arms and toss the vessel— when crockery dances about as if in the hands of a juggler—when a chosen morsel of food which was expected to lodge beyond the *ivories* tumbles into an adjoining plate, and a glass of wine (*la première qualité*) empties itself as readily into a pocket as down that convenient and fit receptacle—MAN's throat! An old fellow on the opposite side of the table was heard to give this homely yet wholesome advice to his wife, who seemed to have no appetite: "It is well, my dear, to lay in, because after awhile you can 't eat." And he practiced what he preached, as was shown in the quantities of food that disappeared from various dishes around. He soon exhausted the bill of fare, and, like Oliver Twist, asked for more. Some parties, perhaps stimulated by the old man's logic, lingered at table; others left to indulge in the last steady promenade on deck.

The passenger-list having been largely added to at

Halifax, many persons came on board to bid farewell to friends, and there remained until the busy stir of sailors and the tolling bell gave warning that they must "be off." It was seven P. M. when the Captain's form appeared on the little bridge that spans the hurricane deck. The officers, too, were at their posts; and the cries of "Steady!" and "Port!" came shortly afterwards, as the ship steamed out of the harbor. One long, lingering look we gave to Halifax, and an oft-repeated *good-bye* to the land.

October 11.—In peace we have slumbered the second night of the voyage, rocked by the lullaby of the wind, and cradled in just as small space as in the days of innocent infancy. Now, fast in old ocean's grip, our ship is played with as if it were a cork or trap-ball bounding to and fro from aquatic walls. Like giant-arms the encircling billows stretch out, to make us feel our dependence on that God who ruleth over land and sea, and whose commanding voice has stilled the tempest and the waves—"Thus far shalt thou go, and no further!"

At mid-day, reclining upon comfortable blankets, spread upon the deck in Oriental style, and quite luxurious, we saw on the tossing waves a lonely little boat, struggling, as it were, in its solitude to get beyond our sight. It held nothing human, and there was naught to tell its story! Perhaps the life that animated it some hours before had gone out through despair in the darkness of the night; had been engulphed in the waves whose eternal motion we were watching. If so, may a heavenly morrow in light and joy anchor the soul in that *Port* beyond the storms of ocean, and where all earthly buffetings cease!

* * * * This afternoon affords an opportunity of making a sketch of some of the passengers; and of the mortal ken around there is a sufficient variety to form an interesting group. Foremost is a young and beautiful girl, with face and form that would eclipse the Venus of the Sea, and entitle its owner to be the heroine of a charming romance. On this occasion, however, the pen is likely to describe an ugly, awkward movement from the motion of the boat, and the writer would prefer to glorify such an object elsewhere than on top of the crested wave. How pleasingly could be woven a tale of a flower-wreathed bark, with a guiding spirit at the helm, who would condescend to say to some poor, struggling mortal in the cold waters of "single wretchedness:" "Enter in, and I will lead you to a haven of happiness even more desirable than the Liverpool dock!" But the idea is at once destroyed of manufacturing a love-history with an agreeable and happy result, as this same lovely creature wears the love-light in her eye for a cavalier on one side of the deck, and brightens anew to another on the opposite side. Oh, woman! coquetry is power, and it is yours to wield in gentle use, or stern abuse. What a dangerous weapon in your soft, fair hand; for whilst its blade flashes over many a trusting heart, it does the work of magnetizing the surface, if not of inflicting by a bold thrust a wound that no surgeon's skill

can heal!   We wonder if our bewitching beauty counts
the hearts seared out or consumed by the inflammable
torch of bright eyes, or if she stops in the march of conquest to sigh over those who have fallen by the cold
steel of her indifference.   We do not regret that she has
attracted *England* at the bow of the boat, and brought
him to his knees, thus making him forget the usual stiff,
conventional salute; but we are grateful that, from love
of country, she has raised *America* to a more elevated
position.

Seated upon a high coil of rope, our countryman looks
to the uppermost rigging of the ship, thinking, perhaps,
that he would be willing to scale the very clouds for her
sake.   Still another vassal to her will, holds a goblet
containing the *champagne* remedy, with this thought
expressed on his countenance, "What if she should be
sea-sick!"   Yet, who will not acknowledge that Beauty
deserves a long train of admirers, and in this instance,
who would not worship very near, and follow the *white
plume*, just as lovingly as the breeze that plays in and
about its soft down?   In contrast with the graceful girlish figure is a jolly little man, hugely corpulent, but the
personification of good humor.   He goes about distributing kind words generally, and is like light in a dark
place.   I, too, would think his company desirable, but
for the narrative he has just poured into my ear of a
dreadful shipwreck that occurred not long since, and
where only a trifling number were saved. Can he know
that his subject is ill chosen, and calculated to affect the
beatings of my heart?   Yet, if we were really in danger,

this comfortable looking individual (provided he would keep silent) might lessen much of the chill of fear. There stand a newly married couple, young and handsome, who excite a whispered comment of praise ; a small group of missionary divines with their wives, bound for the East, in the sacred calling of " Soldiers of the Cross ;" a few British officers, wearing scarlet coats, to enliven the scene ; a chatty and agreeable widow, rich in diamonds, and her maid (a Scotch lassie, very pretentious), wearing a trained robe and a basquine trimmed *à la Huzzar;* a theological student of more than ordinary erudition, whose fund is drawn upon daily without danger of exhaustion, and several gentlemen bearing the *Cunard* name, a distinction at once acknowledged, from the high favor in which this line of steamers is held. There is also an aged lady, whose mild benevolent countenance is lighted up with intelligence. She is the sister of one of our most celebrated historians. Little children fill up the background, lovely, sweet and engaging voyagers, among those whose locks have gathered the hoarfrost of many winters.

October 12.—Last evening six or seven of us seated ourselves *à la Turque* on deck to make jolly the hour with song and anecdote. There was an abundant indulgence in conundrums, one being, " Why is Andrew Johnson like the rudder of our ship?" " Because he steers well amid opposing elements!" If our inclinations had been consulted, we would not have heeded the last strokes of the bell, which sent us away from the

beautiful moonlight to the dimly lighted cabins below.
Eleven o'clock is the latest hour permitted the passengers to prepare for rest, as after that an Erebus darkness
prevails.   Even poor little Cinderella was allowed more
time to reach her ash-barrel couch ! Shoes have dropped
from our feet in the same haste as the little glass slipper
fell from hers; yet, after all, rigid regulations must not
be complained of, the caution observed, and the vigilant
watch on board these steamers being most commendable.
Every voice should join in a stentorian huzzah for England's protecting care on the sea.

Nothing of interest occurred to-day, except that the
waves grew higher ; the sky became overcast, and several showers of rain baptized us.   It is noticeable that
some of the company no longer preserve a steady step,
and that the bounding motion of the ship conduces to
Terpsichorean feats, regardless of music or will.   May
not my qualmy feelings be the precursor of a state of
wretchedness, and dreary times below with stewardess
as friend ? * * * * *   At the hour of 5 P. M., cosily
tucked in on deck under a huge Buffalo robe, and with
eyes and thoughts directed upward as far as possible
from the horrid water, I feel just in the humor to hate
the sea-gods, and all else appertaining to the ocean.   Not
even " wild music from fluted conchs " can pacify me !
The wind is blowing fresh, and the sailors are at work
in the rigging.   Their peculiar song or cry attracts
attention, and we wonder if they can be really happy.
Surely they are creatures of duty ; and may the honest
old tar who sees most of storm in this world find a
greeting of sunshine and calm in the next !

October 16.—Oh! ye days unchronicled! If ye had been put down I would blot ye out with briny tears. Sea-sickness! monstrous malady which, once begun, seems never-ending! Down in the cabin, prostrate, with eyes closed and mouth open, quite willing to be swallowed by Jonah's whale or to get rid of life by any means—obliged to be patient, though bumped every moment and bruised at every angle—scorning food, only to aggravate the feeling of "*goneness*"—wondering why ships were ever made, or why Europe turned a *Circe* to lure one through a whirlpool of distress, to wreck both stomach and brain, leaving scarcely a heart to love with or a soul to pray from! The question arises, why should we be thus punished in our seafaring life, and be denied a further enjoyment of the broad expanse of ocean, with skies to meet its outskirts? Truly its grandeur finds no expression in words—a wrapt emotion alone, paying silent tribute to the great Creator! Alas! that enfeebled frames and a lack of vitality compel us to remain in our state-rooms, which are like the "black hole of Calcutta," the only ray of light being the cheering presence of friends, who report upon what is passing above. Their words of encouragement do not go amiss, and the grapes and peaches they bring save us from utter starvation. Think of a person who has paid his passage-money, a solid lump of $150 in *ore*, (especially in these days of our depreciated currency), being obliged to call himself throughout the voyage a *starved beggar*—an epithet indeed appropriate, for he would like to feed his

c

stomach, but dares not; and although it spurns food, it is still hungry enough to beg. The tortures of *Tantalus* are fully realized by a sea-sick passenger on a Cunard steamer, the fare being of a quality to satisfy a fastidious gastronomist.

I heard that a large schooner last night shot across and barely missed our bowsprit. What dangers thread our course! But God was with us! Why prate, then, of trials and suffering, after such an evidence of divine protection? Thus far we have passed only one steamer, which we signaled with rockets. The sea last evening, roughened by wind and rain, was said to have presented the appearance of a thousand cataracts. The waves were mingling together in appalling sound like heavy thunder, and extending their might and wrath against the vessel. Church service was conducted in the saloon on Sunday, but the impressive scene was lost to me!

October 17.—The *Java* is making fifteen knots an hour, and promises one of the quickest passages on record —joyful tidings for the invalids who have barely strength to crawl up on deck. As we near "old Erin's" shores our hearts beat lighter and happier. Sterile as the rock-bound coast appears, there is a wild beauty about it, so solitary and sea-girt, with only the gulls for company. It is the St. Helena of my imagination! The eye cannot discern a single human being; and even should there be one, the lonely dreariness of the place would make a Napoleonic spirit fret itself away with

only the sound of the sighing winds and the surging
tide.   Tennyson's lines are brought to mind :

> " Break, break, break,
> On thy cold gray stones, oh sea !
> And I would that my tongue could utter
> The thoughts that arise in me.
>
> * * * * * *
>
> " Break, break, break,
> At the foot of thy crags, oh sea !
> But the tender grace of a day that is dead
> Will never come back to me."

These moments, fraught with the bright anticipation
of soon reaching land, can never be dead to memory :
and although Tennyson's verse is ever sweet, still other
poets we choose to greet.   Now, under the inspiration of
Byron's health-bumper to Moore, we propose to drink
to "ould Ireland" with whatever is good; so on with
the champagne, sherry and moselle !

October 18.—Last evening brought us within sight of
Queenstown, and we hove to at a distance of two miles
from her dim showing of lights.   Soon came the tugboat
to bear off the mails and passengers; but whilst the sea
appeared calm, her treachery was at work beneath the fair
surface.   Lashed to our bulwark of strength with stout
cables, the tug meant to be faithful in her embrace, but
she was torn from us ruthlessly, angrily, defiantly.   At
such a juncture, of what avail was the voice of man ?
What were ropes, timber or anything in the face of that
dread element which once destroyed the world ?   Standing upon the deck, we felt our security, but trembled

for the fate of the tug, which seemed to be dashing herself to pieces against the staunch sides of the *Java*. Twice was she thrust away, and bore up again in shattered garb, as if determined to conquer tide and swell. Several sailors, dispirited and exhausted, fell at the top of the gang-plank from the laborious work of winding the windlass, and others pressed on with haste to lay down their burden of heavy mail bags. One narrowly escaped a dip in old ocean, and but for the timely assistance of the first officer would have lessened the number of the crew. Captain Moodie firmly interdicted the transfer of passengers in the face of such danger; and the boom of our guns as the ship moved on seemed like a wail across the waters, or the sound of rolling drums beating a last farewell to the poor little boat. Still trusting that she might reach her haven, we left the mist and rain above, and repaired to the saloon to discuss broiled ham and Welsh rare-bit.

This morning the sun shone brightly, and the cheering prospect of a speedy landing brightened many a face that a day or two since was wrinkled and sour, peevish and sallow. The waters of St. George's Channel, so placid and calm, wore an emerald tint far removed from the deep blue and gray of the bounding billow; and the spirit of animation was indeed abroad, the ships coming on one by one bearing grateful signs of life that had long been denied our sight. I myself began to feel that through whatever clouds or darkness I had passed, the "Star of Hope" had not been lost: may it irradiate all my future wanderings! A double meal in lunch and dinner was served in the saloon, and the steward's kind hand had deposited at my plate a delicious bunch of grapes—doubtless the last of his stock. Many were the eyes that envied me its possession! Some of the company quaffed a parting bumper to the *Java.*—Long may she float a monarch ship of the sea, and bear her living freight in safety to every port! The last thing to be done was to make a visit to our state-rooms to reward the services of the faithful stewardess. Upon returning to the deck, the Liverpool docks—pronounced to be the finest in the world—were in sight, stretching away in one continuous line of six miles; and the scene presented was truly beautiful, in the hundreds of white sails and tiny row-boats that studded the Mersey. Shortly after, when the machinery of our ship ceased its motion, the joy that animated our hearts was in a measure like that of Columbus' sailors when they cried "Land! land!" Thousands of miles had been traversed in a little less than nine days, and one country had been exchanged for another.

The tug brought up the Custom House officers in large numbers, besides friends and relatives of the passengers. Many a joyful meeting was looked upon by some of us in silent sympathy, as our greeting with absent ones could only be through the medium of fond thought and remembrance. Upon the lower deck the luggage of a hundred and thirty-nine passengers was deposited, and the officers in their mock inspections made us exclaim, "What a farce!" I handed over my keys, satisfied there would be a short and neat rum-

C*

maging, very glad that no woman's curiosity and eager search were to be encountered. Several hours were consumed in the transfer to the tug of trunks, boxes, and what-not, all of which were watched impatiently, impressing us with the thought that our belongings were of more importance than ourselves. As the last piece disappeared, I found myself the nearest passenger to the gang-plank—a steep inclined plane which threatened to slide me as unceremoniously as it had done the luggage. The descent, however, was safely made, first officer Brown standing at the head, and second officer Webster coming up half way to proffer aid—who knows but that a hand or two may have been squeezed out of sheer *timidity*, if not *gratitude?*

It was five o'clock in the afternoon, the sun was setting, and with her "parting fires" cast a glow upon the *Java* that lay proudly at rest. If there arose one feeling of regret, it was in sundering our connections with the noble vessel that had performed the good work of bearing us safely to land. The last token of "farewell" from the ship was the waving of a white handkerchief by some hand that did not grow weary,—but perhaps the "invisible fingers of air" kept it afloat! An event sad in nature occurred on the *Java* at the moment of anchorage—the death of a passenger, a British soldier from Halifax, who was returning on furlough to his native land. As he neared the haven that contained all that was dearest to his heart—wife, children and friends— his spirit took its flight. The surgeon whose fidelity to the sick had been remarked, endeavored to move the poor creature to the deck, but the exertion caused the rupture of a blood vessel, and the tide of life ebbed away in three short minutes. Throughout the voyage the unmistakable cough that presages death to the consumptive sounded its knell in the state-room adjoining mine; yet, I did not dream that the Destroyers' hand was so near.

CHAPTER II.

LIVERPOOL, October 19.

TERRA FIRMA was reached last evening at half-past six o 'clock. The docks were lighted, and there was a precipitate rush on the part of the passengers to secure carriages and hasten on to the hotels. My escort led me to a peculiar-looking conveyance called a *hansom*—a cosy little novelty to my American eyes—and the order was given to drive without delay to the Adelphi. For a moment I knew not how the horse was managed, as to me inside it seemed to be guided by instinct; but I soon discovered that it was no Pegasus nag, for the reins passed over the top of the vehicle, and the driver sat aloft at the extreme rear. Passengers for the *Russia*, advertised to sail the next day, had filled the Adelphi and the Washington House, and our only chance was at Queen's Hotel, where a few moments later I had the pleasure of meeting my ship-mate, Miss T——. Finding her in distress, sharing the fate of those unprovided for, I invited her to occupy my domicile, glad of such cheerful company in so dingy and sombre a room. The lack of comfort drove us to the reading-room below. Mr. V—— left shortly after to attend to some matters of business, and as Liverpool seemed a blank within doors, and our desire to survey the city was great, we accepted the escort of an English gentleman, Mr. Archibald—a person of distinguished appearance, tall and portly, wearing a suit of black velvet, that contrasted well with his ruddy complexion and snowy locks. He crossed the Atlantic in the first ocean steamship, and on this trip of the *Java* has just completed his forty-ninth voyage.

We proceeded three abreast through the principal streets, attracting not a little attention from the fact that we were appropriating the entire sidewalk. A heavy mist having settled around, wrappings were brought into requisition. Not less than a dozen beggar-women held out their hands for charity during our peregrinations, and pitiful objects were they in their tattered garments. The buildings are large and substantially constructed, the stores well-stocked with goods of superior quality, and the streets admirably illuminated by trios of gas-jets—like unto a three-leafed clover—which cast a much more brilliant light than the single lamps in use in the United States. The promenade ended, Miss T—— and I sought our room, which we vainly endeavored to light up with two miserable candles. The fire of a badly ventilated stove had died out, and in the chill and gloom we sat down to write to the loved ones at home.

Though it was past midnight when we retired, we found it impossible to get to sleep, for the stately old-fashioned bed, with its dark hangings, seemed to fasten us in to become the victims of burglary. A moment after, just under the window, amidst a scuffle and clamor, came the cry of "Murder! murder!" from a female voice, and this additional horror settled the question of sleep for the remainder of the night. Wearily did we ponder over murderous weapons and throat-clutchings, wondering if all other sojourners in Liverpool experienced the same trials. We, at least, shall carry away an idea of its demoralization and wickedness.

But shadows do not last forever, for now the morning's light is streaming in to revive our spirits, as well as the colors of the old faded carpet. Soon shall we turn our backs upon every discomfort by taking the cars to London. Miss T——, in her eagerness to see the great metropolis, has decided to leave for the present her party, the family of Professor Hall, to accompany me.

London, *October* 19.—Thanks for the wonderful propelling power that transports us so swiftly from place to place, for here we are in this far-famed city, after the travel of only six or seven hours!

Before leaving Liverpool we caught a glimpse of St. George's Hall, a massive and imposing edifice; also, the statue of Lord Nelson. As I write, I feel that I have just completed one of the most agreeable journeys of my life. At eight A. M., comfortably ensconced in a railway compartment—not worthy to be called a *car*, as its capacity is limited to six persons—we had scarcely left the station, losing sight of bricks and mortar, when a lovely region of country was gained, every acre of which proved a garden-spot. England cannot be described in words—tame and inadequate are they to express the great enjoyment afforded by her rural and picturesque scenery. One longs to be an artist of some merit, to bear off other pictures than those stamped on memory. Although it is the month of October, when the leaves and herbage in America are changed into the "sere and yellow" and "russet brown," nature here preserves her verdure, only an occasional tint of crimson in rich and vivid coloring peering out of the green in pleasing contrast. Here and there are magnificent lawns, with stately trees, fields and groves, and neatly trimmed hedges. In the distance the splendid turretted castle appears, and nearer to the eye, the "lowly thatched cottage," which awakens memories of the sweetest song in the world, "Home, Sweet Home." Surely the English lord in his castle is not more richly surrounded by nature's charms than the humble cottager. The word Happiness should be inscribed over the portals of such homes; for are they not a Paradise far more beautiful than any city in its costliest splendor could give to man? Yet, in hurriedly glancing at these Elysian spots, the thought came, Alas! may not the "serpent's trail" be among the fairest flowers; and whilst nature revels outside, may there not be sorrow at the hearth-stone and in the heart's core? Whether this be true or not, there was something enchanting in every view, and "merrie England" did her utmost to convince us that earth is very lovely, and also to make us the more appreciative of the bounteous blessings vouchsafed by a Heavenly hand. We shall certainly carry to "dream-land" to-night the remembrance of the charming panorama disclosed in the last few hours—a bright Arcadian vision! a land teeming with beauty; green meadows silver-threaded by streams of sparkling water, along whose borders comes the sound of "lowing kine" answering themselves with their own tinkling bells; the fresh green moss and bright flowers; the laborer at his daily work; the song of birds to the sweet refrain of *Rejoice and give praise;* the calm sky crowning and bathing in blue ether the scene below, and the joyous sunshine with not one fickle ray! In this range of pleasant scenes, the spirit of romance has the power to enchain so·closely that one knows not how to detach the links.

Upon reaching the Euston Station the conductor unlocked the door, and ·liberated us from imprisonment. Why do they adopt this mode of holding travelers in durance close and fast? My brother-in-law from Paris had arrived, and a few hurried words convinced me of the necessity of his speedy return. Although regretting so hasty a departure, I had to yield to marching orders, the difficulty in the way being a "Report on the Munitions of War," which must be completed in a few days, as the Exposition is fast drawing to its close. But what was to become of my friend Miss T——? it were a barbarous act to leave her in the great city alone! Being thus forced to depart so precipitately, I suppressed my wrath with the determination to vent it on the Colonel at some future day, when he will surely find that to contend against a woman's will is to war with truth and right. A *royal* fate, it would seem, brought me again to a hotel named for the Queen, it being the nearest and most convenient place to brush off the dust of travel. Mr. V—— joined us at dinner, and afterwards took leave of an encumbrance which he had patiently endured for ten days or more; but for the kind care bestowed, I should be willing to engage his services for the return trip.

See, the thought of home and a return has intruded itself even now! I am not unlike the bird that soars to a strange clime, but whose wings are never folded until it reaches the home-nest again.

Paris, *Oct.* 20.—I take up my pencil at the railway station, in order to promote a patient waiting on Custom-house officers, who are busily toiling away at hundreds of pieces of luggage. Last evening, in London, my trunks were deemed so heavy a burden that the pocket had to pay the penalty; the Bible injunction "Why take ye thought for raiment" being recalled as salutary warning for the future. Rightly does the extravagant stock of wearing apparel of these days bring down the maledictions of provoked officials; and would not such an exhibition surprise our great, great grandmothers, if they were living, as much as their economical and modest wardrobe would dissatisfy us? Let those who contemplate traveling on the Continent heed the advice of one who has already paid dearly for experience. Just prior to leaving London we sauntered along leisurely to see the shops, many of which are truly magnificent; stopped at Exeter Hall, a quiet, home-like place, where we found

D

Miss T. enjoying a cup of coffee, and endeavoring to make the best of her loneliness. On the table lay an accumulation of papers and journals, which I greeted like old friends—read some items of American news, viz: a notice of the marriage of Mr. Howard, of the English Legation at Washington, to Miss Riggs, one of our young and lovely resident belles, and a severe editorial touching upon the finances of Mrs. Ex-President Lincoln, a subject foreign journalists evidently like to discuss. A few moments of conversation followed, and then came the parting with my friend and shipmate, who if *lost* in London gives promise of being *found* in Paris. It was a subject of regret not to be able to note down some of the places of interest in that world-renowned city; the little that was seen was by dim twilight, if not veritable night.

A few moments before the starting of the train we took seats in a luxurious compartment, and a short ride of an hour and a half brought us to the English channel—that bugbear of the traveling public. Its effects are described as of a worse character than those produced by the mighty Atlantic; yet very glad was I that sufficient penance had already been paid to old Neptune to secure me immunity at that juncture. What an ugly little boat it was that hugged the stone quay below, and how illimitable was the number of steps that led to it! The moon being obscured by masses of floating clouds, the white cliffs of Dover could only be faintly descried; and then with a puff of black smoke off we shot to describe zig-zags and all sorts of hieroglyphics on the

water. To avert sea-sickness the horizontal position
was advised, and fortunately so, as in some instances it
served to bring kind Morpheus to the rescue: it was
only the familiar cry of "Port!" "Steady!" as we entered the harbor of Calais, that broke the spell. Ten
minutes were granted for supper at the railway station
on the quay, and then we took the train for Paris. A
French couple, the only other occupants of our compartment, gave us the benefit of their valuable conversation one half of the distance, and after their departure
the orange damask cushions afforded me a couch so
pleasant as to render me entirely oblivious until within
a half hour's ride of the fortifications of this queenly
city. My admiration is still for England, whose scenery
is very much more beautiful and attractive; yet I am
happy in the land of vineyards, looking perhaps as wistfully to the green grapes as the fox in the fable. * * *
* * * Now there is a stir of travelers who have passed
the ordeal of inspection hurrying away, and so my scribblings must be brought to a close. Installed in a cab
outside of the station, waiting for my escort and the
luggage, I am rejoiced to inhale the delicious morning
air, believing as it fans my brow that a promise can be
stolen from it to make me "good as new" in this city
of charms. The *cocher* is directed to *Avenue des Champs
Elysées*, and his lazy team carries us slowly through the
streets, some of which are not unlike certain portions of
New Orleans. The women are out in the early morn,
some sweeping the pavements, and as they sweep are
jabbering, or making an attempt at merry little songs,

and others pursuing various avocations. A noticeable feature are the small white bonnets or caps, which seem as indispensable to their heads as apparel is to the body. If Napoleon troubled himself about matters of dress, we should certainly think that the wearing of the cap was enforced by Imperial decree.

CHAPTER III.

Paris, October 23.

SEVERAL days of rest have afforded me an opportunity of musing over the changes which the last two weeks have brought; and all seems like a dream, the waking from which assures me that I am distantly separated from kindred and friends. And here, lest faithful memory should invoke all of the heart-joys left behind, I will omit their record, and substitute a simple quotation in praise of home:

> "There is a spot,—a quiet spot which blooms
> On Earth's cold, heartless desert;
> It hath power to give a sweetness to the darkest hour!"

But what of Paris, this charming and beautiful city which boasts of so many places of interest and historic association?—as yet scarcely seen in the *coup d'œil* cast over its immensity, but the one view of the *Champs Elysées* from our window is truly enchanting, leaving nothing to be wished for by the eye or mind.

This avenue is one mile and a quarter in length, shaded by trees and bordered with walks, from which diverge many little gardens and groves. The white stone dwellings, pavilions, and restaurants, combining with the natural attractions, afford the beholder a blended

D*

picture of city and country; for in a moment or two after leaving the elegantly furnished apartment and gilded saloon, one can be upon the green lawn among the many hundreds of little children at play, or among the flower-beds and gushing fountains. What a lovely playground! how admirably adapted to children's sports, and how varied the amusements! First of all appears a miniature vehicle, drawn by four goats, which leaves the greensward for the broad avenue, attracting almost as much attention as the carriage of the Emperor. The little folks who pay for a ride are as happy as Kings and Queens are expected to be. Their joyous shouts, at least, attest it. Next is a revolving equestrian machine, and then an interrupted circle of boats and carriages, that go round and round to the workings of a crank, if not to the jingle of copper coins dropped by tiny, dimpled hands. The seats and chairs in the vicinity of all this sport are occupied from time to time by pedestrians who sit for hours in lazy indolence or grateful rest. A dreamy langour is produced by the atmosphere and the sunshine of this Elysium, and old age lives over again the happy days of childhood in the merry scene before his eyes. Who would not be a child again? I almost envy the *bonne* as she siezes the trundling hoop and bids her charge follow on. At the *boutiques* or tiny shops (fancifully constructed of wood) which dot the groves here and there with a gay display of toys, are to be seen groups of purchasers. Every fond mamma seems eager to turn over her surplus *sous* to a noble boy or a pet daughter, on whom the vender of pretty things showers innumerable compliments, bestowing a gentle pat or a glance of admiration at long golden locks and beautiful blue eyes. How I wish that my own dear little ones, Corinne and Félicie, could take my place! To them I dedicate every thought that comes to me in this happy spot! Opposite this scene of juvenile revelry, on the north side of the avenue, is the *Palais de l'Industrie*, a magnificent building of stone with a glass roof, about seven hundred feet in length. The Universal Exposition of 1855 was held there, but it is now used for the exhibition of paintings of modern artists. The groves in the rear of the edifice still preserve their verdure, the spring and summer blossoms being scarcely missed in the bushes of crimson holly and chrysanthemums of every hue. *Rond Point*, on this avenue, is a circular space ornamented with grass-plots and large fountains, whose waters fall in murmurings "sweetly musical." In the heat of summer how refreshing must be such a wealth of spray! Thousands of superb equipages, from the gilded coach to the homely *fiacre*, are hurrying by to the *Bois de Boulogne*, or to the boulevards and streets where the shopping is to be done. How much of life all around—of elasticity of step and gladness of spirit! We catch the *fever* of gaiety at once, or feel the exhilaration of *"je ne sais quoi,"*—an elixir, or something with which Paris ever sets the pulses bounding and drives sad thoughts away. To almost every eye the pride and glory of the *Champs Elysées* is *l'Arc de Triomphe de l'Etoile*, the superb monument erected under the Republic and Empire in honor of France. Its erection is due to Napoleon I., that hero whose proud renown justly entitles him to chronicle in imperishable stone his valorous deeds and those of his countrymen. Of what majestic beauty is. this arch, with its groups of colossal statuary, some of the figures measuring eighteen feet high ! The two groups facing the *Champs Elysées* represent the *"Genius of War encouraging warriors to action"* and the *"Coronation of Napoleon by Victory."* Those facing the Bridge of Neuilly represent *Peace* and *Resistance.* *Peace* can be thus described: a warrior returning from battle is met by his wife and children, his sword being sheathed, as if in acknowledgment of an allegiance other than military. *Resistance* represents a young man defending his family from the invader. The wife, holding her dead child, implores the husband to tarry awhile ; but neither life with its dear behests, nor death in its sacred ties, has the power to repress his military ardor. On the northern side, above the arch, in sculpture unsurpassed, is the *"Battle of Austerlitz,"* and on the southern is the *"Battle of Jemappes."* There are also *alto relievos* of the *"Taking of Alexandria,"* the *"Passage of the Bridge of Arcola,"* the *"Surrender of Mustaphar Pacha at the Battle of Aboukir,"* and the *"Death of General Marceau."* The freize surrounding the whole represents the French army departing for Italy, the presentation of flags and banners, and the return of the victorious troops with trophies of war. The view from the top of this arch, one hundred and sixty feet high, gives us beautiful Paris in all its extent ; but the ascent of over two hundred steps is an exercise which one would not like to repeat often. Whilst the *Arc de Triomphe* terminates the *Champs Elysées*, the Palace of the Tuileries looms up, in its historic fame, at the other end. I acknowledge a feeling of discomfort in looking upon this palace, the scene of so many cruel events. Its origin is cotemporaneous with the crimes of Catherine de Medicis, of which none was more conspicuous than the St. Bartholomew massacre; and then the bloody stain of the Revolutions is deep-dyed on its records. It would seem that its brightest and most redeeming fame comes of recent years, since it became the residence of the present Imperial family—the fair and lovely Empress, who is pronounced to be as good and charitable as she is beautiful; the Emperor, bearing throughout the world the appellation of a great man; and the little Prince, who may one day shape the destinies of France.

The *Place de la Concorde*, which separates the gardens of the Tuileries from the *Champs Elysées*, is a magnificent open square, presenting as its central boast the tall obelisk of Luxor, the gift of Mahommed Ali, Pasha of Egypt, to the French government. Its sides are covered with hieroglyphics which many will vainly endeavor to interpret. It marks the scene of bloody tragedies, that evoke a loathing of such an age of butchery, for there it was that Louis XVI. and his unfortunate consort were guillotined. The sorrows of poor Marie Antoinette live not only in history, but in the hearts of all creatures who are not dead to justice and mercy. As we stand in this grand square, now named *Place de la Concorde*, be-

cause white-winged Peace is brooding over it and cast-
ing her happy reflex on all things around, our minds
naturally revert to those dark days when this same spot,
then called *Place de la Révolution,* was shadowed with
the gloom of death—was rife with the execution of some
of the noblest spirits of France. There are eight large
statues representing the principal cities in France, as an
encircling guard to this beautiful *Place;* and two fountains of colossal dimensions, whose basins are fifty feet
in diameter. The designs are aquatically carried out in
spouting dolphins held by mermaids.

Whilst descanting upon the beauties and attractions of
the *Champs Elysées* by day, let us not forget its charms
at night, when lighted by its myriad lamps. It is an
earthly meteoric display, when to the gas-lights are added
those of the thousand carriages which seem never to
desert the avenue. The effect produced is that of fire-
flies gemming the ground, and the constant scintillations
or sparks of light might challenge the stellar firmament.
But this is a sacrilegious simile; for after all, how dim
and dark must every light of earth be, compared with
that starry region which to our vision suggests the ex-
haustless brightness of the inner heaven!

October 27.—These last few days have fled in "circling
dance," whirling me around in social pleasures, in that
friends have discovered me and extended a welcome so
cordial, as to dispel the thought of meeting in "greeting
cold, the stranger's palm in foreign land." Mr. and
Mrs. E. H. Pendleton, of Cincinnati, gave a handsome

dinner-party at their apartments, on the *Champs Elysées*; the guests comprising some of the most agreeable American sojourners in Paris, among whom were Gen. and Mrs. Darling, of New York, and Mr. Hunt, of Louisiana, recently married to a Baltimore belle, the daughter of a talented lawyer of that city. My escort to dinner was an intelligent gentleman, Dr. Robinson, U. S. Consul to Port Mahon, Spain. During the hours of sparkling wit and sentiment, a gallant cavalier remarked that Parisian dinners *à la mode* consisted of food fit for angels; and that the ladies who partook thereof seemed for the time being to lose their mortal identity, and to shine as with light from the upper spheres. But, if we were angels on this occasion, our wings were slow to bear us off from the bright scene, for it was midnight ere we had flown. Mrs. Gilman, of New York, also gave a dinner, and we unexpectedly met there Mr. Tebbetts, of Boston, who seemed gratified to encounter familiar faces. I have often heard this pleasure described by those who have " met by chance " in a foreign land.

Much might be said in praise of the French for the tasteful and decorative manner in which they prepare a dinner; the garnished dishes (the graceful serving of the same), the exquisite flowers and luscious fruits. The dessert embraces fruits of all kinds—oranges (Sicily), pomegranates, peaches, pears and grapes. It is like wandering in a garden with the privilege of unlimited choice. As for the grapes at this season, they are so plentiful that even beggars might buy, the insignificant price of them bearing a marked contrast with what one has to pay in New York! In fullest satisfaction I hail the land of vineyards! France is not only beautiful in her rich clusters of this fruit, but famous for the extracts manufactured therefrom, and with which her people fill high the glass, in utter repudiation of the "cup of cold water." Many of us, however, as true-Americans, cannot renounce the latter, and although exceedingly fond of the grape, can still proudly say, "We need no vine our country's hills to brighten," while majestic streams and sparkling rills are ours. The flowers, too, are beautiful and profuse. Nearly every *salon* or some portion of a house is adorned with *jardinières*, pots of fuschia, carnation-pink, or other plants exhaling sweet perfume. Does not the sight of a little fragrant flower among objects of art, however rich and costly, turn our thoughts from "gilded toys" to God, the author of this humble though sweetest gift to man?

* * * * * This is my birthday anniversary, and, although I am far from home, it brings more than one kind wish that the hour-glass of Time may ever wear for me a bright garland of joy! A portion of this afternoon was devoted to a promenade in the Tuileries garden with little Alice May Norton. She is just four years of age—a miniature picture of beauty, with bright eyes, rosy cheeks, flaxen hair, and plump little figure arrayed in white embroidered skirt and violet *ceinture*. It is indeed a delight to contribute to the enjoyment of children appreciative of beautiful scenes and possessed of enquiring minds. How well they sometimes reason against our own matured intelligence, and how many

busy thoughts range through their young brains! An illustration of the above surprised and interested me: Upon approaching the obelisk of Luxor the query was made, "What is that tall pillar?" whilst sundry other questions led me to mention the sad fate of Marie Antoinette. Instantly the child's face darkened, and with some feeling she said, "And where is the pretty French Queen now?" I responded, "We hope that she is in heaven." "Well, what did God say to her there?" "That her sorrows were ended, and hereafter she would be happy with Him and His angels." "Then, what answer did she make to God?" Here I became puzzled at the swift-coming queries, and remarked rather at random, "She said she was very happy to be received by God." Just at the close of my sentence came her quick retort, "No, she didn't, for how could she talk when she had no head?"

The garden of the Tuileries abounds in trees, and among them are interspersed statues of bronze and marble. Seats are to be found everywhere, for which comfort you pay a few *sous*. The vigilant eye of an old woman observes every new-comer, and notes every departure. Of course, she has help when the grounds are crowded, but her eye is far-seeing at all times, and the pockets of her apron are evidently made to receive large deposits. It is a generally admitted fact in this city, that small change has no abiding-place, as it disappears in the continual *pour-boire*. Very true, the drain upon the finances is small, but its frequent repetition becomes an annoyance to the newly-arrived traveler. We stopped

E

at the large basin to feed the swans with some bread pro-
cured for that purpose, and then walked leisurely on to the
private garden of the Imperial family, which was thrown
open to promenaders.   It is situated immediately beneath the palace windows.   The building loses some of
its sombre aspect in the flower-beds laid out under its
very shadow, *Flora* holding her court amid a variety of
bright and beautiful tints; and this outside *Queen* could
well dispute the palm with *Eugenie* and all her royal
train.   *   *   *   *   *

10 P. M.—I have just left the *salon*, where, in listening to the rough experience of an American sojourner, I
first learned the demerits of the French servants.   Mr.
G—— told me his modest and amiable little wife had
been summoned before a *juge de paix* to combat in feeble
French the voluble tongue of an uncompromising *diable*
of a cook.   The *cuisine* is generally the " bone of contention," but as *it* and the *larder* are so necessary to a
comfortable existence, *la belle Americaine* must often sub-
mit to imposition, and bow to the yoke with imprecations heavy on her tongue.

October 29.—We have been to that fairy-land of
beauty, the *Bois de Boulogne.*   It furnishes a wide field
for the artist, and poets might write of it in enraptured
verse.   Every portion of this world-renowned park reveals natural and artistic beauties, making it an Eden
with no delight forbidden or limited, it being thrown
open alike to royalty and the masses.   The finely graded
roads that thread it in every direction are usually crowded

with magnificent equipages; and some of the finest horses in the world are to be seen there. The Emperor and Empress go, with a military escort, in a coach drawn by four or six horses, two of which are mounted by postillions. Their carriage is generally followed by one containing several ladies of the Imperial household. The opportunity to see their majesties is always very favorable, as the main avenue during the afternoon is too crowded to admit of fast driving. Some American snobs or would-be noblemen assume a pretentious right to State-carriages, etc., recalling the shoddy performances of Central Park, New York. The display of coroneted coaches, with coachmen and footmen in tight knee-breeches, flesh-colored hose, shoe-buckles and gay cockades, is quite bewildering; and so much is there of the aristocratic swell and dignity, that a plain American who witnesses the scene for the first time, sinks back in his hired vehicle, feeling his utter insignificance Besides the personages of title and rank, there is another class of society that unfortunately wields an influence too great to pass unnoticed—the gay *demi-monde*, who woo deceitfully, and barter the pearl of chastity for dazzling gold.

But the *Bois* itself, without bright eyes, gay voices, swift horses or sound of wheels, is a ravishing picture with its lakes, cascades, arbors, bowers, flowering vales, shady groves, and shrubbery touched, as it were, by "emerald fingers."

I saw that portion of the Park called *Longchamps* waked into triple life and beauty on the occasion of the review of the French troops by Napoleon and the Emperor of Austria. The day was propitious in a bounteous flood of sunshine, which made the very air shimmer with its glow. Mrs. McCauley, of California, with her young and interesting daughter, called for me in an open carriage. I was thus persuaded to leave our balcony at home, which had been decorated with American flags, and whither some friends (the wives of a half-dozen U. S. naval officers) had repaired for a good view of the passing troops. The spectacle at *Longchamps* was most brilliant! The soldiers, numbering many thousands, drawn up in line on a perfectly level plain—the glitter of sabres in the sunlight—the blending of colors in the different regiments—the presence of the crowned heads mounted on superb chargers—the Empress and *suite*—the stands for Ministers of the government, and the canopied tribune filled with gaily-dressed ladies—made up the charming *tout ensemble*. France might well be proud of her soldiers, whose manœuvres elicited universal admiration. The *chasseurs* were particularly attractive.

The sound of the bugle, besides inspiriting martial airs, the vociferous cheering of the people, and the usual excitement of a crowd, evoked some military enthusiasm from little George McC——, who, with heart beating time to the music, left our company to stroll around, much to the dissatisfaction of an anxious mamma. Several times both coachman and footman were sent in pursuit of him, and they found it difficult to discover his whereabouts or entice him back. At one time he was found lodged in a high tree, regardless of the danger of breaking his limbs, and shouting to the glory of France.; and at another, hidden away in a clump of bushes with some lolling Zouaves.

Upon our arrival at the *Bois*, very fortunate were we in securing a fine position, the coachman having driven to a high knoll of ground overlooking *Longchamps*, where, through an opening in the foliage, was witnessed what will be a life-memory. At various times cavalrymen passed on the narrow roadside, and gave the command to "move off!" As long as they remained in sight we bowed understandingly, and made a feint at leaving, but as soon as they had departed we remounted the seats, and enjoyed our *lorgnettes* again. Many persons in the passing carriages looked enviously at our position, yet were forced to continue on, not having the assurance and pertinacity of our American party. The review was ended at five o'clock. The hours which brought fatigue to the troops wore away too rapidly to suit our wishes, and particularly those of little George, the coachman and footman, the two latter having once served in the army. With the disbandment of the soldiers, the mass of people departed from the scene in furious haste, as if a hostile army were at their heels. The avenues and walks were literally blocked up, and the *cochers* practiced a successful manœuvre by whipping their horses to a brisk trot in order to elude the *gendarmes*, who in thundering tones were ordering them to follow certain routes. In a spirit of opposition, we passed the gates of the *Bois*, and after leaving the *Avenue de l'Impératrice*, deemed it best to turn into the side

E*

streets, thus avoiding the *Champs Elysées* until within sight of home.   As we were about to enter that avenue a *gendarme*, with a most provoking assumption of authority, held us captive for ten minutes; yet had he not detained us, the presence of our carriage there would assuredly have added to the "confusion worse confounded."   We scoffed at *patience*, a womanly virtue, for it was very hard for hungry mortals to be thus baffled.   A fight of words in *French* ensued, with a sprinkling of English as a spicy flavor; but what availed all manner of spleen against French bravado?   Finally, we resorted to another street, which, although guarded in like manner, did not refuse us passage.   *   *   *

To-day all the principal boulevards were decorated with banners.   The Austrian flag threw out her folds from many a window and balcony, and it was often seen entwined with the French colors, in honor of the visit of *Francis Joseph*.   One thing remains to be said—that no nation in the world equals this in the enthusiasm or the impressive warmth with which her people espouse a cause or celebrate an event.   Their hilarity or excitability may well be compared to their glorious champagne; and if it does not last much longer than the effervescence of the draught, it is none the less attractive and effective.   The Emperor of Austria, out of respect to the unfortunate Maximilian, declines to accept the compliment of a ball at the *Hôtel de Ville*, and thus are many French and American expectants disappointed.

October 31.—Mr. Corcoran, of Washington, called

yesterday, and urged an immediate visit to the *Exposition*, which ere this should have engrossed my time; but Paris admits of no set plans or projects. He is much improved by a recent sea-voyage, but anxiety for his daughter's health represses his usual flow of spirits. He will follow her to Cannes, whose climate we trust will serve her case; yet while consumption may flatter for a season, the spectre of Death comes at last in the mockery.

* * * * * Our first visit to the Exposition lasted from early morning to 4 P. M. How much the word implies with the prefix Universal, for is there not afforded a view of the products, the works of art, etc., of all the countries of the world? It certainly repays the tedium of a voyage across the Atlantic and compensates the distress of its accompanying evil, *mal de mer*. The building stands on the *Champs de Mars*, and is divided into sections, or, "it forms a series of rings one within the other, holding a garden in the centre." The articles on exhibition are all on the ground floor, and from their groupings an idea may be formed of the comparative industrial condition and advancement of each country. Hereto is appended a synopsis of the contents, which are divided into ten great groups, and these subdivided into ninety-five classes: "Group I. Fine arts. Group II. Materials and products of the liberal arts. Group III. Furniture and household utensils. Group IV. Clothing of all kinds. Group V. Raw and manufactured products of extractive industries. Group VI. Instruments and processes of the mechanical arts. Group

VII. Food, fresh or preserved, cooked or uncooked. Group VIII. Live stock and models of agricultural establishments. Group IX. Plants and horticultural tools and models. Group X. Objects exhibited with with the view of ameliorating the physical and moral condition of the working population." The distribution of space to countries is as follows: "France occupies nearly all the easterly half of the building and park, with the exception of corners to Belguim and Holland. Beginning at the western corner of the main entrance of the building, and in an easterly direction we see Great Britain and the colonies, Central and South America, United States, Tunis and Morocco, Persia, China, Siam, Japan, Egypt, Turkey, Rome, Italy, Prussia, Sweden and Norway, Denmark, Greece, Portugal, Spain, Switzerland, Austria and the minor States of Germany and Prussia. Prussia, by being brought near to France, holds a place of honor, and faces Belgium." Thus passing all these national names, one might fancy himself making a tour of the world, without the expense of traveling, though with much of the bodily fatigue.

On our first visit, we availed ourselves of small one-seat carriages, or Bath chairs (as they were styled), drawn by a guide;—a mode of conveyance very convenient for invalids or lame persons ; yet, if we did make ourselves objects of curiosity, and tolerated the snail pace, we at least saved a vast amount of physical strength. The park or outside grounds contained much that was interesting, independent of the attractions of the interior. One space was assigned to Morocco, and the Palace of

the Bey of Tunis. Adjoining the American Restaurant,
I recall a Tunisian Café which regaled us with a minstrel
performance, and the sight of some *acrobatic feats*. A
small fee admitted us into the Chinese and Japanese
houses, where there was nothing specially interesting
except a pretty Japanese woman seated on a gay colored
rug, her fingers plying steadily at some fancy work.
Then came the gardens of Persia, and an Egyptian
Temple, abounding in beautiful and rare sculpture, said
to be the fac-simile of the Temples of the Pharaohs.
The English space furnished several large structures for
"the exhibition and testing of building materials," and
France made a display of machinery, chiefly locomotives,
which are insignificant in size, and inferior in workmanship and finish, compared with those of America. A
Swiss-Italian pavilion by the beauty of its architecture,
appealed to the eye; also, a photo-sculpture building,
furnishing souvenirs that will ever be associated with
the great Exposition. A large metallic light-house was
pointed out, whose revolving light is shed over all Paris
by night, and a building not far from the Emperor's
pavilion, containing the choicest French Art Manufac-
tures; but a description of its colossal bronze statuary
were better left to a masculine pen. Seeing a vast crowd
collected around a statue on our right, our curiosity naturally led us to it. Two of the *cent gardes* gazing up at
its towering height appeared dwarfed in comparison, although much above the average height. Is it the proud
war-horse eager for the fray that most attracts, or the
bold and fearless rider, sitting there like some chivalric
crusader? The foot of the horse is raised as if threaten-

ing to trample down Prussia's enemies, and King William with heavy casque, and determined mien seems ready, if not anxious, to challenge the world in deadly conflict.

Once again in the interior of the Exposition we walked through some of the sections devoted to paintings and sculpture, and gazed in ecstasy at one faultless gem of statuary. The delicate and beautiful form was clad in a web-like drapery, and the face, so perfect in its classic loveliness, might have passed for that of an *angel*, had it not been *Sappho*. Referring indirectly to the angelic, I have caught a radiant view through memory's glass of two figures which seem to belong half to earth and half to heaven. The subject is the *Loves of the Angels*, and such love there exemplified doth shame the coarse passion of mortals. The figures, in gentle embrace, seem about to soar away to the upper world, whilst their feet scarcely touch the flowery vale below. The pedestal of the statue is wreathed in vines and tendrils that stretch towards the receding limbs, and mingle their beauties most harmoniously. A very fine bust was that of the Princess Alexandra! From the look of tenderness in her eyes, there must be something dove-like in her nature. Gentle beauty is apt to strike more pleasurably than that of the spirited type. The *chef d'œuvres* of art were numerous, but a description of the subjects by me might prove a sacrifice upon an altar which has no flame worthy to light them into just notice. Besides, it is twelve o'clock at night, and drooping eyelids bid me drop the theme. May my visions be of absent loved ones!

CHAPTER IV.

November 1.

THIS is All Saints Day, when it is the custom of the French to pay tribute to their dead, in visits to the cemeteries, and in the floral adornment of graves. The Baroness de R —— (an agreeable friend) came to pass the day *chez nous*, and insisted upon my going in her carriage to *Père la Chaise.* Her father, Col. B—— kindly waited on me; and knowing that our rambles would be of long duration, he wisely dismissed the *cocher.*

The street leading to this vast "city of the dead" was crowded with persons carrying wreaths of *immortelles,* and fresh flowers, and upon the faces of some were traces of deep sorrow, which even the tenderest sympathy of strangers durst not intrude upon. The shops along the route were filled with bouquets, anchors, crosses and garlands, all made of *immortelle* flowers, the preferred yellow predominating over the more appropriate and tasteful white and green. I was much disappointed in *Père la Chaise.* It lacks the picturesque beauty of many of our American cemeteries, such as Greenwood, Laurel Hill and Mount Auburn; but like the Congressional Cemetery at Washington, its attractiveness consists in its monuments to distinguished dead. The first tomb sought was that of *Abélard* and *Heloïse*, where faithful love has left to the world a blessed memory. The two lovers lie side by side, and their tomb is surmounted by recumbent statues. A sculptured canopy shields these figures bestrewn with flowers. Devotees to-day had laid fresh offerings there, but the withered tokens that had fallen about the base of the monument told of many a pitying visitor in years gone by. Alas! that *Love's* bright dawn should fade into a sunset of sorrow! The tomb of *Rachel* bears evidence of the estimation in which she was held by the French nation. It is literally covered with names, in the cards so lavishly scattered about, and other homage is paid her fame in lovely flowers with their mute yet eloquent language.

If the great actress could rise from the cerements of the grave, she would find that a fadeless wreath of affection and gratitude had taken the place of the proud coronet she wore all through her professional life. The monument of Count Lavalette is of white marble, bearing a beautiful sculptured design, commemorative of woman's heroism and devotion,—the Countess dresses her husband in her clothes, in order to effect his escape from prison. On a commanding knoll is a sepulchre, with the simple inscription *Schickler*. We plucked some ivy-leaves that sprang from its base. Two half-veiled statues, like vestal virgins, keep vigils over the sacred spot, and a sculptured owl lends alike its ministrations. Wandering on, we came to the resting-place of *Eugene Scribe*, whose bust surmounts a stately shaft. The words

"*Inde Fortuna Libertas*" are inscribed beneath three heads carved on the pediment. Among the tombs most worthy of notice are those of the French Marshals, *Lefebvre* and *Masséna*, and that of Vice-Admiral *Duc Decrès, ancien Ministre de Marine.* On the Vice-Admiral's is a bas-relief both appropriate and beautiful—a vessel in action. At a short distance we find the monument to *Larrey*, the faithful surgeon of Napoleon I. The following inscription shows how much beloved he was by the great General: "*L'homme le plus vertueux que j'ai connu,*"—*testament de Napoleon.* The magnificent marble tomb of General *Gobert* was so completely surrounded by visitors that it was difficult to obtain a satisfactory view of the equestrian statue and the bas-reliefs marking his military career. One represents a distinguished General at the battle of Famars, delivering up his sword, who, as he expires, charges *Gobert* to gather the *débris* of his army. *Gobert's* response, "*J'espére que je l'encore honorerai,*" proved a faithful pledge. Another design showed where *Gobert* rushed to the rescue of some of his imprisoned men in Egypt, and killed the guard who was about to apply the torch to the mine prepared for their destruction. The third bas-relief represents him quelling the insurgents at Boulogne by words that proved weightier than the sword ; and the remaining one, portraying battle and death, I could not make out, being too timid to venture on a ledge which overlooked a steep declivity. Within a small enclosure, a spot devoid of monument, lie the remains of *Marshal Ney.* Upon the gate-sill can be deciphered the words : "*Sta viator heroem*

F

calcas," although half effaced by time and hid by grass and ivy. The pilgrim stops to pay the homage of a sigh over the hero's dust, and to reflect that a just reward is not always meted out to the brave and gallant, for whilst towering marble is reared here and there in close proximity to commemorate FAME, only a few flowers and trailing vines cover up his lowly mound. One of the grandest mausoleums is that of Elizabeth, Countess de Demidoff, *née* Baroness of Strogonoff, died April 8, 1818. A temple encloses the crown and crest, which lie on a cushion, and a thick wall of masonry surrounds the whole. A Russian tomb erected to the Princess de Valachie Marie Bibesco is one of the most costly. It consists of a magnificent chapel, with an iron dome surmounted by a cross. Over the entrance of white stone an eagle is perched, holding in his talons a marble cross, sceptre and sword. Two lions hold in their claws the family crest and crown. The doors of the chapel are of bronze, with figures of Faith and Charity. Not less conspicuous is the tomb to General Foy, erected by national subscriptions, Nov. 28, 1825. Above a massive base rises a Grecian temple, the figure of the General resting against a column, upon which are two olive-wreaths encircling his sword. The bas-reliefs on the side point to his military exploits. The twin-tomb of *Manuel* and *Béranger* is of circular form. Their heads are sculptured in bronze, and over them hang wreaths of laurel. One inscription, in the language of *Manuel,* reads: "Yesterday I announced that I would only yield by force—to-day I come to keep my word;" and *Béran-*

ger's dying request is told in words that proved the strength and fidelity of his friendship: "I wish to be buried in the tomb with my friend *Manuel.*" The tombs of *Molière* and *La Fontaine* also claimed our notice, but the hours were too brief to permit us to loiter at every attractive spot. The Chapel of *Père la Chaise* is situated on a hill commanding a fine view of Paris. It being densely crowded, we were very glad to escape therefrom, yet on emerging, we found the outside avenues alike swollen with the human tide. I feared I was wearying my kind and intelligent friend by my insatiable curiosity to peer into all the grated chapels—to look at the statues of the Virgin draped in lace, lit up by the mellow gleam of wax candles—to count the wreaths of *immortelles* accumulated by yearly deposits, and to read the various records of noble deeds and gentle virtues. It was very sad to behold little children clad in black carrying bouquets to a father's or mother's grave, but still more sad to the heart was the sight of those grassy mounds beneath which sleep little ones from our own far distant land. What trial can be more sorrowful than that of a parent who travels homeward, leaving a beloved child in a foreign grave; for is it not a shrine where the heart forever dwells, and towards which loving feet long to turn? Oft have troubled souls, leaving gay Paris, turned their last glances in the direction of *Père la Chaise*, and found a ray of consolation in the same thoughts that moved the poet's pen:

> " Far, far away, the zephyrs wave
> In silence o'er thy lonely grave!

> And spirits of a foreign air
> At evening love to linger there;
> And roses of another shore—
> (Blooming where thou shalt bloom no more—)
> Shed sweetness o'er the quiet spot
> Where thou liest low, but unforgot;
> While moonbeams of a distant sky
> Watch o'er it like a mother's eye."

Death loses but little of its sadness, even when associated with beautiful flowers, the carol of birds, and the chiming of bells. I witnessed and heard all this to-day, and with the mournfulness of it all came the thought of that heavenly joy which reigns above the tumult of this world. How expressive are French epitaphs! A single word, *Hélas!* contains a volume of sorrow and sentiment; as also "United on earth and in heaven," and "Rachel mourning for her children."

Leaving the cemetery at five o'clock, we had the ill luck of finding no carriage at hand. The *gendarmes* and cavalry officers on duty at the gates were to us a novel sight; but it seems that the enforcement of order in France is paramount to every other consideration. We were directed to turn into a miserable street, as disgusting as the name it bore, *Rue des Rats;* and on emerging therefrom were obliged to walk all the way to *Place de la Bastile.* There the proud *Column of July,* commemorative of the three days of that month in 1830, rises to the height of a hundred and sixty feet, and the Genius of Liberty, a graceful winged figure, caps its summit. A further search of a conveyance resulted in our finding *only* an omnibus, which conveyed us as far as the *Madelaine.* Fifteen minutes elapsed before a carriage came to our second relief, and we strolled about the flower market, enjoying the fragrance of violets and other sweet blossoms.

November 3.—Mr. V——, of London, has arrived in Paris, to attend the farewell banquet of the Commissioners to the Exposition, which promises to be on a magnificent scale. We passed some very profitable hours at *Champs de Mars* this morning, first entering the British section, so rich in machinery, textile fabrics, and furniture. The United States department is emphatically a failure, and contains but little that can entitle us to rank with other nations. The food show, including the wines of California and Ohio, is perhaps her only success, and after this comes a motley collection, embracing some minerals, stuffed birds of gay plumage, fire-arms, ferocious looking grizzly bears, wax flowers, artificial teeth, photographs, and other minor articles. A case of silverware from Tiffany's, New York, reflects no particular credit on that elegant establishment. Of pianos, the *Chickering,* so faultless in tone, must surely win the prize. It is said that on the opening day of the Exposition the array of American ladies was so brilliant as to be remarked by the Emperor, an incident that made some atonement for the shortcomings of our country. In the sections of Egypt, China, Morocco, Persia, and Turkey, are many interesting objects—the white elephant of Siam, Turkish food (not at all suited, we should think, to the American palate), furs, antlers, and rich

F*

fabrics of Morocco. But the most attractive features are life-size figures representing different nationalities— "a closely-veiled lady on the back of a dromedary, and a woman reclining on a gorgeously-tinted carpet;" and in the Brazilian and Haytien departments, "men carrying the lasso, and a hunter in his trappings taking leave of his wife." The latter group is so life-like, and the expression of sorrow on the faces so natural, that we feel the full force of a real farewell. The Turkey carpets are rich and elegant, and so are the embroidered dresses—the raw produce being all-sufficient. Rome presents some choice mosaics, chief among which is the beautiful picture, the tomb of *Cecilia Metella*. A circular table of large dimensions represents the palaces of Rome and its principal monuments of antiquity; and another, more simple, displays a few sprays of lily of the valley, the green leaves and white flowers contrasting well with the polished black ground. They looked as natural as if they had been carelessly thrown there. The jewelry of this section is most tempting, and consists of stone and shell cameos. The ebony furniture is inlaid with ivory; and then come specimens of malachite, and quantities of raw silk, spun and in the cocoon, marbles, etc. The Russian courts embrace hardware and raw materials, furs and heavy caps, suggestive of her cold winters, fancy articles of leather, whose odor was almost overpowering when the cases were opened, and lay figures in the national costume. There is always a crowd around these interesting figures, which are far more attractive than many of the distinguished visitors.

The two magnificent *etagères*, inlaid with malachite and mosaic to represent fruit and flowers, were presented to the French Empress and the Empress of Russia by the Emperor of Russia. The next attraction for us was a white marble mantel of rare device—cupids lying among the roses; but the little "blind gods" were in such cold and stern repose that they would not let fly their arrows. A very curious article is a silver lace handkerchief more delicate than the finest spun glass and of cobweb consistency. A rich Countess had placed it on exhibition with other rare articles. The collection of precious stones exhibited in this department is very valuable. Portugal displays silks, wines, coals and other minerals; but Spain does better in an extensive show of machinery and a large collection of cereals. Greece is charming with her many varieties of oranges and lemons, and their color seen from afar made us imagine we were gaining on a gold region. She also furnishes spun silks and costumes. Switzerland abounds in watches and beautiful carvings in wood. Austria makes a varied display of machinery and hardware, food, glass and porcelain ware, photographs, and *meerschaums* of many shapes and designs. The art of photography, it would seem, is known all over the world, judging by the thousands of pictures afloat here. Prussia unfurls her banner proudly over her treasures, her most solid excellence being in machinery. Berlin saddlery, cane chairs, straw hats, etc., do her much credit. The perfume of *eau de Cologne* of Jean Marie Farina in this vicinity seemed to be diffused throughout the whole atmosphere, as bottles

were opened to invite purchasers. Belgium is specially
attractive in her wealth of laces from the cities of Brussels and Antwerp, some being miracles in pattern and
texture.   In the examination of these fabrics many persons give a thought only to the beauty of design, the
fine quality, and the rich adornment they will make to
the figure or person, little dreaming of the weary hands,
the overtaxed eyes, and the poverty of the creatures who
toil "morn in and day out."   With due appreciation of
the benefit accruing from factories, where so many of
the poor are employed, there is still something sad to
the contemplative mind, which cannot fail to pity those
who pursue their daily round of work in a close and fetid
atmosphere, doubtless more injurious than the roughest
out-door labor.   So I thought years since on visiting a
porcelain and glass factory in Jersey City.   The wasted
figures and pallid countenances stamped themselves on
my memory, from which they will never be erased.   The
ecclesiastical vestments from Bruges are exceedingly rich.
France comes *last* in notice, but, following the old adage,
she shall be *first* in the assignment of rank. We place the
diadem upon her brow ! In justice to some countries, due
allowance must be made for their distance from this city
and the difficulty, trouble and expense of transportation.
France is "at home," and this one advantage would
insure to her victory independent of her very great
merit.   The noting down of machinery becomes so heavy
and tedious a work that its bare mention must suffice ;
but the food topic being something invigorating, I will
add that her courts are copiously stored, and that the

wine districts abundantly display Bordeaux, Burgundy and Champagne. The cutlery is very fine, and the glassware from *Baccarat's* bewildering in its prismatic reflections. The famous dinner-service of white cut-glass set in gold comprises a variety of ornamental pieces, and seems fit for a sovereign's table. Scarcely less observed is the delicate ruby glass and that of the soft amber shade, the porcelain ware richly colored, and a supper-service, each plate varying in designs, such as landscape views, flower garlands, or a single cherub face, in beauty not unlike Raphael's angels. Sèvres' unequaled china, the Aubusson carpets and Gobelin tapestries, bronze ornaments, carved furniture, clocks and watches of celebrated makers, dress apparel made up after the most approved styles, the gorgeous silks and velvets of Lyons, and doll-baby shows (which interest adults almost as much as children), stand pre-eminent; but there are, besides these, thousands of *"articles de Paris"* which it would be an overwhelming task to enumerate. The most magnificent jewels on exhibition are those of the *Countess Dudley*, comprising brooch, necklace, tiara and bracelet. The central diamond of the latter article is a Koh-i-noor in size, and the others that cluster around it are worth a fabulous sum. On the same range with this private display is a case of the most costly jewelry from the house of *Harry Emanuel,* 18 New Bond street, London—jeweler to the Queen, the Prince and Princess of Wales. Chief among the dazzling attractions gleams a diamond eagle set with other precious stones which would more than buy a Prince's ransom.

November 7.—Dates commence to puzzle me, for I find myself making a retrograde recountal of events. These latter days have brought to Paris my friend Miss Tracy and the family of Prof. Hall. We visited together the Exposition. The carriage of the Emperor was in waiting at the *grande porte,* where a dense crowd had assembled to see his Majesty and the Emperor of Austria leave the building. The enthusiasm waxed very strong, but ended in disappointment when the coach moved off, and it was discovered that a more private exit would be made. The attendant upon the Emperor's pavilion, near at hand, had donned his embroidered apparel and powdered wig, ready to throw open the doors of the beautiful miniature palace, the splendor of which few imaginations, however rich and poetic, can conceive. It lacked nothing that taste and wealth could suggest. The floors of the *salon* and adjoining circular rooms were covered with the finest Aubusson tapestry, and the idea of stepping among flowers was poetically carried out as the eye met a milk-white ground, scattered over with roses, violets, and other garden beauties. The furniture, with its rare texture of tapestry, exhibited interesting designs, such as a parlor scene with *Marquis* and *Marquise,* and representations of lovely nature in a greensward with birds and flowers. Thus every chair became a pleasant study. Articles of *vertu* appeared here and there, and added to these were the chandeliers and vases of crystal, the damask and lace drapery of the arched windows, the frescoed ceilings picturing the heavens with faint blue clouds and hovering angels, and the odor of freshly culled flowers, to make it May-day within. With beauty so complete and choice, who would not sigh for royal privileges or the possession of this little fairy realm?

In the reserved gardens is another pavilion, fitted up in sumptuous style, for the Empress. She can sit among the lavish splendors inside and gaze out upon the beautiful surroundings—the parterres of bright-hued blossoms and the fountains—and listen to sweet music, as a charm added to her charmed sight. The Empress generally devotes the early part of the mornings to visiting the Exposition. The fine art galleries seem to be the favorite places of resort; but the crowd there is usually so great, and the time for examination so limited, that the merit of the pictures is often lost. It is perfect rapture to walk through those long galleries, whose walls seem to breathe and speak in the paintings of the "human form divine," and then to turn to the aisles where beautiful statuary also seems ready to spring into life. There are historical, poetical, mythological and religious subjects; and one can wander, as it were, in each of these separate worlds, culling flowers to lay at Memory's shrine. The few I have chosen and gathered give out their richest perfume, and will always sweetly flourish.

England, from general opinion, seems to be lacking in pictures by her great masters. Is it due to oversight or apathy? There were fine portraits of the Prince and Princess of Wales, and a painting, *The last night of Jesus Christ in His Nazarene home.* The inscription, "The night is far spent, the day is at hand," (words of sorrow that should sink deep into every heart), struck me as forcibly as did the sad subject to whom it applied. The United States furnished a gem in Church's *Niagara*, and the *White Girl* by Whistler. Whatever may have been the merit of the latter piece, it attracted more by its oddity than by its beauty. In the Russian section there were some fine battle-scenes; and France was not wanting in pictures of her military eras. A portrait of Joan of Arc after the battle of *Compiègne* revealed a saintly face lit up with the fire of military enthusiasm, yet tempered by "religion's softened ray." One of the finest gems in coloring was *Venus rising from the Sea*, and Leutze's *Mary Stuart hearing Mass at Holyrood for the first time after leaving France*. In sculpture there were Thompson's bronze statue of Napoleon, a splendid success, and a bust of Abraham Lincoln.

In the Italian section we principally noticed the paintings—*Jesus tempted by Satan*, by Bonajuti, and Rapisardi's *Ophelia*; but the statuary was in every instance worthy of that classic land. First and pre-eminent, the statue of Napoleon I., represented in a sitting posture. It pointed to his last days at St. Helena, when the proud spirit was about to seek release from its earthly bonds, and the battle of life was drawing near its close. One felt, in gazing upon this statue so cold and white, the silence of death, or that the last lingering spark of vitality was about to depart. Upon the base of the statue were inscribed these words, *Gli ultimi giorni di Napoleone primo*, and the name of the artist, Vincent Vela, to whom is rendered the just and liberal homage of thousands. There was still another statue of Napoleon, by Romanelli. If I remember rightly, Italy claimed the *Sorrowful Christ* and *Mary*, two figures upon which many an eye turned in pensive thought; and *La femme adultère*, a beautifully executed work. How much of supplication and anguish in that face, and how vividly does it tell us that the loss of virtue stealeth away happiness and drieth up the founts of the heart! Who could fail to mark the furrowed brow, the drooping eye, heavy as with pent-up tears, and the prostrate form crouching low, as if to avoid the gaze of those who knew what her burden of sin was? And yet with all this sorrow, there lingered about the figure an air of beauty and youth which showed that with pollution there may yet remain something to mitigate the world's censure—a something from which purity cannot be altogether driven—and that "one faint trace of heaven is left in her." This statue seemed to lack the sympathy which the celebrated painting of the Adultress finds in the figure of the pardoning Savior, and to miss that balm of consolation to the contrite heart in His words, " Let him who is without sin cast the first stone." Close beside stood a fine statue of *Eve*, by Pandiani, and two busts representing Marie Antoinette at *Versailles* and at the *Conciergerie*—the proud Sovereign, and the dethroned Queen awaiting the guillotine. The proudly arched neck of the Queen is plainly marked in every bust and statue. A critical examination of the infinite variety of statues from the Roman States, or Italy's vast field of marbles, would have engrossed weeks and months.· The

G

gendarmes invariably drove us out at the hours of four or five P. M., and each parting seemed "a farewell to Paradise." It was truly an Eden of delight to minds appreciative of rare creations of art.

* * * A pleasant reception at home brought together some friends whom I had not met for several years. Paris seems to take up the links of friendship, and bind them anew after the old fashion. Many are the familiar faces that greet us in distant lands, and dear are the associations they awaken! Mr. S. P. Dewey, of California, and family, were among our welcome guests. One friend, a mere youth when last seen, had matured into a splendid type of manhood, and acknowledges himself knee-deep plunged and heart engrossed in the pleasures and distractions of Parisian life. A residence in the Latin quarter tells how the hours come and go with some Americans, who would have the finger of Time *rheumatically* inclined, so as to point slowly at the falling sands. The wife of Mr. Martin Zborowska attracted universal attention, possessed as she is of talent and grace. In her recent marriage the American colony has lost a beautiful widow, whose charms enlisted numerous suitors. Then there was the handsome Miss Gordon, of Ohio, unanimously voted enchantress of the hour; and Miss Sharp, of New York, a little heiress so bewitching as not to need the flash of jewels or the aid of golden bait. Among the gentlemen were Messrs. L'Herbette and Kane, French and English bankers, noted for their urbanity of manner; Governor Winthrop, of Boston, and many others, the mention of

whom time and space will not allow. Dancing to delightful music did not cease until nearly two A. M. * *

The great theatrical star in Paris at present is Mlle. Schneider, in the play of *La Grande Duchesse*. Her votaries pronounce her *superbe, magnifique, ravissante*, and exhaust the French vocabulary in their expressions of praise. The charming song, "*Ah! que j'aime les militaires!*" sets all our musical nerves in motion and ourselves in a twirl, which if experienced every night would surely require a soothing potion. We have recently attended the *Théâtre de la Porte St. Martin* to see *Biche au Bois*. What language shall be employed to describe the rich and elegant costumes of the ballet dancers, who were fairly flying in the air under the murmurs of applause like leaves swayed by the breeze; the vivacious acting; the syren-like songs; the dazzling scenery; and all else that bewildered? The play was *Black Crook* intensified, though with a fairer title, the *White Fawn*. Every moment spent within the walls of this theatre proved the correctness of that droll description of *Porte St. Martin* and its dramatic revelry by Moore, in the letter of Biddy Fudge to Miss Dorothy. At the close of the performance, as in Moore's time, a man entered a den of lions, which in this instance were not stuffed, and fought with them furiously. Such dangerous sport should not be countenanced unless there be *Daniels* in these days. A few nights previously this venturesome person was wounded. The prices of seats in the Paris theatres range very high, but one gets the worth of his money in the good performance and in the length of the plays. *Porte St. Martin* contains eighteen hundred seats, and its exterior is adorned with busts of *Sulli*, *Grimault* and *Glück*. The ventilation is miserable, and headaches usually follow an evening spent there.

November 6.—The Exposition is finally closed, and what was a busy scene before, in the masses of sight-seeing people, is equally so now in the numerous workmen who are despoiling the building of its goods and chattels ; robbing it of its beauty hour by hour, so that soon there will be naught left but the great shell which enclosed the treasure. We walked through the dismantled sections and left* their *débris* for the central garden, whose statuary was yet undisturbed, and where the flowers were still sweetly blooming amidst the playing of fountains. From this stand-point an accurate idea was formed of the magnitude of the Exposition, of the immense wealth gathered within and around, and of how nations had vied with one another in their efforts to excel. What a triumph for *Champ de Mars* will ever be the Exposition of '67 !

We found our way to the American soda fount, around which were groups of persons patiently awaiting their turn of refreshment. This simple drink is looked upon by the French as deserving of popular favor and patronage, whilst our own people welcome it with the delight they would a crystal spring in an arid desert. Many quaffed it as though it contained nectar drops "mixed by the gods", and we gave evidence of a similar belief in our frequent *encores,* which fell so fast on the ears of the enterprising vender as to elicit from him an appeal to "stop," else he would not be responsible for our rashness. What a snug little fortune might be made in France with that effervescent draught! One little girl did not see why the apparatus could not be put up at her home, if only to afford her the amusement of turning the spigot.

Our steps were next directed to the *Jardin réservé,* whose beauties wore so rich a glow as to warrant an entrance fee. There was everything to charm the vision. Upon sloping mounds appeared many varieties of vegetables brought to their greatest perfection, and in juxtaposition, a feast of flowers growing luxuriantly in the open air. Specimens of cut roses were exposed in conservatories, their sweet odors filling the atmosphere; and yet to have kept a fresh supply during the Exposition must have exhausted the bloom of many acres, and left a "wilderness" where once "blossomed the rose." After the flowers, came the fruits, laid out most temptingly; but the printed command, *Ne touchez pas,* made one wish that the peach with its ripe blush was of wax, or that the mellow pears and golden grapes were a thousand miles distant. The garden abounded with little arbors, summer-houses, iron-wrought pavilions, flower-beds, clumps of bushes where the hardy berry peeped out, and rustic bridges with clambering vines. But the enchanting scene was the Grotto, which elicited from every beholder an ejaculation of surprise and admiration! A winding pathway led to its summit, which was construct-

G*

ed of rude, jagged stone, over which the ivy grew and the myrtle-vine twined its glossy leaves. The sound of the cascade was here heard, inviting to its discovery. Turning from the point where we stood to the other side, we saw water trickling down the steep, and all of us grew enthusiastic over the beautiful and admirable representation of nature. All these attractions rendered us the more eager to enter the subterranean passage, which by its narrowness necessitated some squeezing in the crowd that was passing in and out. The grotto was circular in form, and along its sides large cavities formed aquariums, the atmosphere being considerably cooled and freshened by the water all around. It really seemed like a miniature insight into the mysteries of the deep, as the finny tribe, among which glimmered some disagreeable looking little monsters, were swimming about among the stones, pebbles and ferns. At one end of the grotto, immediately facing the entrance, which admitted only a feeble ray of light, there came splashing from a rocky height, a sheet of water reflecting an emerald hue, caught partly from the overhanging ivy. A large basin in the centre, with moss-covered sides, received the falling water, and the crystal rill with its tinkling music flowed gently on, and out of sight. So did we emerge out of the darkness to enjoy the brilliant sunset, and to listen to some operatic airs by a magnificent band of music. Chairs were selected near a large wire cage filled with paroquets and other birds, whose warbling notes were responded to by little Alice in a melange of French and English words.

"All things must have an end," was our sad musing, as the sun went down, and our steps turned away from the lovely garden.   The fine afternoon had brought out all Paris, affording one the best opportunity possible to see the people.   Some persons were clad in the picturesque costumes of their respective countries, the bright, variegated colors imparting a brilliancy to the scene; but, very little can be said in praise of the beauty of the women seen on that occasion, the French, in general, certainly lacking it.   In all my wanderings among thousands of the fair sex, I do not remember to have met a half-dozen pretty women, other than Americans. Once in the English restaurant I saw two faces that any land might have been proud to claim.   They were English beauties, engaged in the traffic of sweetmeats and candies.   One was white as Alpine snows (and this comparison is barely just), with hair purely flaxen, bound with a violet ribbon, and adorned with a single camelia.   The other was of a more animated style, with a bright, cheerful face, an eye speaking a thousand fancies by its lustre and twinkle, and with that glorious crown—luxuriant hair—which might have even excited the envy of several Spanish señoritas who were sitting at a refreshment table near by   But now we must make our farewell to the *Champ de Mars*, upon whose site have not only been gathered the products of the world, but thousands, nay, millions of the human race, from Kings, Emperors, and nearly all the crowned heads of this great continent, to the poorest and humblest of mankind—the beggar and perchance the outcast!   As for

myself, I feel a deep sense of gratitude for the good fortune that wafted me to a foreign land.   The long-cher-
ished dream of Europe has become a sweet reality; yet
with all these enjoyments, and the appreciation thereof,
my heart clings not the less fondly to America!

CHAPTER V.

WHAT a relief from the routine of dinners at home is afforded in the restaurants of Paris,—an institution indispensable to the happiness of the Frenchman, and conducive to the comfort of the stranger! A few evenings since found us at the *Dîner de Paris*, in the *Passage Jouffroy*, where an abundant meal can be had for the moderate sum of five francs. The successful management of so large an establishment must be owing to the wonderful order that reigns everywhere, from the cash-counter, that meets the eye at the head of the stairway, to the brisk and polite waiting of the *garçons*. The dinner consists of a fixed number of dishes, including *vin ordinaire*, which the American lady very frequently leaves for the waiter, who acknowledges the favor in the oft-repeated and never-failing *"Merci!"* To glance the eye down the long line of tables, adapted to parties of from two to twelve, is to take in at u view hundreds busily engaged in plentiful repast, which the reader may doubt from the cheapness of the price, but which those bountifully blessed with appetite can conscientiously affirm. And what an array of characters all around! There is a fashionably attired lady, whose

expensive silk robe and jeweled fingers entitle her to a
royal meal, but who seems quite content with the dainty
bits that are being served to her in quick succession.
Her neighbor on one side is a flashy fop, with a massive
gold chain, the huge links of which awake a suspicion
that pure metal is not in all that glitters. His eye-
glasses, doubtless genuine, bear evidence that his travels
over the Continent have impaired his sight, or else their
frequent adjustment is occasioned by the belief that
there is improved coquetry in the stare, if it passes
through the medium of glass. Very near by sits a
plain old gentleman, who, it is evident, speaks not a
word of French, for he grows red in the face whenever
the *garçon* addresses him. How many of our people,
ignorant of the language, present a ridiculous appearance by their gestures, when their mouths dare not utter
a word! Those having a smattering often labor so hard
at a single sentence as to induce a fit of strangulation;
but the latter word comes in *mal à propos* to the *Dîner
de Paris*, with its luscious morsels. There is a saucy
pair of eyes belonging to a *demoiselle* not far off, that
play like light artillery upon her escort, a sedate youth
(an American, I am sure), who seems to be dreaming
more of philosophy than of flippant French love; yet I
wager to a conquest by her in the end. In a word, this
is a nondescript assemblage of persons, whose performances with knives and forks do them more credit than
could a pen-and-ink description.

Recently a large party was given on the *Champs Elysées* by Mrs. Bowler, of Cincinnati, to her son and his

lovely bride. The young couple appeared supremely happy; but how else could it be when

"At God's altar radiant run
The current of two lives in one?"

The presence of the old French artist, the Count Maxamilian de Waldeck, one hundred and two years old, and his wife, about fifty years his junior, formed quite a contrast with the bride and groom in their connubial spring-time. I was presented to the Count, and asked him to confide to me the *secret* of longevity. He quickly replied: "The secret lies in this, my child,—I never allow one pulsation of my heart to be quicker than another." The *charm* of living so long I ween, must reside in an amiable wife that permits him to "pursue the even tenor of his way." It may be well to follow this advice towards preserving youth, for it has certainly enabled the Count to assist at banquets, when others, taking an opposite view of life and its cares, have been "gathered to their rest." Mrs. Dewey, of California, looked as usual, queenly and handsome. Our Minister to Spain, Hon. Jno. P. Hale, and daughters, and Col. McClure were present, their faces reviving many pleasant reminiscences connected with entertainments we had enjoyed together in Washington, ere dire war came to mar the gaiety. The bridal reception closed with numerous good wishes of friends for the *nouveaux mariés*, who are soon to start on a tour to Egypt. It would seem that the love of distant and difficult travel is on the increase with Americans, judging by the numbers now directing their steps to the East; to the shores of the "low, smooth Nile," the Cleopatra land!   *   *

A visit to *Notre Dame* must be chronicled—the magnificent cathedral which has stood through centuries, and has seen enacted pageants that have hallowed its every inch of ground! What were our thoughts as we paced its lonely aisles—did we not people them from the dim yet glorious past with kings, queens, prelates, statesmen and generals? There stood Napoleon and Josephine with the imperial crowns set upon their brows! Then we heard the bridal vow of Eugenie rising to heaven amid the perfume of flowers, and the solemn hush of the august assemblage. But fair ceremonies were not all, for a dark vision floated before the mind's eye in that the sanctuary was invaded and the holy shrines sacked! We seemed to hear the solemn *Te Deum* that celebrated the triumph of the French arms, and again, the mass for the repose of the souls of brave men who had passed forever from scenes of strife.

Several days might be devoted to this edifice, so grand in its naves, columns, arches, stained windows, high altar and chapels. The celebrated marble group by Coustou—the *Descent from the Cross*—is a master-piece; and very beautiful are the illustrations of sacred subjects, delicately carved on the oaken choir-stalls and pulpit. However, it is impossible to stop to enumerate the various attractions in the body of the Cathedral, for the sacristy, with its gorgeous treasures, demands our time. Here are the ecclesiastical vestments worn at the marriage of the present Emperor, and those worn by Pius

VII at the coronation of Napoleon I,—the coronation robes of Napoleon I,—a chalice set with precious stones, presented by Henry IV,—and several croziers and mitres of gold and silver. Our attention was particularly drawn to an ivory cross, presented to Mme. de la Vallière by Louis XIV, after she had entered the convent. The inscription read: "*Louis XIV à Sœur Louise de la Miséricorde Carmelite, Mme. de la Vallière.*" What a commentary might here be made upon unholy love! The unhappiness it occasioned served to turn the heart of the unhappy Louise to God! After musing awhile over the vanities of the deceased Monarch, once so great in his bewigged pride and flowing robes, I turned to the portraits of the Archbishops on the windows, one of whom was Denis Affre, who lost his life in the insurrection of 1848. A splendid monument is erected to his memory in a chapel of the Cathedral, with his ever-memorable words: "*Puisse mon sang être le dernier versé.*" There is also a full-length portrait of Archbishop Denis Sibour, who was assassinated near the entrance of the Church of St. Etienne du Mont, at one of its festivals, in 1857, by a priest named Verger. The priest was executed in the same month that the murder was committed. Another chapel is said to have received the remains of the hapless young Dauphin, son of Louis XVI; and still another contains a monument to Cardinal de Belloy, the distinguished prelate who took part in the ceremonies at the coronation of Napoleon I. South of Notre Dame is the site where once stood the Archbishop's palace, destroyed by the

H

insurgents in 1831. A Gothic fountain, called *Notre Dame*, now marks the spot.

The Church of St. Sulpice boasts a magnificent portico, with a double range of Doric columns, and is reached by a broad flight of steps. The corner-stone of the building was laid by Anne of Austria, but the structure was not completed until after the lapse of a hundred years. Its architecture is of the Corinthian, Doric and Ionic styles. The frescoes in the side-chapels are rare and beautiful, and four of the most attractive paintings are those in the Chapel of Our Lady, representing *The Annunciation, Visitation, Birth of the Savior*, and *Presentation*. The richly-carved organ displays seventeen figures playing on instruments, and chief among them is King David. Before entering the nave we saw the colossal shells for holy water, presented to Francis I by the Venetian Republic. The stained glass windows are of great merit. Fronting this beautiful church is the fountain of St. Sulpice, with statues of Fénelon, Bossuet, Fléchier and Massillon, and four recumbent lions.

During our wanderings in that quarter of the city, on the Boulevard St. Michel, we observed the magnificent fountain of the same name. St. Michael is represented overcoming the dragon. The water falls into five different basins, conveying the idea of a pronged shower. The city of Paris erected the fountain in 1860. These fountains that intersperse the city are great ornaments, most of them being richly sculptured. The sound of the falling water attracts the distant ear, and the sight of it pleases the eye, fatigued by the glare of innumerable buildings.

We threaded the labyrinth of the *Bon Marché*, by reputation the cheapest *magasin* in Paris. Go when you will, there is a surging crowd to jostle you at every step, and the manner in which you are carried along and tossed about recalls the billows of the sea. The buzz of voices, the tramping of feet, the rapid gyrations of countless employés, and the haste with which purchases are made, combine to create a confusion too much for the head-piece, which invariably gives way ere the cash gives out. On leaving this Babel, we gladly turned to the freedom of the street, but soon found ourselves enticed into the *Petit St. Thomas*, another mammoth store, vieing with the *Bon Marché* in fine merchandise and moderate charges, but certainly more orderly, and not so much frequented by the poorer classes.

The *boulevards*, those superb streets, abounding in stores, cafés and restaurants, prove most attractive to the stranger. When one mingles with the crowd, and sees the bustle and fickle excitement of the Parisians, the false glare added to the brilliant show,—takes in an overwhelming glance of shop-treasures, and notes the march of progress everywhere—the mind conceives the full truth of Saxe's lines :

> " Inventive France! what wonder-working schemes
> Astound the world whene'er a Frenchman dreams !
> What fine-spun theories,—ingenious, new,
> Sublime, stupendous, everything but true !
> One little favor, O! Imperial France !
> Still teach the world to cook, to dress, to dance;
> Let, if thou wilt, thy boots and barbers roam ;
> But keep thy morals and creeds at home."

A *cocher* should always be summoned for the Boulevard de Sébastopol in its magnificent extent, but one is always content to wear out shoes on the Boulevard des Italiens. where attractions multiply with every step. How busy and gay, with masses of people pushing on to some aim or business scheme, or for the recreation of mind and body—certainly a wide field for pleasure, as well as for observation and study. Here saunters along the student from the Latin quarter, who, if questioned, would doubtless pronounce the atmosphere about the Grand Hôtel far less buoyant than that of the Boulevard St. Michel. Daintily stepping, appears *une jolie Américaine*, with eyes intent upon some shop-marvel (a treasure of a thing in Valenciennes lace or some finely embroidered *lingerie*) that calls forth an earnest ejaculation of praise, and at once loosens the clasp of her *porte-monnaie.* Here a newspaper vender brushes against a fashionably attired Marquise, just alighted from her *coupé*, and knocks from her careless hand a light parcel containing several pairs of delicately tinted gloves. They catch the dust of the street and are spoiled; but the independent boy rushes on, protected by the "liberty of the press," or that which it gives to its employés. Now passes a distinguished *membre du Corps Legislatif*, wearied from the discharge of parliamentary duties, all heedless of the bunch of violets which the meagre hand of a beautiful flower-girl thrusts before him; then an actress or *danseuse*, upon whose countenance are traces of *rouge* and late hours; the sewing-girl, returning from the *modiste*, where her needle has plied industriously nearly three-fourths of the day; the prosperous banker; the struggling musician, and the rich merchant; lastly, the poor artist and author—the former giving to the world rare and splendid creations of his genius, the latter lofty and poetical thought, for which neither receives more than a tithe of the reward that is justly his. Whilst the ceaseless tramp is being kept up on this great thoroughfare, amid the sound of rolling carriages and many voices, a regiment of Zouaves advances with the French colors waving, and martial music fills the air, the strains dying away to give place to a favorite air of *La Grande Duchesse*.

November 15.—An entertainment, in compliment to my arrival, proved an occasion of much enjoyment to me. Prominent among the guests was Mme. Zborowska, who wore her bridal dress—a delicate straw silk, covered with inimitable flounces of point d'Alençon lace. Miss Eddins, of Alabama, a delicate blonde, arrayed in white tulle, might well have passed for the "white lady of Avenel." Miss Gordon, of Ohio, always lovely; the intelligent and graceful Misses Gregory, of New York; Mr. Jos. B. Varnum, of New York; Mrs. Mygatt, a wealthy and interesting prize; Mr. and Mrs. Coolidge, of New York; Mrs. Fellows, of New York; Colonel Hoffman, United States Legation; Mr. Ryan, of the New York *Times;* Mr. Nicolay, U. S. Consul; and Dr. Sims, our popular American physician, contributed vastly to the brilliancy of the occasion. After supper we entered into the dance with renewed spirit, caring for

II*

naught save "badinage, music and mirth."   *   *   *
A few mornings since an interesting group of children
gathered around our board at a *déjeûner à la fourchette*.
It was a kindly sight—those bright, winsome creatures,
with their *poupées*, dressed like themselves quite *à la
mode*. One of the parents, Gen. McClellan (who seems
to find diversion in the fascinations of Paris), was present; and another, the venerable Commodore Stevens, of
New Jersey, famed for his formidable battery, certainly
gave no thought, on that day, to the pride of his declining years, but seemed to revel in the mirth of rosy childhood. Mr. Edward Gould Buffum, a talented gentleman
attached to the New York *Herald*, looked in upon the
juvenile party. The introduction of buckwheat cakes
was received with great satisfaction, that article of food
being scarcely known in France.

November 16.—Mr. and Mme. Z—— called for me
to drive to St. Germain en Laye, a distance of five leagues
from Paris. The day was a golden one, and will ever
remain such in its associations with beautiful scenes.
How pure and delicious the air, as we escaped from the
boundary of the city! There arose majestically to view
Mont Valérien, one of the strongest forts that defend
Paris! It lodges a garrison of 1,500 infantry, besides officers of artillery, and an immense amount of material of
war. Unfortunate the enemy that should come within
range of its guns! The mount is quite isolated, and from
its summit there must be a fine view of the city. Jerome
Napoleon Bonaparte of Baltimore is said to be stationed

there. We stopped at Malmaison, once the home of Josephine and Napoleon, but were debarred the pleasure of visiting the château, it being closed by order of the Emperor. The persuasive eloquence of Mme. Z—— proved of no avail with the guard, and we had to rest content with a view of its exterior and of the grounds. How much of interest hangs around this spot, which witnessed the happiest days of Josephine, and the sorrowful ones following her divorce—which calls up interesting historical scenes, and is also made sacred by her demise! This last association recalls her sad and loving heart, her heroism under suffering, and the beautiful prayer uttered in her dying moments: "Oh God! watch over Napoleon while he remains in the desert of this world. Alas! though he hath committed great faults, hath he not expiated them by great sufferings? Just God! thou hast looked into his heart, and hast seen by how ardent a desire for useful and durable improvements he was animated. Deign to approve my last petition, and may this image of my husband bear me witness, that my latest prayers were for him and my children." True and steadfast must have been the love embodied in her last words: "*L'Isle d'Elbe—Napoléon!*" At Reuil, not far from Malmaison, the remains of Josephine are interred in the small village church. The monument, which represents her kneeling in prayer, bears naught but this simple inscription: "*A. Joséphine, Eugène et Hortense,* 1825." Hortense sleeps near Josephine, it being her last request to be buried beside her mother. The statue of the Queen is also in the kneeling attitude.

Upon the base of the monument are engraved these words: "*A la Reine Hortense, son fils Napoléon III.*"

St. Germain en Laye is a town of 14,000 inhabitants, and is a favorite resort of English and French families during the summer, on account of its salubrious atmosphere. It is said to be eighty-six mètres above the level of the sea, and sixty-three above the Seine. The streets are irregularly laid out, and the town looks ancient, compared with Paris. After viewing the château (now being restored to its former grandeur), we gained the noble terrace, where the scene presented was one of the most beautiful I had ever witnessed. It is one hundred feet wide, one and a-half miles in length, and affords a promenade unequaled. The landscape glowed with beauty—open fields and grassy spaces, little gardens bright with flowers and the vine, hills and dales studded thick with trees, the Seine in its meandering course, and the girdling forests of Vésinet. Mont Valérien's height was not lost to view, nor was the tower of St. Denis. Even the Arc de Triomphe and the dome of Les Invalides at Paris lent a proud interest to the scene. Such was the panorama, lit up with glorious sunshine! The pavilion of Henry IV overlooks a hollow filled with shrubbery. There is a tradition that the spot upon which it stands was the birthplace of Louis XIV (a finely chiseled cradle on the building attesting it), but another gives it the honor of his baptism. Either event would suffice to invest it with interest; and yet the purpose it serves now, viz.: that of a restaurant, although less distinguished, is certainly more in consonance with our utilitarian views.

The St. Germain forest covers an area of eight thousand acres, with a circuit of nearly thirty miles, and all the routes are evenly laid out, their length being three hundred and eighty leagues. It was the rendezvous for the chase, and the names of many of the most distinguished persons of various eras mark its avenues. Francis I and Louis XIV contributed greatly towards its embellishment. We confined our promenade chiefly to the beautiful avenues near the château, where the sunlight glanced in and out among the trees, which are so regular in line and so uniform in shape as scarcely to vary an inch one from the other. Many a proud beauty has walked under the shade of those forest trees (the chestnut, oak and elm), and down the broad avenues has swept many a courtly train,—the queen and the courtesan,—one throwing the witchery of pure love, the other the spell of unchaste affection over the place and its surroundings. Regretting the close of day, that put an end to our explorations, we lingered awhile in that grand open space fronting the château, where the luxuriant mignonette in beds, all bordered in green, gave out its delightful perfume. Our drive homeward was by lovely moonlight, and the enchantment of the scene had imbued us with a sentimentality which found vent in quotations from the poets, none of which, perhaps, were more appropriate or expressive than Shakspeare's " In such a night as this," etc.

November 17.—An invitation to dinner, extended by my friends, Mr. and Mrs. D——, at the Grand Hôtel, afforded me a favorable opportunity of seeing by gas-light the magnificent *salle-à-manger*. I experienced not a little pleasure in pacing the long corridors of the hotel and the beautiful reading-room—ground that had been so often trod in former years by relatives and friends, and rendered familiar by description. In the course of the evening we were joined by Mrs. Judge Field, of California, and Mr. and Mrs. Findla, of the same State.

* * * A huzzah for our navy has not only gone up from the shores of the Mediterranean, where now the great naval hero looks out upon his proud fleet, but here in gay Paris! A recent dinner-party *chez nous* was composed in part of the wives of those who gallantly wear the stars and anchors, and enjoy the distinction of being attached to the Farragut squadron. Who will not contend that the navy has no right to *widow* such attractive women by sending their husbands on a cruise? Yet they should be willing to yield to a necessity that opens to them the charms of Paris. And Paris might be proud to claim for a season, however short, the brilliant Mrs. Shirk, and Mrs. Moore, whose face Murillo might have chosen for a Madonna subject. * * *

My friend Miss T——, who has the classic land of Italy at heart, has just said farewell. May my hopes in that direction be realized before leaving Europe! At present an opportunity offers to visit Belgium and Holland, and I gladly take up the wanderer's staff.

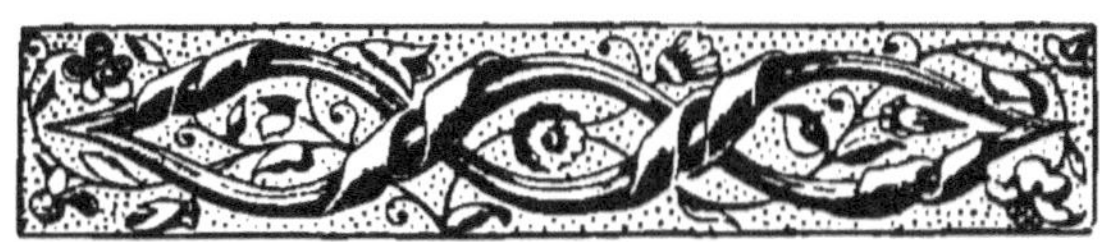

CHAPTER VI.

ON leaving Paris yesterday afternoon, we found at the station Mr. Buffum, the accomplished journalist, who joined our party, and continued with us nearly all the way to this beautiful capital. A heavy shower of rain set in on our arrival here; and from the overcast appearance of the sky, disagreeable weather threatens to attend all our journeyings. How unfortunate for one suffering the persecution of chills and fevers,—my sorry condition at this inopportune time and season!

The *Hôtel de Belle Vue* on Place Royale, true to its name, and from its elevated situation, affords a charming view of the city; for in its vicinity are clustered the finest buildings—the Royal Palace, the Park (affording a beautiful promenade under the shade of fine old trees), the best hotels and private residences. Within a stone's throw of our location is a statue of the valiant crusader, Godfrey de Bouillon, who laid siege to Jerusalem in 1099, and delivered it from the hands of the Moslems. The warrior is mounted on a noble steed, bearing a shield, and holding aloft a banner that never waved in a worthier cause. But the finest monument of the city is that erected to the memory of the men who fell in the revolutionary struggle of 1830, and which stands in the Place des Martyrs, one of the principal squares. Four kneeling angels surround the base, and the figure of Liberty is its crowning ornament. At the Place de Congrès, also, a superb monumental column rises to challenge the admiration.

The lower part of the city is much less attractive than the elevated portion, its streets lacking the cleanliness for which Brussels is proverbial; yet one is constantly reminded of the French capital, and thinks the title of "miniature Paris" aptly applied. The Hôtel de Ville is grand in Gothic architecture, its pyramidal tower rising to the giddy height of three hundred and sixty-four feet. We were interested in the paintings within the building, the Gobelin tapestries, and frescoed ceilings. One peculiarity of the latter is, that some of the figures are painted with an adroitness and skill that seem to make them shift their position in correspondence with the movements of the spectator. At the south end of the room the sweet, smiling face of a goddess was directed towards us, and upon our moving to the north end (where we expected to get only a back view), imagine our surprise at finding the head of the goddess still fronting us. The guide was evidently amused at my wonderment, and was disposed to compliment me by saying, "*Regardez la déesse couchante, couverte de fleurs, —Elle vous aime sans doute, parcequ'elle vous suit toujours avec ses grands yeux bleus.*" A very finely executed portrait of Maria Thérèse of Austria interested me more than it otherwise would have done, from having recently reviewed the life of that Queen in one of Mühlbach's charming novels. The Grand Place, where the Hôtel de Ville stands, contains other objects of interest,—the Maison du Roi, where Charles V signed his abdication; and the bronze statues of Counts Egmont and Horn on one pedestal, erected near the house in front of which they were beheaded. Here is commemorated one of the many cruel and merciless acts of the Duke of Alva, which throughout the countries of Belgium and Holland cry out against the name of that detested tyrant.

I lingered for an hour at the establishment of Mme. Everaert and Sister,—a house rich in its possessions of lace, Brussels, Chantilly and Valenciennes, pleasant reminders of the miracles of that fabric at the Exposition. What a temptation—the shawls, flounces, capes, handkerchiefs, collars, parasol and fan covers, and all other articles that please the vanity of woman! A well-filled purse is needed here, for the polite proprietress is quite irresistible.

A visit to the grand and ancient edifice of *St. Gudule* gratified us far more than the municipal palace we had so recently left. It ranks as one of the most splendid cathedrals erected in the middle ages. Its large square towers and its style of architecture recalled the Notre Dame of Paris. The great attraction of this church is its stained glass, the principal window displaying in gorgeous tints *The Last Judgment*, by Frans Florins, a Flemish painter. On the north side is a chapel illustrating the Holy Sacrament. In an alcove shut in with glass is a statue of the dead Savior, covered over

I

with a drapery of gauze, and around it are gathered the figures of saints bearing offerings. A monument to the memory of a Belgian philanthropist, Chanoine Triste, next attracts the eye; and lastly, the famous carved pulpit by Verbruggen, representing the expulsion of our first parents from Eden. The figures of Adam and Eve at the base are life-size; and crowning the whole is the Virgin, with the infant Jesus, endeavoring to overpower the serpent with the cross. Many beautifully decorated altars and paintings complete the richness of the edifice. Our reluctance to leave the sanctuary and its splendors was mollified by the thought that our route would lead us to many other holy temples, ancient and costly.

Who that has sojourned in Europe for a short time has not observed the faithful attendance of the people of Catholic faith at their places of worship, and how close is the tie between rich and poor in the costliest of tabernacles. On the cold stone before the altar, under the light of tapers and the shadow of the cross, a richly attired personage kneels beside a mendicant; — the fair and innocent child bends in prayer, her garments touching those of an erring sister, seeking forgiveness at the throne of grace; and the laborer in his spotted blouse, leaving his work for a few moments, shows honest devotion to his religion :—thus seen, however, does not the poverty of his attire or his stained garments rise to the significance of Joseph's coat of many colors?

The Hague, *November* 20.—The ride from Brussels to this town made no agreeable impressions upon my mind, perhaps owing to the fact of my being a miserably sick woman from intermittent fever. I enjoyed the sympathy of the traveling public; but the Custom-house officers obdurately closed their hearts against me, in that they desired me to alight from the car, and exhibit myself in conjunction with the luggage. Attempting the dodge of ignorance of the language, I was just ill enough to be spiteful. *"Descendez, s'il vous plâit"* was repeated again and again to dull ears, which could not be made to comprehend, and back was sent the response in a most decided tone: " You must excuse me, sir; I am ill." But the importunate man intending not to be outdone in his duty, soon brought to his aid a person who could converse with me in my own tongue. In retaliation for their victory I felt inclined to plead lameness, and request them to carry me; but not weighing two hundred pounds, I fancied they might not object to the task. At last, forced to yield to my persecutors, a descent was made just as the cry *"en voiture"* rang in my ears, and the travelers were issuing in haste from the Bureau. This proved my small triumph, and I took especial delight in saying in tolerably good French: *"Bon jour, messieurs—Je vous remercie bien!"* In our compartment we found a pleasant and profitable *compagnon de voyage* in a little Frenchman from Havre, who gave us a foresight of the journey, and cautioned us against a petty imposition practised on through travelers by Rotterdam cabmen, who endeavor to make fees by the offer of their vehicles, when the railroad ticket includes the transfer by omnibus. We soon saw it exemplified.　Here it may be well to mention another deception perpetrated by hotel-keepers, viz.: the candle swindle.　Bills are often stretched out to a surprising length with *bougies*.　Mantels have as chief ornaments three or four candlesticks, and though only one candle be consumed, there is a charge for the remainder, which the poor traveler, in a hasty settlement, pays.　Even the fair name of Brussels wears the candle stain, proved by the overcharge of that article on our bills.

We are comfortably located at the Belle Vue, in this pretty little town, to all appearances clean and neat. My room looks out on a lovely little garden, whose remnant of summer verdure, yesterday baptized with rain, is now glistening under some bright rays of sunshine. May they continue for one day at least to help my suffering condition!　A streak of bad luck befell us in the closure of *Maurits Huis*, where are exhibited the celebrated pictures of Rembrant's Anatomical Lesson, and Paul Potter's Bull, and we had to remain satisfied with engravings of those two master-pieces seen in the *salle-à-manger*.

The King of Holland is now at his palace,—an announcement that excludes visitors therefrom.　It is said that his Majesty pays a visit to the Queen's palace, designated "The House in the Woods," only once a year.　Here comment might be made on connubial infelicity which makes inroads upon royalty with the same insidious venom it deals to the common crowd.　No earthly throne is so exalted as to be beyond the reach of sorrow.

Our disappointment was great this morning on learning that our Embassador and all his attachés were absent, as one of the party, bearer of the secret cypher for the United States government, is hunting up Ministers and Consuls. Fortunate are they who hold such missions as to admit of a residence at a point remote from that to which they are accredited. Were this Paris, few would desert their post. The urgent necessity of continuing on our journey deprives us of seeing the forest and the Queen's palace, which is described as a scene of enchantment,—a picture worthy of the *Arabian Nights;* and therefore to imagination must be left its gardens, lakes, and embellishments of art. In a drive through the town, canals were remarked here and there,—an indisputable water-right Holland largely possesses.

In this country houses seem to rise up out of the water. Little children hang out of windows entirely heedless of danger, and sit on the very brink of the canals, whilst their mothers, bare-footed, are engaged with their brooms. Certainly the protection that shields them is from that High and Holy Power that watches over "the children of men." The healthy appearance of the inhabitants, especially the lower classes, is a strong appeal to the pale-faced daughters of America to adopt the duck-mode of living for a few weeks or months. A good-natured Dutch woman suggested this idea, as I glanced at her rounded face, ruddy cheeks, and muscular arms.

AMSTERDAM, *November* 22.—The route from the Hague to this quaint old city lay over a flat country, abounding in wind-mills, causeways and canals. The

I*

approach to the town of Leiden, with its celebrated university of five hundred students—among whom are doubtless many youths of our country—awakened an interest which could not be gratified in a visit, as inexorable business stood in the way. We caught but a glimpse of Haarlem, whose history can never be forgotten in the memorable siege it sustained against the Duke of Alva, when its brave people suffered to the last extremity before yielding to the bloody and rapacious Spaniard. Added to the necessary horrors of war, alas! how doubly sad it is when conquerors become tyrants to strike again a fallen foe, as was the case when this famine-stricken town surrendered, giving up 57 of her best citizens, and saw the terms of amnesty violated, in the ruthless murder of her garrison and two thousand citizens.

Our eyes took in at a rapid glance a portion of the 50,000 acres of land that were redeemed out of the immense lake of 1,000,000,000 tons of water. The famous engines that accomplished this extraordinary pumping are still to be seen at Haarlem. Upon the flats large herds of cattle were browsing, and every cow was kindly cared for in a comfortable blanket to protect her from the weather. The fit was perfect, and it appeared to us that the matronly hands providing these comforts had taken quite as much pains with the cut and stitch as they would bestow upon garments intended for the little ones of the homestead. *   *   *

We have taken lodgings at a hotel thoroughly Dutch in name, Brack's Oude Doelen. I find my apartments overlooking a canal, whose turbid water is far from being a pleasant sight. The bridges are not to be counted in a hasty glance, but one can readily credit the estimate which puts them down at three hundred, and the islands at ninety. This old hotel has been in use two hundred and fifty years, and does not yet look like toppling down : my greatest fear in such an event would arise from its close proximity to the muddy water—a bath in which would not leave me white as snow. The buildings strike one as being very quaint, and deserve the appellation of glass houses, from the number and width of the windows. The bricks with which they are built are exceedingly small, and are laid with great uniformity, showing a vast expenditure of labor and time. The amount of scouring done here in a day is something wonderful, the women seeming to wear away the very stone by the busy application of brushes, and the indomitable will with which they work. They appear on door-step, pavement, and within doors, and verily is their labor plied with a Sampson strength. They wear a peculiar wooden shoe called sabot, which is very suitable to this "Venice of the North." I have several times been brushed along by street-sweepers, whose broom-mania always elicits a smile, suggested by the recollection of a song heard in my childhood: "From Deutschland I come with my light-wares all laden, . . . Buy a broom ! . . . buy a broom !" A picturesque costume is occasionally met with, and the head-gear or bonnet usually calls forth an ejaculation of wonder ; but what excites the greatest comment is the complexion of the women, for would not a peach in its ripest state pale before their crimson flush? Much that is *good* is said of Amsterdam. It has many charitable institutions; beggars are so few as to be at a *premium*, and the inhabitants—whilst not altogether discarding worship at the shrine of *Schnapps*—are not given to intemperance.

Touching upon the bibulous subject, observation leads to the reflection that some of the European countries set an example to our people worthy of imitation. In the *salon* as well as in the thoroughfare, there is a commendable observance of propriety. *Par exemple*, in the gayest capital of the world—Paris—the eye is seldom shocked by the sight of a reeling inebriate, whereas in our large cities such a sight is of no rare occurrence— men of brains and money sinking into a common degradation. Oh! that America would cast off the abomination of strong and poisonous drink, and welcome the milder substitutes!

We visited a choice collection of paintings bequeathed to the city by the late Mr. Forder, and were particularly struck with two small gems. One was a gallant courtier making love after a fashion that looked enrapturing on canvas. The recipient seemed to be the embodiment of "the love that makes summer-tide all the year long," and the possessor of "the heart that is its own heaven." The other was a Moorish group on the shores of the Mediterranean. In pensive mood they stood: the sea had caught the glow of the setting sun. Then our eyes fell on what was certainly a master-piece, occupying a large space at the head of the room. It represented the Saviour performing the miracles that are so abundantly told in the chapters of St. Mark. Suppliant women were there with sorrow and agony depicted on their countenances; chained captives; the blind, and those possessed of unclean spirits. How full of mercy such acts, and how comforting the words : " I come to bind up broken hearts, and to loosen the fetters of captives ! " Near by was another painting—the pious monks of St. Bernard and their dogs rescuing travelers in the snow. Many other pictures were worthy of a better notice than we could bestow; so having indulged in a general view, we drove to the King's Palace, situated on the Dam, a large open square.

The Dutch regard the palace as one of the wonders of the world, and so must visitors from distant lands accord to it their warmest admiration. It is built on 13,000 piles, and was erected in 1648. Fortunately for us, his Majesty was absent; and if we lost something at the Hague by his presence, we gained very much here in a visit to the interior of his palace. After entering the lower hall so superbly grand with its walls of Carrara marble, the attendant asked for our signatures which were forthwith inscribed in a royal big book. Heretofore it has always been my good luck to meet the politest of guides, and on this occasion our names were bracketed *à part*—a distinction on my account, so said the guide. "*N'importe*," said I, "so the beauties of the palace are not withheld from our gaze." Every room wore a gorgeous aspect, but principally the private audience chamber, the large and small *salle-à-manger*, and the chapel, in which were rich paintings and marble mantels with bas-reliefs most delicately carved.   Three scriptural pictures, covering entirely the walls of one saloon, represented *Moses and Aaron,—The reading of the Law at Mount Sinai,*—and *Solomon praying to God for wisdom.*   A painting over a doorway so closely imitated sculptured marble, that even a near approach could scarcely remove the illusion.   The ball-room is considered the finest in Europe, and its proud ceiling spurns support from pillars.   What a scene of sumptuous elegance it must present when chivalry and beauty meet on its floor! The *plafond* is of rich frescoing; and the chandeliers of crystal, are very beautiful and light in appearance, being formed of the smallest fragments strung at short distances on wires so delicate, as to be almost invisible. These myriad bits of glass scintillated like gems, and were diamonds to our bewildered eyes.   At one end of the room is a colossal figure of Altas, bearing on his shoulders *the world*, represented by a blue globe, studded with stars.   The panelings are all of white marble, and the four elements of the universe, fire, earth, air and water are represented by admirable figures.   The attention of the visitor turns from all this splendor to the shattered banners and flags of the eighty years' war, draped on high and black with the dust of time. Gloomily frowning down on the luxury below, these tattered emblems commemorate the valor of thousands that have bled for their country, and in their cobweb aspect are the skeletons of the palace!   A painting in the audience chamber, representing the dauntless Van Speyk firing the magazine of his ship, as the Belgians

were about to board it, won our admiration. In the
Throne-room was extended to me a royal favor, viz:
the invitation to sit in his Majesty's chair! The compliment came direct and flattering, as the attendant in
broad English informed me that no other lady had sat
there for years. A large eye embroidered in conspicuous colors on the back of the royal chair was very awe-
striking in its gaze. What is the signification of that
eye? Can it mean the "All-seeing One" that never
sleeps? If so, how it must ever appeal to the conscience
of the King who sits there to wield his sceptre over the
Netherlands!

This afternoon we rode through several streets that,
strange to say, had no canals; and in inspecting shop-
wares, I was near making the injudicious purchase of a
meerschaum, until the label of the case assured me it
was of Paris manufacture. In Paris there is a better
collection. The drive afforded a view of the prominent
features of the city, which frequently elicited the exclamation, " How strange is all this!" The docks were
a point of interest, filled as they were with vessels of all
nations. We descended from the carriage and indulged
in a promenade on the quay,—the breeze from the North
sea blowing chill and damp, to add discomfort to my
shaking frame; and oh! how I wished just then for the
balmy breath of the tropics.

The navigation of the canals is indeed a mystery, for
the boats are so huddled together that even a child could
step from one to another. Some are clumsy and ugly,
and one would hardly suppose them tenanted, were there

not ocular evidence of it in the occasional appearance of a man or a woman. About others there is quite an air of gentle life, for we observe a flower-pot, a work-box, or a piece of needle-work. It is to be understood that these boats are homes for many of the Dutch people. Our driver said they were "as good as houses on land ;" yet we could only think of the incongruous mingling of pigs, poultry and babies in one little cabin ;—but perhaps the maternal head contrives to keep the babies aloof.   *   *   *   *   *   *

Now as I write, a little village, Broek—six miles distant—is spoken of, where it is probable the American Consul can be found. Before starting on the expedition it would be a good idea to construct a trap for him, so as to make sure of the game. An accommodating maid—who bewitches me by a few words of English, very grateful to the ear after all the incomprehensible jargon around—has just made up a cheerful fire in the stove, and so bright is its glow that I refuse to leave it for the attractions of Broek—a village reputed to be so clean, and so much on the Turkish order, that even the Emperor Alexander was obliged to take off his shoes ere he entered its doors. Acknowledging an inferiority to the Emperor—an unworthiness to tread even on imaginary holy ground, and preferring a trip to Palestine instead — an impossibility — we cheerfully and wisely conclude to remain at Amsterdam.

November 23.—This morning's dawn crept on gray and chill, and for a long time I lay in bed exhorting the sun to come from behind its curtain, and cheer up the gloom of a room at *Brack's Doelen.* An invitation was extended to me last evening to go and see Blondin; but I lacked the courage to gaze upon such perilous feats, remembering too well the emotions excited by the extraordinary one at Niagara. Nearly all night a wide-awake spirit possessed me, and so I heard the exquisite chiming of the bells as the hours rolled by. Some serenaders halted near my window, and in the stillness of the "wee sma' hours" there was a charm of sweet music which awakened visions of home, far, far away. How much of profit to the heart does separation from loved ones bring! It makes us feel the value of one cherished spot, and all that it holds. But should not God be brought into those memories, His claim being greater than all earthly ties, and His home one "not made with hands—eternal in the heavens?"   *   *

I see this moment, crossing the bridge, two little children clad in Sunday attire, on their way to church. They are most cunning specimens of miniature women, with their gingham dresses to the feet, white caps with fluted ruffles, brown stuff shawls folded across their breasts and tied behind. They are just the size of my little ones, who I hope, on this Sabbath morn, are seated in dear old Trinity at Washington.   *   *   *

3 P. M.—Service has just been concluded at the English Episcopal chapel, a building as plain and neat as the modest little country churches seen in America. The altar, equally simple, has the British crest above, representing a gold lion crowned, and a white unicorn with

J

the inscriptions, *Honi soit qui mal y pense*, and *Dieu et mon droit*. Very impressive were the responses of the congregation and the singing, unaccompanied by organ. The hymn selected was " Jesus, Savior of my Soul," the second verse of which—"Other refuge have I none "—must ever strike a chord in the Christians' heart. The text taken from the 1st chapter of Micah, 13th verse, drew forth an able and eloquent sermon and the following prayer was offered with much fervor. "Almighty God, the fountain of all goodness, we humbly beseech thee to bless Albert Edward, Prince of Wales; the Princess of Wales, and all the royal family:—the King and Queen of the Netherlands and the Prince of Orange. Endue them with thy holy spirit; enrich them with thy heavenly grace; prosper them with all happiness; and bring them to thine everlasting kingdom through Jesus Christ our Lord. Amen."

* * * * * * A few more hours, and I shall bid farewell to Amsterdam, to my pleasant apartment, a parlor in dimensions, which presents quite an American or English air in the engravings that hang on its walls, viz: *Moral education*, the father and son,—*Religious education*, the mother and daughter,—*The welcome*, and the beautiful one of *Erin, farewell*. As I look on this picture, the face with its Evangeline type of sadness recalls a dear departed friend,—the low forehead, the wealth of hair, and the large lustrous eyes dreamily looking back to the past. Its words so fraught with tenderness read—

> " Erin, my country, though sad and forsaken,
>   In dreams I revisit thy sea-beaten shore,
> But alas ! in a far foreign land I awaken,
>   And sigh for the friends who can meet me no more."

ROTTERDAM, *November* 24.—" Behind time for once," was the exclamation yesterday afternoon as we drove away at furious speed to reach the railway station. If the term snail could be applied to me, another member of the party who was slow in counting *guilders* also justly deserved the appellation.

But amidst all our difficulties, rain storm included, we arrived just in time to make a graceful entry into the car, which unlike *time* and *tide* had seemed to wait kindly upon our movements. The only other occupant of the compartment was an intelligent University law student of Leiden, who spoke passably the English language. And here I shall relate an amusing incident that might be construed into a compliment to myself. The young man addressed me in these words—" Have you been playing in the city, Madame ? " Thinking I had probably misunderstood him, I requested a repetition of the inquiry, which was granted in a lower tone of voice. The look of ignorance upon my countenance evidently confused him, as did the vague reply—" I have not been long in Amsterdam; I am a tourist in this part of the world." Under continued embarrassment the student explained his mistake in this wise: " I thought I was addressing the celebrated actress Fr. Von Lib-yowski, who goes to Rotterdam to fill an engagement;—pray excuse me!" Yet notwithstanding the explanation made, he still seemed in doubt, looking at me the more critically, and pronouncing the resemblance most striking. Fearing that I might not deem it a compliment to be compared with, or mistaken for an actress, he assured me that *"Madame Von L—— etait bien belle et très distinguée."* We laughed off the mistake, and found the student on better acquaintance quite equal to a guide-book in his complete knowledge of the country, &c. Upon nearing the station of Leiden, a waiving of handkerchiefs from fellow students greeted him. Handing me his card, E. W. B .. g—Juris Studens—Leiden, and expressing wishes for our welfare and a safe journey, he glided from our presence, the door scarcely closing upon his form when from my lips irresistibly fell the music, "Thou art gone—Thou art gone," words from a song in the old opera of Amilie. The *adieu* doubtless proving a relief to him from a mistake that had been so sorely felt, he might have found comfort in another musical strain. "Thou art gone from my gaze!" It was argued that a picturesque appearance had much to do with the distinction I had gained, as I was thus described. "A white and lilac cachemire scarf tied over the head—as protection against neuralgia—a jaunty black velvet hat, with plume, a Scotch plaid shawl, and the prettiest red blanket on this side of the Atlantic." Continuing the journey, we passed Schiedam, of gin-fame, Delft, formerly noted for its pottery ware; and on arrival at Rotterdam secured rooms at the New Bath Hotel on the quay Boompjes.

Having for the last few days lived with our heads scarcely above water, it seemed but natural to find aquatic surroundings here. A perfect forest of masts was visible from my window. The service of this hotel is all that could be desired, as one might infer from our getting an excellent dinner, notwithstanding we arrived an hour after the time for the regular *table d'hôte*. Opposite at table sat a quaint old Irish gentleman who kept supplying me with *entremets*, and kindly handing over everything warm that was brought to him. Finding that we were Americans, he engaged the Col. in a long talk of our country, its commerce, institutions, politics, the late civil troubles, and other topics, and soon discovered that he was conversing with a gentleman of ability and intelligence. The old man seemed greatly pleased with the abundant information gained, and as he became more and more enlightened and interested, he would nervously exclaim "quite so! quite so!" Counting the phrase many times I thought he must have been born with it on his lips, or that he had made a bargain with himself to carry it to the grave. He told us sadly, and with a tear in the eye, that he had been awaiting in vain the arrival of several of his ships from Queenstown, but it was his belief that they had gone down in the recent gales. Almost involuntarily to my mind came the beautiful verse

> " Down to the wharves, as the sun goes down,
> And the daylights' tumult and dust and din
> Are dying away in the busy town,
> I go to see if my ship comes in."

J*

May the poor old man at last not feel the burden of
these lines still sadder—

> " But she comes not yet,—she will never come,
> To gladden my eyes, and my spirit more."

A bright fire, and two candles have enabled me to
inspect some curious, gloomy old pictures that entirely
cover the walls of my room.   The subjects are biblical,
two of which are Cain killing Abel and Rebekah at the
Well ; and over the arch of the fire-place which has no
mantel, is a paneling in bright colors representing Delilah shearing Sampson.

November 25.—The day has been passed in viewing
the town which is better built than Amsterdam, the
houses being much more commodious.   The hundreds
of ships lying at anchor, and the immense docks lining
the quay, that were constructed under the direction of
Napoleon I, amply attest its maritime importance.
What a busy scene was presented !   The women—who
seem to do even more work than the men—were sweeping hides and bagging wool.   We visited the American
Consulate, dispatched some business, and thence were
escorted by an *attaché* to the Cathedral church of St.
Lawrence, built 1472.   The interior is perfectly plain,
but the visitor is impressed with the lofty appearance
of the building.   The floors are almost entirely taken
up with the sunken tablets of stone which mark the
resting places of notable dead, each stone bearing a coat
of arms, with an inscription.   The principal tombs are

those of Admirals de Witt, Rortemaar, and Van Brakel;
the first representing a naval engagement in bas relief,
in which the sculpturing of the ships is nearly as fine as
pen or pencil tracing. The figure of the Admiral lies
extended, his head resting on a cushion of marble.
The organ is as magnificent as its dimensions are great,
having 6572 pipes and 90 registers. Outside of the
church our eyes met a truly Dutch scene in a fish market,
where were congregated numbers of women in smock-
frock costume selling the "finny tribe." It being
market-day, the town wore a lively aspect, and the
canals seemed more blocked up than ever. The dress
of the women here slightly differs from that worn by
their Amsterdam sisters, the calico short basque being
more in vogue among the lower classes. A better and
more expensive style of apparel includes a bonnet made
of white muslin or lace, and those wonderful serpentine
horns, or coils of gilt that protrude from the region of
the ear, giving the wearer a decidedly martial look.
One cannot fail to observe their excessive love of self-
adornment. Ear-rings of gilt are worn so long as nearly
to touch the shoulder, and numerous strings of beads
encircle the throat and chest, the dress-body being generally cut away to favor the display. What a sensation
Les Hollandaises would create on any of our fashionable
streets! Our sight-seeing included the Palace of Justice, and the bronze statue erected to Erasmus—the Re-
former—who was born here in 1467.

ANTWERP, *November* 25.—We commenced our jour-

ney to this place by embarking on the Meuse river, a
change from railway travel quite acceptable, the scenery
being so novel and interesting. At every turn there
were wind-mills whose giant fans—like mighty arms—
beat and beat the morning breeze; and to each revolution a little maiden who sat on deck twirled her thumb,
to keep time with the movement, as she said; but the
gentlemen thought it subserved a better purpose, viz.:
the display of a fair and pretty little dimpled hand.
The coast for miles is ornamented with a double row of
trees, whose peculiarity consists in their being closely
trimmed in pyramidal form ; and now and then appear
little low cottages, with red tiling, and others whose
roofs are covered with green moss. The dykes with
their wicker and brushwood, tall grasses and rushes,
have a soft, feathery look, far more agreeable to the eye
than a hard, pebbly shore, and are intersected by numerous docks and shipyards. Steamers on this river
always summon little boats from the shore to take off
passengers at different points. There was a detention of
twenty minutes at Dordrecht, a town of respectable appearance, and very soon after we were transferred to the
cars at Moordyk. The ride by rail to Antwerp afforded
a varied scenery of neatly laid out vegetable gardens,
dense shrubbery, and hardy pine forests; the latter recalling familiarly those of our own native land.

In this interesting old Flemish city, comfortable quarters can be found at the Hôtel St. Antoine, which has
the advantage of a park in its contiguity to Place Verte.
Place de Meir is a handsome thoroughfare, finer than

any to be seen in Holland.   At 6½ o'clock we dined at
table d'hôte, where there were sixty persons present,
mostly gentlemen.   Such a clattering of foreign tongues
and jingling of wine-glasses I had not heard since my
arrival in Europe; and the holy command, "Love thy
neighbor," seemed to be carried out to its fullest extent
in the friendliness everywhere evinced.   Surely four
languages, independent of English, were distinguishable
in that incessant hum.   At my side was seated a fair
young girl, who had evidently just been relieved from
an academic course of study; and towards the close of
the meal her papa jocularly remarked : "My daughter,
I will call this a matrimonial market, and would like to
know your choice."   There were black eyes near by
sparkling like the bead in the champagne glasses, and
she might not have wandered beyond the fourth person
on the opposite side, but for the fickle instinct that led
her on to the fascinations of a handsome blonde some
distance down.   By that time an answer was exacted,
and by way of compromise between light and shade,
she gave this evasive answer to her gray-haired parent :
"If there was one like you, dear papa, as good and
noble, that man would be my choice; but I have certainly not found him in this field, and may not in *all
the world.*"   The papa looked proud and grateful; but
he was nonplussed, and the meal was finished.   Nearly
all night, and to the disturbance of my orisons, several
of these good-looking fellows in an adjoining room
"made merry," whether with champagne, moselle or
margeaux, I know not, but either might be made a subject of agreeable dispute.

November 26.—Having devoted the entire day to the splendid churches which abound here, we feel like saying: "Of all the spots from which we shall be reft, this one will preserve a holy memory;" for who can wander from such shrines unmoved by religious inspiration? At many of the street corners are to be seen figures of saints or images of the Virgin, set in niches, or resting against the walls of the houses. Thus an Ave Maria is not confined to the grand old churches, but is heard at almost every corner from the lips of humble worshipers. Some of the houses are very low, with pointed gables, and were erected at the time Antwerp was held by the Spanish. Many buildings of more recent construction are six and seven stories high. The two little mirrors projecting in front of the windows of the houses are remarked at once by the stranger,—a very economical method of finding out what is going on in the street, no change of position being required to see both ways.

Our guide led us first to the Cathedral of Notre Dame, first in rank of all the churches, and built in 1300. Its lofty spire, four hundred feet high, seems worthy to pierce the bright, golden clouds overhead. The exterior of the building, plainly marked by ravages of time, impresses the mind more deeply than does a perfectly new structure; just as the sight of an old ruin turns thought into a channel to unravel mysteries, as gray and ancient as the lichens that cling to its sides. Not far from the front entrance is a memorial of Quentin Matsys the blacksmith, who, true to love and its exaction, won his

way up to an artist's fame, in order to gain the hand of
his lady-love. The iron canopy, so admirably executed,
is the work of his anvil. A small stone tablet—a simple monument to his genius—is set in the outer wall of
the edifice, and bears upon its face an anvil, chisel, and
brush. The Cathedral abounds with aisles to the number of seven. One of the cupolas displays a painting,
The Assumption of the Virgin, copied from Rubens'
high-altar piece, by Schut, one of his pupils. At the
high altar, with its grand subject, the worshiper, on his
bended knees, might commingle with his prayers thanks
to God for the genius He gave to earth in Rubens, as
this roof shelters his *chef d'œuvres*, which are perhaps
the most touching of all the pictures that portray the
sufferings of Christ. *The Elevation of the Cross* represents the Savior nailed to the cross, and the Jews raising
it to an erect position. Sorrowing women add to the
sadness of the scene. The lateral pieces, or wings of the
painting, relate to the subject: one representing mounted
Roman soldiers with spears, and the two thieves being
nailed to the crosses; the other, Mary and Mary Magdalene, with other followers of the Savior to Calvary.
The Descent from the Cross—the most renowned of Rubens' paintings—bewilders the beholder in the grand
conception of that terrible scene on the Mount, the anguish and sorrow of which the world can never properly
estimate. We stand before the bruised and mangled
form, upon which the heaviness of death has fully settled, and see the tender removal of " Him crucified " by
Joseph and Nicodemus; then we direct our eyes to the

agonized mother of Jesus, the faithful Marys, and others
who ministered unto Him. Words fail to express our
emotion,—what we feel is told in the silence with which
we turn away. The wings to this sublime painting furnish the salutation of the Virgin, and the presentation
of the infant Jesus in the temple. Rubens purchased
the ground for his home from the sale of this work.
On one side of the Cathedral is the chapel of the Holy
Sacrament, with an altar composed of black, gray and
white marble, ornamented with gilt, and on the opposite side, the chapel of the Virgin constructed of white
marble and decorated with gilded garlands. A rare
specimen of painting on marble is the head of Christ
by Leonardo da Vinci. The tomb of Ambrosius Capello,
bishop of Notre Dame when Antwerp was under Spanish rule, is one of exquisite sculpturing with its life-like
marble figure, robed in ecclesiastical vestments—a perfect imitation of velvet and lace. A large and beautiful
painting portrays the death of the Virgin. Under it,
in a narrow panel, is a white picture producing the effect
of marble, and resembling one to be seen in the Amsterdam Palace. The painted figures stand out in the bold
relief of statuary, and the deception to the mind of the
spectator is as complete, as the artist's conception is
wonderful. The subject of this strange and effective
picture is the Marriage of the Virgin. A finely carved
marble illustrating *The Holy Trinity* especially attracted
our notice ; also, the Gothic stalls for the priests, and
the oakwood choir with its carvings. The church of
St. Andrew contains a fine altar sculptured by Verbrug-

gen, and the finest pulpit in the Netherlands, the subject
being the miraculous draught of the fishes.   St. Andrew
the patron saint of the church—instead of St. John, according to scripture—is in the boat with St. Peter, and
the Savior, walking on the water appears to them.   The
undulations of the water are skilfully wrought, as are
the shells lying on the shore, and a basket, the perfection of wicker, filled with fishes.   The bursting nets
and the well-stored boat testify to the bounteous plenty
from the Divine Command.   A large painting of the
Crucifixion of St. Andrew by Ruben's master adorns the
edifice; also, the portrait of Marie Stuart, a face fitly
chosen to grace the monument of two English ladies
who had served that unhappy Queen just prior to her
execution.   Near the high altar are relics, sent from Rome,
of different saints,—principally fragments of bones enclosed in niches of marble about the size of a common
prayer-book.

The church of St. Augustine has for its altar-piece
the celebrated picture of Rubens, *The mystical marriage
of St. Catherine.*   Saint Catherine surrounded by a host
of saints, whose names are brightest in scripture, kneels
to receive the ring from Jesus, the infant being supported by Mary.   The painting is on canvas, and in
this respect differs from all the others of the Great
Master.   In it, Rubens has copied the faces of his two
wives, his own, and those of his grandfather and son.
His family are thus handed down by his imperishable
genius, and will ever live in holy association.   Napoleon
bore away this picture among his many prizes, and it

K

was not restored to the church until after the battle of Waterloo. In the interim, its place was supplied by the *Ecstasy of St. Augustine,* by Vandyck, a famous picture. How many sacred shrines have suffered by the ruthless hand of war and insurrection ! *The martyrdom of St. Appolina,* by Jordaens, is another triumph of the Flemish school. A large side chapel contains some rare and exquisitely fine old paintings. The figures appear to stand out from the burnished background which looks as though it was illumined by a strong light,—certainly the painter's brush here dropped its richest coloring to vie with the golden hue !

St. Jacques is one of the costliest churches in Antwerp, and is perhaps the most attractive; its embellishments displaying a splendor rarely surpassed. The side chapels owned by distinguished families are constructed chiefly of marble; and the walls adorned with paintings and statuary, should not fail to arrest the gaze of the most indifferent beholder. But how little is the genius of the past appreciated by the majority of tourists ! Often is memory too sluggish to preserve even a skeleton-picture of the rich treat that has been afforded. Thus are privileges abused by many who have means at their command, whilst minds, intellectual and appreciative are denied the pleasure of a search after the beautiful. These, alas ! can only indulge in a mental view of the works of genius through the medium of books, catching as it were the sunset-gleam, whilst others walk amid the veritable splendors of noon-day ! The first chapel we entered on the right, proved one of interest to my escort

who unexpectedly saw the tomb of some of his ancestors,
the family crest on the tablet corresponding precisely to
his own.   Shortly afterwards, the priest who opened for
us Rubens' chapel, was attracted by the name in the
Col.'s hat, and remarked—"If that is your name Sir,
permit me to lead you to a monument not far from the
high altar."   There was read the following inscription
"Anna Guise, widow of the 6th son of George Blount,
Knight Baronet—died 1752."   The chapel erected by
Rubens fifteen years prior to his death is the chief spot
of interest in the church, it being his burial place.   A
slab of marble in the floor marks where he lies, and
near him rest his two wives, and all the other members
of his direct family except his mother.   On the right
and left of the chapel are handsome monuments, female
figures beautifully executed ; and over the marble altar
hangs the picture of the Holy Trinity, in which he again
paints the faces of his kindred.   During the French
revolution this chapel was the only one spared by the
conqueror.   We looked in a spirit of quiet and glad
content at one massive treasure which resisted even the
great Napoleon.   It was the magnificent *chef-d'œuvre* of
Vervoort, *The elevation of the Cross*, sculptured in high
relief out of a single block of stone.   Next in the
order of our route, came St'. Paul's church.   On the
outside is a representation of Mount Calvary, calculated
to excite a feeling of mingled pity and horror.   The
crucifix is erected on a high eminence of rock, and statues of saints, prophets and priests in various attitudes
surround it.   All the stone-work was carved by the

monks. Winding our steps around this jutting eminence into a narrow and dark passage, we saw a woman kneeling in prayer before a small aperture cut in the rock. Not wishing to disturb her devotions, our guide led us off hurriedly to the opposite side, where he requested me to look through a small grated space, not exceeding the size of a man's hand. This was a grotto, said to be an imitation of the Holy Sepulchre at Jerusalem. Out of the dim, sepulchral shadows I descried a recumbent figure representing Christ as he lay after burial. Many offerings were strewn around, such as gilt crowns, garlands and wreaths. A feeble ray of light was sufficient to reveal the sorrow-stricken face of the old woman we had just left, who several times sighed as if from the very depths of her soul. She had sought a shrine, very sad, lonely and silent, at which to unburden her heart. I hastened away although influenced to linger, and forthwith turned my eyes to something very fierce contrasted with the peaceful sepulchre. A painted wood-carving attached to the face of the rock represented hell with its lake of fire, and its victims writhing under torments,—a fearful picture of the terrible wrath that cometh to sinners!

We stopped at the entrance of the church to allow a funeral procession to pass in ; the coffin being borne on the shoulders of priests. The strange sight outside, and the solemn scene within impressed us gloomily ; and not wishing to disturb the last rites being paid the dead, we walked very noiselessly around, directing a rapid glance at the best paintings, viz: *The Scourging of*

Christ, and *The Adoration of the Shepherds*, by Rubens; *The Savior bearing the Cross*, by Vandyck; *The Shipwreck of Saint Paul* by Peckar, and *The Seven Works of Mercy* by Teniers (father). The confessional boxes were carved by Verbruggen who seems to have left in almost every church a monument of his work. At the Museum is a large collection of pictures comprising the choicest specimens of the masters of the Flemish school. *The Adoration of the Magi; St. Theresa interceding for the souls in Purgatory*, and *The Crucifixion of Christ between the Thieves*, by Rubens, are among the most meritorious. The latter scene is portrayed in its worst horrors. A soldier has broken the limb of one of the malefactors, who in his agony has wrenched half of his foot from the cross, the nail standing out, wet with the gory stream that trickles from the torn limb. The executioner is plunging his spear into the Savior's side, and the Magdalen is crouched in an agony of sorrow at his feet. *The dead Christ* extended on a stone table, covered with straw—a picture of exquisite pathos—is by the same master; also *The Holy Trinity*, another example of that peculiar art which makes · an object look towards the spectator whatever his position may be. My chief interest hung about a half-finished picture on an easel, which had been left but a few moments before by the artist who, having no hands, is executing this fine specimen with his toes. Thus, we see that nothing is impossible with necessity. Until that moment I had never dreamed that a foot could attain to such artistic fame, thinking only of the ordinary uses it subserves;—

K*

of the functions it performs for the maintenance of
health; of the wearisome marches it accomplishes; and
of the grace and beauty with which it completes the
human form, as designed by our Heavenly Maker.
Several citizens of the United States have purchased
pictures of this remarkable artist. We hoped that he
would return to the museum ere we left, and that we
would thus be enabled to witness the extraordinary
feat; but even the vacant stool and the half-drawn
sketch had power to impress us with his strange merit,
and to elicit another pæan for the name of Valu.
The Siege of Antwerp, a painting of huge dimensions, presented a woful scene, calling up out of the
"long ago," the wrath that fired the hearts of men; and
The Death of Rubens formed also an impressive scene,
the second wife in her widowed grief being one of the
most conspicuous figures. *The Descent from the Cross*
by Quentin Matsys is singled out as one of the works of
merit by which he secured his matrimonial prize. The
inexorable father of the maiden,—Frans Floris—found
himself at last excelled in art by the poor blacksmith,
turned painter. *The Crucifixion*, a masterly conception
is by Antoine Van Dyck; *The Resurrection* by M. de
Vos;—the master of Rubens' master—*The Boors smoking* by Teniers; *The Nativity*, and *The Fallen Angels*
by Floris. There is a fine bust in black marble of
Rubens, and a chair that once belonged to him. Indeed
the very name of the dead master creates a sacred spell
among the people of this land! Not far from the
museum stands a marble statue of Vandyck.

We bestowed a passing glance at the Hôtel de Ville, its stone-work and gilt tracery, and concluded our explorations at a lace-venders, where articles sell much cheaper than at Brussels. The bells chime in this city as in Amsterdam; and last evening they had all the soft tones of a musical-box. How sweetly, in these countries, does night steal away, and like a "mystic hymn" lend heavenly thoughts to the soul. Curiosity prompted us to look over the list of American names registered in a fine album belonging to the hotel, and we found those of a number of friends who had wandered to this interesting land. How like a magnet is the name of one's home, never failing to attract amid all the magnificence of foreign scenes!

BRUSSELS, *November* 27.—Back in Brussels, and at the Belle Vue! The pleasant sunshine invited a stroll in the Park, and we found an hour of quiet relief after the excitement and fatigue of nearly ten days' travel. Such a retreat, with its sweet tranquility, affords not only a grateful *abandon* of the body, but repose to the busy and overtaxed mind. A lack of time and a desire to visit the Wiertz museum of paintings cut short our stay in the Park.

We drove first to the United States Legation, where we were cordially received by Judge Goodrich; and thence to the museum, a lovely spot situated on the brow of a hill, accessible only by a footpath. There seemed to be a classic spell over all the surroundings of the place; in the bright verdure of the height; in its geo-

graphical garden, laid out to indicate the routes to some
of the principal European cities; and in its old ivy-
wreathed columns, that might pass for the ruins of a
Grecian or Roman temple. It was the conception of
the artist to enclose his works in a reproduction of one
of the temples of Pæstum ; and here are collected some
of the most marvellous paintings of modern times.
Some interest might be felt in the painter before the
works of his genius have been seen, and that interest
must increase as his history and character are told.
Without guide or help in his earliest years, but with an
inspiration of soul to follow the glorious art, he fought
every obstacle that crossed his path. Disappointments
he cast aside, as he would have dismissed an evil
genius, and yearned for the gilded heights of fame,
where he hoped one day to be crowned with proudest
laurels. How often does stern reality thrust into our
paths a stumbling-block to dwarf our noblest efforts
and blunt our finest sentiments! Not so with this
young artist! At the age of fourteen, at Antwerp,
whither his desire, dazzled by the bright genius of Rubens, had led him, he took up his abode in a very humble place—a sort of cell or granary, not impervious to
the snows and frosts of winter. There he worked away
in solitude, with nought to illumine his path save the
bright and beautiful dream of success, born of will, energy and hope. His dreams were colored with the resplendent glory of Michael Angelo and Rubens, while
an innate literary and musical taste inspired him with
Corneille and Mosart. Then sickness came to abate his

fervor and dull his enthusiasm. That passed; he awoke
to a renewal of his occupation. It is recorded of him
that, one day at Antwerp, when still the creature of
poverty, he was offered by an amateur a good price for
one of his sketches, and that he quickly replied, "Keep
your gold! this is the death of the artist"—words
freighted with truth, as his application to the art did
one day prove. He was content to live upon the small
pension of one hundred florins allowed by the Belgian
government; and placing the strongest barriers against
whatever might tempt him from his studious seclusion,
amidst the jeers and sarcasm of some of his fellow-men,
he faithfully followed the rigid course of life that had
been laid out with a dignity that recoiled upon his as-
sailants. The paramount idea and desire of Wiertz was
to retain his paintings, believing that the work of im-
provement must ever go on; and therefore even after
his fame had been fully established, he never sold any
save from necessity. When he received the Emperor of
Russia's offer of three hundred thousand francs for his
Triumph of Christ, he refused to sell, giving as excuse
his belief that to-morrow he would find something to
correct. Upon a meagre sum Wiertz traveled to Paris,
where he prosecuted the study of art; and thence to
Rome, Venice, Naples, Florence and Milan. At Rome
he wrote a eulogy upon Rubens, which proudly chal-
lenged the admiration and applause of the public. From
time to time he answered the criticisms of his enemies
in various pamphlets.

Thus did this wonderful artist, poet and musician—

a combination of talent not often met with—struggle through most of his life, without fortune, counsel, aid or protection. To give up his art was to him equivalent to death, and he feared death only because it would cut short those wonderful creations with which he intended to endow his canvas. One year ago ended his mortal career; and the artist, in the dream-land of his poetic fancies, has doubtless found more garlands of happiness than were wont to spring up about his earthly pathway. In the paintings bequeathed to the Belgian government, he has left a monument which future generations will love to cherish; and over the entrance to the museum might be written *One Wiertz*,—for when shall come another?

The attendant of the museum discovering that I was an enthusiastic admirer of the artist and his works, took great pleasure in relating little incidents in the life of the deceased. He led me to his portrait, three-quarters length, and in profile, the face of which is classically sad and tending to the spiritual. The artist is represented clad entirely in black, relieved by a narrow white collar. The arms are folded across his breast, one hand holding a black drapery that falls from the right shoulder. A pallette and brush are introduced, and on the background of the canvas can be distinguished the words—"*La critique en matière de peinture est-elle possible?*"—the title of his pamphlet published in 1851. Above the portrait was a smaller one of Wiertz's mother, painted by himself. Her calico gown, a ruffled cap and pin-a-fore, though tastefully adjusted, indicated an humble position. On exhibition were various medals presented to him by crowned heads, also his flute and the other musical instruments he played.

One can scarcely describe the impression felt on entering the painting gallery, for the four walls treat of imposing, awe-striking subjects so extravagantly dealt with, as almost to defy analysis or comparison; and with what great variety of subject,—war, hell, Christ's sufferings and victory, the past, present and future, all spread out seemingly to lead the mind into a train of serious thought! Here and there, amidst the painful and the sublime, appeared a gem of beauty simple enough in subject, to touch the fancy of a little child, and once or twice I was glad to turn from the thorns to the roses. *Le Triomphe du Christ* is a painting of such merit as would vanquish a world of Wiertz' enemies, just as the subject shows the defeat of the legions of hell by Christ. How gigantic a labor and conception to paint countless numbers in combat, with all the fierce passions stamped upon their countenances;—the arch-fiend and leader himself resisting the flaming sword and the thunder-bolts of heaven, until before him the vision of the cross appears wrapped in celestial glory! Satan has raised his right arm to protect his eyes from the divine light, that condemns him to the burning lake below. Then the other figures! The arch-angel Michael with spear, wild and grand in his destroying agency,—the angels near the cross chanting the hozanna, --the Seraphim armed with thunders, and those sounding the trumpet-notes of victory,—the mangled bodies fallen under the lance of St. Michael,—the condemned masses writhing and burning in the flames; and high above all this despair and agony, the immortal victim of the sins of men, with a look of serenity amid the sufferings of Golgotha!

This picture reflects in a measure the sentiment of Paradise Lost, and is a faithful expression of the Savior's Passion as recorded in the Bible. *Le phare de Golgotha.* has a mysterious power also, and partakes of the same character as *Le Triomphe*, in the struggle between the powers of light and darkness. *Le dernier Canon*, represented by a goddess and her train, portrays the triumphant march of civilization despite all obstacles. The scene of carnage, and all the attendant evils belong to this age, but the pleasant contrast of love, amity, progress and right is claimed for the future. Some of Wiertz' figures are from twenty to thirty feet in height. My eye caught a glimpse of a giant form, the limbs of which seemed to find no limits:—it was too big for an hour's study, and it remained on the wall a monstrous mystery. There was a mythological series besides the Homeric, and the one which most attracted our notice was *La forge de Vulcain*. The group is formed by Vulcan, Venus and Cupid. The lame god sits on his anvil. Venus the blonde and beautiful daughter of the sea, as nude as when she rose from the waves, appears to her husband with some indiscreet demand, and with blandishments and caresses wears a most irresistible look. One arm is cast around his neck, and with her left hand, she receives grapes from a chalice tendered by glowing nymphs, and wine from golden flagons with which to tempt and seduce her ugly spouse. On Vulcan's knee rests Cupid, a pouting little god who seems intent on seeing Venus victorious. *La seconde après la mort* is treated in this wise. A mortal having put on immortality is ascending to the skies. Stars and planets are passed in his flight, and from his grasp has fallen a book inscribed *Grandeurs humaines.* The pallor of death still lingers on the features of this immortal spirit, that has seen the littleness of earth, the shortness of life, and the vanity of human greatness.

The Appel à la Bienfaisance, the work of a few days of continuous labor, was touching in the extreme. A rude coffin, marked with a black cross, and containing the body of a murdered man, has just been removed from a house by several persons. The grief-stricken wife and children have rushed frantically from the abode, as if to call back the precious one. Two little ones have dropped on their knees from exhaustion in their haste to stop the men, their outstretched hands clutching at the box. *The Old Concierge Asleep,* a happy illustration of forgotten cares, and *The Keeper of the Bastile Key,* suggesting the dark days of the Revolution, were both excellent; whilst two charming figures and faces of Hebe loveliness, thrice beautified with youth and grace, were near keeping us an entire day within those walls.

*   *   *   *   *   I add my farewell regretfully to Brussels! Having a few moments to spare before the time for the starting of the train, I employ them in convers-

L

ing with a female bookseller at the station, who evidently counts upon making a heavy drain on my purse,
judging from her untiring efforts to please. I shall at
least purchase, as souvenir of this beautiful city, some
views handsomely bound. Here we have the unexpected pleasure of meeting again Mr. Buffum, with
whom, by chance, we began our journey, and shall soon
end it.

CHAPTER VII.

PARIS, November 30.

A· RETURN to Paris, amidst all her brilliant attractions, confirms my opinion that very just is her
claim to the traditionary title of Queen-city of the
world. It was my good fortune to arrive just in time
to do honor to our President's Thanksgiving Proclama-
tion in a dinner-party composed of American friends.
Others of our resident colony did not fail to observe the
day—judging from numerous cards of invitation for
dinners and small parties,—and if it was not permitted
them to meet in consecrated places, to " Praise Him
from whom all blessings flow," they could, at least, evince
their gratitude in home-festivities. Among our friends
were Mr. Valentine, who had come all the way from
London to lend his genial presence, and Mrs. Gregory,
of New York, and family, whose agreeable society we
must soon lose, as they contemplate a trip to Italy.
Many seem inclined to that poetic land, whilst others
cannot give up the cheerful, dashing life of Paris. To-
day's multitudinous show on the Champs Elysées and
the Boulevards, was one of the finest panoramas conceivable. The first query that arose in the mind was
" Where do all the people come from ?" Like a swarm

of wind-beaten insects that sometimes suddenly fills the
air, so they crowded upon our vision, and frequent came
the cries, " more room—save me from being trampled
upon!"   How varied must be the purpose, promise and
sentiment of so mighty a crowd, representing as it does
all the civilized nations of the globe!   The French element it is plain to see extracts the most enjoyment out
of life, accepting the situation of *peu d'argent, ou beau-
coup d'argent* with equal grace ; and it is only heavy
sorrows and afflictions that can turn them from their
philosophic course.   In their outward appearance we read
nothing of troubled life ; yet there must be some weary
souls whose woe is locked up in secret chambers.   Behold
in that throng the proud statesman, who wears on his
breast the emblem of the order of the "Legion of Honor."
He has perhaps this day been engaged in laborious
debate, arguing with his compeers, even to the wielding
of the fire-brand of anger, but nevertheless, there lingers
not a trace of it on his features.   He is out of the Chamber, and whatever passion may be lurking in his breast,
he obeys the characteristic impulse of concealing it from
his fellow man.   And female character is no less emu-
lous of this policy, the most unhappy of them wearing
the society look of contentment.   We rather like this
cheerful mien, whether worn by the brainless dandy, or
the distinguished man of letters ; by the flaunting
Camille, or the Sister of Charity ; by the flippant adven-
turer or the gallant soldier ; by the tottering old man,
or the youthful student.   How truly wonderful to find
this in a nervous, restless people whose every fibre is

like an electric wire, and whose every vein runs with
the blood of animated passion! However this counterfeit life is not barren of good results. It wields a good
and kindly influence, removing much of the rough coating that forms on the face of society. It is that which
brings about the marvellous agreeability of manner
which meets us in the shop, in the church, in the *salon*,
at the table, at the ball, and everywhere. Whatever
may be the errors and immoralities of the people, this
trait of character is certainly very pleasing.

Place Vendôme! how charming, with its fine houses,
and popular hotels, of the Corinthian style, encircling
the magnificent column of Napoleon! The bronze bas-
reliefs of the shaft rise in a spiral coil to the summit,
where stands the figure of the great General. The designs of the bas-reliefs are not only interesting, as illustrating the memorable achievements of the French army
against the Prussians and Austrians in 1805, but from the
fact of their being cast out of the 12,000 pieces of cannon
captured in the campaign. Around the base of the
monument is an iron railing, which never lacks annual
offerings of immortelles at the hands of the French
people. To the faded wreaths of former years are added
fresh garlands, and the effect produced is that of a flowery
chain.

December 2.—My love of the drama is showing itself
now and then; and were it not for the miserable ventilation of the theatres, here, the enjoyment would be far
greater. *Robinson Crusoe* is being performed to crowded

L*

audiences at the Opéra Comique, situated in Place des Italiens. Some of the sweetest love-melodies run through the play, and the singers are so engaging that even those uninitiated in the sentimental passion must catch an inspiration and a thrill. Robinson Crusoe when cast upon the dreary island—with the sweet memory of an absent lady-love in his heart—explains to *Friday*, his new-found savage friend and servant, what love is. The mere description of the passion wakes up to new life the untutored savage, who shows, by the fire in his eye, the novel joy that needs only an image of worship. Soon a fair and beautiful creature arrives on the island in search of her lost Crusoe, accompanied by a waiting-maid, who has brought her lover along. They are at once siezed by the savages, who struck with the charms of *la belle*, separate her from her attendants, proposing to make her their queen or bride, and then to immolate her at a fire-altar. She is led forth to the stake, and commences to chant her death-song, when Friday suddenly appears on the hill-side. One single glance at her beauty has sufficed to make him feel the full power of love, and he loses not a moment in endeavoring to rescue her. Concealed behind some brush-wood, he fires several shots among the blood-thirsty red men, who, panic-stricken, take to flight; and thus the fair prize is rescued by one of their own race. Friday bears off the fainting girl to Crusoe's tent, and ministers to her wants, watching her as she sleeps, until the return of his master. All this time love is taking deeper root in his heart, and when the curtains of the rude shelter are pulled aside and Crusoe's form appears, there are no bounds to his ecstatic bliss as he leads his master to the couch.

What a sweet surprise to Crusoe; but his happiness soon meets with a check when the poor savage insists that the idol is his! An unhappy scene ensues in the contest for the prize. Alas! how fatal is the love of two men for one woman! In such cases how shall the difficulty be settled? When women become objects of contention, would it not be wise to make them nuns, or send them from this lower world to join the angels?— and as for the men we would suggest a grated cell, and a monk's habit. Friday suffered on, fighting Crusoe's argument with this logic. "I have been your faithful friend through every danger that has threatened your life on the island, and have not forgotten your promise to share with me all things in life." He wanted his adopted master to hold to the contract in the case of the lovely woman, and was deaf to every explanation of the sanctity of an engagement of marriage; nor could he be made to appreciate the purity and justness of the tie that binds two loving hearts in one. How was a provision to be made, and where would the quarrel end? At this juncture the coquettish little waiting-maid, who had just escaped from her rude captors appears, and Friday learns as if by magic, that it is as easy a thing to love the second time as the first. His savage rage melts away before the comforting glance of an eye that says, "let my mistress alone, and I will befriend you," and the work of atonement goes bravely on until the rustic swain—who has just been released from "durance vile"

—comes suddenly upon the scene, and enters his claim for the maid, as Crusoe had done for the mistress. Lastly, through difficulties and sorrows, Friday having been taught a lesson of life, and two of love, discovers that there is something sad in both. An escape of Crusoe and the party is shortly effected by the arrival of a friendly ship, and the savage band falls an easy prey to the vengeance of the white man. Friday accompanies Crusoe, and we do not doubt that he will try to love a third time. May success attend him! This was a story of *mal de cœur*, but we do not always have to go to the stage to see it played. Many spirits pay with bitter sighs and tears, for the fleeting pleasures of love misdirected and unrequited,—"trees of hope, with lifeless stems!"

The interior of this building is elliptical, with three tiers of boxes, and seats for fifteen hundred persons. It possesses the advantage of being fire-proof. The decorations are chiefly in white and gilt—preferable to the heavy and sombre styles of some of the theatres. * *

Several days since Commodore and Mrs. Stevens entertained us very handsomely at dinner. The Commodore, although far advanced in years, is the personification of vivacity and gallantry, and Mrs. S. has genial and engaging manners. General and Mrs. McClellan were present.

December 5.—To-day our hearts are linked in sympathy with one of our esteemed countrymen, who mourns the death of his only child. Mrs. Eustis died yesterday at Cannes, bidding farewell to life with a calm and beautiful resignation; her hold on earth being riven amid that sublime faith to which her fleeting breath gave utterance—"Thy will be done!" To the friends who are left these words must seem the harbinger of that peaceful slumber over which angels keep vigils, and of the spirit's welcome to eternal joys. Ere the chaplet is woven to deck the pale brow, memory leads us back to trace her gentle life. A few years since a happy bride, and the idol of a fond parent's heart, she left her home to seek another across the Atlantic surge; and here, in sunny France, with love and hope, and friends and blessings, she has sung the songs of gladness. Tiny hands and brows of beauty have nestled on her bosom— these little children having yet to learn and understand the fearful mystery of death. And thus has the lesson of fleeting life again been read to us! The sun may glow in splendor, and the air be filled with tropic warmth; the flowers may bloom, and happiness be shed around; but all this beauteous landscape must fade upon the vision, and pass away forever before that brighter "greenwood of the soul!"

December 10.—The last few days have embraced a variety of occupation, amusement and instruction,— drives through the most ancient parts of the city and the environs,—visits to the bazaars, those pet places of Americans,—a peep into some of the *cafés*, whither the Parisians flock in search of the indispensable *demi-tasse* and *petit verre*,—the Bourse, with its frantic stock-bro-

kers, and bustling merchants,—the Italian Opera, with
the bewitching Patti,—the corn market, and the one
which supplies our daily food.   The market in Paris is
a sight that ought not to be overlooked by an American
lady; and she would do well to take the place of her
cuisinière for a day, to see the brisk trade going on in
fish, vegetables, flowers and fruits.

A witch of a woman, or a true representative of one
of the Furies, assailed our coachman ostensibly because
the carriage had blocked the way for a moment, but we
fancied that it was in revenge for our *bonne's* not having
patronized her stall.   There was something about her
akin to the angry and vindictive spirit of the fishwomen
who marched to Versailles after Marie Antoinette.
Amidst the brandishing of arms, clenching of fists, and
the thunders of a voice that might have intimidated
Cæsar or Alexander, we shrunk away, hoping never to
look upon her like again.   I found that in my alarm I
had unconsciously crushed some delicate sprays of white
lilac that lay on my lap.   How truly tender and peaceful a contrast they offered to that harsh and unfeminine
ebullition of passion!   Women and flowers poetically
affiliate, but the connection for the moment was rudely
sundered by that one creature of our sex.

December 12.—A lovely Sabbath favored an attendance on church service at the Hôtel des Invalides.   The
building is in every respect worthy of its great-purpose,
—the maintenance of the decrepid and aged soldiers at
the nation's expense.   There they are provided with all

the comforts of a home. The service, held in the ancient Church of St. Louis, is rendered the more impressive by the presence of gray-haired veterans, whose age and battle-wounds have taken away much of the joy of living. Many a tottering form nearly ready to leave this earthly scene for a heavenly tabernacle, is here refreshed by the influences of religion; and what would this world be without its precious aid?—a dark and dreary waste,—a desert without a spring! Added to the Mass is the music of the military band, the selections of which are frequently from choice operas. The heart-stirring tones of the *Miserere*, in *Trovatore*, floated through the arched nave,—a melody which loses none of its power by being divested of scenic accompaniment. Would it not be better for our clergy to sanction the introduction into churches of harmonies that sweep the innermost chords of the heart? On hearing the *Miserere* it did not follow that we should call up the tower-scene and the sorrow of love there set forth, for it came to us to-day more like a dirge in the associations of the church that had suffered by a mandate of war and by fire,—more like a requiem to the few reposing within the walls, and to the thousands whose memories are identified with the faded and tattered banners. Upon the arches supported by Corinthian pillars are inscribed the names of deceased Governors of the hotel who died holding office. The pulpit, of white marble, is the only object particularly attractive. A visit to the refectories and kitchens was permitted, notwithstanding it was the Sabbath. The dining-rooms, of which there are four, one hundred and fifty feet in length, contain thirty tables each; the officers occupying one, the sub-officers and privates the remaining three. The frescoed walls represent towns conquered by Louis XIV; but their merit seems indifferent. Outside in the quadrangle formed by the hotel are arcades, whose paintings afford an interesting view of French history from its earliest period. Beginning at Clovis and Charlemagne, we made the acquaintance of other monarchs, and some of those fierce queens who loved rapine and crime so well, that they were blindly forgetful of *good* names and the opinion that future generations might form of them. In this advanced age of civilization we could but frown upon the figures so unfeminine and cruel! As yet, the paintings have not been brought up to the First Empire, or to the reign of the present Emperor. Unfortunate it is that the artist's pencil has not portrayed the character of Eugenie, that it might be contrasted with that of some of her infamous predecessors. Upon our homeward walk we saw the imperial carriage with the fair burden just named.

December 14.—A visit by special permit to the Palais Royal, the residence of Prince Napoleon and the Princess Clotilde, afforded us great pleasure. Several days previously I had made the circuit of the arcades of the building, under which are some of the most dazzling shops in Paris, the prices here being much more reasonable than on the Boulevards. This is one of the gayest places in the city, the crowd rarely ever diminishing until a late hour of the night, so much is there to attract,—the glittering treasure of diamonds, gold and precious stones, and, near by, the faithful imitation of the real article,—the restaurant windows, with fruits of mammoth growth, and flowers artistically arranged,—the tempting game at Chevets, and last, but not least, the rectangular garden, seven hundred feet long, with its lime-trees, bronze and marble statues, central fountain, and the noted little cannon fired by the meridian sun! How charming a scene this garden must present on a summer's day with its crowd of idlers, and its band of music! We might even now wish for a change of season. Some of the associations of the palace,—the most exciting in history—mark the turbulent period of the Fronde and the first revolution; and recall its occupants, Cardinal Richelieu—the founder,—Louis XIII; Anne of Austria, regent for Louis XIV; the Duke of Orleans and Prince Lucian Bonaparte. The late Prince Jerome Bonaparte resided there prior to Prince Napoleon, and to him has been attributed much of its present magnificence. The only rooms not visited by us were the private apartments of the Princess Clotilde, which our attendant said he would have exhibited, had she taken her usual morning promenade. However, a door was thrown open leading to that reserved portion of the palace, where we espied several lacqueys in knee-breeches and gold lace, pacing to and fro as if on sentinel duty. A magnificent stairway of marble amply rewarded us for the brief glimpse granted. The lower landing, from which branched off two noble flights of stairs, was filled

M

with rare exotics, their lively tints setting off to great advantage the snow-white marble. The *salon aux armes*, so-called from the armor hanging on the walls, contains marble busts of Napoleon and Hortense; a superb dinner-service of Sèvres china; a chess-board of solid gold with chessmen carved most ingeniously out of the same rich metal, and many curious antique articles under glass. The *salle-à-manger* is ornamented with numerous busts of the family on handsome marble pedestals. On the upper landing of a massive staircase were several ungainly antique figures, bearing a strong resemblance to Egyptian idols, but having no fancy for the unattractive, we did not inquire into their meaning. The *galerie des grands hommes* abounds in busts of celebrated writers, among which is that of the great Racine. A ponderous crystal chandelier heightens the beauty of the salon, and under this brilliant reflector are two models in wood, the first, a Grecian temple, and the other, Prince Napoleon's yacht, said to be the fac-simile of the one now lying at some neighboring port. A compliment is paid to the French favorite Rachel in a piece of statuary, representing Tragedy. The *salon de Colonnes* has life-sized portraits of the Emperor and Empress, Victor Emmanuel and his Queen, and busts of Victor Emmanuel and his son Umbert; whilst the marble mantel-piece richly gilded, holds the single bust of Napoleon III. Passing through a corridor, we observed a painting representing Marat in his bath, just after he had received his death-wound at the hand of Charlotte Corday. Next *en suite* were salons fitted up in the Pompeian

style,—a gallery chiefly devoted to Italian paintings,—
a library with Gobelin tapestries on walls and ceiling,
treating of mythology; and a room of much smaller
dimensions called the library of Napoleon I, containing
some very ancient books—his property. The marble
busts arranged around the sides of the salon were taken
at different periods of his life—1780, the scholar at
Brienne—1797, the Revolutionary attire—1801, General—1806, the Emperor, crowned with laurel—1812,
prisoner at St. Helena. The last, showing the great
man fallen, awakened a sad, salutary thought. We live
to pursue the allurements offered by fame—we clothe
ourselves with glittering robes, and feel the pulse of the
mighty world throb to our deeds, nay at the very mention of our names. Suddenly the diadem falls, and the
temple that once enshrined so fondly, holds no longer a
niche for us. Then comes a little isolated spot—like
unto Napoleon's rocky isle—distant enough from vain
ambition, pomp and glory, to turn the heart to more
solid joys; to fortify it with the strength of wisdom
until the coming of that angel whose icy wing shall
spread over all of earth! A painting of Napoleon in
his coronation robes, and a cast of his face taken after
death, completed the interest of the room; and we came
next to the beautiful statue of Meditation, and some
rare gems of painting by Eugène de la Croix—thence
to the Throne-room beautiful in frescoed pictures, and
with its fine statue of Napoleon I. It was there that
Louis Phillipe received all the deputations of France
in 1830. Adjoining is the ball-room decorated with

the usual stately appurtenances—a salon lined with
Gobelin tapestries, and lastly the *salon des bijoux* with
many articles of vertu, among which is the magnificent
colossal vase bearing the following inscription—*donné
par Frederick Guillaume IV à Prince Napoleon, à
Berlin.*

The morning ended with a visit to the studio of Gustave Doré, situated in Rue Bayard,—a spot towards
which my inclinations have often tended. Beautiful as
are his illustrations of the Bible and the Wandering
Jew, his oil paintings have far greater merit in my
eyes, doubtless owing to a partiality for coloring. The
famous picture, *Le Tapis Vert*, which represents a
sprightly scene at Baden Baden, has been recently
sold for a large amount. Having seen a drawing of
the same, I regretted all the more the absence of the
original, which, however, was in a measure compen-
sated for in his *Dante and Virgil visiting Hell*. The
sombre, sad and indistinct features of that painting were
agreeably relieved by the two prominent figures, robed
in light rose and blue drapery. *The Massacre of the
Innocents* was executed with a force true to the brutal
event. A mighty genius alone could have delineated
such fearful modes of slaughter, and depicted the agony
of fond, bereaved parents; but there was too much of
the painful in that one scene for us not to desire relief
in a kindly subject, and where could it be better found
than in the spirited representation of Spanish peasantry?
The artist's taste chiefly runs on the olive tint, black
hair and eyes; and, of this style, were *Two Gitanos—*

The Fortune Teller; a scene in the suburb of Triana-Seviglia—*Manca Peasants*—and a *Beggar Girl.* What can surpass the brilliancy of color, the expression of animation or woe that speaks from the eyes—those "windows of the soul," into which we look to read either happiness or misery? The very canvass seems endowed with life, at one time invoking pity, at another admiration. Several half-finished Biblical subjects were *Christ leaving the Temple,* and *Christ Insulted.* Among other pictures the most striking were *Francesca da Rimini—Judith arriving at the Camp of Ashear—Moses discovered on the banks of the Nile—Diana surprised by Actæon—A Nymph seeing her reflection in the Water—Red Riding Hood,* with the sweetest of faces struck with terror at the approach of the wolf—and *Europa carried off,* who, wreathed with flowers, wears a happy look, and seems most comfortable on the side of the huge bull. With due deference to the great god Jupiter, we thought the animal too highly favored. Then came landscapes with mountain and stream, forest and dale, castle-ruins and cascade to vary the extensive grouping of figures. As we were about to depart from the studio Gustave Doré entered, and after an introduction to us, nearly lost his balance under an avalanche of compliments,—the promise of his autograph and photograph to one of the party being a little incident related afterwards with girlish blushes and excitement. And now a word of the artist, whose appearance does not indicate the profession he follows. Very youthful and gay is he, with a face almost boyish, and bearing no imprint of the melancholy

M*

studies he has pursued. Can this be the man who has
illustrated great volumes,—who has walked in thought
with the deepest sorrows to make his sketches the embodiment of suffering? We can only recognize in him
the merry talent to picture a bright-eyed peasant, dancing to the music of the tambourine.

December 16.

WE dined at Véfour's restaurant, Palais Royal,
yesterday, and afterwards attended a reading by
Mrs. Leigh Ward, at the Hôtel de Palais Royal. How
unique and artistic are the French in decorating their
places of abode! Sometimes a vestibule has all the appearance of a miniature garden, with its *jardinières*, its
ivy-vines, pendant baskets and herbariums. Along the
staircase of the hotel runs an artificial vine, and interspersed among the leaves are bunches of grapes made of
green and purple glass globules lighted up with tiny
gas jets. Like soft moon-light seem the rays that come
mellowed through the stained glass. Many times heretofore in ascending to the various *étages* of a hotel, I
have weariedly frowned at the numberless steps; but so
pleasing a sight as that of last evening would surely
lessen, in a great degree, the tiresome ascent. The reading was given under the patronage of the American
Minister, Gen. Dix, Sir Joseph Olliffe and others.
Among the best recitations were Edgar Poe's Raven,
and Clarence's dream in Richard III. Of the comic
readings, the most amusing one was Bumble's Courtship,
by Charles Dickens, which was delivered with much

spirit, eliciting prolonged applause from the audience. The entertainment was varied with songs by a little Irish singer, Rose O'Toole. At the conclusion we sauntered through the galleries of the Palais Royal where our eyes were fairly blinded with the gorgeous display of jewelry, rendered all the more dazzling by the reflected gaslight. Thence, we strolled along the Rue de Rivoli, when suddenly we confronted the entrance to the Passage Delorme with its doll-babies. It is only the visitor to Paris who can understand the importance of the *poupée*, or form an idea of the large amount of money spent on toys. Huge glass cases exhibit hundreds of dolls arrayed in beautiful costumes of the latest styles; and, at first glance, one might imagine them really endowed with life, so natural are their attitudes. Our thoughts revert at once to Tom Thumb, and the fabled *Puk-Wudjies*, of Hiawatha's song, save that in the latter instance the "little people" flourished "airy war-clubs" by the light of the early moon. The only war-cry here heard, is from the little children outside who cannot successfully storm the citadel. First, we come upon a parlor-scene, the hostess standing in a becoming position to receive her company, and wearing a trained robe, with jewels on her fingers, buckles on her toes, and hair dressed under the elaborate manipulations of the *coiffeur*. Then, the guests, presenting a picture true to fashionable life—a flirtation in the corner, a partner accepted for the dance, and a couple engaged at a game of cards. Next are the mysteries of a lady's *boudoir*, separated by a slight partition. The dressing-case has its *poudre de*

riz, rouge and *cosmétique*, and the officiating doll assumes
a graceful pose before the mirror with head tossed on
one side as if to show what vanity the women of the
19th century have, and what arts they resort to in order
to beautify themselves. Then follows a fashionable
promenade scene, with much of the Champs Elysées
dash about it. In an open carriage is seated a doll, with
foot protruding in fancy boot, and ankle saved from
further freedom by the white skirt and fluted ruffles;
the parasol screening a multitude of curls, and the eye-
glass resting carelessly in the left hand. Close to the
bewitching demoiselle is a jockey on a fast nag, and on
the side walk an English fop, with gold-headed cane,
and a wondrously arranged moustache. He seems to
be taking a view of the fast horses, and perchance the
faster people. One can almost hear him say—" How
shocking!!" Society does not lack any of its elements,
for here we find even the *bonne* with her immaculate
cap, and baby in arms. Certainly that baby's mamma
never counts the cost of its Valenciennes robes! Should
not these toy establishments be classed among the institutions of Paris? Do they not in their mimic-life,
illustrate the Parisian *beau monde* far better than any
picture that could spring from pencil or brush? Oh!
that the fascinations of doll-babydom could be seen by
those little eyes so dear to me, across the sea!

December 20.—Who has ever fully described the joy
felt by persons in a foreign land on the receipt of home-
letters? Tidings from loved ones must not fail us—

days are counted—steamers watched for; and the sight of one little envelope affords more real happiness, than all other pleasure-giving things in the world. Even newspapers seem like familiar words. A visit to some of the reading-rooms thrown open to the public, convinces one that new interests, occupations and amusements cannot alienate the heart from its native land, or render it indifferent to current events—for fealty springing from will and pleasure needs no protective armor against the most seductive fascinations.

Our political troubles furnish the most important news that reaches us through the sub-marine telegraph. Can praises ever decline, or gratitude slumber, as we ponder over the wonderful invention that unites the old world with the new? Only one thought connected with the electrical link strikes us sadly—tidings of death or other misfortunes.   *   *   *   *   *   *

This date must ever bring to me a sorrowful association. Denied the usual offering of flowers at the grave of a cherished little sister, I can only give my tenderest thoughts to the gentle spirit above, praying that it may teach me heavenly faith,—that sweet solace which far excels earth's greatest joys. In view of a Christmas *fête* to be given by my little niece, who bears dear Alice's name, I have commenced to dress a mammoth tree. How much we love this season! Both old and young rejoice at its coming! How hopefully the love of that child was told when she begged her physician to make her well for Christmas day. Pleading thus to be spared to prepare gifts for others, she was taken by Him of

whom it is written—"Suffer little children to come unto
me, and forbid them not, for of such is the kingdom of
heaven."

December 25.—The last few days we have passed
under the shadow of a tree that has grown in marvelous
beauty from hour to hour. Paris is indeed the only
place where one can get up perfect *arbres de Noel*, there
being no end of pretty things made expressly for their
adornment. Our labor ended, every bough bent gracefully under the weight of glittering stars, tiny lanterns,
miniature flags of every nation, flowers, wax fruits, flying angels, birds of gayest plumage, and toys, which for
number and beauty could not have been surpassed.
Around the base of the tree was grouped the doll's
household furniture, complete from attic to cellar, many
articles of which were gifts from kind friends. At the
moment of dismantling, the question naturally arose,
"What will become of all these trinkets?" but the destructive propensities of little children will soon solve
that problem. The *salons* were decked for the *fête*, and
appeared like floral bowers with evergreens, flowers and
holly; the only serious emblem being a large cross of
white camelias, typical of the rite of baptism. General,
Mrs. Dix and I stood sponsors for the youngest member
of the house, who received the sprinkling and the holy
sign on a high key and with big tears; but our mortification at the uproarious conduct soon died away when
we were assured that it augured well, long life, etc.
Rev. O. W. Lamson, of the American Episcopal Church,

conducted the ceremony. It was said that Christmas-eve in Paris had never brought together so brilliant an array of American juveniles, many States of our country being represented. A very enjoyable sight were those wee faces lit up with delight at the revelations of the tree; little feet tripping merrily along, eluding the vigilance of mamma and nurse; cheeks the color of *rouge*, and eyes as bright as diamonds. It was only when several branches caught fire and the candles were nearly out, that the miniature world sought a new diversion in *Guignol*, more commonly called Punch and Judy. This is nothing more than a theatrical representation—comedy on a very small scale—the dialogues being conducted in a squeaking voice by a man under a tiny stage, whilst the most bizarre and comical little figures bob up and down, and strut about, as if they were really things of life, endowed with brains and the power of speech. Actions are suited to words in an extraordinary manner, whilst the dancing and fighting are so spirited and droll as to excite screams of merriment from even the most dignified spectator. We do not wonder at the clapping of little hands, or the joyous laugh of those who witness these comic scenes.

Among the guests of the evening were Colonel and Mrs. Hoffman, of the Legation; Mrs. General Derby, and her beautiful daughter Daisy, whose bloom excels the pink blush of the flower; Mrs. Blake, of New York; Mrs. C. H. McCormick, the dearest prize of all her husband's "*reapings;*" Mrs. Mechlin; Mrs. Fellows, of New York; Mrs. Costin, an intelligent widow, beaming

with the lustre of her *signal-lights;* Mrs. Francis, of
New York; Mrs. Judge Field, of California; and the
Princess Savalan Kahn, whose Armenian beauty might
have been the theme of the evening, had not all praise
been pledged to the children.

A tempting invitation was sounded in my ears to
attend the midnight Mass at the Madelaine, where voices
in song and prayer were heralding in this blessed morn.
How beautiful the thought to forget night and its shadows, and to be lighted to some hallowed altar in the
remembrance of that one bright star of Bethlehem,
which told the Savior's birth.

Everything tended to make our *fête* happy with a
single exception—the sudden death of an invited guest,
Mr. Buffum. A note of acceptance, evidently fresh
from his hand, was followed a few hours later by the
intelligence of his demise. These tidings brought sadly
to mind the Brussels trip, his last earthly journey.
Who of our party thought then of the prophetic words,
" Behold, I come quickly ! " Surely the day and the
hour were not foreshadowed.

* * * * * Added to a wealth of flowers to-day are
some exotics from Nice. They wear a peerless beauty,
and make me long to see that spot, so lovely in its endless spring. The Emperor and Empress are out for a
promenade, and in so unostentatious a way as to elude
the popular favor usually extended to them. Their
Majesties do not often lend their presence to public
promenades, but this happy anniversary must have
prompted the inclination.

N

December 26.—Last evening the Boulevard des Italiens drew together crowds of promenaders, eagerly gazing into the *boutiques* or booths arranged along the sidewalk. The government permits the poor to sell their wares on the principal thoroughfares during the holiday season; and their simple little sheds, neatly painted, afford a marked contrast with the magnificent shops and stores that confront them. For the first time we saw the beautiful Avenue des Champs Elysées almost deserted in favor of the boulevards. The leaden clouds overhead had shifted, and the cessation of the obstinate showers of the past few days—so discouraging to the poor venders—gave a sort of *rainbow* promise, that culminated in the appearance of moon and stars. All the world was out to say, "Hail, happy season, and may we live to see many!" Who will not add, "Give me Paris in sunshine, and save me from storms?"

The stores enticingly displayed articles of the richest description, the confectionery establishments bearing off the palm in novelties emblematical of the season. Some miniature Russian sleighs made of steel were filled with candies and fruits; and windmills for the same purpose admirably represented that conspicuous feature of Holland. At Siraudin's, on Rue de la Paix, at least an hour could have been pleasantly spent in inspecting the windows, which abounded in tasteful *cadeaux* awaiting purchasers. The boxes of sugar-plums seemed too beautiful to be despoiled, or even handled, in their lilac and rose satin garniture, embroidered in flowers; as also the gilded baskets, entwined with green garlands and purple velvet grapes. The temptation did not consist alone in the large plated-glass windows, as there was beauty among flowers and gas-light within. Behind the counters were several very pretty French girls *très bien coiffées*, and fashionably dressed, who handled twenty-franc pieces with all the dexterity of a Wall-street banker. One possessed such attractions as to electrify a man outside, who exclaimed to the lady on his arm—certainly not a jealous wife or sweetheart—"*Regardez cette demoiselle,—sa beauté est ravissante,—Je ne peut pas la quitter, —Oh! qu'elle est belle!*" That individual had evidently reached his seventh heaven of delight on a ground-floor, and so did not ask for wings to soar higher.

We visited a museum of wax-figures, at the entrance of which was stationed a sentinel of ponderous appearance, and in complete armor and helmet. The sight of this formidable figure so frightened a little child about to enter the door, that its parents were compelled to lead it away in order to quiet its nerves. After we had made the tour of the windings, and had seen below stairs, the dread impression felt by us was quite in sympathy with that of the terror-stricken child. First to greet the eye, was the lovely figure of a martyred virgin, which seemed to have a strange fascination for all around;—a form stamped with beauty's lines and curves; a tiny foot and dimpled hand;—no model was ever more perfect,—a sweet, infantile face with closed eyes, whose long black lashes threw a soft shadow on the waxen cheek; the hair disheveled lying on the bosom, and the red gash of the murderer's knife across the delicate white throat. It really seemed as if some human being lay there, wearing a smile in death. Next came grouped figures, *Samson overcome in his strength by the beauty of Delilah*, and *Don Quixote* mounted on horseback. If knights can thus be made so handsome, then we care not for the genuine! The head of John the Baptist with its severed vessels and muscles was horrible to contemplate. A landscape view very near by proved an acceptable diversion, viz: a sheet of water—formed with glass—reflecting on its surface waving grasses and lilies; and the back-ground thickly shaded with palm leaves, revealing what may have been a Hindoo slave,—something ugly and hideous enough to be of the Devil's making. A beautiful female form lying in a hammock, suspended over the stream, possessed so much natural loveliness as to disdain all other drapery save her enshrouding hair. The figure was enviously fair, compared with the one stamped with ebon blackness. A military scene next claimed our attention,—Frederick the Great surprising a soldier who—prompted by devotion to his absent wife—was writing a letter, in violation of the order to extinguish all lights. The loving words the soldier had written in those lone, still moments by the light of a flickering candle became the preface to his death warrant. "Add but one line to what you have written,—that by to-morrow's noon you die!" was the withering sentence that fell from the lips of the stern Frederick. Their countenances were stamped with the emotions they felt. In that of the doomed man we read consternation and despair, and in Freder-

ick's—just here the title of "Great" must be dropped,—
a look of implacable anger. In close proximity was a
similar scene bearing upon a disregard of military orders,
yet showing the clemency of Napoleon. A sentinel
under fatigue has fallen asleep, forgetful of his trust.
The General assumes the duty of the post, and when
the soldier awakens, he hands his sword in silent reproof.
In passing very near a figure seated on a bench,—a man
ordinarily dressed, with old felt hat, and eye-glass in
hand,—I was heard to exclaim "Pardon Monsieur,"
perfectly unconscious of my mistake until startled by
bursts of laughter behind me. However I made no
excuses for being so completely deceived, as sharper eyes
than mine had been cheated by that same figure. A
pair of winding stairs led down to a cellar dimly lighted
and very lonely, where an old man closely followed the
party, eager to describe the *horrors of the Spanish In-
quisition.* He was mumbling out a petition for money;
and several francs served to dispel the gloom from his
face, which was quite in keeping with the surroundings
of the place. A large grated cell contained twelve or
fourteen figures, and in the distance, before a red-hot
furnace, several men stood heating irons for the torture.
The principal victim in the foreground was chained
down, with arms pinioned back, and jaws thrust open,
whilst a man poured water down his throat from flagons
kept constantly replenished. A priest stood by as if to
extort confession. The torture of slow drowning was
visible in the bloated, distended stomach, the staring
eye-balls, and the agonized countenance. We passed

N*

from the sickening sight; and the guide—whose underground life was to be pitied—conducted us into a narrow passage-way that disclosed "dead men's bones." We were in the Catacombs,—but not the famous ones of Paris which cover miles—and saw numerous skulls and skeletons, grim and shadowy reminders of what we shall one day become. An additional fee admitted us to the Floating Head, a wonderful sight which we had witnessed before in New York. A mirror is said to accomplish the wonderful delusion. We talk to a pale, sad face, which seems to be set on a table, and to have lost connection with its mortal frame, the head moving wearily about as if on a pivot. Apparently the body is missing. A gentleman attending this performance, once mischievously asked if a glass of good old rye would not do much towards alleviating the sufferings of decapitation, whereupon the head betrayed itself by a broad grin and laughter. Emerging from the museum, and out again among a more jovial population than the *wax-people*, we refreshed ourselves at Peters' in the Passage des Princes, that celebrated Anglo-Franco-American establishment, furnishing every style of cookery. The turtle soup, choice edibles and wine were capital, but the oysters had a decidedly coppery taste, which was very objectionable to us Americans, who are accustomed to such fine ones at home. If our bivalves could be introduced here, both England and France would be put to shame. At a short distance from us sat one of our handsome country-women, who was not too discreet to decline the offer of a *demi-douzaine* in these words:

"Take away those small, shriveled oysters,—their acrid flavor would not sweeten this night's 'dreams!'" And the fair lady wisely chose *truffles aux champignons* with a glass of sparkling moselle.

CHAPTER IX.

December 27.

MR. and Mrs. C. H. McCormick entertained their friends last evening at the Grand Hôtel, and several hours were agreeably disposed of in dancing, music, and in listening to recitations by Mrs. Leigh Ward. The daughters of Dr. Sims sang very artistically, as did also the grand-daughters of Governor McDowell, of Virginia. The beautiful hostess dispensed the hospitalities with the most charming grace, appearing from time to time among her guests at the *round tables*, and was pronounced by all, the radiant light of the golden circle.

This bright day, with a touch of frosty cold, betokens a return of good weather, and we rejoice that our appeal to Old Sol to come again in his glory has at last been heard.

December 28.—The necessities of the poor have not been overlooked in these festive days. A Fair for the benefit of the suffering Poles in Paris, took place to day at the Hôtel Lambert, the residence of the Countess Dzialynska, *née* Princess Czartoryska. This lady is at the head of the society that befriends these indigent exiles, and most generously does she throw open her palace, rich in art and splendor, adding thereto the fragrance of a deed of charity. Some of the most distinguished women in Paris presided at the tables, which lined the long gallery; and a few fair Americans assisted in a salon adjoining, the varied and tasteful display of their fancy articles bringing good prices from ready purchasers. This table was under the direction of Mrs. Dix. The historical associations of the Hôtel Lambert made the visit one to be desired. It was there that Napoleon in 1815 held a last conference with his minister, M. de Montalivet, when reverses had so multiplied that all seemed lost; and there Voltaire lived, and with his brilliant genius planned *la Henriade*. It was also the abode of Lambert de Thorigny, an opulent President of the Parliament of the 17th century, and the residence of the financiers, Dupin and Delahaye. The entrance is remarkable for its staircase, and the beautiful scroll-work of its balustrade; and the *tout ensemble* of the grand edifice reflects glory upon the name of Levau. The *salons* abound in profuse ornamentation of gilding and painting, the fame of the great painters Lebrun and Lesueur speaking from the ceilings, and being handed down in such verse as—

> " Lesueur, Le Brun, ces illustres Appeles
>   Ces rivaux de l'antiquité,
> · Ont en ce lieu charmant, étalé la beauté
>   De leurs peintures immortelles."

Ere we left the cheerful scene within doors, the moon had risen in all her brightness, and our drive in an open carriage did not prove uncomfortable, notwithstanding it was December, far advanced. The situation of the

Hôtel Lambert is in the Rue St. Louis en l'Ile. The river gives a picturesque appearance to that portion of the city; and at various points along the banks, a spirit of life, and active trade are manifest. There are venders of papers and books, some of the latter looking as if they had been printed a century ago,—then, jutting out from the embankments are bath-houses; swimming-schools for ladies and gentlemen; and the *Lavoirs* with their busy *blanchisseuses*. The Seine impresses one also sadly, as it recalls many unhappy lives given to its flood—a favorite mode of suicide of the French people, who court life in the hey-day of fortune and pleasure, and cast it away when the clouds of adversity gather.

December 29.—Under bright sunshine, and with heart cheered by the receipt of letters—whose crumpled pages were hastily consigned to a pocket—I repaired to the American Episcopal church. Some fair hand had prepared a beautiful Christmas garb, green scriptural texts adorning the walls and the altar. From out of the dark cedar and glossy holly-leaves, peered a single star, the emblem of hope, love and redemption. As in ages past it directed the wise men of the east, so does it now lead the ignorant to the shining road, scattering the mist from unbelieving eyes, and giving to troubled souls the promise,

> "That not unto the highest, here
> The highest place is given;
> But they who serve below, may wear
> The starry crown in Heaven."

On my return home I found Hon. and Mrs. Thos.

H. Davis, of New York. Mr. D. has the sympathy
of numerous friends in the late illness which nearly
terminated his life—his remarkable fortitude winning
the admiration of many besides his surgeons. May he
live long to be an ornament to his profession and country! Mrs. D. is a brilliant conversationalist. Her
description of Italy makes it a "golden dream—the
vision of all that is lovely and fair."

December 31.—New Year's eve! The pen is inclined
to make a slow and solemn movement as it traces these
words; for are we not about to leave the beaten track of
a twelve-mouth's journey for an untried pathway,—to
launch our barques upon a new tide, yet to learn whether
we shall be "care-worn or pleasure-bound?" Stepping
thus upon the threshold of a new year, the remembrances
of old pleasures will linger, and we press fondly the
withered bouquet of those joys, as if to extract all the
perfume that remains. I have recently parted with the
sweetest young rose-bud of all the American colony,—
little Bessie Scholey, modestly answering to the choicest
type of beauty, with her tender-lighted eyes, soft brown
in hue, fair skin, and hair of golden chestnut. I have
locked her up in my heart with the recollection of her
rare intelligence, her gentle manner and affectionate caresses, and wonder if she will ever come to me again,
except in memory. We feel like saying with a sigh, as
we lose the charm of a fair face, or other delights—

"Ah! well-a-day!
Life leaves us so.
Love dare not stay.
Sweet things decay."

* * * * *   The midnight chimes are just now answering to the dirge-like command of England's poet—

> " Ring out, wild bells, across the sky,
>   The year is dying in the night—"

Out of this death will there not come a good angel, to guide our feet into new and pleasant mysteries ?

January 1, 1868.—The Parisians celebrate this day as we do Christmas, there being a free interchange of kindly sentiment, gifts, etc. Of the American residents, a few followed the custom of keeping "open house," and offering cheer to friends and acquaintances. The visiting hours, cut short by twilight's dusky shadows, embraced the usual incidents,—a bit of mock idolatry to bright eyes over a glass of egg-nog; saucy speeches— only that and nothing more—from some who are straight-laced on all other days than this; a *bon-mot* and a blessing religiously bestowed by a gray-haired sire, who may have dropped a silent tear last night at the ghostly hour of twelve, feeling that life, with him, was slipping away like the years; a sparkling verse and witticisms, that will make memorable the author and the beautiful object who received it naively—her blushes deepening to the ruby of the glass ;—light and capricious things to drive seriousness from the hours. This is a day for the *belle* to wear her sweetest smile and finest robe, and for that *belle's* mamma to think with pride of the flower-strewn path her daughter treads ;—a day for *beaux*, new kids, and a *sans-souci* air,—in a word, a day for every one to rest in a shadow no darker than the *couleur de rose*, and to weave out of it bright dreams and hopes for the future.

CHAPTER X.

January 4.

MERRILY speed the hours, said some of us a few evenings since, whilst assisting at two brilliant parties; one hostess being a charming Princess of the "blood," and the other, an American, whose beautiful *salons* are not to be excelled in Paris. How shall we describe the two, rendering equal praise to each? The foreign mode of entertaining has its advantages, no formal introductions being required, and the hostess not being obliged to go through the laborious duty of providing partners for her guests. It is not an unusual thing to see a young American girl, uninitiated in the custom, receive the salute of a Frenchman with a hesitation she regrets the next day, if only on account of the awkward appearance she may have presented. But the cavalier does not mind such a rebuff, attributing it to a lack of *savoir faire.* Last evening we heard one generously exclaim, upon the refusal of his hand by one of our country-women: *"Elle est bien belle et gracieuse, quoiqu'elle ne veut pas danser avec moi;"* and then he pulled at his waxed moustache—whose length certainly needed no extension—and walked away to claim another partner, who did not wince behind her spangled fan and

o

say, "*Non, monsieur.*" Who does not feel the gay inspiration of Strauss' waltzes, and find in a waxen floor more utility than beauty? In the parlors of the American hostess hung many rare paintings, reflecting great credit upon her taste. How refreshing the *buffet;* how sumptuous the supper; and how lovely our women, rendered doubly so by their Parisian toilettes—those odd yet beautiful styles of the time of Louis XIV,—those wonderful creations of Worth, the magic ruler of fashion—to say nothing of Pangard, Savarre, and Fanet et Beer. What an extravagant outlay of money! Thousands of francs swept by in the numerous laces and other rich fabrics, whilst husbands and fathers looked on with pride, and did not seem to miss the gold that had vanished from their pockets. Brightest of all the stars was Miss du Hamel. According to some, New Orleans claims the honor of her birth, but Cuba takes up arms against the assertion. Be it as it may, Princes, with all their prerogatives and wealth, might rejoice in such a prize.

January 7.—Already has memory woven out of the Christmas festivities a garland that wears a warm and fresh glow like the berried holly still decking our homes. Have not the pleasant events of the past week imparted a zest to the incoming year, and made us accept more resignedly the farewell of 1867? And although '68 has received our greeting in a frosty, snapping humor, we should not make complaint when such glorious frolic is vouchsafed to us at the skating park.

The snow may fall to the fierce-sounding title of a storm; the ice-king may wave his sceptre, hanging every bough with glittering pendants, and leave not a vestige of green on the Champs Elysées; the current of the Seine may be converted into a rock strong as Gibralter; but what care we for all this, when January brings out the skates, and makes a gay carnival for the mirth-loving people of Paris? It is only the knowledge of the suffering poor that should make us denounce this month's rightful claim in the "circling seasons." The Parisians rejoice in being suddenly Russianized by this cold spell, and we believe they would willingly resign the greatest attractions of their beloved city for a few days of skating sport. Several days since the large lake at the Bois presented a grotesque sight, with representatives of every class engaged in the *glissant* motion. How animated was the scene, as we witnessed it from a little knoll overlooking the locked-up stream that shone like a mirror, and how excitedly the crowd skimmed along, marking their love of the novel amusement! Some one said, within my hearing, that this was Paris on a Toodles-drunk; and so it seemed, as round and round they went,—some on their knees, and others lying at length, wholly unable to keep their feet. Just beyond the rustic bridge that spans the narrow curve of the lake, a broken surface of ice revealed a number of ducks and swans, who were making the most of their imprisoned space, and seemed to be imitating the frolics of the people. How cheerful looked the picturesque Swiss restaurant on the opposite bank, so snugly embowered in shrubbery—still green—and how busily ran the *garçons* to and fro outside, distributing glasses of hot punch! *Le cercle des patineurs*, a reserved rink in the Bois—under control of a club—collects together some of the choicest cullings of American society, and is frequently graced by the Imperial family and Court retinue. The Prince Imperial, on the 3d inst., glided courageously along, entirely enwrapped in the jovial sport, and totally unmindful of the cares which the future may unfold—in a word, the great responsibility which ever rests on the shoulders of royalty. Distinction, however great, cannot evade the penalty of a wrong move, or an awkward tumble; and even the most experienced are not always exempt. Let this be proclaimed for the comfort of those who go tremblingly forward as beginners! Victory cometh after a hard-fought battle; so, with skating, is there, at first, a struggle to gain secure foothold with the polished *steel*, which *cuts* but never *slays*. Woe to us when the full-orbed sun shall come with its thawing power! But hie to the crowning feature, the night-carnival, held by a pageant of gaily-costumed people, in innocent dissipation by the light of the moon, and amid the variegated lanterns that shed a crimson and golden lustre on the glossy ice! The groves of the Bois on that night lost their usual stillness, re-echoing the tramping of horses' feet, besides the tread of hundreds, nay, thousands of human beings. The air was cold and bracing, and furs might have sold at a premium, at a midnight auction in the woods, with old Boreas as crier. The lovers of wintry pleasures came out in full force, courting perhaps abuse from the stay-away world; but we, who appreciate the icy sport, and that hardy type of nature capable of a Siberian endurance, will not withhold our approbation.

We doubt not that last night a husband or two, after leaving the scene of fashion and beauty at the house of the popular American Embassador, became cross and peevish as the horses' heads were turned away from home and repose; and that, on the other hand, some domestic angel—wives and mothers deserve the title—waited through the "wee sma' hours ayont the twal" for the sound of footsteps that came not; at last becoming drowsily convinced that a skating carnival has no bounds. If an unseen magician presided at this carnival and brought out enchantment after enchantment we are not aware; or if the fairies tripped over the snow-covered paths to the scene of busy action, and shook the wand of beauty, we cannot say; but this we will assert, that nothing could excel the dexterous use of limb and the swiftness of pedal motion there exhibited. The old man of sixty put the calendar of time behind him, and began a renewal of his school-boy days, and his companion of the gentler sex entered into the sport with equal enthusiasm. Here and there, like stars shooting across the horizon, came young and lovely girls, with bright costumes, short dresses and bewitching ankles; and then followed their cavaliers who were roguishly inclined to pretty and rapid compliments when guardians were not by. Here a countess brushed her velvet garment against a handsome marquis, attired quite *comme il faut;*—there

o*

an English barrister, a graceful skater, was rudely
sundered from his lady friend. And who was guilty of
this breach of etiquette? Why a mischievous little
sprite who sped like an arrow through the crowd, up-
setting all of lighter weight that lay in her path. A
little further on, a Russian Count, in comfortable fur, was
making love to a pretty little damsel in a tasteful costume of Tartan plaid. But of what value are *les modes*,
and what is dress?—a perishable fabric scarcely more
enduring than the flower which yields its perfume for a
day and is withered the next? Is not its most important use rendered subordinate by those dictators, fashion
and vanity? But, of the joy, happiness and content that
come of innocent amusements and jovial exercise we
might grow eloquent, were it not for lack of time. These
rouse the blood to healthful action, causing it to circu-
late evenly and gratefully; whereas the cares and guilty
dissipations of the world freeze the sensibilities, making
the heart heavier and colder than a river turned to ice.
If the goddess of this realm, the charming Empress, was
not present on the occasion, we will assert it was for
some reason not derogatory to the event. However, the
glory was enough in the delight of hundreds whose glad-
some shouts pealed through the wooded glens, making
music, whilst the night breeze bore away exultantly the
last lingering sound that told of the carnival. To-day
the Emperor was on skates for a half hour; also the
Empress, who appeared in a Bismarck velvet costume,
and if not skilled in the accomplishment, she at least
displayed that perfection of grace which never deserts

her.   Our people cannot fail to notice the marked differ-
ence between his Imperial Majesty and the President of
the United States in regard to the indulgence in amusements and active sports.   It is evident that royalty
siezes at pleasure, where Democracy stops to consider.

January 9.—O! merry world of Paris! how many
altars and shrines of pleasure ye erect to lure the senses
and win the heart,—how much valuable time ye demand
from us worshipers who madly call the hours idle, and
count them not as they pass forever from us!   The life
we lead is surely one of felicity, if not of earnestness.
It has the garnish or tinsel that sparkles on the surface
even though it may lack the virtue of solidity.   We go
on in one giddy round, catching at sundry delights amid
the swell of music, the hum of gay voices, the dance of
pleasure, and the garlands of grace and beauty.   The
scenes we frequent are picture-worlds where lights and
colors blend harmoniously; and if there be a dark spot,
it escapes our dazzled eyes, like the serpent that lurks
unseen in a bed of flowers.   One kneels to the fragrance
of the blossoms, yet the venomous breath is there!   We
do not stop to become artists of our own existence, but
leave others to paint us in our butterfly flight; and even
memory, whose store-house begs to be filled with the
aliment of our joys, is left hungry, because days and
events bear no chronicle, and are confusedly slipping
into the great abyss of oblivion.   Worthy deeds and
labors bring richest treasure to our minds—profitless
pleasures wound our spirits even in their warmest em-

brace. These crown the festival, but they poison the wine! But all such philosophy in Paris shuts itself up in a remote hiding-place; its teachings being hieroglyphics that defy understanding and practice. The cry is "*vive la bagatelle*," and, with that shout, a thousand feet spring forward, and as many voices take up the key-note, locking us in the arena of exciting gaieties, and walling us around with fortifications stronger than granite, which we would not batter down if we could. And why? Because we are creatures passing away, whose poor unwise natures grasp at the most evanescent joys.

Several days preceding the 8th, a day memorable in our country's annals for the great battle of New Orleans of 1815, there were rumors of a ball to take place at the Tuileries, and from twenty to .twenty-five Americans were preparing for presentation; the gentlemen donning garments of fine cloth embroidered in gold; the ladies costly and effective dresses of satin, silk, tulle and lace, each of which was pronounced a miracle of fashion. I had the honor of being escorted to the palace by Gen. Dix, who, in entering the presentation *salon*, turned with some pride to his country-women, so elegant, graceful and beautiful. The *Rue de Rivoli* from the early hour of eight o'clock was enlivened by an unusal number of carriages, many of them coroneted, and quite as attractive with gorgeous livery as the fabled Cinderella coach manufactured by fairy genius. Princes, Dukes, Counts and titled dames occupied the seats, but their's was no royalty transformed out of obscure poverty as in the instance of the persecuted child who left the chimney-corner in rags to become a princess by reason of her beauty, and not by inherited rank and fortune. If there was nothing outside the palace—as seen by other eyes than ours—to awaken the fairy story, there was within enough of splendor and enchantment to create a glowing tale which the world would stop to read and admire. The spacious court-yard which we entered through a beautiful arch from Place de Carousel was guarded by soldiers whose simple grade was but the stepping-stone, at the threshold, to the inner-court where military and civic titles dared approach a throne and salute an Emperor. The presentation *salon*, notwithstanding its dingy ceiling and sombre aspect, was rendered bright by innumerable lights and gay costumes. A superb piano, recently presented to the Empress by the Emperor of Austria, engaged the attention of a few of us until the hour of ten, when there came the cry—*L'Empereur! L'Empereur!* In a long line England and America were drawn up in brilliant array; and some military officers—their nationalities unknown to us—completed our *comet-trail;* but this luminous body paled before two stars of regal magnitude, the Emperor and Empress, who passed around the encircled space in dazzling glory. When America's turn came in the order of presentation, our Embassador called the names of his people with a readiness that drew forth from their Majesties, this compliment—"We would desire our memories always to serve us as well as yours has on this occason." The Emperor in demeanor was cold, and he wore the air of one heartily weary of

etiquette, yet proudly true to all of its exactions. The
Empress with unpretending charm of manner, and in-
effable grace, glided before us like a lovely vision, her
dress being simple, yet elegant. Alternate stripes of
gold and silver ribbon upon a satin ground, shone
through the soft tulle like vertical rays of sun and moon,
and the drapery floating from the shoulders bore so
striking a resemblance to wings that she well deserved
the appellation of *angel*. The *collier* of fringed diamonds was of unexcelled magnificence. Butterflies of the
same precious stone shimmered here and there through
the tulle, whilst some brilliants of equal beauty glistened
in her hair,—a fitting coronal for such a brow. After
the presentation ceremony, which was simply a recognition of each person by a bow, an occasional word
from the Empress, and a cramped courtesy from us who
sighed impatiently for space, their Majesties repaired to
the Salle des Maréchaux, where they were joined on the
daïs by the Princess Mathilde, and became spectators of
a scene truly radiant. Gas and candle-lights innumerable beamed down on a variety of court-costumes and
gorgeous regalia. The gold garniture created a blaze
of dazzling light that quite oppressed the eye, and a
pleasant relief was found in viewing the more subdued
toilettes of lovely women,—pearls and dew-drops amid
the golden sheen. A simplicity of dress among some of
our ladies, Miss du Hamel, Misses Beckwith, Miss Lippincott, Miss Dix, and a few others was remarked,
but it was confined to those just unfolding their youthful beauty in budding warmth, and who have not yet

reached that mature age when ornament is necessary to enrich nature. Mrs. Duncan, of New York, a regal beauty, in white satin dress with *demi-jupe* of black Chantilly lace, and a scarlet velvet *ceinture* contested the palm with Mrs. Caldwell, of the same city, who wore a white silk covered with flounces of *point appliqué* lace, over which were clustered marguerites amid a profusion of wavy grass. The Princess Metternich was attired in pink, her *toilette* being the perfection of style, and the Princess Mathilde was robed in white, adorned with multicolored roses.

Delicious music with ravishing sound helped to keep up the magic spell of the hours, and from the varied scene we drank in continually draughts of pleasure. As we drifted here and there to new beauties, it seemed like sailing over a sunny sea, whose surface was of burnished gold, with melody in the air, and flowery odors in the gale. The Salle de la Paix, with its mirrors, gilded ceiling and superb crystal chandeliers,—the Salle du Trône, with its red velvet draperies, and canopied throne all studded with golden bees,—the *Salon blanc*, with its decorations of gilt and white, and furniture of green damask, were all open to the guests; and at every door were visible the *Cent Gardes*—the handsomest specimens of men in France. They stood like statues in their imposing height, wearing glittering silver breast-plates, and helmets with long white plumes. The beautifully sculptured statue of the little Prince, with the greyhound at his side—Royalty and Fidelity matchlessly grouped— graced the long supper-room, where was spread out a "feast for the gods." Royal feasts must be showered with drops of nectar, else why were persons loth to leave, forgetting that others were to come after as beggars of the crumb? At one end of this room—the Galerie de Diane—was a fine display of silver-plate surrounded by flowers.

The Imperial party left the Salle des Maréchaux at one o'clock A. M., and passed through the long line of *salons* into the supper-room, after which no more was seen of them. Besides the *diplomats*, rich in decorations, there were present military chieftains and other celebrities; a brother of the Tycoon, in his native costume, and some members of the Japanese Embassy. A face black as midnight, and peering out from behind some jeweled coronets, indicated a fire-worshiper. If the precepts of Zoroaster had e'er been forgotten by this follower, he would have again returned to his idols amidst the myriads of lights that flashed everywhere in the Tuileries that night. A Spanish duchess wore a crown of diamonds whose height could be measured by inches. A brigand might have become rich off a single jewel, whilst any banker entrusted with the treasure would feel compelled to guard it with Argus-eyed vigilance. Looking down from niches in the wall, in the Salle des Maréchaux, upon this brilliant scene, were seven or eight superb figures—statues of gallant generals and brave naval commanders—and of the portraits of the Marshals of France, the mention of the intrepid Ney will suffice, without intentional slight to others, for was not Cato's image once left behind? Upon leaving

the ball no gloomy historical association came up to
overshadow the rose-colored tints of what we had seen.
We feel assured that France, in these days of glory and
peace, would gladly blot from her record the stain of
every ruby drop that flowed from her guillotine.

January 13.—The day after the ball at the Palace,
the Empress honored with her presence the *Cercle des
patineurs*, where she enjoyed several hours' skating.
Her attention was attracted by the extraordinary feats
of a young American girl, upon whom she lavished
many gracious compliments. This morning we were
prevented from visiting the *Cercle*, on account of preparations that were making for a repetition of the night-
carnival, and had to go to Longchamps instead; but the
skating rink there lacked the gaiety for which the former
is noted, as well as the comfort of a heated saloon near by.
However, the large bonfires proved most acceptable to
the old folks who clustered there, like Macbeth's witches
around the seething caldron; and claret punches, selling
readily beneath a temporary shed, served to take away
the numbness of many a skater. The *traineau*—a tin
chair with runners—is in frequent use with beginners
on the ice. It being very light, the inexperienced skater
with its aid moves rapidly along until, by some accident,
it escapes his grasp, when suddenly down he tumbles, to
the infinite amusement of the lookers-on. We saw a
Marquis undertake the instruction of a fair young friend
from one of our far Southern States. Her exclamation,
"I could abide by such fun all the year round," proved

P

her willingness to give up the delights of her cheerful,
sunny clime for winter's sports in Paris. The Marquis, a cruel teacher, soon left her to her own resources,
—sternly forbidding proffered help; but the Southern
spirit bravely met the challenge to come forward, and
ere the hour was spent, fairly astonished the natives.
The first trial of a pair of lovely little feet from California, that crept along like tiny mice, elicited the com-
plimentary remark, *"Regardez cette jeune Américaine—
quels jolis pieds !"*

A day at Vésinet succeeded the one spent at Longchamps. This pretty little village, only a few miles distant from Paris, with its neat white cottages, forest and
park, lake and rustic bridges, presents a most romantic
picture. Its pride is an Asylum for sick working-
women, the building having accommodations for three
hundred. We found that Gen. Quincy, of Boston, and
a few other Americans, had resorted thither, felicitating
themselves on reaching a spot more quiet and retired
than the Bois de Boulogne. The forest paths still re-
tained traces of snow, soon to be dissipated by the bright
sun, whose fervid rays were threatening like destruction
to our delightful sport. To add to our fears, there came
at dusk a provoking shower of rain; but it quickly
passed over, and then the moon peeped slyly out, as if
to tell all loiterers to betake themselves home. My
English friends declared my triumph complete in the
circuit I had made of the lake, and that was happiness
enough to make me bestow a cheerful farewell upon
Vésinet. Bundling up with our skates all regrets at

departure, we hastened on to the station, where a large, bright fire animated the waiting-room. Twenty minutes were at our disposal, and then came the plunging, noisy engine, the last remembrance of the day. I doubt not that the new scenes and pleasurable exercise made my pillow seem the softer and dreams more light and airy.

January 15.—A love of flowers guides hundreds of feet to the Place de la Madelaine. On the eastern es·planade adjoining that grand and beautiful church, wreaths, garlands and bouquets are arranged on booths and benches, and sweet odors mingle with the breeze. The spot bespeaks the bloom of summer, and yet it is frosty winter that has proved itself a glorious season for roses, jessamine and tender violets. "In Eastern lands they talk in flowers"—so shall our language, in praise of France, be woven of the richest and most fragrant blossoms,—the pink hyacinth, with its star-shaped clusters; the snowy camelia, making the rose at its side blush the deeper in crimson; the geranium, in scarlet blossom; the delicate fern; the fuschia and the daisy; the lilac and the pansy.

" Come gather a wreath from these garden bowers,
And tell the wish of thy heart in flowers."

12 P. M.—We have just returned from an amateur musical entertainment, at which two nieces of Hon. Horace Greeley assisted. A Shaksperian recitation was given by the host in a style that might have done credit to the stage. A piano composition, the *Rêverie de l'In-*

venteur, floats up now with all its exquisite softness and
melody, obedient to my invocation:

> Oh! sweetest Rêverie! come to my soul,
>   And with dream-like music beguile the hour,
> Steal from my life every sorrow and toil,
>   Make me to worship thy magical pow'r.
> Come to me like the blest visions of night,
>   With peace and with joy enwrap me to rest.
> Cease not thy melody,—bringing delight—
>   My heart to thee clings like a bird to its nest.
>
> Thou hast entranc'd me! soft floating murmur,
>   Whose musical cadence seems from above,
> Leading my spirit to all that is pure,
>   Wooing my thoughts to the sunshine of love.
> There are chimes in thy measure sweetly sad,
>   That ring thro' the heart like bells in the night;
> They banish rude passion, cheer, and make glad,
>   And still through the shadows point to the light.
>
> If all the fond joys that now are so sweet
>   Should perish and leave me a mourner here,
> I'd ask but one mem'ry ever to meet,—
>   That of thy music, its charm rare and dear.
> And like some lov'd flower I gather always
>   To lay on the heart, its perfume to keep,
> So shall I cherish these vanishing days,—
>   Echoes that 'll ne'er let thy melody sleep.

CHAPTER XI.

THE second of a series of entertainments at the house of the American Minister came off last evening, the assemblage comprising many distinguished personages, and the loveliest of our country-women,—America's bouquet of beauty standing pre-eminent amidst politics, diplomacy, literature, science and the military. The spacious *salons* were thronged up to the limited hour of midnight when the music and the dance ceased. Nearly all the Americans who were presented at Court on the 8th inst., participated on the occasion, and among them were the handsome Mrs. Lippincott, of Philadelphia, and her daughter, who is soon to form a matrimonial alliance with the Secretary of the United States Legation at Rome; Mrs. Caldwell, of New York; Miss Paine, of Boston; Miss Blood, of Tennessee; General Quincy, of Boston; Mr. C. H. McCormick, of Chicago, and Mr. Walsh, of Japan. The wife of the Tunisian Envoy was present, her oriental style of beauty and magnificent jewels commanding general admiration, also M. Michel Chevalier; Lord Lyons; Chevalier de Nigra, the Italian Minister; a noted representative from Persia wearing a Tartar cap; and one of the editors of the *Constitutionnel*.

January 21.—A votary again to-night at Pleasure's

P*

shrine; but "the serious things come after awhile" whispered a gray-haired sire of the *beau monde* as we stood in the midst of the gay dancers. This ball given by Dr. and Mrs. Johnston, Boulevard Malesherbes, gave evidence of distingué and liberal taste. The flowers scattered here and there in profusion would have formed a luxuriant conservatory. Among the numerous guests were Gen. Dix and daughter, Mrs. Blake; the gifted Mrs. Schleicker; Dr. Evans; Col. Heine, of the United States Legation; Miss Eddins, of Alabama; and the Messrs. Dewey, of California. A distinguished belle, fairest of all, was observed to wander off from the dazzling scene to drink in the more dangerous light of a pair of black eyes, whose power lay very deep under the heaviest fringed eye-lids; and our wager is that out of the wooing will come a chiding, and yet no harm need have been done. *Nous verrons!*

January 26.—Day receptions and evening parties continue to make up the schedule of time. At the ball of Madam Anstey—an English lady, with a trio of lovely blonde daughters,—were mingled the beauty and grace of at least five or six nations. Following this, came the reception at the Hôtel de Ville, by Baron and Baroness Haussman, and on the same evening another brilliant *soirée* at 6. Rue de Presbourg.

January 27.—A notion siezed us this pleasant day to visit the *Morgue,* that dismal place which clouds the spirits even before its portals are crossed. On visiting a cemetery where the dead lie shut out from sight, and

where only green mounds or stone-tablets meet the eye,
sad emotions fill the mind, widely differing from those
evoked by the sight of a dead body, whose end has been
a violent one. The *Morgue*, lately renovated, presents a
neat exterior. Numbers of persons were flocking in
from sheer curiosity, but in the throng there were a few
wretched mourners looking for lost friends. A scant
calico apron received the tears of one poor woman who
turned her sorrowful face towards us as she brushed
by—her quick, nervous tread betraying her mission,
whilst our slow steps told that we were only sympathetic lookers-on at grief and death. The building is
appropriately situated near the Seine, as this river furnishes most of its occupants—unfortunates that must be
claimed by friends within a specified time, or else be
consigned to unknown graves. The bodies are exposed
to view three days, their clothing being hung up to assist
in the identification. A grating separates the visitor
from the corpse which lies extended on a sort of inclined
plane, a constant stream of water trickling down upon
the form. When we first entered, the curtain had not
been raised, and those few moments of suspense seemed
a century to several persons, whose hearts were swelling
with anxious emotion! Soon were revealed two victims
—a man and a woman—and a single glance sufficed to
impress upon our minds the sin of life taken, or life
surrendered without the hand of God in it. I turned
away to the sunlight, welcoming the street with its
animated aspect, but not without a wish that the sorrows
of mortals might be lessened, and that our heavenly

Judge might show mercy to the self-destroyer, and to
him who imbrueth his hands in the blood of his fellow-
man. A drive around *Notre Dame,* which is in the
vicinity of the *Morgue,* afforded us a more correct idea
than ever of the magnificence of its architecture. It
would require a giant eye to take in all its beauties, and
a mind co-equal to invest and treat each pinnacle and
portal with the merit it deserves. Victor Hugo's pen
has brought out the sculptured ornaments as boldly as
did the artist's chisel, making them shine with a glory
as golden as the light that streams down upon them
from heaven. His description so faithful and true, has
gained for him one of his proudest laurels. * * * *

The Marquis de Geoffroy in a visit just made to us,
conveys the gratifying intelligence of a friend's recovery
of health in Italy. How many seem to shake off the
burden of disease and *ennui* in the freshness of that
bright land!

January 29.—I attended to-day with the Princess
Savalan Kahn, the reception of Mrs. Dix, who, by her
accomplished graces, always imparts to her re-unions a
charm, independent of the attractiveness of her guests.
Then followed a drive to the Bois, where we found the
usual display of stylish equipages and gay people. The
spectacle there presented, at certain hours of the day, is
most imposing. A soirée musicale given this evening
by a friend residing on the Avenue de l'Impératrice,
whose apartments are the *ne plus ultra* of elegance, embraced some of the best professional talent of the city,

besides the graceful amateurs, Miss Sims and Miss du Hamel, who won bountiful praise.

February 2.—The Greek church in Rue de la Croix is built in the Byzantine-Muscovite style, and the effect of the dazzling sunlight is very fine upon its burnished gilt cupolas. The interior of the central one is painted to represent *Christ imparting His blessing.* Upon entering this chapel we are reminded of a family oratory by its diminutive proportions. All the appointments, however, are of the most gorgeous character. It was erected by the voluntary contributions of Russian families at the cost of two hundred and forty thousand dollars,—a sum sufficient to make it one of the brightest jewels of the crown that Paris wears in beautiful churches. The paintings on the walls are *The Adoration of the Shepherds; The Sermon on the Mount; The entry into Jerusalem;* and *The last Supper.* The finest velvet tapestry covers the floor ; and a railing near the entrance separates the spectator from the inner shrine, so marvellously grand and enticing, as—

> " To rouse the heart and lead the will,
> By a bright ladder to the world above."

* * * * * * The Park Monceaux—a more appropriate designation would be garden-spot,—is one of the most attractive resorts, it being situated in the very heart of the capital. Magnificent gates of gilded iron lead to the grounds, which are embellished with handsome trees, green shrubbery and bright flowers. The main walks are supplied with seats, but there are more

secluded windings where the beautiful greensward invites one to recline *à la paysan.* Many visitors drive through the park, but a *promenade à pied* is preferable, for it enables one to wander along the banks of the little lake called Naumachie, to view the broken columns of the Corinthian colonnade; or stand at the stone bridge, a short distance off, and let fancy weave some romantic history out of the mock-ruin. But there is a real history connected with the park, and which is told in the fragmentary remains of a pyramidal tomb. It was in the days of Louis Philippe, that Monceaux, owned by the Duke de Chartres, was a spot consecrated to pleasure, and where games involving heavy losses of money were indulged in. A young German possessed of considerable riches came to Paris, and soon fell into the fascinating pastime of gambling. He lost at the play, and thereupon very excitedly cast imprecations upon those who had led him into the game. A gentleman attached to the Duke de Chartres, reminded him that "he must not speak thus before his master," to which he tartly replied—"among fools, there are no princes." The crowd fell upon him and killed him, and secretly buried his body in the gardens. Another of the attractions is a small grotto whose rocks, almost entirely overgrown with mosses and grasses, are constantly bedewed by a showery waterfall. The interior is very curious, abounding with stalactite formations. We left the grounds rather reluctantly, our parting glances falling on the rotunda, now occupied as a residence by the park-keepers; and, on our homeward route, stopped at the

church of St. Augustine, an ornament recently added to
the Boulevard Malesherbes. The building is in the
style of the 14th century, with a magnificent dome, surmounted by a gilded ball, and has statues of the twelve
apostles as outside decorations. The lateness of the hour,
however, excluded us from the church-proper, but we
gained admission into the basement, where vespers were
being held. On reaching the Avenue de l'Impératrice
the scene was excessively gay for a Sabbath afternoon—
at least so we thought! But, in Paris, this day of all
others, is selected for a general turn-out by the rich and
poor; the former in their luxurious carriages, and the
latter on foot—the hard-toiling man and his family enjoying the wealth of bright, beautiful sunshine, little
caring for the vain accompaniments of riches.

February 10.—A week consumed in frivolities, and
another ball at the Tuileries, which passed off with the
usual *eclat*, has left scarce a moment for reflection. But
while fashion and gaiety reign, we are sometimes forced
to turn from the rose-strewn path to the pale lily, emblematical of death. Nowhere is the coming of death
more poignantly felt than in a strange land, when it cuts
down the tender bud, or the stately flower that has
bloomed in grace and beauty upon our own shores. In
the demise of an estimable lady from Alabama we share
the sorrow of the bereaved family and the regret of
friends far away. The blight of disease, whose destroying touch takes from us our loved one, still leaves like a
perfumed incense the memory of every gentle virtue;

and we know that through "the valley of the shadow
of death" we shall catch a gleam of the light that leads
the spirit from the darkness of this world to the "perfect day."   Such is our consolation in bereavement; and
so doth hope turn us from the ashes of the tomb to the
sweet promise of immortality—from the withered earthly
garland to the imperishable heavenly crown !

February 14.—St. Valentine's day !   A pleasant reminder comes in the shape of a sweet-scented *billet* from
England.   We stopped this morning at Charlie's restaurant—noted for its excellent buckwheat cakes and
pumpkin pies—to add our mite to the fund of praise
accorded it by many Americans.   From its very humble
appearance one would hardly expect such cheer within.
The windows present no such luscious and tempting
morsels as those of the Grand Café and Maison Dorée,
and no fine plate-glass attracts the eye, but a snow-
white muslin curtain partially drawn back reveals the
neatness of the little saloon.   The absence of glittering
mirrors and chandeliers is agreeably atoned for by the
little bouquets scattered about, and by that *one dish*
which the best of French cookery can never make us
forget.   Madame Busque, to whom the establishment
really belongs,—a nice old dame full of compliments—
came in from the culinary department to welcome us.
Let none of our people pass by this Franco-American
institution, as a breakfast served there is sure to recall
"Home, Sweet Home," and a pleasant word of English
will greet the ear should Madame B. enter to wish a

"Good morning." If an invading army threatened
to overthrow Paris, would there not be enough lovers of
hot cakes and *American eagles—one* is perched over the
entrance—to protect from harm this one little spot?

To-night another *musicale* is added to the pleasant
entertainments that friends have been constantly offering. Among the celebrities were Gustave Doré; the
accomplished Doctor Martinez—Maximilian's late Embassador to Turkey and Greece; and the beautiful
Madame T., wife of Gen. Tour of Italy.

February 16.—In our promenade around the lake, in
the Bois de Boulogne, it was a delight for the eye to follow the graceful, easy motion of the swans, as they came
up to the banks to receive the scattered crumbs. The
gorgeous sunset was succeeded by a flood of crimson
light that tinged all nature with beauty and made me
think—if earth is so lovely, what must heaven be?

February 20.—Let there be a truce to gaiety as my
pen records this date, so fraught with sad memories!
Through many years we may drink sweet draughts at
pleasure's fountain, yet at some moment there will surely
come the Marah-drop. A sage has truly said that painful memories are of the greatest benefit to the soul. As
the summer storm spends its fury over the lovely landscape, imparting purity to the atmosphere, and bringing
out the sweets of the flower, so do the bitter waters that
sweep over our souls purify and chasten us to the beauty
of holiness!

Q

CHAPTER XII.

February 22.

THIS anniversary, so fondly cherished by our nation, auspiciously dawned upon us here; and our patriotism was stimulated by the brilliant celebration at the residence of the American Minister. The assemblage numbered nearly a thousand persons, including a few foreigners who united in doing honor to the memory of the immortal Washington. The balustrade leading to the *salons* was wrapped with the *Stars and Stripes*, and a flag of huge proportions draped the doorway. Tasteful hands had decorated the rooms with garlands of red and white camelias, and with pendant baskets of flowers. The entwined colors of France and America graced the portrait of Washington, whilst a beautiful banner—presented to General Dix during our country's late struggle—was conspicuous with its Goddess of Liberty, and its motto—the General's own words, attesting his love of the flag. This morning several American residents and sojourners in Paris presented a handsome marble bust of the "Father of our Country" to General Dix, as a testimonial of the high esteem in which he is held. The ball-room was appropriately decked with numerous flags—not confined to the glory of one nation

—and under their variegated folds met the brave, the gay, and the beautiful, to mingle in the dance. That pleasure, however, did not last long, for the surging crowd that swept into the *grand salon* broke up the order of quadrilles, nay, even the usurping *galop*, that always enforces space. Dresses were damaged beyond reparation; headaches became a sort of patriotic martyrdom; complexions faded in the toilsome circuit of the *salons*. A veteran, who in the early part of the evening had admired the carnation-glow of cheeks, said at a later hour, "The only colors that remain true are those of our banner—the *red, white and blue!*" France was represented by M. Rouher, Minister of State, and M. Moustier, Minister of Foreign Affairs; England, by Lord Lyons, and several attachés of the Embassy; and Italy, by Chevalier de Nigra. Dr. Martinez wore decorations numerous and large enough to form a breastplate. Fair names come to my thoughts as thick as "leaves of Vallambrosa." Miss Ware was pronounced one of the sweetest flowers of this strewing by the great French artist, who everywhere wins "golden opinions" like the lustre of his name. Miss Torrence appeared to all eyes the stately lily; and Mrs. Ronalds a beautiful rose. Lastly, a word of praise is due to my escort, Captain Drake—the sole representative of our navy—whose uniform was to us quite as attractive as the glittering decorations bestowed by the hand of the Emperor.

February 23.—The holy Sabbath! and to think that on this solemn day of Christian worship there should be

a frolicking, reckless throng of people following *les bœufs
gras*—a *cortége* numbering five hundred, on foot and on
horseback, in chariots and in cars—all clad in grotesque
costumes, some wearing masks that pointed back to the
dark ages. The procession, starting from the Palais de
l'Industrie, moved in the following order: A regimental
display, consisting of a drum-major of the old Imperial
Guard; a huzzar bearing the French standard of 1804;
a band of music, and a number of soldiers. A chariot,
representing France, was drawn by four horses, and held
the goddess of the year 1868; also, the four seasons and
the months of the year personified. Then came America, with additional music, red-skins and allegorical characters; Asia, with horsemen, slaves, and a big elephant
carrying a Princess of India; and Africa, with her sable
band. The remaining chariots, tastefully decorated with
wreaths and garlands and mixed devices, represented
Agriculture, the Four Ages of Life, and the Olympian
Deities. Conspicuous in the show were the poor oxen,
sporting ribbons of rainbow hues—their horns wreathed
in flowers—and wearing, we thought, a sad look, as
though conscious of their certain and near-approaching
doom. These animals parade the streets for a period of
three days for the amusement of the citizens, and then
are led to the *abattoir* to be killed. But who can describe these people in their wild revelry, with screams
and shouts, fanfares and brass horns? The Champs
Elysées re-echoed the Bedlam-noise long after the Arc
de Triomphe had been passed; and we wonder if the
distant country did not catch a sound that disturbed its

tranquility? What a sight, and how nearly lost was
dignity! But it would be *mal à propos* to suggest mod-
eration to this excitable race, for is not gaiety the very
essence of their lives?

February 25.—Prominent among the festivities of the
Carnival was the magnificent costume ball of Mr. and
Mrs. Downing, of New York. Arriving at a late hour,
we found the scene one of dazzling beauty, in its groupings of rich costumes, from the oriental, mythological
and historical, down to the plain Venitian mantle. Re-
viewing the beautiful picture, worthy of first notice is
the hostess, whose commanding figure and elegant appearance admirably adapts her to the choice personation
of a *Marquise*. Let all stand off to admire the elaborate
costume, and to avoid crushing any of that shower of
roses, dropped so gracefully on the *point d'Alençon* of
her velvet robe. Take in, at this pleasing glance, the
sparkle of her jewels, which are not confined to neck
and arms, but help to make up the becoming *coiffure;*
and then pass on beyond the stately *Marquise* to the
loquacious character attracting, with her genuine wit, a
host of friends, who gaze at her as if she were a total
stranger. Her disguise is perfect. Can this old maid
from Boston be Mrs. Blake—daughter of General Dix?
—if so, would not her husband, three thousand miles
distant, be glad to receive, from the inexhaustible reti-
cule, some of the apples and nuts that are being dispensed alike to *beaux* and *belles?* Behold how lost in
wonder she is at the curious things seen in a Paris *salon!*

Q*

—she thinks the men look like mere toys compared with the stalwart swains of way down East, and considers none prizes who cannot sew buttons on, make a good cup of tea, on a rainy day, and nurse the babies in a case of emergency. Besides, her country is not given to such short dresses as that pretty girl, across the way, wears, who is spangled all over, and shines like the moon on a cold, frosty night. Surely, Jack Frost ought not to be blamed for paying court to such ankles. The old maid, however, is not hard-hearted, and will give to the shivering girl, should she suffer with *engelure*, a little of her healing balsam—only a little—for she does n't believe in wasting, as that brings "woful want." Then she adjusts her scant yellow gown;—"That man's spur nearly put a rent in it, and a military Court gentleman ought not to be awkward;"—bridges her nose over with her spectacles, and resumes her knitting, believing that hay can be made under gas-light as well as in sunshine. She thinks that, although candles may be cheap in France, too many are placed in a row, and that reminds her of soldiers in time of peace on parade—too much *shine* for the little good they do. Oh! that she could impress on these people the importance of economy! Would n't six lights answer as well as a hundred; and why should soldiers wear long lines of buttons so close together as to pinch their fingers, when six would do the work? She advises that *Bedouin*—as they call him —to take off a part of his long, funny gown, and stop clasping his head, and bowing down to *her* and the Muse of Poetry as if they were Egyptian idols. The Muse is so overcome by his queer antics that there is no longer any reason or rhyme in her. *She* don't care if the Muse does call her old Mother Hubbard, for was n't that old lady considered very smart in poetry? Of one thing she is sure—that the sights that fall under her observation are enough to make folks stand on their heads, like Mother Hubbard's dog. She is afraid that one of the musicians will be troubled with *goître* if he don't stop blowing that trombone so hard; it don't make little feet go round any faster, and certainly Mr. Strauss did n't compose music with the view of killing either the performer or the dancer. Her Yankee "thinking-cap" had not set so closely for a long time. She had thought a variety of things in a few hours, but trusted that her strength of mind would stand the test of Paris shows, and enable her to return to dear old Massachusetts just as she came,—only, perhaps, with a bit of foreign air which she could n't help sniffing from the atmosphere.

Then we left Massachusetts, and sought Italy, in red and gold attractions, saying, *for the nonce*, "This is the magic-land," not even excepting *la belle France.* See, in that corner, how sweetly cluster three flowers—*Eglantine*, who gives a wild-rose from her basket; *Pansy*, whose charms make hearts-*ache*, and the *Lily*, as pure and white as the regions of snow! Keep up your trio-band of fragrance, beauty and love, for we shall wander back ere long. Near this sweet quarter, comes *Oiseau-bleu*. Have you not flown from Paradise on heaven's azure wings, and does not your pretty plumage elicit many a—"Wont you have me, or let me be your mate?"

Captive here must you be held until you warble the sweet little answer *yes!* Then, and only then, may you flap your tiny wings, and seek your native sphere. See, in the path of the Dianas, the gallant worshipers who fearing not silver bows and arrows, kneel in rapture to the crescents that sparkle on their brows! Who would not fall a willing victim to such archery, even though it cost them a sojourn in Spain, or a voyage to America? And *you*, the brightest of *Vivandières*, tinged with El Dorada's glory!—have you not fired the hearts of a whole regiment by a gentle look from softly-veiled eyes? But the most disastrous and gorgeously grand element is *Fire*, represented by a bright and beautiful daughter of Cuba! Raging everywhere, damaging and consuming hearts without number, still, for *some*, she proves a genial ray. Winter keeps far away, for her frost-crown would melt before that mighty power, like mist before the sun. An Armenian group forms a dazzling circle, the Princess S— in a dress of gold embroidery, and girdle of precious stones, and her daughter; the Countesses L—— and B—— in rich satins of orange, red and blue. Turn, now, to a tiny Page whose face is a miniature picture of beauty, and ask again and again if to her belongs the ponderous title of Madame; and behold the fair Marguerite, with blonde hair that can scarcely be eclipsed by the radiance of Golden Wheat. A Water-Nymph floats by, the shade of whose apparel indicates that she comes from the "pale-green sea-groves," bringing with her grasses and corals, "starry spangles and shells." She speaks with another goddess of the sea, who must have sprung, Venus-like, from the pure white foam, for she is enveloped in snowy tulle, and wears pearls and water-lilies. Tennyson's "Who would be a mermaid fair?" finds a fitting answer on this night·

"I would be a mermaid fair—
 *   *   *   *   *   *   *
With a comb of pearl, I would comb my hair;
And still as I combed, I would sing and say
'Who is it loves me? Who loves not me?'"

Here strays a Gipsey who salutes a lady of rank from Warsaw; and there a Spanish Gitana dances with the Count de B——, an Andalusian nobleman in maroon velvet, flashing with diamonds. And thus continues the kaleidoscopie view; new angels and new heroes investing the scene with interest, until a streak of morning light creeps in, and these *stars* vanish from the scene, like those that are paling in the skies.

February 26.—Yesterday being the last of the Carnival, the northern Boulevards were crowded with the merry revelers up to mid-night, when they repaired to the Bals Masqués to finish their sport. Numbers gathered around Duvals, the famous butcher-shop, which was illuminated and garlanded with flowers; a sort of high carnival being held there over the slain oxen. Very few will credit the assertion that such a place could be made attractive; but let the unbeliever come to Paris, and see how the magic hand of the Frenchman invests with a polish and grace things that are coarse and unseemly—how it transforms ugliness into beauty, and develops out of very little marvellous greatness.

We attended the brilliant concert of an American pianist, Mr. J. E. Haner, at the splendid Salle d'Erard, where some of the most distinguished artists met to greet the *debutant;* among whom were Henry Herz, Camille Stamaty, and Damcka. The crowded saloon, and the enthusiastic applause, from time to time, gave proof of the high order of talent and the excellence of the performance. Before leaving America, this young and accomplished artist was a pupil of Gottschalk and Mills; and he has since pursued his studies abroad, with Stamaty; at the Conservatory of Vienna, and more recently with Damcka. The pieces selected, admirably displayed the facility of his execution—*la danse des Fées*, by Prudent—*the fugue of Hummel*,—the duet of Mozart's *Don Giovanni*, by Lysberg— performed on two pianos—Mlle. Laure Caulmaehe assisting; and his *Rêverie de l'Inventeur*. This last sweet melody, succeeding loud and brilliant executions, fell gratefully and soothingly on the ear, like the sound of rippling waters after the din and roar of a tempest. M. Ponsard, of the Grand Opera, and Mlle. de Beaunay received flattering applause; also M. Tayau, who, in several comic *chansonettes*, suited to his words an extraordinary play of features. A little boy who saw his wry faces and puckered lips, remarked that he must have been eating persimmons. His accomplished little daughter, as violinist—the recipient of the first prize at the *Conservatoire Impérial*—was indeed a prodigy, and in her budding fame might stand beside the great Ole Bull and Vieuxtemps. At the close of the concert some beautiful floral offerings conveyed good wishes for the *debutant*. May America, at no distant day, richly crown him as her pride!

Wending our way homeward, we struck the stream of revelers who were cutting the most absurd antics, one of which was the thrusting of an abominable, long, artificial nose into our very faces. It was not difficult to fancy, from a glance at their horned heads, that they were akin to the *diable*, or, if not, that they had clothed themselves under the eye of his satanic majesty. The only escape opened to us was Hill's English Restaurant, with its inviting treat of truffles, champagne, and tiny oysters. On the door of the room into which we were ushered, we read the name of our beloved Washington, to whose memory, joint homage was paid by the party, consisting of representatives of England, Ireland and America. The other saloons were honored by names of some of the most distinguished French poets. The night wore a carnival-splendor in bright stars and cloudless sky. More than once, on the Champs Elysées, we glanced up at the moon to see if there was mischief in it to account for these "quips and cranks, and wanton wiles; nods and becks and wreathed smiles," but every beam was chaste; her fair, full face looking down upon us serenely bright. With the *concierge's* sleepy response; the sound of a tiny clock that struck 2 A. M.; and the heavy closing of porte-cochère, gay, audacious Paris was shut out. I plead for slumber with an easy conscience, having indulged only in the mild offence of witnessing a portion of the Carnival.

February 28.—Yesterday, at the Hôtel de St. Petersbourg, a pleasant dinner-party was given us, enlivened by an interesting description of military travels, through Egypt, by an Italian army officer. Professor Morse, of New York, seemed to enjoy the impressive manner and warmth of spirit with which the various ancedotes were told. Later in the evening the young and piquante wife of M. Luchese—the celebrated singing maestro—rendered to perfection those plaintive melodies—*The Last Rose of Summer,* and *Home, sweet Home.* In our hearts never was a chord more deeply touched, responsive to memories of our native land. Selections from choice operas also were sung by this sweet nightingale, who promises to give to the stage, at no distant day, the charm of her voice and the beauty and coquetry of her person.

March 1.—Sunday, and the Holy Communion, amid the distractions of Paris and society-life! How can we serve God and Mammon too? Do not our wayward feet lead us oftener to the latter shrine, and are not our devotions there the most faithful? Passing the Madelaine towards the close of evening Vespers, we concluded to enter the spacious and beautiful temple, and found it thronged with worshipers. Twilight glimmered faintly through the windows, and wrapped the marbles in gray and purple shadows. You, who have stood in some grand cathedral at the dim hour that defines neither day nor night, can appreciate the solemnity that reigns at such times. Music floats more softly through the arches; vespers sound low and sweet, like the nun's prayer;

and the very sanctuary, the finite sphere where we give praise, seems to merge, with the mysterious shadows, into the great infinite:—religious thought finding fullest scope in that perfect calm and harmony.

March 3.—A day so beautiful and so antagonistic to the reputation of this blustering month, suggested an open phæton and a pair of splendid horses,—the latter full of spirit, swift as lightning, proud and dashing in style,—reminding us of the mercurial French people. Many fair *equestriennes* were at the Bois, imparting grace to the scene—some escorted by handsome cavaliers, and others followed by their *valets.*   *   *   *   *

To-night the play or operetta of *La Fanchonette* came off at the Théâtre Lirique, Place du Châtelet. Our party occupied the Imperial box, whose spacious dimensions and proximity to the stage greatly enhanced our enjoyment of the performance. On previous occasions we had been so cramped that there even seemed to be a limit set for breathing. The lighting of this house by a reflector, on a crystal ceiling, is not only beautiful, but soft and pleasant to the eye, and the new method should gain rapid favor. The purchase of refreshments, in the *foyer,* seems to be much in vogue, and affords a pleasant pastime during the *entr'actes,* which are always exceedingly long. Madame Carvalho entranced us with her vocalization, for hers is a bird-like voice, made up of trills and cadenzas. Flowers lay thickly strewn at her feet. The simplest offering, a white lilac-spray—perhaps the *artist's fleur de préférence* — was gracefully

R

picked up, and added as an ornament to her rustic peasant attire.

This night of flowery ovation recalled an evening at
the Opéra Comique, when Mlle. Marie Roze warbled
the delicious music of Auber, in the "*Premier jour de
bonheur.*" How beautiful a priestess! Thou "charmer
of the gods of India" and star of the "far Orient," do
not longer veil from our gaze the soft beauty of thine
eyes! Sing to us forever, in poetic, dreamy strains, *La
chanson des Djiume;* and, for the one night of pleasure
thou hast granted us, may all thy days, like *le premier,*
be full of music and happiness!

March 5.—Rain, after the fashion of a deluge, and
much to be regretted, as we were in possession of a ticket
to see Paris underground, or the great sewers! "*N'importe!* Variety is very acceptable," said we, as water-
proof wrappings were donned and a carriage summoned.
The round-faced, jolly *cocher* whipped up his old white
horses all the way to Place du Châtelet, to ensure our
arrival in time, not seeming to care a whit for the cold,
pelting rain. He was dismissed with an additional *pour
boire,* which caused him to smile upon us, and say to our
escort, "*Vraiment les dames sont bien courageuses!*" The
spot from which we made our descent of twenty feet,
underground, was near the Châtelet fountain, that com-
memorates the victories of the Republic and Empire.
Several *gendarmes* stood at this aperture, which disclosed
a winding stairway; and from the depths a sepulchral
voice shouted, "*Vous êtes bien tard—descendez vite, s'il*

vous plaît." With scarcely a moment to glance around
at our subterranean quarters, we were stowed away in a
little uncovered truck, at some distance from the company that occupied the car ahead of us. One of its passengers styled us " the three Graces," and why he should
have done so we know not, as our merits could not pos-
sibly have been distinguishable in so dim a light. Dr.
C——, one of the trio, did not relish this feminine title,
but we ladies rather liked the joke, and rejoiced in the
feeble glow of the lantern, hoping that our nearer approach would not neutralize the delicate compliment.
The track extends over a channel about ten feet wide,
whose current of water is entirely inoffensive; and the
car is drawn by men. Having turned the first corner
with a sudden jar and a grating noise that made me
grasp at the arm of my escort, and that called forth a
cry of alarm from his timid little wife, we merged into
a still darker *route,* whose only light came from a reflector a mile or more distant; but it served as a beam
of hope to Mrs. C——, who wanted to know "if we
would stop there, and how long it would take to reach
that one dear little spot." Troubles are often more imaginary than real. We passed many openings of smaller
sewers, bearing numbers and names to correspond with
the streets above; and, at some of them, a ray of day-
light momentarily flashed upon us. Still another fear
and discomfort came to my frightened little companion
in the drops of water that now and then fell upon her
from the pipes overhead; but she was re-assured when
told that we were not going to travel the full extent of

three hundred miles; and so said not another word of complaint. High up in the tunnel are suspended immense iron pipes, that convey water to various parts of the city, and on the sides are leaden ones containing telegraph wires. There were no gas-pipes visible, and upon inquiry as to the reason of it, we learned from our conductor that they were yet to be added. Having swiftly passed over several miles, the time came for a transfer from the "low-back cars" to the canal boats, which turned off in the direction of the Place de la Madelaine, our destination. At the point where we took the boats the stream was considerably wider, and the dark tide upon which we committed ourselves, together with the dreary surroundings, called up the horrors of the Styx and the Plutonian shades. An additional number of men was employed to do the laborious pulling. They wore dark blouses, and seemed inexpressibly relieved when they had brought us to a final halt. To the cry of *"Montez,"* we left the feathery mist and the dampness below for the upper regions, where we were greeted by the same obstinate shower that had pelted us on our start. Hereafter, when we shall wend our way through clean streets, breathing an untainted atmosphere, we will give a thought beyond palatial structures, busy marts, and gay people, to the great sewers that run, below, like veins and arteries, and whose purifying agency is felt all over Paris. Nor shall we forget the faithful workmen, who live there, day and night, on duty.

March 9.—A bunch of violets gathered in Nice was

a sweet greeting to wearied eyes this morning, after the late hours of a soirée which had brought to us seventy or eighty friends. What a medley of grace and loveliness there was among the ladies—two or three of England's fairest type; a merry, winsome face from Scotland; a soft-toned, dark-eyed daughter from Ireland, with the lily on her brow, and the rose on her cheek; a *Morse* rose-bud, transplanted from America to lend awhile its beauty, with other flowerets from the States; and, added to all these, the *esprit* and coquetry of France. Under the sway of such captivations how numerous were the devotees! The Pall Mall Gazette wanted to embrace the whole *coterie* of charms in a *column* of praise, but let Capt. B—— hesitate ere he dedicates to perishable beauty an *English monument.* Mr. Fitz H——, if he seconds the Captain's motion, shall be made the corner-stone, a worthy position, though not as charming as the angle he occupied last evening opposite a "diamond-eyed" daughter of the South. There were also Italy, with Prince Eugene Ruffo, and the Dukes d'Artalia and Carrociola; Russia, with her handsome representative answering to the name of Rumplert; Prussia, with her courteous Captain, *gallant* in peace as well as in war; Gen. Quincy, of our own army; Professor Morse, of New York, whose snowy locks add to his other honors; and Paul Morphy, the king of chess-players, cheek-mated for *once* it seemed, *Science* surrendering gracefully to the gentler power *Beauty!*

March 10.—We discharged a heavy debt of visits

during the day, and, of the foreign element, saw Madame Nuba, the wife of the Egyptian Embassador, and her young daughter Zeba, whose striking style,—large almond-shaped eyes, olive tinted skin and jet black tresses—led the imagination to the grand Cleopatra. The Pasha was at home, and entertained us with great agreeability of manner. Their home is luxurious, odd, and rich in all its appurtenances. A visit was also made to the Countess de Lindermann, whose matinées present a reflex of Parisian *haut-ton*.

March 13.—We went to see *La Vie Parisienne* at the Palais Royal last evening, just as if the theatre only afforded an insight into French follies and pleasures. The plot of the play abounds with amusing incidents. The grand finale—" *Célébrons Paris. Oui, voilà la vie Parisienne, du plaisir à perdre l'haleine. Oui, voilà la vie Parisienne! Après toutes ces folies un pardon général,*" is sung by a chorus of merry singers. Amid all those exaggerations of human nature and reckless delights, there now and then flows an under-current of truth and fidelity to work a happy result. Every available space in the house was filled, showing the popular favor with which the play has been received.   *   *   *   *

This afternoon a drive, in company with Mr. and Mrs. Jonas C—, of California, was much enjoyed. We passed along the outskirts of the Bois and saw the Rothschild villa; also the villa of the Emperor, and Mt. Valérien in the distance. The surrounding landscape was showered over with vernal beauties, for Spring is not a tardy goddess in this fairy realm.

CHAPTER XIII.

March 15.

I RECEIVED a card of invitation to attend mass at the chapel of the Tuileries this morning. The Court being in mourning for the late King of Bavaria, those favored with invitations were required to appear in *demi-deuil.* The rain-storm that set in at an early hour and grew fiercer towards eleven o'clock, proved no obstacle to an attendance, for a chance to see the Emperor and Empress at their devotions was not to be lost. The chapel was crowded to its utmost capacity. An under-chamberlain secured me a good position on one side, almost facing the Imperial party. A few gentlemen followed rigidly the instructions as to dress, whilst some wore white vests, cravats and gloves. The majority of the ladies were attired in black; others in gray and *mauve* silks and ermine wrappings—a feeble mark of respect I I thought to a dead King—yet, of what value is outward appearance, if, from the souls of that assemblage, there went up a prayer that the deceased may have passed to the "*Courts of the better Land,*" exchanging the worldly diadem for the immortal crown. The doors were thrown open to admit officers of the Imperial household and ladies of the Court; and immediately afterwards a voice heralding the approach of the Emperor banished all thought of him whose sceptre had fallen by the hand of death. There was a general stir and uprising; a swaying to and fro of figures, and a bowing of heads as His Majesty entered, attended by the Empress and the Prince Imperial. They advanced quickly towards the balustrade that encloses the space before the altar, and, crossing themselves, passed into the enclosure to occupy the State chairs. The organ, for a time, pealed forth in swelling sound, and then the service of the church began amid profound silence. The Empress was clad in black silk and velvet, with bonnet to correspond. She wore a look of deep solicitude,—as did the Emperor—and often turned her gaze upon the Prince, of whose religious training she has recently become the guiding star. The solos of the mass-service were sweet and soft, and rendered with peculiar pathos, by an exquisite female voice, to the accompaniment of the harp. The discourse of the Archbishop was particularly interesting in the allusions made to the Prince Imperial's first communion in May, and to the pious, gentle influence of the Empress. Seeing her engaged in prayer, I recognized only the *mother*—that simple, sacred name, compared with which the proud title of *Empress* sinks into insignificance— and ceased to associate her with the paraphernalia of Court, bestowing a thought rather on her many noble virtues and charities. May she be rewarded by a happy reign, and the fruition of all her hopes in the child of her devoted love! At the close of the service, and after the exit of their Majesties, I loitered a few moments to obtain a cursory view of the chapel, in which were a few Doric columns, a simple altar with lighted candles, and several paintings: *The Assumption*, *The dead Christ*, and *The descent from the Cross.*

March 16.—To-day is the anniversary of the Prince Imperial's birth, and Paris wears a holiday aspect, especially noticeable among the little folks. The schools are closed out of respect to the day, and on the Champs Elysées are many happy, bright faces, perchance the index of the kindly wish that the young Prince's career may redound to the honor and wisdom of his august parents, and that he may be guided aright all through "the march and battle of life!" * * * *

.This evening at a charming dinner-party *chez* Madame H—— I was escorted to the table by a veteran cavalier, Mr. Monbeltet, a member of the Corps Legislatif, and an intimate friend of Hortense, the daughter of Josephine. Both witty and gay, he had not the appearance of one that had lived three score years and ten, and quaffed the sparkling wine with an ode to beauty that would have done justice to famous Tom Moore. Long may he live, and through all the bright years that shall come may kind friends continue to add sweetening drops to his cup of pleasure! A soirée dansante, with light and jovial mirth, followed closely on the dainty comfits of the dinner.

March 19.—The picture of an *Italian Peasant* in the private gallery of a French Baroness enters into the closely packed bundle of pleasant remembrances of yesterday ;—the canvas, in rich and warm coloring, the reflex of a beautiful, sunny land—the flesh-tints wonderfully true to nature,—the sparkle of the eyes, deeply grand, – the brightness of the variegated costume, and the trellis-work, with its clustering grapes of topaz hue—a most tempting delusion.   Oh ! Italy, glorious in sculpture and song, and all that is classic and beautiful, thy peasants do also add a charm, if all are like the one we speak of !   To-day is *Mi-Carême,* and the frantic excitement that prevailed this morning, on the Boulevard des Italiens, beggars description.   Men and women made themselves hideous with masks that represented all sorts of animals from the squirrel up to the elephant.   Even little children of five and six years were falsified to add to the grotesque spectacle.   Passing through the crowd in a carriage, and hearing the clatter and screams, I thought how terrible such a people would prove in a mob or insurrection, and looked very gratefully on several *gendarmes* who asserted, in positive language, that no more orange-skins should be leveled at our vehicle, or at the one that followed us.   A little farther on, a rash fellow finding our carriage blocked up by the gathering masses, thrust his head right into the window, and *such* a *face* as his was might have startled the most courageous ; but such antics must be tolerated as a Carnival license.

March 20.—A mask-ball at the opera-house ! Though journalists write from morn till night, and artists diligently ply their work ; though voluble tongues exhaust their rhetoric, yet, to such a scene, neither picture nor language can render justice! They may give an approximate idea, but that is all. Go you must, if a lady, with the nose bridged over with black velvet or satin, the chin peeping through frills of lace, the head covered with a hood, and with a monkish tunic extending below the knee.

The midnight clock tells that the hour is come for the gayest revelry ever witnessed. Before emerging from the *boudoir*, a glance into the mirror—revealing a sombre disguise and stealthy look—almost makes you hesitate to proceed further. The expression of the eyes under a mask is not unlike that of a pussy-cat, nor are your actions unlike her pranks, for pussy has often been known to run into the *jam* with a view to theft, and so are you going into the *jam*, that you may steal pleasure. The sensation is novel, and grows on one as the evening progresses. Ensconced in the private box, the question naturally comes, "Where am I, and am I myself?" On reflection "I don't think I am, nor are those around me *themselves;*" but the bewilderment is so great that all things logical are put behind, while Satan keeps in the foreground, because, on this occasion, he will not take the rear rank. Your lady companions whisper into your muffled ears, "Oh! did you ever see anything like these people?" "Never," is the laconic reply; for if the mind could wander to all the quarters of the vast globe, surely it would not find their match. Behold Strauss, the mighty chief of the grand orchestral band! In what frame of mind did he compose that maddening music to which thousands, like spinning-tops, whirl round and round? To the waltz, with its ever-varying airs, are suited the *laisser-aller* movement and capers of the dancers; and sometimes, in keeping with the Pandemonium, the soft musical strains give way to the thunder of big drums, the clash of cymbals, and the squeak of fifes—a burst of indescribable noise that deafens most mercilessly the ears, and shocks as rudely the nerves. Look at those feet in rapid motion, every muscle of the frame seeming to act in concert, and note, besides, the sauciness and mischievous humor of those faces! Where is the artist that can catch enough of the spirit of the ever-changing countenances to enable him to make a satisfactory counterfeit? Is it not gone in the twinkling of an eye, or in less time than it took that man to turn a somersault, or that damsel to kick a hat off? Lean over the plush-covered railing of your box, and take in the thousand glittering lights; the endless variety of costume—satins and velvets spangled all over—and the antics and extravagant gestures, winked at by the *gendarmes* because it is a night dedicated to fun and adventure. You will discover that the *demoiselles* are allowed to appear with a small amount of dress, and that the *messieurs* can stand on their heads if they please, squeeze forms of *embonpoint*, or snatch kisses, without repairing to the *foyer*. An invitation urges you to leave, for awhile, the terpsichorean devotees, and promenade in the corridors. The crowd there is quite as great as on the dancing floor. Peering through that precious, deceptive little article, a mask, you see a friend—not in

disguise—and you pass him by without any token of
recognition, enjoying the advantage of observing his
flirtations without his being aware of your presence.
This friend may be an old married man, whose silvery
hair does not prevent him from laughing at that coquettish little vixen; and, although he cannot conscientiously
approve of such roguish freedom as hers, yet it bids him
think of bounding life, and shuts out old age with its
concomitant aches. "It is all in a lifetime," says he,
"and so I will go again to a *bal masqué*." Passing
along, you meet a lady friend whom you choose to recognize, when a spicy little adventure may be confided to
you. A Frenchman goes in raptures over a pretty little
foot wearing an American boot; but the husband is hard
by, and the Frenchman, who thinks it a hard thing,
speeds on for fear it will be a hard matter between them.
Then the restaurant offers cooling refreshment in iced
beverages. You think you have seen enough of exhilaration in the vivacious people, but, as the temptation is
the sparkling widow—Cliquot—resistance is impossible.
During the inspiration of the moment, from the serious
chambers of your heart, there comes a feeling of pity for
those reckless sprites, who—many of them, perchance,
orphans—have been thrown upon the gay world of
Paris, and are lost in its seductive pleasures.

The hours advancing towards day-break, we returned
to the box. Our escorts having left us for a moment, it
was a French liberty for a handsome young fellow in
the adjoining *loge* to address us in these words: "*Honi
soit qui mal y pense;*" besides to guess at our national-

s

ity, which we would n't avow on such an occasion. We
coolly endeavored to pass off for English; but the
Frenchman was not to be thus deceived, and continued
to compliment America; whereupon, seeing there was
no escape, we quietly acknowledged our allegiance to
the *stars and stripes*, trusting its folds would shield us
abroad as safely as at home. A few more glances were
bestowed on the plunging costumed masses, and the time
came to bid farewell to the exciting scene; to leave the
tempest-noises and the frantic concourse for the fresh,
pure atmosphere of the quiet outside world. Paris, at
that hour, had hushed its mighty throb, and was locked
in slumber.

March 22.—Tired nature refused the attractions at
the Hôtel de Ville last evening, and this day of "holy
rest" has come soothingly amidst the worldly altars at
which we have been lately kneeling. Church service
was attended at 11 A. M.; and some simplified Biblical
readings entertained the juveniles in the afternoon.
Sweet little Bessie Scholey, an interested listener of several months ago, is greatly missed; yet, Master Clifford
Clarke—always bright and handsome in his Scotch
plaid—takes up the broken link.

March 24.—Prussia came forward last night to obey
the roll-call of pleasure, Mr. and Madame L—— entertaining a brilliant company at their apartments, on the
Champs Elysées. The hostess, a divinity, shone brilliantly in her gilded saloons; and all around her was a

golden harvest of beauty and fame, with ladies in sparkling jewels, and gentlemen in blazing orders. What shall be said of the extravagance in dress—that enticing passion to which all who breathe the air of Paris seem to fall a prey? A handsome form was clasped by a golden girdle—a serpent-coil—inlaid with various tinted enamels, rubies, sapphires and diamonds; a snow-white throat was encircled by a necklace of solitaire diamonds, each stone set in black enamel, star-shaped; luxuriant golden tresses were adorned by a *crown* whose amethysts and emeralds formed delicate flowers and leaves,—and, although not worn by a *royal* brow, yet it was fitting for the most fair. After all, balls and parties are but repetitions of splendid show, pretty women, gay courtiers, rich banquets, brilliant lights, music, and fragrant flowers.

March 26.—A sprinkling of snow startles the community,—only a few farewell flakes falling from the hoary crown of Winter, about to be supplanted by the rose-wreath of Spring! *Chez nous*, preparations are making for a fancy masquerade, despite the assertion that a private mask ball, out of Italy, must ever prove a *fiasco*. Friends assist in weaving garlands to make the *salons* a fairy bower; and, added to the floral decorations, are numerous flags, among which is a French and a Persian one, contributed by General Dix. To-morrow, then, masks may puzzle; lovers of gaiety may sport in fancy-dress embellishment, and intrigue, harmlessly, under private protection.

March 29.—Like the short-lived perfume of exotics an enchanting scene has passed away, but its picturesque details are still floating through our minds. Let us review characters as they shine under a magic light. At first, costumes are hidden by provoking dominoes, and faces by various colored masks; but, in some instances, the charm of incog. falls before keen and steady scrutiny. A *major-domo*, stationed in the vestibule, appointed to receive cards of invitation, makes a bow of obeisance to Charles IX, as his Royal Highness is about to enter. At the threshold, the King is greeted by a Swiss Peasant who gives up a rose-bud, on demand, saying "I surrender it to your Majesty, for a peasant dares not disobey a king." A Shepherdess, with a lamb in her arms, is teased by being asked what she carries that dog for. As an American, she repudiates the French custom, and says spitefully, "Go into the country, where you will probably learn to discriminate animals." Mr. Z—, who personates Mephistopheles, is startled, on looking into a mirror, to find that he is as ugly as the d—l. A recognition of Miss *Pepper* is told by a loud *sneeze* in her dignified presence. The Countess C— breaks not less than a dozen hearts, and mends only the one belonging to the Vicomte L—. Mr. B—h—who cannot hide his Saxon court-dress—will be brought to trial for following on the tiny footsteps of little Red Riding Hood. His marital relations do not give him this right, and therefore *he* shall be condemned to *wolfish* fangs, after one more glance into her bright, bright eyes. Mrs. D— of the Derby Races, has been assailed, and makes a *fast trot*—brandishing her riding whip—after the audacious creature that pinched her through her scarlet jacket. *La Fille du Régiment* regales a thirsty Fenian from the canteen at her side. He is a militant about to join his regiment, and thinks that one drop received at her hands is worth the full measure of the famous Heidelberg Tun. A Fisherman draws his nets, and is intent on catching something that will stand by him through sunshine and storm; but the pretty little *gold* fish he thinks he has caught, gets frightened and glides away, saying "Not this time, my *laddie*, I'll come again!" Cupid, the archest and prettiest god ever seen, with blue and silver wings, pierces away at a hundred hearts. For all the wounds he makes, and will not heal, he should be placarded.—"Thy pleasure my sorrow has proven; then fly, love, away! Oh! fly away, love!" Raphael will leave in memory a *green spot*, so fast in color, that its emerald loveliness need never be retouched by a magic brush, for youth, grace, and talent are always charming. Bright Cuba is under a snow-storm of powder, that refuses to be blown away to reveal her raven tresses. How we long to see the roses of her cheeks glow the warmer in contrast with the white mockery above, but her tiny mask still denies us that boon, leaving unconfined only a little mouth to warble five or six languages! Wrapped in her cerulean drapery, she bids defiance to 12 o'clock—the hour for unmasking—and continues to coquette awhile longer. Here is a gay French Baron, as the Queen of Hearts. If he desires to tread on hearts, and hold them captive,

6*

he will surely accomplish it by his diminutive feet, which are the wonder of Paris. Let all guessing now cease. A moment since it was "Know thyself," but now comes the *command* "Be thou known." Lo! here wanders an Indian Princess, possessed of a mixed beauty, America's choicest charms breaking through an aboriginal imitation. How perfect the dress, to which are clinging innumerable crimson and gold-flecked feathers that lie as close, as those that nature provides for the warmth of the forest-bird! Luxuriant black hair sweeps around her form, contrasting its ebon hue with her red-tinted skin. Near by is a handsome Baron, clad in a velvet court-dress, and resplendent with costly diamonds. Among the flowers decking the saloons, and vieing with the tulips and camelias of France, is one gathered from a far off American State, the "Rose of Nevada." Her robe is of white satin with silver garniture, and wreathed over with pink roses, out of which peers the motto, "*L'Amour et Fidélité.*" The honor of one State is thus charmingly upheld; and another fair lady undertakes the *glory* of the whole *Western Continent.* So bewitchingly does she combine all the attractions, that she is banded around with a circlet of admirers; and, whilst challenging the homage of *tout le monde* on this side of the water, she still preserves her devotion to her native country. The dress is of red, white, and blue satin, embroidered in maps illustrating the geography of America, whilst some symbols point to the wealth of certain portions of the country, suggestive of gold-mines; and a rare diamond vein is struck, sparkling in *collier* form. From "the enchanted, golden, Gipsey-land, the Valley of Bohemia," come two wanderers; and Italy does not pretend to count her peasants. More than one Troubadour is singing to those olive-tinted daughters of Venice, and the *Cantadinas* of Florence, to the neglect of Spanish dames and damsels, who flirt most charmingly behind their fans, and look love most rapturously from dark-fringed eyes. A *Magicienne* with beauty in her glance, and magic in her voice, leads away captive *Fra Diavolo*, and robs him of his heart. Suddenly he loses his love of plunder, and does not grasp at the golden serpent lurking in her tresses, or practise sleight of hand on the other costly ornaments. The shot that brings him low is not from mountain-ambush, but from bright eyes; and on the flowery stairway at the feet of the beautiful slayer, he dies. Would that the wound might be healed, life renewed, and hopes accomplished! Royalty waves its sceptres, and displays its crowns among Flower-girls and Shepherdesses. Kings Henry I—II—III seem to be reigning at the same time with Louis XIII—XIV and XV,—Napoleon III having no show at all. Saint Denis must have some vacant tombs on this occasion; but, in the resurrected sovereigns we see no sign of Death's withering stroke, nor do their voices echo aught that is mournful of the past. The Seasons assert an influence lovely to behold. Spring and Summer trail their vines and flowers among the dancing feet, making the floor a tinted one with all the colors of precious stones—amethyst, sapphire and topaz, ruby, emerald and pearl. Autumn drops traces of the forest's rich glow, in gold and crimson leaves; and Winter scatters hoar-frost and snow-flakes. Day and Night contest for the highest rank—the sun, moon and stars disregarding the law and order of the planetary system, in the shorter orbits described in the giddy waltz. Turkey sends beauties of the harem;—Greece, a slave, whose chains are loosened, yet with charms to enchain a bevy of admirers. Arabia keeps a tantalising secret. Who is the veiled personage? Her piercing black eyes make us wish the more to solve the mystery. Folly, in orange and blue satin, shakes her bells in gleesome humor; and the Princess Scheherazade, gorgeously oriental, is wrapped in golden glory, her locks floating in masses to her feet. An arch and coquettish mouth whispers *Bo-Peep*, and two lovely eyes flash around the corner. See a gallant knight, in armor clad, has tracked her lurking-place, and pursues the hide-and-seek game with as much earnestness as he would go forth to show his prowess on the battle-field. Before the evening's close he will learn the meaning of the little song, " Beware ! she's fooling thee." A saucy maid-servant knocks the powder from many a court-wig with her dusting brush, and the cry is for a *gendarme*, to place the presumptious *domestique* under arrest. At the throwing off of her simple disguise, accusers turn suitors, for a more lovely Polish damsel never graced a French *salon*. The Count de Montebello could find no terrestrial costume suited to his tall and manly figure, and so he dived under the water to learn what an Alligator could do on shore. Glittering in scales that rattle, his presence is made

known wherever he goes, and every one exclaims,—
"What a head!" About the caudle extremity cautious
steps are taken by little feet in spangled slippers, and
carefully guarded are queenly trains all bordered in ermine. Monsieur Morlot, as *Petit Crevé Anglais*, seems
to have caught the reflection of a gold and silver mine,
and his peaked shirt-collar looks as dangerous as do
some of the ferocious mustachios with their wiry ends.
Vicomte de l'Angle, the hero of *L'Etoile du Nord*,
brings up recollections of its sweet music. We are not
shocked at the many saucy things whispered here and
there, which every one, married and single, accepts, because for the evening the cry is *La Liberté*, and we are
in France.

March 31.—We took advantage of this day, so bright
in sunshine, by first driving to the Champ de Mars,
where the Exposition building, a few months since,
loomed up in all its grandeur; and continuing our route,
passed one of the grandest viaducts of Paris. How imposing, with its numerous arches, handsome balustrade,
elegant lamp-posts, and extensive sweep, besides the
animation above and below, in pedestrians, carriages and
rail-cars! Not far distant are the fortifications, *bristling*
now only with *blades* of grass. Tradition says that Louis
Philippe, in disguise, made his escape from this section
of the city. We soon came to the Park d'Auteuil, in
which spot nature has left her best and proudest touches
—beautiful wood scenery and green bowers; light landscapes, with streamlets, wild flowers, velvety moss and

ferns. The Bois de Boulogne, contiguous to this park, brings out bolder beauties, the offspring of art. Its broad avenues and promenades invite "Fashion's glittering train," but d'Auteuil affords quiet sylvan shades for the meditative mind. Soon after entering the Bois we stopped at the Croix Catelan, a relic of the fourteenth century. It is a monument partly demolished, and marks the spot where a "Troubadour of the Court of Beatrix de Savoy" was murdered by Phillipe le Bel's military guard, who had been deputized to conduct him in safety to the King. The treasure he bore as a present to the Sovereign, and on account of which he lost his life, proved to be nothing more than a few bottles of *perfume.* We visited the Vacherie, at Pré Catelan, and saw some splendid cows. Many persons resort to this place to indulge in a glass of fresh milk or cream. It is brought to an humble little cottage, whose furniture consists of a few plain tables, presided over by a neat waitress, and whose only ornament is the Madeira vine that trails up and along the windows, relieving the glaring effect of calico print. The honest face of an old white *tabby* was there to-day, and she purred again and again at my side, looking as if she had not forgotten the days of her kittenhood, when it was her privilege to lap the sweet milk.

April 3.—As we ended March with a series of nocturnal pleasures, so do we begin this month. A soirée musicale came off at Madame T—s, Avenue de la Grande Armée. The performance of the artists and amateurs was a perfect success, as was the supper in the artistic grouping of fruits and bon-bons, miniature bouquets and tiny baskets of strawberries. Then followed a soirée dansante, with great eclat, at Mrs. McC—'s; a *cotillon* at Mrs. D—'s, towards the morning hours; and a dinner at the Hotel Westminster, by Mr. G—, of Cincinnati. We left a delightful matinée at 4 P. M., to accompany friends to the Bois, choosing the quiet routes at first, and only turning into the spacious avenue overlooking the lake to get a view of the Emperor and Empress, who had alighted from their carriage to indulge in a promenade. All eyes were directed towards them, the Empress acknowledging by sweet smiles, and an occasional inclination of the head, the many evidences of admiration bestowed, whilst her Imperial spouse wore an air of quiet indifference.

CHAPTER XIV.

April 6.

THE morning of the 4th opened bright and lovely for *Versailles*, whose palace and art-splendors, gardens and natural beauties exhaust the vocabulary of praise. Our party filled a railroad compartment, and so speedily passed the time in gay conversation that dark tunnels, and all the little towns and villages on the route were scarce remarked, until our eyes met that grandest of structures, appropriately dedicated "to all the glories of France." The visitor, standing in the spacious court facing the palace, is overwhelmed, at the first glance, with the magnificence of the surroundings. The range of buildings forms an irregular square ; the central and oldest one of which, erected by Louis XIII, and embellished with antique trophies, presents to view the balcony that cites one of the proudest and noblest examples ever known of woman's heroism. It was there that Marie Antoinette appeared to appease the infuriated mob that had burst the gates of Versailles. As the bright sunshine played down on it, in noon-tide splendor, no dark shadow flitted across, save the thought that came to us, of that brave queen's misfortunes. From the same spot, in the event of a king's death, is proclaimed "*Le Roi est mort,*" and, a moment afterwards, the successor is announced in "*Vive le Roi!*" Above the balcony is a sort of attic, with the clock that has been set only twice, each time marking the hour when a sovereign expired. On the left side is the chapel, where the marriage of Louis XVI with the beautiful Austrian took place. A large equestrian statue of Louis XIV eclipses all the others that adorn the court, and rightly so, for that invincible monarch wielded the greatest sway over Versailles and France, reigning longer than any other of the name of Louis, and only dying, it would seem, when he himself was ready to go. But now for the interior, that great historical museum which stretches out miles of glowing canvas, marking grand military exploits ; chivalric deeds ; court and coronation scenes ; and displaying portraits of all the French kings, the most celebrated warriors, marshals, &c.! Near the battles of the Crusades is a splendid picture, *Godefroi de Bouillon,* the chivalric hero of the Cross, who, preferring the title of " Defender of the Holy Sepulchre," declined that of "King of Jerusalem "—who refused a crown of gold for one of thorns. Another very striking one, is *Joan of Arc,* whose patriotic zeal brought deliverance to France ; her heroic life falling a willing sacrifice. Two large tear-drops rest on her checks,—a baptismal, redeeming offering of love and devotion to that country, whose *crosses* she bore to the end as bravely as, in battle, she carried the " lilies on her standard." After exploring the series of rooms—fourteen—on the ground floor, we craved a staff to facilitate our ascent to those

T

salons where the horrors of the Crimean war are portrayed, in *The Storming of Sebastopol* and *The Malakoff*, with all their bloody slain.   In the long galleries devoted to statuary, busts and full length figures rose up in countless numbers; but, an incomparable gem—superb in form and feature—was a recumbent statue, bearing the inscription *"Beaujolais—Louis Charles d'Orléans, Conte de—*1808."   One also of *Joan of Arc* did proudly prove that it is not the masculine hand alone that can wield the artist's chisel with perfect grace.   In the gallery of the great battles, a painting touched our hearts, bearing upon American military glory; the siege of Yorktown—" Gen. Washington and Gen. Rochambeau give the last orders for the attack—October 1781." In the Salle du Sacre, we found that famous picture by David,—*The Coronation of Napoleon and Josephine in the church of Notre Dame, December* 2, 1804; for which the artist received the sum of twenty thousand dollars. Immediately facing it was one representing *Napoleon distributing the Eagles to his Army, December* 5, 1804. Among the portraits of queens, there was only one of Marie Antoinette, in which she appeared the impersonation of elegance and fashion.   The Galerie des Glaces 242 feet in length, and with proportionate breadth and height, is reputed to be one of the most splendid in the world; and so we thought, as we paced over its polished floor, gazing now at the ceiling, made wondrous by the master-hand of Lebrun;—then at the beautiful mirrors filling the arches; the pillars of red marble, and the statues of the gods and goddesses.   It must have occurred

to all of us that we were tracing the footsteps of many
beautiful favorites of the court; of thousands of courtiers
that had hung on the skirts of royalty; nay, even of the
great monarchs themselves. The gorgeous bed-chamber
of Louis XIV was one of the places of greatest interest
in the palace, for there stood the bed upon which the
king died. It is protected by a gilded railing, but I
managed to get near enough to inspect the embroidered
satin coverlet, whose sombre tint was quite in unison
with my thoughts. Yet all did not share these reflections, for one of the party exclaimed, "This is the bed
in which his Majesty every day received his six-inch
wig from the end of a pole; and this is the room where
he decked himself in diamond-embroidered velvets,
before he went out to receive the adulations of thousands." Then the names of La Vallière, Montespan,
Maintenon, and others came up in our minds, suggested
by a little table, at which he had, doubtless, indited
billets-doux to each of these fair ones. The ceiling
reflects, in gorgeous coloring, the taste and talent of Paul
Veronese, in one of Napoleon's trophies from classic
Italy. Adjoining this apartment is an ante-room, called
Œil de Bœuf, where used to meet, in the days of the
"Grand Monarch," his courtiers and worshipers; the
gifted and beautiful—all in servile subjection to one
who, at last, was found to be made of perishable clay.
There is no adjective forcible enough to describe the
Escalier de Marbre, composed of various colored marbles.
It surely cannot be excelled in France. Rare and
magnificent art could have detained us for hours in the

palace. All of us agreed that the name of Louis Philippe, who did so much towards restoring and embellishing it, should be stamped everywhere about in golden characters ;—for he who worthily ruled this kingdom has well glorified its proudest palace. A ramble over the beautiful *Tapis Vert,* whose verdure was catching the sombre hues of declining day, ended our privileges.

April 8.—The captivating Patti, within the last week, has revived a very old opera—*Joan of Arc*—in which Verdi does not seem to have bestowed the same force and beauty that distinguishes his other productions. But the plot itself is replete with interest ; and then the influence of the Diva's voice—whether chanting prayerful notes or trilling merrily—is so potent, that a lack of spirit or beauty in the composition is scarcely noticed. The Libretto is not true to history ; but it may be that *love,* in operatic rendition, is privileged to break down all sorts of barriers. Niccolini, the tenor, admirably seconded the little warbler, whose precious throat of song is held in greater estimation here, it seems, than the crown jewels of France. Dame Rumor whispers that a Marquis of the Imperial household is soon to win the adorable prize.

On the 5th instant, Baron and Baroness Haussman gave a grand reception at the Hôtel de Ville, followed by an operatic concert. As I glanced at the worthy Prefect of the Seine I thought how well he merits the admiration of the thousands that meet in his palatial residence ; for is it not conceded that Paris owes much

of its grandeur to his good taste and indefatigable energy? The Baroness, although not beautiful, has an
amiable countenance, and her manners are easy and attractive. As the concert was about to commence, several
French officers secured us seats in a *salon* adjoining the
reception-room. Very few Americans were present, but
chief among our representatives was Professor Morse—
his tall, lithe form rising above all others—wearing upon
his breast the decorations justly won by his distinguished
services. The programme embraced all the principal gems
of *Le premier jour de bonheur.* First, the grand over-
ture, by the full orchestra; then, the *Air du Sommeil, de
la Muette,* by Mr. Capoul, whose tenor notes fell softly
on the ear, making all woman-kind, at least, acknowledge
the fascinations of the voice, to say nothing of the *per-
sonnel* of the artist. Next, the *Chœur "Pâque fleuries"* of
Fra Diavolo, the solo being sung by Mr. Solon; followed
by the *Air de l'Ambassadrice,* by Mme. Cabel, who
has all the melodious trilling of a bird at her command.
Succeeding those delicious strains came the lovely Marie
Roze—robed in pure white, like the flower of her name
—singing that favorite air of the opera, in which she
personates the Oriental Princess, and mysteriously attracting all eyes to the one little spot where she stood,—
plaudits breaking in upon her magic tones from time to
time. Capoul took up the *Romance d'un premier jour,*
and Cabel and Roze the beautiful *Nocturne.* Lastly,
fragmentary *morceaux* by the orchestra; after which,
the tide of fashion swept through the brilliantly illuminated *salons,* where the hand of art has most lavishly

T*

scattered her beauties. On ball occasions, the Galerie des Fêtes, with thousands of guests, must form an enchanting picture. Various crowned heads have had honor shown them amid the gilded splendors of the Hôtel de Ville; and, to go back to the days of revolution, it was here that the dauntless Lamartine proclaimed that "the red flag should not be the flag of France as long as he lived." Here, too, Robespierre sought to take his own life; but it was not ordained that he who had wielded the rod of such despicable tyranny should escape the guillotine. As we were leaving the *salon*, Baron Haussman rose from a sofa and saluted us in a most gracious manner, and his lady met us on the stairway, as she passed to her private apartments, concluding the *adieu* with a pleasant smile and bow.

April 9.—This month is gladdening every eye with its budding beauty. The nursery gardens in the vicinity have contributed their plants to adorn the public promenades. On the Champs Elysées—southern side—violets and pansies are peeping up near the grassy slopes, and, around the fountains at Rond Point, beds of wallflower yield to the soft breeze a sweet perfume. A very charming drive, at this season, is in the direction of Pont Neuilly, and on the banks of the Seine, where cottages and small villas lie embowered in shrubbery. A pleasure it is to ride along by calm waters, where trees bend low their branches; to watch the boys at their mimic sport of sailing tiny boats; to hear the twitter of the

birds, and feel the peace of all things around. Truly
do rural scenes bring out the poetry and sentiment of
one's nature, after a surfeit of fashionable city life.

April 10.—Good Friday! the saddest day of all the
year, to Christians. After leaving our place of worship,
we repaired to the church of Saint Eustache, arriving
too late, however, to hear the exquisite orchestral music
appropriate to the day; but there was still some melody
issuing from that grand organ, reputed to have cost
seventy thousand francs; and a number of persons were
yet engaged at prayer. The exterior of the edifice is
peculiar, in its single turret, with carved Corinthian
pillars, the corresponding one never having been completed. The interior partakes of a rare grandeur in
memorials of love to Christ and the saints—paintings
commiserating their sorrows, and testifying to their
labors. The chapels containing these frescoes are named
after the saints, and all of them hold *relics*. Those of
St. Eustache can be seen in the chapel that illustrates
passages of his life. A priest sat within, and one of the
altar-boys held in his hand a gold crucifix, to which
numbers of persons brought moneyed offerings—the
poorer classes not failing to contribute their mite.
Everything was gloomy, the high altar and the choir
being almost entirely draped in black; but a few
lighted tapers, imparting a faint glow, relieved, in a
measure, the sombre surroundings. The rose-stained
windows, the carved pulpit, and the statues of the twelve
Apostles are all in accordance with the elaborate decora-

tions everywhere to be seen. Among the distinguished dead interred in this church are the poet, Voiture; the painter, Chas de la Fosse; Admiral de Tourville, and Chas. David, the architect of the edifice. The tomb, *par excellence*, is that of Colbert. The statesman is represented kneeling with hands clasped. On the black marble cenotaph the inscription reads, *Jean Baptiste Colbert, Ministre d'État. Mort en* 1683. On each side of the monument is a female figure, in sitting posture, one representing Abundance and the other Fidelity. The former, partially veiled, holds a cornucopia; the latter, looking upward, is drawing her drapery around her, and holds a key in her left hand,—a dog is crouched at her feet. Upon leaving the church, we went to *Place des Victoires*, and saw the equestrian statue of Louis XIV, in the garb of a Roman Emperor; but, to us, his habiliments seemed more like the trappings of an Indian warrior.

April 12.—Easter Sunday! The American Episcopal church this morning was crowded. The hymn, "Christ the Lord is risen to-day," was sung with rejoicing; and testimonials of that happy thought, in beautiful flowers, decked the sanctuary. The crosses were composed of camelias and white lilac; and, on the altar canopy, in white and red letters,—formed of delicate flowers—were the words, *Bread of Life*, typical of the Holy Communion. The sermon by the rector, Doctor Lamson, was able and eloquent, and accorded fully with the holy occasion.

April 14.—With the French, the presenting of Easter-gifts is a custom much like their New Year's observance. In the stores may be seen a rather startling display of eggs of all sizes, from that of the mammoth ostrich, to the wee shell, not larger than a thimble; and what charming disclosures they make, with their silver, gold and precious stones! There is an old query, " Where is the goose that laid the golden egg?" but we would rather know where to locate that motherly old Hen, that broods over all Paris, dropping donations here and there, and cackling merriest at Easter. To-night Othello's prayer in plaintive music is a prelude to my home-directed orisons. Of what wondrous power is love, and how sweet its angel memory!

April 15.—Finding it impossible to secure seats for the opera of Hamlet, we abandoned our *ghostly* inclination for something very droll at the Cirque Napoléon, on the Boulevard des Filles du Calvaire. The word Circus, in the United States, is suggestive of a tent with uncomfortable seats, and chilling draughts, that give M. D.'s work to do in curing rheumatism and pleurisy; but, in this city, it implies a large building, fitted up with the comfort and taste of an ordinary theatre. The seats are circularly arranged, on an inclined plane, and the walls are frescoed to represent equestrian sports. Numbers of soldiers were present this evening. Free tickets are nightly granted to a certain number, by the Emperor, who esteems it a duty and pleasure to offer regular amusement to those who faithfully serve their country. The music and the performance were excellent, and the horses were of the most spirited mettle. Some well-trained dogs made grown people clap their hands as diligently as did the little children. One little dog—whom we chose to call *Frisk*—was always ready to perform, and would come out of time to do everything wrong. He was Major-general of the party, controlling his master, and shirking the *baton* with an ingenuity that raised the canine race a degree higher in the estimation of the audience. His master, though apparently vexed at first, in the end, gave evidence of forgiveness in a smile, on the principle that a lenient father often overlooks the misdemeanor of a mischievous sprig, and places him on a footing with unoffending exemplars of the law. A little rhyme that I made, seemed to tickle the ears of our juveniles.

> Six fine little dogs sat in a row,
> And each was to stand on his head when called;
> One, not content unless on the go,
> Snapped at his brothers, and raised a big *squall*.

The most wonderful part of the performance was a diving feat—a man remaining submerged in a deep bath for five minutes, in which time he drank a bottle of wine, and ate a piece of bread. His amphibious qualities were clearly shown, for he seemed as much at ease, in the water, as when taking into his nostrils the oxygen of his native element. Doubtless this narrative will be received by many as another version of the ancient, fabulous fish story; but, at any rate, it shall be described as it was seen. An immense glass case, iron bound,

being wheeled into the centre of the ring, and filled
with water by means of a hose connected with a pipe
under the turf, there appeared a splendidly formed man,
in stocking-net, of the athletic type, and with a complexion that told of frequent ablutions. He mounted
the box, or case, by means of a ladder; bowed to the assemblage, and made a graceful plunge into its ·cold·
depths. At one moment, we saw him turning somer-
saults with the same agility as if he were on terra firma;
at the next, kneeling against the glass sides with his
mouth wide open, the bread and wine disappearing, to
the mute astonishment of the spectators. One lady,
however, who could not control her emotion, cried out,
" He will drown ! " but lo ! the wonderful creature rose
to the surface, and shook the water from his hair, like a
dog, after a dive. Many were the conjectures as to how
so extraordinary a performance could be accomplished.
It is said to be effected by the frequent practice of im-
mersion, the powers of endurance increasing each time.

April 18.—The breath of orange-flowers is on the
gale, and a lovely bride has just worn the coronal. I
allude to the marriage of Miss Dix, on the 16th instant.
The ceremony, conducted after the Episcopal ritual, by
Rev. Mr. Lamson, took place at her father's residence,
at 1.30 P. M. A distinguished company was present,
eager to bestow congratulations upon the fair bride and
the happy groom, Mr. Walsh,—the latter looking very
proud of his new possession. A toilette *à la Noce* is
indeed a *spécialité* in Paris, and should not be over-

looked, because of the perfect taste displayed by the *modiste*. The bride, on this occasion, wore a trained robe of white *poult de soie*, with tulle puffings, and a narrow flounce of *point appliqué* lace, which was met by a tunic similarly trimmed, and looped with sprays of orange blossoms. The lace garniture of the *corsage montant* corresponded with that of the skirt, and a graceful, tulle veil fell over her blonde hair, which many thought too beautiful to be thus imprisoned. To the holy *bond* that united this pair, let us add the *link* of poetry:

> " But happy they, the happiest of their kind !
> Whom gentle stars unite, and in one fate
> Their hearts, their fortunes, and their beings blend."

Mrs. Dix seemed to feel most deeply the solemnity of the event, and vainly endeavored to force a smile through her tears. Who can measure the depths of a mother's love, and her solicitude at such a time? But a truce to sadness! preferring to turn to the emblems of joy that were everywhere around— the beaming smiles of the fair women, and the exquisite flowers—one crystal basket measuring three yards in circumference, with a crown of orange-blossoms attached to the handle.

Among the company, chiefly Americans, were the ministers from England, Turkey, Switzerland, and the Argentine Republic; the Duchess de Cambacères; and Mr. and Mrs. Milner Gibson. Capt. Jerome Bonaparte, of Baltimore, was acknowledged to be the handsomest gentleman present, and Col. Hoffman, the efficient Secretary of the Legation, one of the most agreeable. Mrs.

Ronalds and Mrs. Moulton, beautiful as sunlight, and
Miss Morse, a sweet flower, need to be seen only once
to live forever in memory. The toilettes most remarked,
and whose colors, like rainbow hues, shifted here and
there, were worn by Mrs. and Miss Lippincott, of Philadelphia, Mrs. Dewey, of California, Mrs. Gen. Ward,
and Mrs. Durant, of New York. The daughters of
Mrs. Blake graced the scene like little rosy faries, receiving quite as many kisses as the bride. The sumptuous repast added but another proof of the liberal and
elegant hospitality which has always characterized the
entertainments of the host.   *   *   *   *   *

The English Charity Ball, held in the magnificent
salle-à-manger of the Grand Hôtel, on the evening of
the wedding, was a splendid success. As Lord Lyons
entered the room, which was most brilliantly illuminated,
and profusely adorned with flowers, the band played
God save the Queen. Then the music merged into
quadrilles and waltzes, which were kept up until a late
hour, for Strauss never flags a moment, nor do the dancers
who come under his happy influence. An old English
Admiral was seen engaging in the swift galop with the
spirit of a boy; and a distinguished *Français*, whose
epicurean suppers seemed to have located themselves in
the pedal extremities, hobbled through the square dances
with several golden-haired daughters of England,—they
unmindful of his slow measured steps, and he only
thinking of the joy which *charity* bringeth. Many
others, who had swelled the fund of *Napoléons*, in favor
of our good old "mother-country," shared this joy, for

U

they too feasted on bright, beautiful faces, and carried
to their homes the remembrance of a charming scene.
Of the Americans present may be mentioned the fasci-
nating Mrs. Slidell and daughter, of Louisiana; Mrs.
Judge Field, of California; Mrs. Gilbert, of New York;
Doctor Evans; and Mr. Balsh, of Philadelphia.

CHAPTER XV.

April 22.

THIS morning I accompanied Mrs. T—, of South Carolina, to Lady Cowper's residence, 17 Avenue Friedland—to hear Lord Radstock preach. He is an Englishman of rather pleasing appearance,—his delivery quiet, simple and effective. The crowded parlors bore testimony to his efficiency in the holy work ; and although not educated for the ministry, he has the reputation of rousing the sluggish heart to a love of Jesus, teaching it to explore beyond the vain attractions of the world. In the absence of instrumental music Lord R— led the hymn, which began with these simple words, in allusion to the surpassing love of the Savior, "Ah! how He loves!" The morning was bathed in sunlight, yet there still lingered on the foliage, in Lady C—'s garden, some trembling, pearly drops from the recent showers— those gentle fertilizers that April so lavishly dispenses.

April 25.—The French Charity Ball, at the Grand Hôtel, was a repetition of the one given a few nights since, except that the crowd, at a late hour, grew so dense as to render a promenade almost impossible. Our party, arriving at half past nine, found the dancing space of the *salon* encircled by ladies (most of whom were seated), all evidently waiting for the ball to open. To prevent a further waste of delightful music, Miss Morse, with Col. McClure, the Duke d'Artalia, as my partner, and several other couples, inaugurated the movement. At the conclusion of our quadrille, hundreds of dancers appeared, as if by magic; and, ere long, tulle, flowers, and other millinery *débris* were strewn over the floor—stifled humanity vainly sighing for space and air. The large corridor adjoining the ball-room afforded temporary relief, and the only opportunity to see, to advantage, the beauty, grace and gallantry that had responded to a noble call.　　*　　*　　*　　*　　*

To-day we attended a brilliant matinée at the house of the Duchess Riario-Sforza, where was gathered the flower of French aristocracy.

April 27.—After a late dinner, the beautiful twilight, so soft and mellow, lured us to a promenade. The moon peered out in crescent shape, and the lovely evening star, a bride among her legion sisters, made many eyes wander admiringly towards the heavens. All Paris seemed to be out for a stroll. In the Champs Elysées little children had extended their hours of recreative sport, and were riding around a circle on hobby-horses. A pretty little boy, in a blue coat, with spear in hand, *à la* tournament, fairly jumped for joy, when, at the third attempt, he successfully bore off the ring; a feat of difficult accomplishment, simple though it seemed, and requiring great steadiness of eye and aim. The pavilions, cafés and theatres near by, were all brilliantly lighted, and threw their gleams upon the shrubbery and trees which already boast a "leafy pride." To-day I heard the celebrated professor and composer, *Jacques Potharst Alsini*, sing. His voice is sympathetic, and his compositions, *La mer se plaint toujours*, and *L'Innocence*—sung by Patti—are worthy of the highest encomiums.

April 29.—Lord Radstock lectured again this morning to a large company, French, English and American, at Lady Cowper's. The exercises concluded with the hymn, "Oh! I have found a friend! Jesus is mine!" which was sung with much fervor. The remainder of the day we passed at the Bois, rambling through the shady groves, and gathering wild flowers, quite indifferent to the *gendarmerie* whose duty it is to prevent such depredations. The sun shone out in full splendor, lending to the atmosphere a genial, balmy warmth, and everything was so inviting, that we were glad to linger longer than the short hour or two which the fashionable world in fine carriages, usually devote to seeing, and being seen. Several brides, in white attire, and flowing vails, were enjoying a promenade with their husbands. It is not an uncommon thing for one to see here,—*à pied*—couples who have but just left the hymenial altar—a custom of the *bourgeoisie* too conspicuous to accord with our rather reserved American notions. An opportunity was offered for a row across the lake, in a little boat that displayed the tri-colored flag; the dip of our oars, and the sailing of the stately

U*

white swans creating the only ripple on its surface. Then followed a lunch in front of the Swiss Chalet, on the green lawn, where divers ducks soon gathered, all covetous of the dainty crumb. An ugly black duck gobbled up all the nice sponge cake, freely dealt out as *bait* to a pretty white one, which we discovered was fairer than it was smart, impressing us with the idea that stupidity is often linked to beauty. Another spot, cool and shadowy, the beautiful Cascade de Longchamps, was most inviting. Its craggy mound rises to the height of forty feet, and stretches out in width, one hundred and eighty. A limpid stream, with glistening spray, dashes down from a little lake above into a large basin, whose borders are studded with rocks. Passing through a rugged labyrinth, under the cascade, the visitor can wind his way up to the summit, where a fine view of the picturesque country around is to be obtained.

April 30.—In our morning promenade, along the Rue de Rivoli, we met numbers of young girls, dressed and veiled in white, on their way to the churches to take their first communion. It was beautiful to behold youth thus arrayed in the garb of purity, for a consecration to God and the church. How impressive is such a sight; and what an example to those who have lived long years in the darkness, without the light of faith and Christian love! Added to the sweet spring delights of buds and blossoms, that make me happy to-day, are home-letters freighted with a mother's love. Truly it is

"'The gushing spring,
    That sends a sweet and silver stream
(Beneath whose low, dim murmuring
    The soul lies down to dream
Of vanished good, from present ill,
When all its other harps are still !)
Along life's dull and narrow vale
To haunt us like an ancient tale,
And on our path, where'er we roam
Go, singing of its home."

* * * * * * To-night, by invitation of Prof. Morse and family, I attended a concert at the Conservatoire de Musique. The rapid movement of fans every where around indicated the intense heat that prevailed; but who would not have patiently endured even a sirocco, for such superb music, vocal and instrumental? The compositions of the great masters, Beethoven, Rossini, Weber and Boieldieu, were performed by at least a hundred instrumentalists. Mlle. Battu received an encore on that charming Neapolitan song, *Santa Lucia;* and Mr. Theodore Ritter executed in dashing, brilliant style several piano-pieces, one of which was his own composition—*Les courriers.* After this delightful treat of music, Mme. Madelaine Brohan, the celebrated actress, appeared in a short comedy, *Le cheveu blanc,* by Octave Feuillet.

May 1.—With the morning's earliest sunshine came a gentle chirping—not a knocking at my door, or a gloomy raven croaking—the twittering of some little birds on the balcony railing, seeming to say :

" Thy life is in its time of flowers,
    Gather May-garlands while 'tis May."

And this is the merry day when queens are crowned with roses bright, and maidens dance on the village-green; but, apart from the associations of the good old-time festival, it is dear to me as the anniversary of an event linked with gladness.   *   *   *   *   *

To-night, Musard's concert proved an attraction. A lyre, at the entrance, studded with tiny gas jets, served to beguile many a passer-by into the enclosure, which affords a truly brilliant promenade, *al fresco*. The musicians, numbering fifty or more, occupied a pavilion, where they discoursed delightful operatic airs—the sweet gems of *Martha* being among the selections. Nothing is more consonant with the feelings and tastes of the French people than an open-air concert, for they dote on the freedom of the gardens. The seats, arranged around the pavilion, are usually occupied while the band is playing, and perfect order reigns. In the intervals, the promenades present a lively appearance, with a varied assemblage, from the vain coxcomb and the dashing belle, to the serious, plain, old man, who only goes for the entertainment of the young daughter clinging to his arm.

May 3.—After another charming day at Versailles, I have returned, with heart and brain filled to pleasurable excess with its myriad, unrivalled beauties. There I visited Madame Santa Cruz, the widow of a distinguished South American, who filled the positions of General, Marshal, and President of Bolivia, and who also won proud renown in uniting that country with

Peru. Her home is a miniature *château*, furnished with the most *recherché* taste, and abounding in paintings; her family most cordial and hospitable. Before the carriage was ready to take us to the Grand Trianon, the delicious morning had enticed us to a promenade in a little garden attached to the dwelling, where the fragrance of orange-flowers and lilac was heavy on the air. I tried my luck at target-shooting, with two youths, Andres Santa Cruz and Robert Meeks, who were decided adepts in the art. Each aimed at a lilac-branch full of bloom, bringing it down with a single shot, and made me the recipient of a floral trophy. Then followed a drive through the noble avenues leading to that charming villa which the munificent Louis XIV prepared for Mme. de Maintenon. As we passed through the apartments, a large crowd closely followed on our steps, it being the day for the fountains to play. Owing to the great rush, it was with difficulty that we kept near the guide, who, evidently anxious to get through his work, hurried us along, describing, at telegraph-speed, the principal objects of interest. How attractive the suite of *salons!* — the reception-room, with its portraits and paintings; the saloon that takes its name from a valuable malachite—Alexander's gift, in honor of the " treaty of Tilsit;"—the gallery where superb tables and vases, in rich mosaics and malachite, vie with each other in beauty; the royal apartments, profusely gilded—the most conspicuous one containing the bed whose proudest association is that it was used by Josephine; and the council-room, where Napoleon signed the fatal articles of

divorce!   In a building not far from the Grand Trianon
we saw the state carriages, which impressed us more
with the pomp of royalty than all we had seen in the
glittering palace.   The most magnificent one was built
in 1825, for the Monarch Charles X, who rode to his
coronation on its soft velvet cushions; but the gilding
has been retouched, and it is otherwise newly decorated,
to serve him who now wields the sceptre of France.
One was used by Napoleon I when he was First Consul, and another is distinguished as having borne infant
royalty to the holy rites of baptism.   After counting
seven, our attention was directed to the sledges that belonged to Louis XIV.   The painting on the side of one
of them is exquisitely fine.   Not the least in interest,
though last in order, was Marie Antoinette's sedan-chair,
which bore her person in the days of her queenly triumph.   Alas! where were comforts and honors a few
years later?   The Petit Trianon, another mansion built
for a King's favorite, was closed; but all disappointment was soon forgotten when our steps reached the
grounds—a lovely Paradise, adjoining the residence.
If we did not fear to incur the sin of sacrilege, we might
say that this spot is a reflex of the bright land above.
The handiwork of the Creator is manifest in the green
sloping vales and hillocks, the tender flowers and foliage, and the silvery streams; and added to God's imperishable seal—man's art.   We do not wonder at Marie
Antoinette's throwing off for a time the crown, to become a rustic queen; at her being beguiled from the
wearisome formalities of the Court, to accept some mo-

ments of freedom in the quiet groves; at the little Swiss cottage, or at that more humble spot, the *laiterie*. The little brook near by still murmurs the same music that once gladdened her ears, and thousands come to wander over the soil that has borne the impress of her footsteps. And what are the reflections of the visitor as he treads this ground? At what a fearful price is worldly station sometimes gained!—the soul, in clinging to its flimsy allurements, finding failure and disappointment; and reaping, from a few brief joys, a harvest of sorrow! Her bust in plaster, much defaced by the scribblings of tourists, occupies a bracket attached to an outside wall of the *laiterie*. The theatre once used by the Court would have received more than a flitting glance, had there not remained much more of the fairy-land to be explored within a certain time—some verdure-clad bowers; a labyrinth; and a little conservatory, on whose outside walls thick bunches of lilac were trained, presenting at a distance the appearance of clusters of grapes. Resuming our carriage, we drove along the banks of the great canal, which, at one point, gives off two cross branches. Mlle. Santa Cruz told me that pleasant rowing parties often met there during the summer months. Who would not be lulled to peace and happiness, floating over these still waters, bordered with curtains of "living green" from a thousand trees, and with a fair sky above to shed bright sunlight?

Upon our return to the principal grounds, where the fountains had begun to play, we found an admiring *world* in the fifty thousand persons that had collected to

witness the rare and beautiful sight.   The various fountains played in succession, the smaller ones leading off;
and, thus, were our feet kept busy in moving rapidly
from point to point. The crystal spray flew around,
regardless of handsome silks, and imparting to the
atmosphere a moisture very acceptable, inasmuch as old
Sol's rays, like *les eaux*, were fairly flooding Versailles.
Guide-books have described so minutely these interesting adornments, that a word from us who come after,
is like a single drop added to their ocean of thought,
yet we cannot refrain from mentioning the Bronze
Nymphs; the Animals and Cupids; the Tritons and
Syrens, holding laurel crowns; the Dragon; the Pyramid; Latona's Victory; Diana's Nymphs; the Four
Seasons, with their representative Gods and Goddesses,
Saturn, Bacchus, Flora and Ceres; Enceladus, the Giant,
revengeful against Heaven; Apollo at the Bath,—his
grouping Nymphs and all the other surroundings being
of the most perfect sculpture; and lastly, Neptune, who
as God of the Sea, justly presides over, and names the
largest and most splendid of all the fountains. As we
stood on the green lawn opposite, the myriad jets that,
at a given signal, simultaneously rose from various parts
of the immense basin, seemed like shot-off rockets,
lighted as they were into prismatic colors by the slant-
ing sunlight; and then a volume of water burst forth
from the colossal groups of leaden figures, until, far and
wide, a showery mist settled around. Not only were
foreheads and garments sprinkled, but the mossy banks
and leaves caught many a sparkling drop. The cost of

Neptune's dominion was three hundred thousand dollars; and the expense incurred, when his oceanic majesty plays on State-occasions, is said to be many thousands of francs. With this magnificent sight, the pleasures of the day terminated, and there was a general rush for the railroad station. In the shortest possible time, the grounds that had been filled to overflowing, presented a very lonely aspect—nature reigning supreme. I dined with Mme. Santa Cruz, and, upon leaving, was presented with a picture of her husband, the Marshal, in full uniform, a strikingly handsome and dignified man, of whose memory they are very justly proud.

May 5.—How bright and gay was the Champs Elysées this morning; streams of men, women and children, and hundreds of equipages, and gay, prancing steeds, wending their way to a grand review of 70,000 troops by the Emperor! The State carriages came rolling by, to the shouts of the multitude. A few moments after witnessing, from my window, all this heaving, beaming life, in the tide that went out to the sound of martial music, I saw a spectacle of an entirely opposite character—a funeral cortége, presenting all the insignia of mourning. Besides the hearse, profusely draped in black, with ponderous, high, nodding plumes, the carriages were all of the same sombre hue. Even the followers on foot bent low their heads in sympathetic sadness. What more desolate feeling could sweep o'er the mind, than that evoked by such a sight, contrasted, as it was, with the volatile, shouting crowd

v

that had just passed by ?   Yet such extremes are everywhere to be found, but especially in Paris, where gaiety
assumes the most flashing tinsel, and where sorrow wears
the darkest cypress !

CHAPTER XVI.

May 6.

THE opera of *La Juive,* most charmingly rendered last night, must ever remain a sweet memory. A tribute of vociferous applause was paid to the acting and singing of Mme. Marie Sass; and if "honors" had been divided, as in *whist,* the tenor would certainly have received an equal share. How deeply interesting the plot, the Jewess clinging to her religious faith even to her martyred end! The curtain fell as she was being led to the fiery caldron, and the last notes that reached our ears sounded the knell of her sad doom. To dispel gloomy thoughts, we drove to a brilliant café, on the Boulevard des Italiens. Amid the flashing lights, the smiling faces at the round tables, the gay voices, and the sound of popping corks, no ghost of trouble ventured a seat at our board.

May 7.—A card of permit admitted us to the Emperor's stables, which contain one hundred and forty horses. The stalls, of carved oak, were marked with the names of the animals that occupied them, and their high-sounding titles kept us busy wondering what could be the merits to justify such distinction. The war horse of

His Majesty, named after the great Sir Walter Scott, was specially pointed out by the attendant. He is quite old, and, having successfully passed through the din of battle, now finds respite in luxurious ease. The two favorite riding ones are *Hero* and *Marignan*. The stud embraces several of American breed, but those from Russia are deserving of highest praise. It is a regret that so many noble specimens are kept in lazy durance, when they could be healthfully and profitably employed in agricultural pursuits. The Empress and the Prince Imperial do not find it necessary to draw from this overwhelming stock, for their stables at D'Orsay contain about the same number, and not inferior in quality. These stables, handsomely embellished, are admirably constructed, having every convenience, and are well managed by a superfluity of grooms.

We passed next to the coach-houses, where the State carriages, about twelve in number, are kept. Besides these, there are sixty other vehicles of different descriptions, many of which, like the horses, are seldom ever used. Very attractive is the coach that bore the Emperor, on the occasion of the opening of the Industrial Exposition of '57. It is of superb workmanship; but we left its huge magnificence for the wee *voiture* used by the baby Prince, during the first year of his life, and walked several times around the enchanted ground that held the unique and costly little gem. Its downy cushions, covered with white satin, were just fit for tiny bones and dimpled flesh. In glass cases, in an adjoining apartment, hangs the harness, the brightness of the rich

mountings showing the careful attention bestowed on
them; and, in another room, are the saddles, some of
which were presented to the Emperor by the Sultan of
Turkey, the Embassador of Japan, and other foreign
potentates. They are gorgeous in gold and silver and
silk embroidery. Finally, we were shown the riding-
school. General Fleury's sons—friends of the young
Prince—had just mounted two horses, proud and beautiful, with their arched necks and flowing manes.

* * * * * The Prince Imperial receives his first
communion to-day. May the church prove a bright
fountain to him, yielding draughts of heavenly grace;
and, when earthly springs of joy fail, may its refreshing
dews fall gently on his head!

May 9.—It was with great regret that I, this morning, missed the visit of a friend whom I have not seen
since the happy days preceding our national troubles,
viz.: General Breckinridge, the courteous gentleman
and dignified statesman. He will shortly leave for
America.

* * * * * About 5 p. m., when the gay world were
returning from the Bois, and the Champs Elysées was
crowded, there was witnessed a sad accident—a runaway
horse, attached to an open barouche, dashing furiously
by. The driver held manfully the reins, but was pow-
erless to control the terrified animal. On this avenue,
where vehicles were so numerous, it was, indeed, a mystery how he described his zig-zag route, without inflicting damage on others. From many a balcony persons

v*

followed, with their *lorgnettes*, his frantic course, eager to ascertain the fate of the brave woman who sat quietly awaiting the result. But soon came the.tidings of a fatal issue. At Rond Point, where escape seemed possible, the lady, contrary to the advice of the shouting multitude, leaped from the carriage, and sustained a mortal fracture of the skull. Thus, in the midst of an arena teeming with pleasure, a sudden stroke has hurled a being into eternity. Truly, life is like a bubble on the air!

May 10.—Last evening, by lovely moonlight, we went to another of Musard's concerts, and at its termination, a drive to the Bois was proposed. To see that place, deserted by its frequenters, and under the charm of lunar rays, was a pleasing impromptu idea. Thereupon, several *cochers* were summoned, and they soon spirited up their horses, under the promise of that little round sum which ever meets favor in the Frenchman's eyes. After passing the grand triumphal arch, whose proud summit seemed to meet the blue and favoring sky, our carriages entered the Avenue de l'Impératrice, gaining at rapid speed on the gates of the park. Its solitary, moonlit avenues lay open to us, white as snow, the silence being broken only by the hum of insects, or the croaking of frogs. Oh! beautiful Night! how lonely is thy spell over mount and plain, valley and lake, and shadowy paths! How rude for mortal song or jest to disturb the hour of nature's repose! The bowers are still, and who, save the moon, has a right to glance into their hidden recesses, unless it be her own Endymion, venturing to steal from her a kiss in secret?—and what sound should dare intrude but gentle notes from lute or lyre? For several hours, by the lake-side and in the silent groves, we loitered, until a little time-piece warned us that night had wings as well as day; and it was past twelve o'clock ere we went home to slumber and to dream.

A misty rain set in with the early hours of this morning, and thousands, bent on attending the races at Long-champs, would have been wofully disappointed, had not the clouds broken away at noon and disclosed a perfect day. The whole *route* was a scene of excitement, with the grandest of equipages, some—four in hand;—the ladies in new spring toilettes; the fleetest riding animals, and the sporting Jehus, who, seeming to have caught the spirit of the occasion, were challenging every one to a race. Our party reached the Tribune and secured seats just as the jockies, with their horses, made their appearance. They were not one moment behind the appointed time; punctuality and order attending all things in France. All around, bets were being made, and several Englishmen of our party induced us ladies to fall into the fascinating error. My judgment, as a novice, was based rather on the handsome appearance of the animal, or the fair sounding name, than on a knowl-edge of qualities essential to speed. Indeed, it was often more the beauty of the jockey's costume, than aught else, that influenced my selections. The first race, of sixteen horses,—*Prix des Tertres*—2000 francs, taught me not to be dazzled and ruled by appearances, as the three horses I had chosen were ingloriously defeated. The same spirit that makes the professional gambler continue to play, after a loss, surely animates those who bet on racing horses, else why did we hear everywhere around, "Let us try it again!" Before the commencement of a race, all the numbers of the horses entered appear on a black-board, near the Judge's stand, and are withdrawn during the race. At the conclusion, the number of the successful horse suddenly flies out, sending a thrill of gladness to the winners, and one of sorrow to the losers. The second race,—*Prix du Trocadéro*—3000 francs, did not seem to engage as much interest as the one that followed,—the *Prix de l'Empereur*—10,000 francs given by his Majesty. To retrieve bad luck was to place my hopes on that noble animal *Suzerain*, owned by Count de La Grange. The jockey wore cherry and white satin, and came up victorious, to the huzzahs of thousands. At this point, the excitement was tempered by a short interval, when many persons descended from the stand to promenade, and seek refreshment. The scene was one of brilliant animation, as on the velvety lawn, that spread out a mile or more, masses of people were moving to and fro, and many groups were arranging bets for the remaining entries. A racy, though somewhat inelegant quotation, came to our ears; and as it bore upon the sport of the day,—but not on the condition or appearance of the horses,—it may be given.

> "I like to see the waving grass, before the mower mows it,
> I like to see an old grey horse, for when he goes, he goes it."

The great race, *Prix du lac*—Handicap—8,000 francs, proved more interesting than all the others, on account of its large number of horses, viz., eighteen. The *Prix de Neuilly* was the last, and sweepstakes were proposed by a member of our party. Of the fifteen horses, I had selected numbers 3 and 11, but 3 being withdrawn, my chances of success were lessened, and the other number seemed ill calculated, from the poor start the animal made, to bring good luck to me. However, in the grand circuit of 2,900 mètres, *la Tracone* made most charming speed, retrieving all that he had lost in the beginning, and winning for me the *sweepstakes*. A prolonged huzzah was given for the jockey in his *rouge et noir!* The Emperor's absence was accounted for by the announcement that he had gone to Orleans. Our drive home was through the loveliest and greenest part of the Bois. The trees on the borders of the lake bowed under the weight of their pink and white blossoms;—beds of marguerite and myrtle vine greeted the eye;—the boats were filled with pleasure-seekers; and one thought alone occupied the mind, coming in the spirit of Eve's lament, "Oh! must I leave thee, Paradise."

May 11.—Several hours have been pleasantly whiled away at the Palais de l'Industrie, opened within the last few days, for the exhibition of paintings. Of the many meritorious pictures, the most attractive were *Mary Stuart distributing her Jewels the night before her death; The Adultress; Inspiration*—a child at prayer with an angel at her side,—*La Pieta*—the dead Christ, with Mary bending over the body ; and *The Three Ages*, represented by three apples, green, ripe, and withered, and under the fruit, a child, a man in the vigor of life, and decrepid age. A painting exquisitely fine and delicate was called *The Gavotte Step*, where the figure of the beautiful Madame Récamier is introduced. *Vestris* makes Mme. R. repeat a gavotte, which she is to dance the next day with Lady Georgina—Duchess of Bedford —at a ball given by the Duchess of Gordon. The lesson was given to the sound of the harp and the horn. The face of an Italian girl, with eyes of deepest feeling, held many visitors enchanted, and the name of *Maria del Marco*, so musical in sound, with the beauty of its owner, might have adorned a romance, or inspired a poet.

This evening a dinner-party came off at the house of a friend, and towards its close a disastrous crash of finest glass and porcelain paid the penalty of a German baron's tricks. He attempted the feat of making a pyramid of decanters and wine-glasses, which was at the first and second trials successful, but the third brought a great fall, to the infinite amusement of the guests, to the mortification of him who aimed too high, and to the vexation of the host at the foot of the table, who was utterly unable to suppress a groan. Leaving the scene of shattered crystal and porcelain, we repaired to the *salon*, to listen to some skilful performances on the piano, by the hostess—the keys being moved to a medley of sweetest sound under her graceful and accomplished touch.

May 13.—On the route to the Bois de Vincennes, this bright and beautiful afternoon, we saw the house—*à la Fiancée*—noted for its connection with the revolution of 1848. From one of its windows was fired the first shot, and then followed the horrors of bloodshed in a furious blast of passion, which has left a mournful echo in this land. We passed the Tower of St. Jacques, one of the grand monuments of Paris, leading the mind to conceive how elaborate and rich was the taste of three centuries ago. This is all that remains of the church of the same name; and a perfect specimen of Gothic architecture it is, rising from the centre of a square that has all the designs and beauty of a flower-garden! But what a little Eden is the Vincennes Park, its glens redolent of sweet odors, the pansies growing as thick as field-daisies, and every tree in blossom, dropping its feathery burden upon the pathway! The beauties of the Bois de Boulogne, for the time, are forgotten in the more simple and natural charms seen here—the bowers of vivid green, formed by the interlaced branches of trees, whose leaves are more delicate than the finest ferns; the shady paths leading by the side of the rivulet; the thicket or the wood, which still retains its primitive wildness; and the large lake, where canopied boats offer pleasant excursions. At a short distance from this beautiful sheet of water is a cottage restaurant, with garden walks and shaded recesses; and nearer its margin are small tables, suggestive of punches, hot or cold—take them as you please. The ducks and swans are so tame that they come up like old friends, treading on your toes, and looking up wistfully for something to eat. All around is a pleasant witchery. It may be the charm of spring, a happy heart, a quiet conscience, kind friends, or gratitude—*N'importe!* it is enough to know

> "'Twixt joy and joy I be."

CHAPTER XVII.

May 17.

ON the afternoon of the 14th, our party, composed of thirteen, left for Fontainebleau, where we had previously secured apartments at the Hôtel de Londres, near the Imperial palace. A dinner that would have done justice to a first-class Parisian restaurant had been provided for us in a private apartment; and, after the meal, the public parlor being placed at our disposal, we repaired thither towards the hour of 7 P. M. Some fine music, followed by dancing, consumed an hour or more; and for the *lovers* of moonlight, a balcony was near at hand. Know you that in this age, as of yore, fair Dian smiles down upon Romeos and Juliets?—and why should n't it be so at Fontainebleau? A few soldiers of the palace, off duty, were attracted to the house by the violin performance of an accomplished Southern gentleman, and by a lady's sweet songs, that seemed to woo as gently as the night breeze floating through the open windows. The beautiful evening tempted us to a promenade, and, as the clock struck ten, we found ourselves on the outskirts of the forest, threading our way down a magnificent avenue lined with trees whose giant proportions seemed to point scornfully at our pigmy selves.

W

As far as the eye could stretch there was one interminable sea of foliage, which, witnessed in the stillness and solemnity of night, and with the long, unending vista ahead, appeared like a vast eternity. Next in grandeur to the ocean are the forest-wilds, causing the beholder to exclaim, in acknowledgment of God's greatness,— "How marvellous are the works of Thy hands!" Upon our return to the hotel, the moon was still so bright that we could not forsake its company, and sleep being entirely driven from our eyes, we sat in the court-yard among the flowers, singing the old American ballads, "Oft in the Stilly Night," and "Home, Sweet Home." Is not the sentiment of the latter song as dear to the wandering traveler, and as religiously preserved in thought, as is the faith connected with a blessed medal,— a little rustic cross carved out of a saintly relic, or some other amulet that is never permitted to leave the person?

The next morning we took carriages for the forest, with the view of exploring a portion of its forty thousand acres; and soon found ourselves in the midst of thousands of oak, beech and black-fir trees. The scenery is wild and rugged. At one point, from huge gray rocks, irregularly piled up—as if deposited there in some violent convulsion of nature—can be obtained a fine view of the Gorge de Franchard. The name of Franchard is famous in its association with a monastery that once existed, founded by Philippe Auguste. Through the Cave of the Brigands we were led by guides, bearing torches, who mumbled out something about the dread

Thissier and his band that lived there three years without discovery. It seemed that the lapse of a century had not divested the spot of terror, judging from the haste of the guides to get out of the gloomy hole, and our own desire to return to sunlight. The fatigue, consequent upon our wanderings from grove to grove, made us look wistfully for some kind of rest, and it was not denied us. A pic-nic under the verdure-clad canopy had been happily arranged by the gentlemen of the party, and so, in default of chairs, we sat down on the leafy turf, before a feast of salads, meats, fruits and native wines. And thus the hours waned away until the tristful shadows closed around us. * * * * *

Bright and early, the next day, we made our way over to the *château*, first taking a stroll in the garden laid out after the English fashion, and afterwards, standing on the bridge over the large pond to feed the big old carp, that rose in great numbers to the surface. Centrally situated there, is an octagonal pavilion, said to have been constructed by Francis I, and noted as being a place where some of the most important conferences connected with French history were held. A fitting spot, it seemed in its lonely situation,—like a rock in the sea—for lofty minds, untrameled, to plan their mighty schemes. Then was opened to us the palace, which had been the scene of so many notable events. Its gorgeous apartments form quite a contrast with the ancient and unimposing exterior. The chapel, situated on the ground-floor, is beautifully frescoed; and, just within the door, is an exquisite statue, representing a woman in the attitude of prayer. It must imply a refuge from earthly sorrow, in the consolation that comes from above. Ascending the staircase, we came to an *antichambre* graced by a picture of Madame de Montespan, and to several rooms that seemed to tell mournfully of the departed glory of Napoleon I; the first being the *cabinet de travail*, where he labored in thought and writing; the second, the *cabinet particulier*, where he signed his abdication. There, with a single stroke of the pen, was laid aside that vaulted ambition, with which he had met nation upon nation in valiant fight; and outside, not far from that little room, did he learn, in severing the tie that had so long bound him to his comrades, the bitterness of the word *farewell*—more grievously felt, perhaps, than the misfortune that occasioned the divorce from his beloved Josephine. In this very palace was that painful sentence pronounced. On visiting the *Salle des bains*, with its glassy walls, allegorically painted, one might well exclaim, how beautiful and appropriate the conception of the artist! There are sea-nymphs reclining among rushes and grasses, and cupids clutching at flowery wreaths and garlands. It only wants the mysterious love-language of the tiny gods to complete the charming illusion. The council chamber, with Gobelin tapestry, splendid ceiling and panel paintings; and the throne-room, with the conspicuous chair of state, the portrait of Louis XIII, and rock-crystal chandelier, valued at twenty thousand dollars, are truly magnificent. *En suite* are the apartments—once familiar to the tread of Marie Antoinette—occupied by the Empress on her annual visits to Fontainebleau; the *Cabinet de toilette*, with its grand ceiling representing Aurora, and the two vases presented by the Emperor of Austria to Marie Antoinette; the bed-chamber of that unfortunate Queen, the walls being covered with embroidered white satin, a gift to her from the city of Lyons; and the *Salon de Réception*, with a superb table from Sèvres, allegorically portraying the Four Seasons. The *Galerie de Henri II* is the most imposing of all the apartments. How inviting to the lovers of Terpsichore is its glossy floor, richly inlaid with various colored woods! Diana of Poitiers' crest is linked with that of her enamored king. The Salon de Diane is attractive as a feast of literature, forming, as it does, the library of the palace. There are two articles near one of the windows, a sword and coat of mail, that fill the mind with the horror of secret murder. They were worn by Monaldeschi, secretary to Christine, Queen of Sweden, when he fell, assassinated by her cruel orders. In a recess near by is a white vase, with handsome bas-reliefs, from the Sèvres manufactory —a present to the Duke of Orleans. The Prince Imperial's bed-chamber holds a cunning little bedstead, as simple and unpretending as the rest of the furniture. The Gallery of Francis I is wainscotted in oak, and has a wonderful ceiling, made up of massive scroll work, richly gilded. Here and there appear the initial *F.* and the *Salamander*, his Majesty's coat-of-arms. In the bedroom of Catherine de Medicis we saw the first lookingglass that was ever manufactured, and a glance at it made us fancy that we had suddenly grown very aged.

W*

In one room stood the equestrian statue of Francis I, and the gaming-table at which that royal personage often played.   Another *salon* was remarked for its floor, inlaid with the tiniest pieces of wood, to correspond with the ceiling.   The rich ornamentation of that one apartment afforded sufficient evidence of the superior taste of Louis Philippe, who, during his reign, restored palaces to their former splendor, adding thereto his own embellishments.   A white marble mantel of large dimensions, with a sculptured block set in the wall, and extending to the ceiling, struck us as being the most massive piece of workmanship, of the kind, we had ever seen.   The apartments of *les Reines Mères* are associated with the name of that holy Father of the Church, Pius VII, whom Napoleon held captive for two years; and, more recently, with the Duchess of Orleans, who occupied them after her nuptials.   Here we saw a beautiful table, of Italian manufacture, presented by the Pope of Rome to the Prince Imperial, and lately exhibited at the Paris Exposition.   Finally, we came to a small room named for its frescoes, but far more attractive were its porcelain paintings—gems of Sèvres—inserted in the wall, some relating to the history of Fontainebleau, and others, views of celebrated places, such as Versailles.   Niagara Falls, our country's boast, was the subject of one of these unique plates.

Descending by a stairway of brown and white streaked marble, we passed into the outer court—the spot where Napoleon bade adieu to the remnant of his old guard. In treading over these stones, something akin to deep regret was felt for the hero, who, amid the tears and sighs of his faithful band, yielded to the dire decree of fate. But, back to the forests we went roaming, stopping first to bow to a venerable patriarch—a tree one thousand years old—and, if age be honorable, we might forever sing praises to that wonderful parent tree! Some pieces of its bark were brought off, as mementoes. Under its vast shadow two of our merry party grew sentimentally poetic, though with an utter disregard of rhyme.

" Now that we 're in the silent woods,
   With nature's grandeur all around,
   My heart leaps out to meet thine own ;
   Say, dearest, can you love me now ?"

" Yes, dearest, I can love you now ;
   As hart leaps out from leafy grove,
   And glides with swiftness o'er the plain,
   So doth my soul, imbued with love,
   Fly out to meet thee, charming one."

The next object of interest was the Croix du Grand Veneur, situated at the intersection of two roads, and named for the legend of the "Spectral black Huntsman ;" but we were not disposed to look into the thicket for that unwelcome personage, and even had he appeared to us, as he did to Henry IV, our jolly peals of laughter would surely have frightened him away. It did not seem necessary to alight from our carriages at the Croix — noted as a rendezvous of the chase — to report, as did the hunters of yore, for only two deers— *dears*—were said to have been shot in the region of the heart, and their recovery seemed probable, with the valuable aid of *Doctor* Gatling, the inventor of the famous *gun*, whose thunders have already reached Imperial ears. We did alight, however, to peep into the hollow of the oak tree *Clovis*. It has gone to decay, like the sovereign whose name it bears; but the fresh, green ivy-leaf still entwines its withered form, like memory, that wreathes departed worth. Another tree had been shivered by the lightning's blast—the missile that does its work more swiftly and effectually than the woodman's axe. After clambering over rocks and thorny bushes, an eminence was gained commanding a magnificent landscape view. Calling the roll, we missed one of the party, who, in attempting a leap that would have tested the agility of a mountain fawn, had slipped and bruised her ankle, the recollection of which must ever call forth a groan—not a blessing—on Fontainebleau.

Resuming our carriages, we visited the Iron Spring, situated under a shelving rock, and embowered in dense foliage. A woman near by sold articles cut out of wood from the forest-trees, such as canes, boxes and other notions. A little whistle that seemed to say, " Whistle, and I'll come to thee, my lad," was shrilly blown, but there was nary a lad to call unto me ; the only sound in the forest-glade being the cuckoo's voice, so tender and true. The *trembling rock* proved a great curiosity, balanced as it is on a pivot-like edge. Its giant form was shaken by the weight of a small boy, who performed the tilting experiment on the promise of a few sous. The next stopping place was the Fort de l'Empereur. A very old woman, on top of the high tower, furnished a telescope, by the aid of which, she asserted, various objects could be seen at the distance of forty miles; yet it yielded us no satisfaction, as we were either too old or too young for the glasses. Nature pleased us well enough, viewed with the naked eye. That dumpy old dame, apparently as durable as the stone pedestal where she has long been a fixture, brought to mind " Little Nan Etticoat, in a *white* petticoat, the longer she stands, the shorter she grows "—only her's was a *brown* one. Long may she be the guardian of the old crumbling tower, and when she is gone, may the winds that sigh around it, be her requiem! From Mont Calvaire, another height, we saw the town of Fontainebleau, cradled in great beauty. It snugly lay in a hollow, mantled with cliffs and rocks and trees, forming one of the most perfect pictures conceivable. Over the Sponge Rock, so called from the porous nature of its stone, the French flag was waving. Doubtless there is some romantic or historical interest connected therewith? Lastly, we came upon a chapel in the woods, erected in the reign of one of the Louis; and if it elicited a prayer at all, it was that we might often visit such glorious scenes, where to the murmur of the breeze in the grand old forests, our hearts could thrill in answering chords. With this weird music, tuned by nature, lingering on our cars, we returned to the hotel, and, with the regret that comes upon leaving a place that may never be seen again, took up our line of march. Our *adieux*, as sad pilgrims, were freighted with something of the same feeling that was depicted in the face of the Savoyard girl when she bade farewell to her mountain-home.

May 18.—To-day was begun with a visit to the *Conciergerie*, a place of saddest interest, marking scenes of imprisonment and carnage— some of the most pitiable suffering ever endured by mortals. How painful were our emotions as we stood before the prison-cell of Marie Antoinette! With the grating of the key that opened to us the dismal chamber, came vivid spectres of all her woes—the cherished ties rent asunder; the dignity and pride of the *Queen* scoffed at; the gentler feelings of the *woman* abused; the loneliness and suspense of incarceration; the denial of religious communion, such as she favored; and above all, the horrors of an ignominious death! A stone-tablet in the wall, bearing a Latin inscription of her death, and a crucifix that had helped to solace her sorrow, and direct her prayers, first arrest the attention—one investing the cell with the solemnity of death; the other, a memento of her pious trust and faith. Against the walls are two pictures, swung on brackets, that admit of their being brought to the feeble light that struggles through the grated window. One is commemorative of her *adieu*—at the Temple—to the Duchess of Angoulême and Mme. Elizabeth, in presence of Simon, the cobbler. It seems, indeed, the farewell of sorrow amid the perishing glory of a noble career. The other represents her taking the sacrament just prior to her execution, at the hands of the Abbé Mangin, disguised as a *gendarme*. In an adjoining apartment Robespierre was confined, and there, in part, he paid the penalty of his crimes, suffering the same misery that he had dealt out to others. A picture of Marie Antoinette,

like an avenging spirit, is the only thing that breaks the
loneliness of that barren cell. She is represented in prison,
her figure seeking support against the couch, as if overcome with exhaustion, and her face wearing a look of
serene composure, with eyes upturned to heaven. In
the window is the crucifix. In these three paintings
the artists have finely portrayed the majesty of the
Queen, amidst the trials and dejection of the prisoner.

> " In thy beauty's deathless pride
> Thou lookest up once more　*　*
> To play a queenly part."

We saw naught else of the building, but the court-
yard, where a few unfortunate culprits were pacing to
and fro, wearing the traces of some offence with which
stern justice has all to do. And so, in pity, did we look
upon these poor creatures, for the compassionate heart,
as well as the Bible, says, "Let the sighing of the prisoner
come before thee!"

We next visited the Panthéon, whose magnificent
dome rears itself proudly, as a monument to the great
men of the past. The interior has all the attributes of
a place of public worship, whilst certain distinguished
monarchs, once wrapped in the ermine of France, are
allegorically portrayed by the master-hand of Gros,
whose painting, on the dome, spreads out in exquisite
beauty, and is continued, on the pendentives, by Gérard's
scarcely less attractive pictures of Justice, Glory, France,
and Death. The first is a female culprit, perishing by
the sword of Justice; the second, the figure of Napo-

leon, arrayed in state robes, receiving the embrace of Glory; the third, a figure representing France, proudly grand, crowned with laurel; at her side an angel engages in the gentle office of garlanding the tomb of a dead hero; the fourth is Azrael smiting down the strong man. Besides the high altar, there are three others, richly ornamented and enshrining relics. A priest sat before one, to receive floral offerings dedicated to the exquisite marble statue of the Virgin — her pale brow being decked with a chaplet of lilies, whose faint odor, like the first breath of spring, descended to us tenderly, aye, even religiously. Altogether, the temple, to-day, was in keeping with the beautiful month of May, for the cold marbles here and there were brightened with roses of every hue, and other blossoms just as gay. A guide, bearing a lantern, conducted us below to the tombs of Voltaire and Rousseau. That of the former is very plain, with a garland of laurel and a harpsichord on top. On one side of this small locked enclosure—the cenotaphs of these great writers being separated from the others—stands the full length marble statue of Voltaire, with a book in one hand and a pen in the other. Rousseau's tomb is a vault, with a half-opened door, out of which is thrust a hand holding a torch-light, typical of the refulgent genius that has helped to enlighten the world. Following on through various windings, we were brought to the monuments of Marshal Lannes—Duke of Montebello—and of some of the first Senators of the Empire;—there, in the black stillness of those vaulted

chambers, is shrouded forever their light and glory!
The guide requested us to preserve silence, in order that
we might hear the remarkable echo of the crypt. His
stentorian call was responded to with equal force, and
his lowest whisper came back with a distinctness that
was quite startling.

In the neighborhood of the Panthéon is the Library
St. Geneviève, which contains many interesting curiosities, and over two hundred thousand volumes. There
are numerous pastel paintings of the Kings of France;
busts of distinguished writers; and one of Cardinal de la
Rochefoucault, the founder of the library. Some of the
most ancient books on the ground floor are those given
by Rome to Napoleon, in payment of her war debt. A
curious old clock, made in 1546, represents the planetary system ; and a map, with the design of a wide-
branching tree, illustrates the genealogy of Jesus Christ.
There was shown to us a Bible, printed in the year 900,
and another of the date of 1200. A cast of Henry IV,
taken one hundred and eighty years after death, seemed as
perfect as if it had been made when he was in the full
vigor of health. Saint Denis must assuredly possess the
power of preserving its dead ; but, if the deeds of good
men live after them, why should not the features of a
worthy monarch remain unaltered long after the day when
funeral pomp has paid him honor? At a short distance
from this cast is the skull of Cartouche, the celebrated
robber and assassin, the sight of which awakened the
most uncomfortable sensations. And this is all that is
left of the man whose career, it would seem, from early

x

youth, was presided over by the evil genius! Thus, in earthly places, are crime and virtue not far separated; but how shall it be in the great hereafter? Opposite the landing of the staircase that leads to the grand library, three hundred feet in length, we found that very striking painting, *The School of Athens*—a copy of the one in the Vatican, at Rome, by Raphael. May such artists long continue to add to the imperishable glory of the philosopher and the sage! The reading-room, with its closely stored books, contains a wealth of knowledge. Four hundred seats bear evidence of how

> " The mind—an antiquarian—loves to pore
> Amid the dust of ancient volumes still."

Principally in the autumn months is every chair filled, from eight in the morning until sunset; and then, when night is made attractive elsewhere with dance and mirth, this hall is the delight of the student, who deems the sable hours far too precious to be devoted to frivolity. All things considered, learning is a *something* whose value is greater than gold—outlasting trivial pleasures—a companion, when the world is as a desert, and one that rarely ever abandons us until the heavenly decree goes forth that mind and body shall perish.

We stopped next at the gorgeous St. Chapelle, connected with the Palace of Justice. The interior is one mass of gilding, tinted by the variegated colors of the windows—a scene that might be compared to a glorious sunset, blending colors with its gold. The chapel owes its great fame to St. Louis, who designed it for the reception of that greatest of all relics, the crown of thorns, and also a piece of the true cross. Service is only held on the exhibition of these holy relics; and, although our eyes were not saddened by the painful sight, still our hearts remembered that

> " Thus it was ! a diadem of thorn
>   Earth gave to Him who mantled her with flowers;
>   To Him who poured forth blessings in soft showers,
> O'er all her paths, a cup of bitter scorn! ''

The exterior of the edifice is a reflex of the inner splendor, and its gilded roof and spires were beautiful to-day as seen in the bright and glorious sunlight. A short walk brought us to the Café St. Michel, whose neat little tables on the side-walk, tempted us beyond resistance. It was a study to sit and watch the passers-by on this boulevard. One little man, who had been reduced to a skeleton, carried an umbrella, which, without its cover, would have been a fair representation of his own anatomical structure. This wiry ghost was the sharp foreground of another picture entirely his opposite—a plump *Grisette*, in a flashy red dress, which not even the pearl-colored trimmings could subdue. The face of an Italian Savoyard peered out from under a broad-brimmed hat; his large eyes filling with tears as he drew the bow across his violin, and, in plaintive voice, commenced an *addio* to his native land. Just then, a rumbling omnibus passed with a number of smoking, chatting students on top, and thus, for the moment, our thoughts were diverted from the little home-sick wanderer. Next came a foppish fellow, stepping, in fine patent-leathers, and flourishing a cane, who took up a note or two of the sad Italian melody, and then whistled off the merriest air, as if to intimate that, under gay sunshine, nothing should partake of a melancholy character.

Towards 5 P. M., we drove to the Bois de Vincennes. This park has sylvan retreats on the lake-shore, where repasts are furnished, and on a warm spring or summer evening the green, vine-clad bower is preferable to the *salon* of the restaurant. How quickly the hours pass when quiet ease and pleasure control them! Thinking thus, a friend raised her glass with this happy quotation—

> "Ah, never doth time travel faster,
> Than when his way lies among flowers."

And this was followed by a toast—"May the hinges of Hospitality never grow rusty!" How could they under the brightening influence of champagne, and the *oil* of a French salad? Returning home after night had set in, we saw an electric-light on Porte St. Martin, shifting its dazzling glow, in various directions, over the city, and appearing like a vast meteor in the sky.

May 19.—A grand concert took place to-day, at the Cirque de l'Impératrice, for the benefit of the Arabian and French orphans at an asylum in Algiers, founded by Madame la Maréchale de Mac Mahon. The building is spacious, containing six thousand seats, and does not lack ornament. Around the sides are panels with paintings of horses' heads; designs inappropriate to the occasion that assembled us, as something of a more

classical taste would have answered better in presence of
that great artist Duprés, of the Imperial Academy of
Music, who was conducting his Grand Oratorio—*The
Last Judgment.* Arranged in three parts, *La Terre,
l'Abîme, et le Ciel,* it partakes of the inspiration of Michael
Angelo's world renowned picture. The musicians numbered one hundred and seventy, and the performance
proceeded with the truest precision, every note being in
perfect time, and rendered with such eveness as to convey
the idea that the sound came from one mammoth instrument. Duprés carried out most ably the composition,
as bearing upon the three parts above-named,—the soft,
delicate tones, like harp strings, gently swept, whispering of heaven;—the grand swelling burst of sound in
imitation of the thunders of a wrathful sky, warning
the sinful children of earth ; the angry discordant clash,
representing the fury and turmoil of hell. A symphony,
sweet and dreamy, was now and then introduced, making
many regret that the finale had ever to come. After an
intermission of fifteen minutes, the second part of the
entertainment began—a vocal concert, in which some of
the most celebrated artists appeared, riveting the undi-
vided attention of the audience. Mozart's duo, from the
Enchanted Flute, by Mlle. Roze and Mr. Crosti, was
followed by Mme. Marie Sass in that sweet melody,
Sancta Maria, by Faure. Mr. Consolo, an Italian
violinist, gave the *Ave Maria,* and one of Schubert's
delicious morceaux, with all the passionate, pathetic
feeling that characterizes Italia's strains. A duo was
admirably sung by Duprés; and Mr. Leon Duprés,

x*

rendered the *Air de Joconde*—Nicolo—in a highly
creditable manner. But the most attractive piece, was
the *Valse de Mireille*—Gounod—sung by Mme. Vanden-
heuvel. Had a little bird suddenly flown in and
breathed out its soul of song, it could not have excelled
her delicious notes. Each of the lady singers received
a green wreath, and worthy were they to wear the
artist's crown !

May 21.—The Hôtel de Cluny is calculated to interest
those who love to roam among relics of the past. First
of all, the ancient building, with its turrets and quaint
little windows, inclines us to inquire into its history and
associations. Once invested with the sanctity of religion,
it formed an asylum for the abbot and abbess—a refuge
for the papal legates; and, besides, became a home for
the widowed queen of Louis XII. The whole building
wears a quiet nunnery-like air, and the neatly laid out
gardens that surround it are picturesque, and possess
the charm of antiquity in the Gallo-Roman ruins and
monuments, partly overrun with ivy, pointing back to
the days of the Cæsars; the arches and portals of old
convents covered with lichens and mosses, and the large
cross that looms out of the shrubbery with the inscription "From the church of St. Vladimir at Sebastopol."
The Palais des Thermes, adjoining the hotel, is the
oldest monument about Paris, being nothing more than
the ruin of a magnificent pile which was erected in the
year 360. The only portion in a state of tolerable pres-
ervation is the hall called the *frigidarium*, or chamber

for cold baths, which contains some curious relics—fragments of altars, colossal heads, crosses, and bas-reliefs in sculpture. One altar bore an inscription showing that it was dedicated to Jupiter, in the reign of Tiberius.

An examination of all the curiosities of the Cluny museums would engross a whole day. What a treat, with their valuable furniture, tapestry, sculpture, carving, armor, jewelry, paintings, glass-ware, and a little of everything that ever was made on this round globe of ours! There stands the bed of a king—a rare specimen of carving, with knights in armor on the posts—with its thread-bare coverlet; silk and embroidery having yielded to the hand of time, like its owner has done to the fell destroyer, Death. What dreams and schemes did Francis I engage in and enjoy as its occupant? Alas! for poor humanity! The cradle outlasts the smiling, dimpled babe, and the couch of the great and robust man remains long after he is turned to dust and ashes. Next, a piano of the time of Louis XIV, of gold-tinted wood, painted with a diversity of rich coloring. It reminded me of my old grandmother's patchwork quilt; but why bring up association with ancient dame, when, perchance, the hands that brought music out of its keys were those of a blooming, gay Princess, wearing the roses of "sweet sixteen?" A valuable painting of Christopher Columbus elicited our greatest praise, as we thought of the noble spirit that had braved the fury of ocean, a thousand difficulties, and endured the torture of long and dreary suspense, to find a land that every day and hour does something worthy to make her rank

among the best of nations. We also saw a piece of the
jaw-bone of Molière, an insignificant fragment of that
man of genius; a chess-board of rock crystal, that belonged to Louis IX,—another reminder of a "vanished
hand" that once had castles and knights under command; a Venitian piano of the sixteenth century, with
thirty keys; a bed with cherry velvet hangings, now
faded and worn—the property of the Marquis d'Effiat,
Marshal of France in the seventeenth century; the portrait of Mary Stuart, in enamel; and the altar screen of
pure gold, an imperial gift to a cathedral church. The
chapel is of the most singular construction, the heavily
sculptured ceiling being sustained by an octagonal column in the centre. The architecture is pure Gothic;
and, in reference to the altar chairs, it may be safely
said that, for carving, the fifteenth century will never be
excelled. The strange, pointed windows, admit only a
sickly, miserable light—not the gracious rays that God
intends for His sanctuary. Out of the dark little chapel
we passed down, by a curious, cramped, winding stairway, the frequent ascending and descending of which
must have proved a severe penance for the portly old
monks and the good angels of mercy; and, once more
in the gardens, we were disposed to seek our homes, yet
not without a strong desire to turn antiquary soon again.

May 23.—The Louvre! a little word, yet how full of
meaning! Who that enters its spacious halls is not
dazzled by its grandeur and wealth?—Are not increased
organs of vision and bigger hearts needed at this shrine

of the beautiful? Go, first, to the Museum of Antique
Sculpture, and pass statue after statue—meritorious as
they may be—until you stand before the Venus of Milo.
It will not be that you depreciate the little gems in your
admiration of the grander stone; for do we not gaze
upon the skies and skip the beauty of the stars, to give
our first love to the "queen of night?" This crowning
specimen of the majesty of womanhood, serene and calm,
has caught the poet's eye, and thus has been immor-
talized :

> " What thought triumphant moved this woman's mind
>   To such sublime controlment that the Gods
>   Smote her with marble stillness?   Generous earth
>   Whose womb, preserving through the crush of years,
>   Hath given this fragment of a mighty age,
>   To shake the shameful bitterness of this
>   With the rebuking awe of one great look,
>   As if the meaner thoughts of meaner minds
>   Had sent, all quivering into lip and eye,
>   The curve and terror of defiant truth.
>   How lifts the torso grandly into light
>   The fullness of a womanhood complete,
>   Broad breathing in an amplitude of grace,
>   And strong, as is the solemn strength and calm
>   Of midnight moonlight.   Imagination
>   That would restore thine armless majesty
>   Doth strangely grope, pleased with the blind distrust
>   That, in thy rare beginnings, sees no end.
>   Thus art crowns art with art's divinest aim,
>   Leading the wrapped observer from himself
>   To finer issues and immortal flight."

After leaving this grand statue, our attention was
given to many other rich marbles, among which were
the beautiful Venus, by Praxiteles, several graceful

dancing Fauns, the mighty Hercules, and the handsome Apollo; and then we passed on to the splendid hall containing Jean Goujon's Caryatides, which made all else seem diminutive. The glorious treasures displayed in the upper galleries in the thousands of paintings, seemed to appeal for a larger appropriation of time, but it could not be granted, on this day at least; and so, after traversing the court of the Louvre, admiring the ornate style of architecture; the fresh and flowering shrubs, not to be despised even among the proudest things of art, we repaired to the Luxembourg Garden. As the sun was at treacherous play, and chose to hide himself behind some frowning clouds, streaked black and blue, and threatening rain, we were compelled to hasten our steps through the pleasant walks, bestowing only a rapid glance at the many little spots stamped with beauty. What a bright, bright picture in the groups of statuary; flower-beds, shady terraces; chestnut groves and rustic seats! In the massive back-ground of a fountain, is a niche holding the figure of an athlete, overlooking two lovers who lie in each others' embrace, like two pearls in an ocean-shell. A growth of ivy at their heads, clambers about the limbs of the intruder, giving him the appearance of one springing out of a thicket to surprise the careless lovers. Connected with the basin of the fountain, is a miniature lake, completely embowered in green; and the trees, equi-distant apart, skirting its borders, are festooned with garlands of evergreen and ivy. Such is the fairy-bower!—just the spot for music and song, or the poetry of love! Let us, who are grave and unsentimental, pass out and make room, for here comes a pretty maiden, whose cavalier looks as if the quiet, green little spot whispered hope and happiness. Perhaps she may here surrender up her *heart*, and if it be a *true* and *faithful* one, he will have secured earth's brightest jewel—connubial joy, and be sheltered in that haven of love, where beating storms and struggling sorrows are soothed to rest.

CHAPTER XVIII.

May 24.

OUR party of six, bound for the Chantilly Races, on reaching the Northern railway, witnessed an uncommonly gay scene—a Paris station, on such occasions, differing widely from its every-day appearance. Hundreds of persons were scrambling, jostling and running to secure seats by the earliest trains; and such a variety of ladies' costume, from the high-toned colors, pink, orange and Metternich green, to the delicate dove, gray and pearl, was never before seen. After a ride of about ten leagues, we found ourselves near the busy scene of action, the race-course being only a short distance from the depot. The promenade leading thereto, was through a fine grove of trees—a leafy avenue, such as is often seen in bright, beautiful France. Just as we reached the Tribune, towards the conclusion of the first race, an accident occurred. A horse threw his rider, and injured very severely a man who attempted to cross the course. The animal, trained to the work of running for a sum, regardless of injuries inflicted, and not disconcerted by the absence of a rider, pursued his way, coming out ahead, but, inasmuch as he had carried no weight, the prize was not awarded to him. The *Prix du Jockey Club*—

25,000 francs—was won by *Suzerain*, to the discom-
fiture of many of the betting English gentry, who had
wagered large sums on the Duke of Hamilton's horses.
Our mother-country was represented in large numbers,
and it was rumored that the Prince of Wales was present, but whether his Royal Highness participated or
not, there were enough of watchful eyes and strained
pockets to keep up the spirit of the races, even to the
latest moment. In the *Prix des Etangs*—2000 francs—
Count de la Grange's horse, *Airel*—surely, the light and
pleasant sounding name deserved success—saved me a
modest little sum, but made a rash Englishman near by
look like a thunder-cloud, even on this bright May day,
because he had lost seventy-five pounds; and we should
not be surprised if the disappointment yet cost him
twenty more—avoirdupois. At the termination of the
races, the rush of persons for the railway must have
been very comical to a looker-on; it certainly gave
a striking proof of the lack of patience in this world.
Into our car, in somersault fashion, tumbled several
persons, who barely escaped with unbroken limbs. One
man had lost his sweet-heart, in the confusion, and blank
appeared his face, when, from a car in the rear, she
called out *"Je ne suis pas seule"*—most unwelcome
tidings, and poor consolation to the disappointed swain,
who sank back into his seat, and began to work into
place the strained muscles of his neck. Locked in with
us, he vented his ire in an occasional *"Sacre!"* the roll
of which, between his clenched teeth, was listened to
with an irrepressible smile; our lack of smpathy enfuri-

Y

ating him all the more; and yet we did not mean to be
unkind. At seven o'clock our party sat down to dinner,
at a restaurant on the Champs Elysées, corner of Rue
d'Alma, where, with fraternal spirit, the bond between
England and America was strengthened. If the thought
came up—soon must all these happy hours pass, and
friends be called to separate, the reflection seemed mournfully true to me, a few moments later, on hearing of the
sudden death of a friend at Florence. How sad to die
away from home, with no kindred sigh or tear to smooth
the passage to the grave; yet stranger-hands and hearts
fulfilled well the office of paying the last tribute to one,
who, coming to breathe the soft air of that delicious
clime, and to look upon its fair scenes, was suddenly
wafted into eternity.

May 25.—The tomb of Napoleon! How grand and
majestic its situation under the dome of Les Invalides,
where, secure from the destructive influences of weather,
its beauty will be preserved through long ages! Who
can stand by the marble balustrade, and gaze below into
the crypt, without feeling reverence for the valiant hero,
whose fame has shed such brilliant lustre throughout
the world? The sarcophagus is magnificent, though
strikingly simple, the only ornamentation upon its surface of highly polished red granite being several carved
laurel crowns. On top, lay a wreath of violets, tied
with a ribbon of the same color; the chaplet of flowers
lending an emotional charm to the solemn shrine. What
hand could have dropped that eloquent memorial?

Perhaps, some war-scarred veteran had wandered there to lay the sweetest and gentlest of all tokens over the remains of him, who, having passed through a world of strife, now reposes on the field of perpetual peace. The pavement of the crypt is beautiful in its fret-mosaic design. A garland of laurel, mingling its vivid green with strips of lilac, forms a circle around the tomb, and from its outer edges shoot golden, sunlike rays ; also, like a halo of glory to Napoleon, is the inner circle, embossed with the names of his victorious battles—and, commemorative of some of those events, are twelve large statues, holding symbols, and tattered ensigns grouped above. Under the circular gallery hang the funeral lamps, whose flame should light up the gloom daily, instead of only once or twice annually, if but to bring out the beautiful bas-reliefs so deeply enshrouded in shadows. On a slab over the massive bronze gate, leading to the monument, is a dying wish of Napoleon, as expressed in his last testament—"*Je désire que mes cendres reposent sur les bords de la Seine, au milieu de ce peuple Français que j'ai tant aimé;*" and, near by, are two sarcophagi, to the memory of Marshals Duroc and Bertrand, his faithful followers in glory and misfortune, and, therefore, fit sentinels to guard the sacred spot. The high altar of Les Invalides is reached by ten steps, at the base of which are Cupids holding cornucopias. Spiral columns of black and white marble sustain a rich gold canopy, surmounted by a cross, and two little angels bear in their hands gilded palms, which meet to form a half-crown over the gold crucifix. The ceiling frescoes, above the altar, are rendered doubly attractive by the golden light that streams in through stained windows on the sides, bathing them with the *glory* that comes from the sky; and then the magnificent dome, resting on four arches, beams with pictured *glories*—the labors of some of the best masters. In this edifice there are other tombs besides that of Napoleon. Those of Turenne and Vauban are *chef d'œuvres*. The former represents the Marshal sinking in death, and Immortality, holding a gold crown, as the reward of a well spent life. At his feet stands the eagle of conquered Germany, with folded pinions. The cenotaph of Vauban, in the opposite transept, is surmounted by a reclining statue of the hero, and is surrounded by all the paraphernalia of State—the crown, the sceptre, books and flags. Genius and Prudence are the side statues. Jerome Napoleon's tomb is of black marble, with gilded garlands, in imitation of laurel, and with gold eagles at the side. That of Joseph Napoleon— very massive, but of extreme simplicity—consists of a block of green and white streaked marble, on which a wreath, in black marble, stands out in bold relief. Upon leaving the temple that enshrines so much monumental grandeur, and that deserves more than a passing word of praise, we were besieged by venders of books and medals. Brass and paper could not have better told the dead warrior's fame than the words of an old woman, who, parrot-like, kept repeating—"*Achetez un livre s'il vous plaît—Voici le portrait de l'homme le plus célèbre de la France, ou du monde.*" On our way home, we passed a small garden of refreshing shade, at one end of which was a restaurant, "*au petit moulin rouge*." At tables, under the trees, sat groups of thirsty mortals, holding huge mugs of Bavarian beer; but the morning being intensely warm, ice-water seemed to us much more desirable than a heating beverage.

The Hippodrome formed a part of the entertainment for the day, but the equestrian exercises were not more remarkable than many I had seen before. The arena being uncovered, the sun's hot rays proved quite as objectionable to the riders as to the audience. A liliputian jockey was thrown from his pony, and received some bruises on his head; an unfortunate result, inasmuch as the receipts of the box-office, we should judge, hardly amounted to a sum sufficient to pay for a surgeon's services. A woman performed many wonderful feats on the tight-rope, but the ascension of a balloon was a more interesting *feature*. Three trips were made to the regions of "thin air," and if our party had not been timid, we, too, might have enjoyed the salubrious change. Several friends expressed themselves satisfied with soaring aloft, the only unpleasant sensation they experienced being the swaying motion of the balloon before the start.

May 26.—Showers of rain, accompanied by thunder and lightning, brought gladness to the denizens of Paris this morning, serving, as they did, to lessen the intense heat, and to render an afternoon drive to the Bois the more agreeable. The Emperor was out in a small *coupé*, and showed less consideration for *state* than some of his

Y*

Ministers, who rode in splendid coaches with fine liv-
eries.   He looked quite pale, and there were furrows on
his brow that not even the bright sunshine and bland
breezes could efface.   We thought that, though he held
an empire in his grasp, he was not as free and happy
as we who were on our way to Pré Catelan, to drink
delicious milk, served by pretty waiting-girls, under
snow-white tents on the greensward.   Their costume is
very picturesque—a black skirt, a yellow cap, and a
scarlet corsage, open at the throat, to show a large black
cross suspended by a ribbon.   Indeed, they looked more
like Swiss or Italian peasants than French women,
which was, perhaps, owing to the absence of the universal white cap.   Their bronzed faces plainly told of
the *al fresco* life they lead.   Many happy young people
had alighted from carriages to sip of nature's sweets, and
several panting steeds, in the grove, impatiently champed
their bits, while the lithe, fair riders that had wielded
the whip, glided off to coquette with their escorts, and
to teach them the fatal power of beautiful eyes and hon-
eyed words.

This evening we went to the Cirque de l'Impératrice,
taking several juveniles, whose tiny hands went as busily
to work as those of the hired *claquers*, upon the appearance of a wee little girl on the tight-rope—Mlle. Chia-
rini—dressed as *La Fille du Régiment.*   Her performance was wonderful, and elicited frequent applause.
Bockrill, an American rider, made his *début*, and accomplished very successfully the feat of jumping through a
number of hoops with his ankles tied.   In *Le jeu des*

barres, Mmes. Thérèse, Sternath and Palmyre rode most
recklessly, their horses making such rapid turns as to
weary our eyes in the watching. A performance on the
violin by Mr. Price, burlesquing several operas—Trovatore and Lucia—was a rare combination of the "sublime and the ridiculous;" and I thought—Shall such
sweet notes be whined away any longer on a crazy string?
—will not Verdi himself appear somewhere in the crowd,
and cry out against the ridicule of his grand and melodious compositions? But the people are convulsed with
laughter, for, at one moment, louder goes the squeaking,
and, at the next, more tremulous goes the shake. Has it
ended in that slight whisper of sound? Pray keep on
awhile longer, to make us the more merry. Should the
immortal Beethoven walk in, I wager he would help us
to laugh. Next came *les jeux Icariens,* by Mr. Russel
and his two little boys, whom he handled like India-
rubber balls, leading us to think that circus performers
are differently made from ourselves, their bones seeming
to bend like whalebones, and their craniums to be possessed of wonderful elasticity, else why should that little
fellow be tossed across the ring, lighting on his head,
and still live to be tossed again? Grace and motion
certainly found their meaning this night in the performances held in the very pretty building named
for the fairest of women, the beautiful Empress. The
Indian fight, dashing and wild, caused me to turn away
solicitously from the dark red-skins to the little ones at
my side, who timidly shrank back at the sound of the
war-whoop, their roses vanishing in an instant, leaving

a marble-like pallor on their faces. Lastly, appeared the celebrated gymnast, Avolo; young, handsome, and finely developed. The close of the performance was a regret; but why deplore it, as entertainments are by no means scarce in this gay, volatile city, and hours die here to be born again with pleasures still more attractive.

May 30.—*Lost*, for the past two days, in a whirl of varying emotions at the Louvre, whose charms, like a love legend, haunt the memory!—for do not its walls a thousand times and more give the history of some heart-passion, some religious worship, some sad martyrdom, some mighty fame, some mental anguish, and some joy and happiness bright as the flowers of spring? What a charmed spell and delicious thraldom in the countless colors that stretch away and seem never to end, and out of which are woven images and shapes of noble beauty and perfect grace! So faithfully delineated are the subjects that we seem almost to breathe the blue air, to inhale the perfume of the flowers, to hear the whisper of a love strain, to catch the anguished cry of a broken heart, to look upon the writhing of the tortured body, to start at the trumpet-sound of war, and to weep over the still immobile features of the beautiful dead.

We found ourselves before the mournful, loving *Magdalene*, who gazes upon the cross as if ready to fall down in worship. It is her fond spirit's shrine where tearful woes are calmed, and where faithful trust is anchored, safe from the waves of passion. Other beautiful paintings are *St. Paul*, the devout apostle, in his lonely cell, wrapt with an expression of holy thought; *The Guardian Angel*, who turns the wayward feet of the sin-beset mortal to brightest hopes and heaven; *The Angels appearing to the Shepherds*—on the clouds they soar, invoking adoration for the " new-born babe," who is represented in a group with the Virgin and St. Joseph; *The Annunciation*, where Gabriel, bearing the white lily, holds communion with the Virgin—the " handmaid of the 'Lord "—to whom, on glad mission, come also the Holy Ghost and a host of angels; *Jesus Christ giving the Keys of His Church to His favored Servant, St. Peter*, who, in a kneeling attitude, in the midst of the apostles, receives the holy charge; *St. Sebastian*, suffering martyrdom—an arrow piercing his body; *Hercules killing the Hydra*, the monster rising in wrath against the descending club; and *Hercules on his Funeral Pyre*, offering himself to Heaven, his mighty earthly labors being ended. A joyously bright picture is *Cupid's triumph*, the young god sitting in his chariot, drawn by doves, who tread among flowers strewn by a winged child; he holds the arrow, so destructive to hearts, and smiles at the sight of it; and another gem is Murillo's *Beggar-boy*, so lazy, fat and saucy, with a jug and a basket of fruit at his side—a delicious treat for the hungry youth.

Rubens has admirably portrayed scenes in the life of Marie de Médicis, from her earliest youth to her death; and the spectator, following the glory and misfortune of the Queen, feels that life, unto the highest, sometimes brings less security against care and grief than promise

of pleasure and ease.   We first see the young Princess
in happy childhood, when Minerva presides over her
education, and she herself is under the influence of the
Gods and the Graces—next, Henry IV receiving her
portrait, and acquiescing in the behest of France to
enter into a matrimonial alliance,—then the proxy marriage scene before the altar of the church,—the landing of
the Queen at Marseilles,—the scene at Fontainebleau,
when a mother's joy is blended with a nation's delight
that an heir is born to the realm,—the voyage to Pont
de Cè, in Anjou, which city, through her agency, is conquered—she is mounted on a white steed, and wears a
helmet with white and green plumes—the flight of the
Queen, at night, from the castle of Blois, where she was
imprisoned by her son Louis XIII,—the reconciliation
with Louis XIII, and the Triumph of Truth, the latter
showing that in heaven there is union and pardon.
The Queen and her son are represented holding a medallion—two joined hands, and over them a heart.   From
the Flemish school we passed to another apartment, to
see the *Wedding at Cana*, by Paul Veronese; *The Immaculate Conception*, by Murillo; *The Last Supper*—
Vinci; *The Return of Marcus Sextus;* and the sad,
though ever attractive painting, *Atala in the Tomb.*   If
grief was ever poignantly portrayed, it is in that struggle
of Choctas against resigning the beautiful dead body of
Atala, and if the vanity of human life needed to be
strongly impressed upon the mind, it would speak from
that canvas, from the pale form, the marble-like hands
grasping the cross, and the inscription from the psalms

of David—" My days are like a shadow that declineth, and I am withered like grass." *Endymion sleeping !*—so peaceful and calm does he rest under the plane tree, that he seems not to heed the presence of Cupid, in the form of Zepherus, pushing aside the foliage, that the moon may look down kindly and lovingly. *Pysche receiving the first kiss of love !*—how beautiful is the goddess, invoking love, as she sits upon the mossy bank, with her arms clasped to her heart! Cupid might imprint a thousand kisses on her fair forehead, for the purity of her soul would keep him lingering on in the gentle wooing. Then to the war-like paintings we turned—the fray of Romulus with Tatius, and the Sabine women delivering up their offspring to the darts of the soldiery; the lictors bringing to Brutus the bodies of his sons; and the oath of the Horatii as the three brothers receive their weapons from the hands of their father.

June 1.—As a farewell to the flowery month of May, we passed yesterday at St. Cloud, where thousands had gathered to celebrate Whit-Sunday. Gazing at the château, none can fail to think of the important events that have transpired there, and of the many proud inmates that, like obscure mortals, have had finally to succumb to the power of fate or death. It was here that Henry III was assassinated ; that Queen Henrietta of England died ; that Napoleon expelled the Council of Five Hundred, laying the foundation of his future greatness; and that Charles X signed the fatal ordinances which brought about the Revolution of 1830. Here come up, also, the names of Josephine and Marie Antoinette, who esteemed the château a favorite residence; and the preference now given it by the Imperial family adds but another graceful charm to the olden interest. Some of the *salons* are hung with Gobelin tapestry, rich and beautiful, representing the same scenes in the life of Marie de Médicis that Rubens has given to the Louvre; but the Gallery of Apollo, the most gorgeous of all, is fitly named for the favorite god. A full length marble statue of the Empress Josephine looks cold and solemn amid the profuse gilding, the reflecting crystals, and rich paintings. The parks surrounding the château have much of the same ornamentation as Versailles and Fontainebleau,—flower-pots, statues, vases, fountains, and the picturesque rural attractions, water, woods and hills. Velocipede racing formed a prominent feature of the day's amusement, and, at the end of each course, a full band of music struck up a lively air. The crowd being uncomfortably great, we wandered off through the shady park, and, after a short stroll, found ourselves in the midst of a varied entertainment—a catch-penny, at every step, in Guignol or Polichinelle, fortune-telling, hurdy-gurdy, fandango, and what not. There was a little village of stalls, displaying articles of every description. Incongruous sounds from shouting venders, boisterous *gamins* and beating drums rent the air, and so harsh and discordant was the din that those who had a consideration for their nerves hastily retreated from the Bedlam. This was, indeed, a *melange*, characteristic of the French.

Returning to the town, we repaired to a favorite restaurant, elevated above the level of the street, and quite
ornamental in its terraced gardens, trained vines and
flowers. Some of the most exquisite moss-rose bushes
attracted our admiration, and the proprietor very gallantly presented us with a choice cluster of their fragrant
buds, in gratitude, perhaps, for the liberal order that had
been sent to his *Cuisine.* Time, that never hangs heavily
in this land, had vanished unawares, and when we left
our cosy little board, some straggling lights were to be
seen outside, and great was the reduction of the vast
crowd, that a few hours before had jostled about in the
bright sunshine. Some gay music beguiled us into a
building a few yards distant, where a country ball, with
its pell-mell, grotesque dancing was taking place.
Femmes de chambre, Cuisinières, and sturdy lads, in short
jackets and tight breeches, tripped over the saw-dust as
contentedly as fastidious dancers would over a polished
floor. Many spectators sat around the ring, paying
nothing for keeping quiet; but those who "made merry,'
on the toe and heel, were asked to hand over a few *sous*
to a man who went around collecting, with a fathomless
hat, and a jabbering tongue. Towards nine o'clock,
strolling in the gardens of the château, we were gratified by the fulfilment of our wish, that the sky would
frown its blackest, or conceal its every star, in order to
favor the grand pyrotechnic display that was to come
off a few moments later; and, when it began, the glare
of light revealed to our astonished eyes thousands of
persons who had patiently lingered to witness the beau-

z

tiful spectacle. The Cascade of St. Cloud, so architec-
turally grand, with its statues, tablets, urns, dolphins
and shell-work, was even more beautiful under the
influence of a shower of fire than of water, for the marbles seemed to be imbued with life by the reflected
colors, together with the crimson, green and blue tints
that occasionally flashed upon them through the vistas
of the dark background. At intervals, Bengal-lights, in
sapphire beauty, burst high up in the air, and others
scattered down gold upon us like the fabled Danaë
shower. Honors, it would seem, are paid to Napoleon
everywhere, and in every shape, and he was not forgotten
on this occasion, the initial *N* glistening in the centre of
a laurel wreath, around which fell a diamond-like spray.
The hovering eagle, a part of the beautiful design, refused to fade as quickly as did the rest, for, after turning
away, we caught, for some minutes, a view of its gilded
talons. The programme of the evening ended with a
torchlight procession, accompanied by delightful music.
The town was illuminated with colored lanterns, whilst
from posts, arches and doorways hung garlands, wreaths
and other flowery devices. Thus we passed from a
blaze of brightness, floating banners, mirthful sounds,
and shortly afterwards found ourselves in Paris, at an
hour when *cochers* sigh for a night-cap, and other folks
for the luxury of an eider-down pillow.

June 2.—Poetry should coin a new and graceful word
of praise for the entertainment that has been given by
Baron de la T——; and we, who have read of a " Feast

of lights and a Bower of roses," can attest that it is not
fancy alone that invents bewitching scenes.   Last evening was a bright and beautiful reality—*salons* festooned
with rare exotics; walls draped with faint rose-colored
silk and soft lace; a huge pyramid of bouquets in the
centre of a room, dropping as if by magic touch its
flowery favors into the hands of fair dames and damsels;
delicious music stealing in from a balcony garlanded
with nature's green ; waxen tapers beaming and lighting
up smiles of beauty and forms of grace; the banquet
rich as an Oriental Feast, with rare delicacies; fruits
mingling their gold, purple, crimson and pink; variegated ices, in the forms of flowers and cupids, resting on
frozen pinnacles, and doomed to short life, for suddenly
the lily and the tulip vanish, and the God of Love is
ruthlessly decapitated to please a Psyche near at hand;
lastly, the sprinkle of all such *fêtes*, the rosy champagne,
that tells, with its glow and sparkle, much more of enchanting France than we who write after the goblet is
drained and the ball ended.   The June heat must soon
terminate *les soirées dansantes!*

CHAPTER XIX.

HOW sumptuous is the Luxembourg Palace! Beginning with the lone ornament of the *Salle des Cent Gardes*—the life-size marble statue of Jeanne Hachette, with its firm, proud and heroic air—and continuing on to *salons*, where the regal taste of Marie de Médicis still lingers, we feel that we are under some magical guidance, and are not soon to see the end of lavish splendor. Nowhere is this feast more abundantly grand than in the *Salle du Trône*, with golden beauty flashing from ceiling and wall; with the history of France, embracing some of its early epochs, and extending up to the present rule, glowingly set in the artists' colors—with the magnificently decorated Throne, where sat the first Napoleon, and the superb statues, representing the four principal powers of Europe. The gallery of Busts presents a distinguished array of statesmen and generals; and the Cabinet of the Emperor furnishes several historical scenes in the life of Napoleon I; besides two of more recent interest, the triumphal entry of Napoleon III, into Paris, after being proclaimed Emperor, at St. Cloud—flowers strew his pathway; banners wave above his head; music and fair lips send forth a welcoming shout,—and

the marriage of Eugenie.   Beauty's spell always hovers
o'er a nuptial scene, and holy tenderness freights the hour
when the most sacred of all obligations is blessed on
earth, and "registered in heaven."   The Senate Chamber, with its sedate, legislative air, and wood-work of
carved oak, is in sombre contrast with the glittering
grandeur of the rest of the Palace, but it has some bright
features in the allegorical paintings of Law, Justice,
Patriotism and Wisdom; the two large side pictures by
Blondel, and the statues of Charlemagne and St. Louis.
The public are always excluded from this chamber
during the debates.   Descending the staircase, the visitor enters a little room, which is graced with the celebrated picture of *Christ on the Cross*, by Philippe de
Champagne, valued at two hundred thousand francs.
Four or five artists have recently been engaged in copying it.   One young man, to-day, was bending over
another pensive subject, *The Mater Dolorosa*, on whose
face there dwells an agony of grief, the sullying shade
to beauty's brightness.   How many of earth's children
wear, like this holy mother, the stamp of suffering, and
carry like a dove with bruised wing, the smart and burden
of a wound!   The bed-chamber of Marie de Médicis—
sans lit—is profusely ornamented, the doors being tinted
in gold, with gay colored designs.   The exquisite medallion paintings around the wall, are by Nicholas Poussin and Phillipe de Champagne.   Rubens has *crowned*
the Queen with all the glory of his brush, as she looks
down from the plafond in majestic state; and we, who
gaze upon her, irresistibly say, Oh! fatal mirage—ye

z*

gilded thrones and jeweled crowns! Oh! deceitful, flattering voice of power, out of whose melody come groans and weeping, and sorrow's curse! What vicissitudes have marked the career of this woman! Here she dwelt in the magnificence of station, treading a bright, velvety path, and foreseeing no shadow, or stumbling-block in the future; but sunny smiles and joyous hopes are fleeting, for now the scene shifts, and there appears a lone garret at Cologne, where rags, poverty and obscurity take the place of regal grandeur, and finish the last act in the drama of life. The chapel, although not covering much space, contains a few large paintings, representing the Samaritan labors of the Apostle Philip, the clemency of St. Louis, the Marriage of the Virgin, and St. Louis in Palestine. But the statue of the Guardian Angel, and two little children, hewn out of a single block of marble, is the most engrossing object of art.

The gallery of paintings, in the eastern wing of the palace, is very creditable to our contemporary artists; and, in singling out Rosa Bonheur and Eugène Delacroix for the largest meed of praise, we do not mean to depreciate other artists, some of whom are quite up to their high standard. Subjects of the remote past and of the present blend like the colors of a kaleidoscope, and of the great variety may be named *The Glorification of St. Louis; The Levite of Ephraim* finding the dead body of his wife, who fell a victim to the tribe of Benjamin; *The Death of Cæsar*, with Mark Antony carrying the bloody mantle among the Romans; *The Death of Cleopatra; The Kiss of Judas; Le Mont de Piété*—pawnbrokers; *Jane Shore* reviled as sorceress by the London populace; *Raphael at the Vatican; Homer Deified; St. Cecilia's Body* being carried into the Catacombs; and the graceful *Psyche*, leaving hell with the box for Venus. Cerberus stands at the entrance, formidable and uninteresting, beside the lovely figure draped in white, with flowing, golden locks and blue wings. Another picture, heart-rending to behold, is the *Incendiary Scene*, representing a family cut off from escape—a mother holds her babe, and two older children cling to her knees, terror-struck at the flames bursting through a half-open door; the husband, at an open window, is driven back by the volumes of smoke. There is an adjoining gallery devoted to sculpture—groups and single statues. Of the former the most attractive are *The Mother of the Gracchi*—firm, loving and true; *The Infancy of Bacchus*—Pan holding aloft the young god; and *Agrippina and Caligula*. The grace, dignity and courage portrayed in the last statue, strike very agreeably the spectator. She is leaving the tent of her husband, Germanicus, with her child in her arms; and, again, she is taking her departure from Syria for Rome, carrying her husband's ashes. Of the single figures, the most beautiful are— *Minerva*, after the judgment of Paris; *Truth;* the tearful, grief-stricken *Ariadne; Psyche; A Young Girl confiding her first secret to Venus* — for love must make known its joy; and *To Seem and To Be*, in which the mask is introduced.

From the palace we went to the Madelaine. Standing in front of its elevated and noble portico, where column after column rises in Grecian beauty, and ornate sculpture stamps the majestic *façade*, we could but unite in the universal opinion that it is, *par excellence*, the classic church of Paris. The massive bronze doors—after the style of which our national Capitol at Washington has lately received an adornment—are illustrative of the ten commandments. On entering, we first see the fine marble groups of *The Baptism of Christ* and *The Marriage of the Virgin*; and then we move on to the centre of the vast nave, impressed with a spirit of the beautiful, and deriving a holy lesson from arabesques and paintings that tell of the Evangelists and Apostles, of martyrs and saints. The high altar, with the figure of Mary Magdalen, redeemed from the sins and sorrows of earth, and carried on angel wings to Paradise, and the Archangels at prayer, accord with, if they do not surpass, the other marbles that incrust the walls of the side chapels. Everywhere in this temple-shrine is there a claim to admiration, and it may be very aptly quoted, " I could not one moment live the guest of such a scene without the springs of prayer overflowing all my soul."

The church of St. Germain l'Auxerrois engages special interest, its site being one of the ancient landmarks of the city—a religious shrine sacked by the ruthless hand of the Normans, in 886. Reconstructed more than a hundred years later, and taking its present name, it rose rapidly to distinction, and, by degrees, grew into royal favor. It has passed through the trials of insurrection, and it gave that dread and mournful signal, in 1572, which carried out the atrocity and dissimulation of

Queen Catherine's plot. Now, the visitor sees this church with the mist of erring fate cast aside, where the public go to worship in quiet devotion. Deep in its recesses has the prodigal hand of art scattered beauties, and from window, aisle and altar, we have Christ before us, and the ministrations of saints. In the chapel, dedicated to the Lady of our Compassion, is a magnificent specimen of carved wood, in altar form. A gothic altar, illuminated, is in another chapel, the painted windows of which are exceedingly rich, one being by the celebrated Amaury Duval.

St. Roch, one of the most beautiful, if not the most costly of church edifices, is deeply interesting in its several associations with the revolutions of Paris, if only to name the occasion, when the excited mob gathered on its broad steps to witness Marie Antoinette led to execution. Eighteen chapels abound in paintings and marbles, and bas-reliefs in plaster, portraying scenes in the life of Jesus and the Saints. St. Augustin, St. André, St. Denis, St. Geneviève, St. Léon—*le Grand*—and St. Marcel are perhaps the most admirably exalted in sculpture and colors. The altar, most curiously wrought—a blaze of golden light, shooting off into rays which lose themselves in dark clouds—has for its ornament, the figure of the Infant Jesus in swaddling clothes, attended by Mary and Joseph. Tablets and monuments also find a place at St. Roch, and the one which most eloquently appeals to the heart of the visitor, is " *à l'Abbé de l'Epée,*" showing the gratitude of the deaf and dumb for the founder of their institution of learning. The chapel of

Calvary, adjoining the church, is a faithful, yet *triste*
representation of the name it bears. In a niche, mid-
way between the floor and ceiling, there is a cross, with
the figure of the Savior and the two Mary's—the sunlight streaming down upon them—and in lower niches
are plaster carvings, illustrating the passion of our Lord.
A sepulchre, constructed of rough stone, completes the
sorrowful scene.

June 4.—This day has been warm enough to make
idlers of all persons, except those whom necessity com-
pels to labor by the sweat of the brow. I remain at
home, with no other occupation than to gaze from the
balcony at the promenaders, and then to lounge in a
comfortable arm-chair. Armand, the bright-faced little
boy of our *concierge*, makes his appearence in a straw
hat, with a band of sky-blue ribbon, and brings me for
"*un petit cadeau*" a basket of strawberries and a bunch
of roses. Lucie, the *bonne*, has left off her black serge
dress, and donned a figured lawn. The hair-dresser,
needing to be refreshed, treats his handkerchief to a
shower of cologne from one of the bottles he has offered
us for sale, and even the cook leaves the kitchen-range,—
that "furnace of affliction,"—thinking *charbon* a dreadful thing, and asks Madame for "*un peu de glace*,"
which is cheerfully given her. Old Mr. R—, who,
every day, paces up and down the Champs Elysées, with
gray overcoat, and always looks so thin and cold, is
actually using a fan, and wipes his face, and stops to
blow. Mlle. G— lies back in her open *landau*, and

holds her parasol with the air of an *ennuyée;* Mme. H—
wears no longer her velvet hat and bird of Paradise,
but a leghorn trimmed with daisies; and the *Professeur
de Chant,* excused from a lesson at our number, says
adieu with inimitable grace, knowing that he can go
off and sing the song of *"Je suis libre."*

We did not venture out until the sun had gone
soundly to sleep, and then the beautiful, starry night,
led us down in the direction of Avenue Montaigne, where
our eyes were dazzled by the brilliancy of some gas-jets
that spelled out the word *Mabille.* Shall we go in
among the lights and flowers, groves and grottoes, where
Terpsichore is throwing a spell over the evening hours?
Yes!—this little syllable never seeming more mischievously disposed—we entered by an avenue softly lighted,
that lay under arching foliage, and arrived shortly afterwards in the crowded circle, just to the left, where flying
feet were pulsing the air with that vibratory motion,
which, once seen, is never forgotten. But the magical
beauty of the scene! At our feet, on mossy beds, glimmered numerous lights, some of the Tyrian dye, and
others springing from the hearts of tulips and roses. All
that was needed was the presence of a fairy, who might
whisper, "Thou shalt stray among flowers, and thy footsteps be lighted." Moore wrote of a summer *fête,* and
Mabille has realized his dream.

> " Here shone a garden—lamps all o'er,
> As though the spirits of the Air
> Had tak'n it in their heads to pour
> A shower of summer meteors there ;"
>   *   *   *   *   *   *

> " Lamps, with young flowers beside them bedded,
>   That shrunk from such warm neighborhood;
>   And, looking bashful in the flood,
>   Blush'd to behold themselves so wedded."

This scene lacked a limpid lake, but, in other respects, was so charming that softer music than the harsh fiddle and clarionet was looked for,—some witching, gentle harmony from lyre or harp ; the song of the bird or the voice of a fay. And yet, where were the nymphs? Hidden, perhaps, in the lonely grotto ! The *demoiselles* that meet here wear not the semblance of etherial life, but are solid enough to rush—as the battle cry says— "To arms, to arms !"—for into such do they bound, yet linger not; and to follow them through their numerous darts and poises would be more difficult than to work out a problem of Euclid. No ballet costume is allowed at this garden, the short walking dress prevailing ; though, occasionally, a trailing robe may be observed sweeping the green lawn, where mademoiselle sits down to a tiny wine-glass, bending o'er its contents with dancing eyes and merry words. The band performed the *Œil Crevé* with brilliant effect, and, if the lookers-on could scarcely keep their dignified feet still, imagine the excitement of the spirited *danseuses*. Following the peculiar mazes of the dance, my vein of thought ran to the measure of that old familiar rhyme—" This is the house that Jack built." This is the white and ruffled skirt that meets the boot, that covers the foot, that France alone knows how to use; and here is the girl that raises that foot, to kick at a hat, to strike at the

stars, or set the clouds in motion. This is *Mabille*, and
here is *Ma Belle*, and where will you stop on the end of
your toes? With another leap to Egypt you'll fly, but
dance once more ere you say good-bye. If this is demoralization, we are out of the giddy round in a little
while—we have only looked at the gay *Parisiennes*, in a
fairy-like scene; and what avails our opinion against
that of the merriest city of the world, whose supreme
aim is *amusement*, and which would order our arrest for
stern, philosophic advice, and the repudiation of that
which she loves most. Therefore, adieu to the idols we
cannot break down! At 12 o'clock, to-day, our party
further explored the Louvre, passing in review the
Egyptian, Grecian and Roman museums, with their
wealth of olden and curious treasure. What a huge
memory to bring away!—the tombs and sarcophogi of
past ages, from the sphynx size to the pigmy fragment—
the Italian and French earthenware and pottery—the
models and patents—the drawings, pastels, miniatures,
enamels, and the myriad things that the whole world,
it appears, has contributed, no more to be counted than
the sands of the ocean! The frescoed ceilings, whose
beauteous tints seem to have been stolen from the pea-
cock, overspread all these collections, antique and modern,
just as the coronet, that glistens on the brow of the king,
gives the highest beauty to the rest of his gorgeous
apparel. Especially in the *Salle des Souverains*, is the
visitor prone to linger longest among the relics of monarchs, and of famous women, some of whom have reigned
in glory, then suffered and died. The mind busily runs

AA

from period to period, associating events with the articles closely grouped, the most interesting of which are the suits of armor, numbering six or seven—the sword and sceptre of Charlemagne, who was so renowned in conquest, so just and good a monarch; and the chair of Dagobert, reminding the spectator, that since the Merovingian sovereign sat there, twelve hundred years have been added to the history of France. Then, there are two prayer books—by whom were they used? The eyes of fair Marguerite of Valois have wandered over the pages of one, and the sorrowful Marie Stuart found religious solace in the other. There is the mirror, set around with agates, cameos and emeralds, that reflected the face of Marie de Médicis; but the saddest things of all, are the old black silk shoe of Marie Antoinette, and her farewell letter to Mme. Elizabeth, the words of which send a sympathetic thrill through the heart of every reader. Of the numerous memorials in the room dedicated to Napoleon I, none impressed us more than the cradle of his son, the King of Rome. What must have been the joy of this ambitious man, when he saw fulfilled the hope of long years,—that hope which induced him to silence the voice of conscience; to forget love's tender pleadings, and to banish from the throne a true and noble wife! But alas! how soon did Waterloo's gory strife sunder the fabric of that cherished dream! We stopped a few moments at the Church of St. Clotilde, inaugurated in the year 1857, but the description of churches is so much of a repetition, that allusion shall only be made to the exquisite painted windows, after

the designs of Amaury Duval and Galimard, and the
bells that comprise a whole octave, and whose music is
sweeter than that of any other chimes in Paris. An
hour of this serene and pleasant day was devoted to the
Artillery museum, where our footsteps led through
cannon, cast-iron coast and siege-ordnance, fire-arms of
every description, and various trophies of battle. On
viewing, in an enclosed space outside, some monster
specimens, we conjured up scenes of the siege of Sebastopol, and pictured the fearful havoc that had been made
there by those dread engines of war. In the *Salle des
Modèles*, with a fond American eye, we descried the
Maynard rifles, close by the arms of Britannia; and a
glow of pride was felt at seeing here the famous breech-
loading gun of one of our countrymen, whose talents in
other departments of science and art have won substantial recognition from several of the crowned heads of
Europe. The saloon of armor contains every implement
of war—helmets, shields, coats of mail and weapons,
some of which belong to the Merovingian age. One
suit of armor, owned by a Marshal of France, dates
back to 1556; and there are many others that were
worn by brave and distinguished men. Glass cases
enclose some of the most curious and costly objects of
centuries ago, a few of the fire-arms being set in precious
stones, and others being inlaid and wrought in silver
and gold. After leaving this place, we took the boat
on the Seine, and made a pleasant little trip to the
Jardin des Plantes, which is one of the bright, lovely
spots of Paris. It has other attractions than the nursery,

for, besides the botanical garden and the conservatories
—one of which abounds in aquatic plants—there is a me-
nagerie and a museum of anatomy. The first anatomical
study that met our eye, on the ground-floor, was a whale,
whose skeleton showed capacity sufficient to have accom-
modated at least half a dozen *Jonahs;* and, up-stairs,
were dissections of all the animal kingdom, from the
mightiest work of God's creation, to the reptile that
crawleth on the earth, and the bird that fendeth the
clouds. The mummies, fossil-remains, and skulls came
next in order, but, having no love for Hottentot blackness, or "dead men's bones"—however refined the
race,—we passed on to a gallery, containing some things,
a little less abominable—hyenas, porcupines, and apes,—
and were not sorry to escape from them as soon as it
was practicable. With a friendly pressure did our feet
touch the greensward, it being pleasant to get out among
the flowers; to look upon the little artificial stream,
meandering through the grounds, and to walk around
and among the netted compartments that held the birds
and the parrots, the chickens and the doves, and all the
contributions, it would seem, that had helped to make
up Noah's ark. Kindly glances were bestowed upon
the little frisking deer, the goats, and all that there
was of gentle make; and then, we went on a few yards
further to see grum, ugly bears, and such wild beasts as
acknowledge the presence of visitors with a growl and
a clutch.

As we took our departure, by the gate, a soda-fount
was refreshingly revealed, with a sparkling vanilla drop

to quench our thirst, and prepare us for further fatigue
at the *Buttes de Chaumont.* The sun had just set when
we reached this park, which differs so widely from others
of Paris, in the wild grandeur of its natural scenery.
Of the few ornaments, thus far added, is a quiet lake,
with a suspension bridge, in airy height, and some leafy
bowers, one of which we selected to take dinner in,—
being obliged to look after the material life, although we
should not have starved on romance. Afterwards, ascending higher and higher with every step, and by dint
of perseverance, we reached a rocky mount, and stood
in the little Temple of Sibyl, where, under the charm of
its name, we might have imagined ourselves at Athens
or Tivoli, had there not prevailed in our minds a thought
of those sanguinary days in the history of France when
this same spot and the environs gave fierce battle, and
the gallows and grave-pits cut off hundreds of men and
women. Here, also, did Catherine de Médicis and
Charles IX—accompanied by a gay cortége—come to
see, hanging on a gibbet, the mangled body of Admiral
de Coligny, one of the victims of the St. Bartholomew
tragedy. This remorseless woman, only a few hours
before, had gazed upon the head, that had been cut off
by an Italian, and carried to her at the palace. Not
content with the terrible sight, she lent her presence to
the scene where fiends in human shape were yelling and
dancing around the remains of the venerable martyr.
It would seem that the acts of atrocity here perpetrated
should almost forbid the place to smile in verdure; but,
to-day, all was bright and lovely, calm and peaceful,—

AA*

the grass growing, the flowers blooming, where were formerly reeking, gory trenches; and the breeze wafting our light words, that once bore the sound of lamentations. True it is that though "states fall,—arts fade," and man passeth away, "nature doth not die." From the heights, a charming panorama of forty leagues lies spread out before the eye. As we viewed it, a misty veil hung over the splendid city of Paris, the bosom of the Seine, and the many little nestling villages around; yet, the landscape did not seem to lose much of its beauty by the mellowed aspect it presented. Leaving the upland view, we descended to the rock-grotto, and rested awhile under its stalactite arch. Our route home was by the circular railway that belts around so much of interesting space.

CHAPTER XX.

June 5.

TO-DAY we journeyed five miles from Paris, and visited the ancient abbey church, consecrated in honor of that great Christian martyr, St. Denis. Various sovereigns helped to restore and add to the original chapel, that was built centuries ago, designing that within its walls their ashes should rest in undisturbed slumber; and thus, the long range of a thousand years converted the spot into a vast sepulchre. If ever a desecrating mandate went out from council or convention, it was the one of 1793, when the tombs of this edifice were thrust open, and bones and ashes were disinterred that should only have been summoned forth at the last great day. Thus did rash man decree that Princes, who had worn the proudest of crowns, should no longer sleep in peace, but be hurled into a common trench, as unbefitting to their rank as the order to disentomb them was sacrilegious and wicked. Who that beholds the antiquated monuments, in their defaced condition, does not denounce and deplore the scourge that made these places empty, and ruined these sacred shrines? Interesting as is this church, in its ancient and royal associations, it has an additional claim in the possession of the remains of

Louis XVI and Marie Antoinette, that lie in the under-croft.   Verily do we stand above the dust of these un-fortunate ones, who suffered so keenly for the errors of their people; but vacant are the tombs of Dagobert and his consort, Nanthilde; the superb monuments of Louis XII and Anne of Brittany, with effigies and kneeling statues; and the still grander tomb of Henry II and Catherine de Médicis.   It seems strange that this Queen, who planned so much suffering for others to bear, should have been represented so perfectly placid in feature. One might say, in looking at the calm, composed face, "There was nothing cruel in that woman's nature;" and yet history leaves upon the fair marble the crimson stain of blood.   A side chapel contains some rich treasures, excellent paintings, and a massive plate of steel filled with figures executed with wonderful merit.   Everywhere about the building does the work of restoration go on, and what with the obstructions incidental thereto, and the hurried steps of the guide, many of the minute de-tails of art were lost to us.   Louis Napoleon, like his illustrious uncle, will continue lavishly to expend from the coffers of France, so as to make this edifice a fitting burial-place for Imperial dead; and it has been rumored that Les Invalides may yet give up to St. Denis the revered dust of him whose last wish was that his "ashes might repose on the borders of the Seine."

After a ramble through the town, decidedly uninter-esting, we stopped at a little garden near the station, and enjoyed for awhile the green shrubbery.   Strange to say, there were no flowers in bloom; but a pleasant surprise awaited me at home, in the gift of some beautiful magnolias and roses.

June 6.—A pleasant drive, this morning, with some English friends, brought me to Sèvres, a village very ancient in appearance, founded in 560, and whose principal attraction, at the present day, is the porcelain manufactory, of whose splendid treasure the government may well be proud. Some of the rooms display specimens of rare beauty, from colossal vases and table-services, down to the tiniest article, the exquisite painting of which will tell of hours expended to make it the perfect gem. Here are to be found faithful copies of some of the *chefs d'œuvre* of Raphael and Michael Angelo, and so smoothly delicate and beautiful are these porcelains, that canvas, ever grand and noble, seems, for the moment, to yield the palm to the newer art. Titian and Guido are also imitated with a mellowness that is like summer twilight, lovely to behold. Prices are fabulous, a single picture commanding from forty to fifty thousand francs; but what is glittering gold, compared to the possession of that beautiful Psyche, whose beauty, dwelling at Sèvres, will haunt us when we are more than a thousand leagues away? The ladies of our party were interested in some charming little articles of *bijouterie*, particularly a brooch of porcelain with a tiny rooster on it, that looked as if he were ready to crow; yet, when we were forced to say "good-bye" to chanticleer, he did n't utter a single cry. Doubtless the charm of these choice specimens dies out with many a visitor, when he reaches the workshop and sees the process of manufacture—the rough clay; the whirling tables; and the workmen, in blouse, moulding into divers shapes the plastic material. Not so with us, as the various means employed in making these crude things reach the goal of perfection rather interested our inquiring minds; and our pleasure was certainly enhanced by the accommodating spirit of several of the artisans, who made cups and saucers, plates and vases, and a little of everything, for our benefit. Holding a special permit from the Minister of State, we left no part of the establishment, even to the furnaces, unseen. In the museum there was a large collection of earthenware and pottery; foreign specimens of every design, shape and size; stained glass, enameled metals, and a good deal more that must be left unmentioned. In the gallery, where sat the busy painters, with vases and plates strewn around them, dwells my most faithful memory. A gray-haired old man, with feeble frame, raised up for a moment's rest from work,—his brush glided away from the petals of a delicate flower, and a sort of greeting smile lit up the wan eyes at a word or two of praise from me,—a tribute to the genius that was evidently making a vast sacrifice of health; and at what price? It ought to be princely, thought I, and may it at least be comfortable under Imperial patronage! * *

To-night being warm enough to favor out-door strolls, we repaired to a *café chantant*, on the Champs Elysées. Like all Americans, we evince something of a breakneck spirit to sieze at all kinds of entertainment, in the shortest possible time, mixing the serious with the frivolous; passing from solemn shrines and classic art, to scenes of mirth and buffoonery. So it goes in Paris! We weep at one moment, and laugh at the next. The poet writes

> "Pleasures are like poppies spread,
> You sieze the flower—the bloom is shed,"

—so is the charm of our amusements here very soon gone. An orderly crowd,—the *bourgeoisie*, had gathered at this place, and no noise was heard, save the murmur of conversation, half lost in space and air, or some animated applause, occasionally called forth by the eccentricities of the performers. What a melange of entertainment did the brilliant Kiosk afford! Singing, skating, dancing, recitations and dialogue. The duet, with a male and female voice, in imitation of fighting cats, was inimitable, and so was the skating of a *demoiselle*, clad *à la Polonaise*, who pirouetted equal to Fanny Essler. Admission is free to all this merry show, but those who play the fiddle, and dance to its music, expect every one to lay out a reasonable sum in beer and ices, which are served by garçons, who trip around with a speed and a spirit peculiar to this people, and which cannot be improved upon. If one is not much refreshed by what he has eaten or drunk, he, at least, goes away in a *good humor*—the great promoter of comfortable sleep—being that much happier than some of his neighbors, for all the world is not so privileged as to be able to lounge at a *café chantant*, in the beautiful month of June, with stars overhead, and music in the air.

June 7.—The grand races took place at the Bois to-day, the prizes amounting to more than a hundred thousand francs. Their majesties, the Prince Imperial, and other dignitaries were present, and added much to the interest of the scene.

June 8.—We marshalled our forces, *i. e.*, our little remaining strength, at 11 A. M., for the *Gobelins*, purposing to include the world-renowed tapestry among the sights that battle so hard now with the fast-speeding hours; but, upon a slight eminence, the factory stood as formidable as the castle of the giant that Jack killed, and the guard at the gates, as cross as that same ogre, who "smelled the blood of an Englishman "—only, this time it was not *un Anglais*, pleading for admission, but a German Baron, more eloquent than politic. Not even the charms of a comely English maiden, one of our party, could do aught towards gaining entrance: we had mistaken the day, and soon discovered that rules and regulations in this country, rarely ever yield to the most persistent entreaties. Politeness is a predominent element of French character, and the omission of it, on this occasion, shall be excused, in consideration of the courtesy that is usually shown to the stranger. The best remedy for a disappointment is a search for something else, and it were well, indeed, if all could find consolation as did the fisherman of old, who lost his pearl, yet wasted no time in weeping, because he believed that the sea would soon yield him another. With this reflection, we turned away, and went to the *Chapelle*

Expiatoire, where glowing worsted colors soon faded out of the imagination before the pale, cold marble, sadly commemorative of Louis XVI and his Queen. Over this little chapel, erected to their memory by Louis XVIII, will forever hang the shadow of their terrible fate; and a bitter thought must arise from those, who, bending o'er the sculptured stone, read the last instructions of Marie Antoinette to the Princess Elizabeth. It is a farewell, wrung from a breaking heart, in the severance of earthly ties, but withal, shows the firm spirit that sustained her in the closing scenes of life—"stern endurance conquering fate." Her figure is mournful and beautiful, as, kneeling, she extends her arms towards an angel. The opposite monument, of the king, represents him sustained by religion, and bears on its base an inscription of his last testament. A few moments were spent in the subterranean chapel, in contemplation of the hallowed ground, whither the bodies of these sovereigns were brought direct from the guillotine, and consigned to a most obscure sepulture, in order that they might be saved from desecrating hands. Here their ashes rested for twenty-one years, and were then transferred with all becoming pomp to St. Denis, which sad ceremonial scene the visitor will find represented in a bas-relief in the upper chapel, near by the monuments. No day is allowed to pass without some religious recognition of the sanctity that clothes the precincts. Other victims of the revolution, including the faithful Swiss guards, also found burial in the adjacent ground,—once the grave-yard of the Madclaine. Tread lightly, stranger,

BB

over this greensward, for under its mantle hath lain embosomed many a sleeper, to whom memory still loves to pay her sacred tribute.   *   *   *   *   *

Such balmy nights as these are sure to beguile to a promenade or drive. Somewhere on the way to the Latin Quarter, we came across several rag-pickers, who were industriously raking among the piles of rubbish in front of shops and houses. Stop we must, to see a member of this Bohemian class, wondering if, with his long.hook, he would extract anything of value from such a mass of rags, bones, broken china, etc. With lantern close to the ground, he seemed determined to discover something worth carrying off, and at last, found a piece of iron, and a half smoked cigar. He cannot make much by the sale of the former, but the latter, although taken from the filthy garbage, may give him some comfort when he sits down at home to overhaul his basket. What a sorry occupation, yet, it is extensively followed in its several orders, which embrace the poor, miserable raker of the river-banks; the shabby Diogenes—too poor to own a basket—with a coarse sack thrown over his shoulders; and those of more decent appearance, the labors of one of whom we watched with some curiosity and interest! These *chiffoniers* are mysterious beings, prowling about in the silence and darkness of the night; and, during the hours when sleep befriends the couch of the man of luxury and riches, they are gathering the crumbs that have fallen from his table, and the refuse of his mansion. As insignificant as this class might seem, these ragged wretches—possessed of passions like

other men, yet, exercised with less reason and fore-
thought,—can render themselves very powerful, even to
the overthrow of the dominions of their opulent brothers
—and how?   The changeful tide in the affairs of France
affords them, now and then, an opportunity to make
themselves objects to be greatly feared.   In a revolution,
they rush forward to pillage, aye, even murder.   Their
bent and stooping forms are straightened and strengthened to the work of destruction; and then, truly, are
the manacles of *les misérables* placed upon the tender
hands of aristocracy.   We hear of singular reverses in
the lives of persons all over the world, but they are
more observable here; especially, when it is told that
men of the position of a marquis, and of professional
title, and women of beauty and intelligence, have fallen
into this low condition.   It will only sadden my lady-
readers to draw a picture of one of our own sex, reduced
to so miserable a state,—to tell of delicate features hard-
ened, and soft complexion marred and bloated; of fair
hands stained with the mud of the streets,—therefore, I
throw a veil over the sepulchre of the hopes that must
have perished in some hearts that loved her, and leave
unrevealed the inscription of so unhappy a fate.   .*   *

Another phase of Parisian amusement!   What shall
be said of the *danseuses* at *Closerie de Lilas*, and the
frolicsome students, who, by hundreds, are throwing
themselves away physically, if not morally in the frantic
whirl?   This is the student's ball, his hope and aim
after the hours that he has devoted during the day to
medicine, law or art.   He is the dignified, intellectual
man whilst the sun shines, but, when, at the hour of

9 P. M., he lights his cigar, and struts off to this resort, he seems altogether another individual, looking only for recreation in a swing, a bound, a twist, and every kind of antic wild and grotesque. Gazing at all this wonderful twirling, we might ask if any bones have been broken, or if that youth has dealt with so many dead bodies, that he imagines his own sinew and muscle have no longer a spring of life to be snapped or injured. This place has not the beauty of *Mabille* in its ornamentation. The attire, too, of the girls who dance here, is less pleasing than that seen at the other garden; but the true coquetry of the nation is not missing—discernible in the toss of the head, the mincing laugh, the flash of the eye, the sprightly air,—and may be as harmless as it is attractive, if only like *les fleurs passagères*. From the Moorish-like hall or gallery, designed for winter use, one may look down upon this strange, comical scene, and make his own reflections. He will observe numerous *gensdarmes*, and soldiers pacing to and fro; for the government eye watches very closely over this mirthful quarter, lest the students, exhilarated beyond the dance, bring stern politics into the arena—yet, why should they do so, when they have bright eyes, beer, and cigarettes to regale themselves with?

June 9.—Breakfast at 6 A. M.,—and in Paris! The record is startling to myself, and will doubtless be discredited by friends. The fashion here is a *déjeûner*, at noon, that makes life seem very lazy, easy and luxurious. This morning, for the first time since my arrival, I saw the sun emerge out of the gray shadows, and kiss into light the sky ; and the air came refreshing and grateful, after the excessive fatigue and late hours of the last few weeks. A party of three of us started for the chapel of St. Ferdinand, and, in passing numbers of men and women on their way to the workshop, and the sewing room, it occurred to us, that they were not so unfortunate, as they are represented, for does not their early rising give to them the freshness and purity of the morning air,— a boon unknown to the *paresseuse ?* Whilst waiting for a carriage on the route, we overheard the following conversation between two *femmes de chambre : " Nannette, comment se porte Madame G— ? On m'a dit qu'elle etait malade."* *"Oh ! non ! vous vous trompez,—pas malade, mais elle dort à cette heure comme un sabot. Elle ne se leve jamais jusqu'a midi. Quelquefois à dix heures, elle sonne pour des raisins et un roman."* This description was indeed characteristic of a Parisian home. Smiling at the truth—for haven't we fallen into just such habits as Madame G—'s ?—we continued our way, and arrived at the iron gates that enclose the little chapel, not later than seven o'clock, when the *concierge* looked still drowsy, and his broom had not done its morning work.

The building is of the Lombard-Gothic design, and was erected soon after the Duke of Orleans lost his life, over the place where he was brought to die. Standing by the black marble cenotaph, on which rests his recumbent figure, clad in uniform, with breast bared, and features stamped with the peace of approaching death, we recalled these lines, as appropriate to the melancholy interest of the spot:

BB*

> " Remember, life is but a shadow,
> Its date the intermediate breath we draw.
> Ten thousand accidents in ambush lie
> To crush the frail and fickle tenement,
> Which, like the brittle hour-glass measuring time,
> Is often broke ere half its sands are run."

The angel, kneeling at the head of the expiring Duke, was executed by the Princess Marie. Thus did a loving sister—who went before him to dwell with God's angels—leave a memorial of her genius, little dreaming that it would one day decorate his tomb. A bas-relief on the monument is too beautiful to pass unremarked—France weeping over a funereal urn, the French flag drooping at her feet. Triquetti's laurels are very fairly won in a portion of this tomb, as also in the "Descent from the Cross," in marble, over the altar; and it is due to the industry of old age to allude to several chairs, the tapestry work of Amélie, Queen of the Belgians. Just behind the altar, in the sacristy, is a painting representing the death-bed scene. The royal family surround the couch, and marshals, dukes, curés and physicians, add to the mournful group. We were shown a clock of black marble, whose design was the lament of France, over a broken shaft, the hands pointing to ten minutes to twelve, the precise time the Duke fell from his carriage. In the court, among the sombre cypresses, is a flourishing cedar tree, brought by him from Lebanon, and which was transplanted by his son, the Count de Paris—its thick branches fitly wave near the spot where he breathed his last. After leaving the chapel, we appropriated an hour to the *Jardin d'Acclimatation*, bright, cheerful and sunny, and green as the greenest of Parisian gardens. How picturesque are those thirty-three acres!—the pleasant rural walks; the rivulet, where ducks, geese and swans, from Egypt and the Sandwich isles, float harmoniously together; the rustic bridges, spanning here and there the winding stream; the little islands, with their emerald turf; the aquatic plants; the fine trees, transplanted from foreign soils, the most conspicuous being the Greek fir; the flower-beds, fragrant and showy; the conservatory, three hundred feet in length, bright in tropical bloom, with a miniature rivulet coursing along, and a tiny grotto lending a mysterious charm; the aquarium, one of the most animated attractions of the place, with finny occupants large and small; the department of silk-worms, Chinese and Japanese; the aviary, containing a brood of doves, peacocks and pheasants; and the stables of donkeys, horses and camels. I made my adieu to the Bois in all its freshness and sunlit beauty, when smiling nature seemed to whisper the glad promise, "These places shall know thee again."   *   *   *   *   *

10 P. M.—I have just participated in a dinner, a farewell compliment, tendered by friends, at the café of the Grand Opera. If the choice dishes served to make me carry away a remembrance of the excellent *cuisine* of Paris, how much more did the many pleasant associations of the city, its attractive scenes, and the hospitality of its people, crowd in upon the mind this evening, asking an abiding place in memory. Some one remarked that the name of Paris should be inscribed upon our hearts, and wreathed with the *pensée*—a flower as beautiful as its emblem is appropriate.

CHAPTER XXI.

TOO much has already been written of that little word "good-bye;" of the heaving sigh, and the fast flowing tear, but I cannot refrain from saying, that Paris was given up with something of a struggle, the thought creeping into my mind, that the key that had opened its enchantments, might lock me out forever, or that, to see it again, would only be by the light of memory. As a sad theme is more apt than a pleasurable one, to make the pen grow poetic, and run away with itself, I, therefore, do the wisest thing in coming to a full stop. Our journey was attended with but little inconvenience, the squeamish troubles of the channel being escaped, and though, fortunate ourselves, we still had compassion for the woes of other travelers, some of whom must, even now, be wretched under the bare remembrance of their sufferings. Here is a rough picture—not an artistic one,—for having only *sour* material to work upon, the plain, unvarnished truth will present itself. A murky looking boat that rocks about, emitting now and then a volume of black smoke, and sending down cinders in a regular shower,—one white parasol is ruined, and so is a man's white hat;—a narrow, uncomfortable deck with passengers, closely packed,— our

party, five in number, are so *jammed*, that we are not
unlike the *ginger-bread figures*, all joined together, that
we used to buy when little children. A sallow-looking
man is the first to take to the railing in a *pas de trois*
that he could never have accomplished so successfully
after a year's tuition with the best dancing master. He
opens his mouth—an unmeasurable one—as if to yawn ;
then shuts, and opens it again, and would like to close
it finally, but cannot, as the pressure from within is too
great. He drops into a seat on the convenient bench,
but does not stop there long; rises again, and then
sinks down another time. It 'all looks very funny
to us, this antic of opening and shutting the mouth,
and particularly the bobbing up and down, which
reminds us very forcibly of *Jack in the box*. Poor
man ! would he not, just now, rather be that little
red devil, bought for a shilling or two, than himself?
He is not alone in his *performance*, for there is another middle-aged gentleman looking a little pale,
who takes a pinch of snuff, and turns blue around the
corners of his moustache. The snuff he believes a remedy for *mal de mer*, but five minutes more prove its utter
inefficacy. Our party, still safe, keep quiet, much like
cowards, afraid to speak or comment, believing that if
our lips should part, we would do even worse than our
neighbors. On the central settee, stretched out at full
length, as if owner of it by favor or double fare, is a
closely wrapped *Anglaise*, attended by a maid, who
stands ready to administer cologne, although very un-
steady herself, and looking quite ill. The hot sun glares

with maliciousness right into the face of the lady, and
she glances up at it, as if to say, "Get thee behind a
cloud!" but as it does not obey her wishes, she wears a
cross expression, which, we fancy, under the *heated influence*, must ere long culminate in *boiling wrath*. ·No one
accuses the madam of being sick, for she reads very ear-
nestly a work of fiction; but the maid succumbs, after
the example set by others, and wanders off in search of
a wash-bowl. This article, on the Channel, is not entirely associated with cold water ablutions, as it is frequently seen subserving another purpose. Surely, sea-
sickness changes everybody and everything! By the
time the maid returns, somewhat relieved, the *Anglaise*
becomes tired of the recumbent posture, and proposes to
sit up awhile; thereupon, her feet are arranged upon
shawls, that take the place of a cushion. My sweet,
matronly friend, Mrs. Gregory, desiring to change her
cramped position, modestly steps to a seat at the end of
the lady's bench. It is not possible that so amiable a
countenance and gentle a manner can be repulsed; yet
it is even so, for the English lady now unbottles her
wrath, and says peremptorily that the seat is *hers*. This
unexpected treatment causes the *blush* to deepen on my
friend's cheek,—a beautiful contrast to her silvery hair—
still it does not prevent her from asking the privilege of
at least a few moments stay. Even this small request
is refused by the Madam; and, in order to carry out her
imperious selfishness, she assumes the horizontal position
again, and thus gets rid of what she calls an intrusion.
We wager that this stern dame, who lacks good-will and

charity, will soon be punished, if only by the infliction
of an additional *crow-foot* to the many that surround
her lustreless eyes.

Discomforts are on the increase as the boat jogs on.
A little baby "tunes up," we suppose, because it is on
the Channel — not on account of any bodily distress.
Boy No. 2 rather likes the "ups and downs" of the
trip, and tumbles over his mother's valise, by way of
adding to the commotion. A dog, also, is frisky, and
do n't know what to do in the limited space, but to poke
his nose into the lunch-baskets of two little Misses. A
rickety maiden lady, wonderfully tall and gaunt, comes
up from the cabin, whose low ceiling must have mashed
in her bonnet-frame, or else she lay down in it, forgetting, in her misery, the price of millinery. The lovely
Miss F—, inclined to eat an orange, begs the steward to
believe that this is her first experience on the Channel,
and that fruit is, therefore, essential to her comfort. At
this moment she does not look as rosy as when she
danced, in Paris, at the Empress' balls, a charming
divinity among scores of French officers, who would
willingly have led her through miles of orange groves,
and laid at her feet quantities of the golden fruit. But
those days are past, and now she eagerly craves a single
orange at the hands of a greasy steward. Monsieur A—
follows in her footsteps. A few hours since he was fresh
from the hands of his barber, who arranged his full,
waving moustache, with all the care requisite for one
about to appear at Court, and not for rough waters that
disturb the stomach, and, when there happens a blow or
a breeze, every well laid hair. He is too polite and ele-

gant to swear, but he tells Miss F—that he cannot like
England, if everything there is as *degoutant* as the
Channel; and that, if it had not been for her, so fair
and lovely, he would have preferred to remain in dear
Paris, where *vin rouge* is drunk, and not seltzer water.

June 12.—Charming weather, very desirable for the
gay London season! Carriages were ordered for a drive
in the 'west-end, and we finished the morning hours with
a visit to the Houses of Parliament and Westminster
Abbey. Broad, stately and plain is Westminster Hall,
where we paced up and down, and found a liveried guide
to lead us to those chambers where some of England's
greatest statesmen have sat in council. In the Court of
Exchequer, there were a few members in gowns and wigs
of horse-hair curls, which gave them an air of grandeur
and importance, as compared with our American judici-
ary. In the House of Lords, an appeal was being made,
the most quiet dignity prevailing in that august body.
The House of Commons disappointed us as to size, and
the fact of its being vacant, may have greatly lessened
our interest in it. We stood at the seats of Bright,
Gladstone and Disraeli. Who that has read the glowing literary sketches from the pen of the latter, would
not desire to hear his voice in an important political
debate? It is a noticeable feature that the gallery for
ladies is enclosed with a grating, so as to obscure their
features, England refusing to *openly* compliment—as
America does—feminine beauty and grace. An adjoining corridor contains a large array of statesmen, under
the cold and motionless stamp of marble, but, we could

at least glance at their features, and guess at the high
order of intellect, which, though passed away, has insured
for them an honored niche in their country's palace, and
in her memory.   Thence our steps were directed to
Westminster Abbey, that lies within a stone's throw of
those legislative halls, where so many exciting issues
have transpired.   Who that stands in the great temple
of the dead is not wrapped in solemn thought?   How
still and lonely, after the noise and bustle of the crowded
streets,—how far removed it seems from the cares and
pleasures of the great outer world !   The eye meets the
sumptuous monument, new and untarnished, and the
crumbling stone, with its half-effaced letters, curious
devices and ancient date.   Go when you will, the gay
and proud spirit must be veiled; the springs of life
checked apace, in order that they may correspond with
the sacred spell that broods over the place; whether it
be when the gorgeous light of mid-day bursts in to gild
the epitaphs on the marbles; when the mellowed evening ray lingers softly on the carvings and figured glories ;
or, at the hour, when soft music breaks the silence, and
every " stone is kissed by sound, or the ghost of sound."
Of royal sepulchres, that of Sebert, who died, 616, is the
most ancient.   Over it is a costly gemmed altar decora-
tion that belonged to the fourteenth century.   Then
follows a long line of sovereigns, who held the sceptre
during a period of twelve centuries and more, among
whom is the proudest of queens, the virgin-mistress of
England, at whose words minions quailed, and whose
verdict sent the noblest of courtiers and statesmen to

CC

imprisonment and death. Not far from her sleeping dust are some great names that flourished during her reign, and in that register are those of the "Immortal Bard," Shakspeare, and Edmund Spencer, author of the "Færie Queen." In the chapel of Henry VII is a monument sacred to Mary Stuart, whose neck came under the rod of the august Tudor. How can these two slumber calm and peaceful, under the same temple-arch? Our sympathy makes the jeweled sceptre fade into insignificance before the innocence of the unfortunate Scottish Queen. After all, how incomprehensible is the human heart, for did not the hand that signed the death-warrant of the hapless Mary, place upon the brow of that Queen's son the diadem of England? Very near the sepulchre of James I, is an altar bearing a Latin inscription,—the bones of the murdered Princes Edward V, and Richard, Duke of York, finding there appropriate sepulture. The most venerable attraction of the Abbey is the shrine of Edward the Confessor, the former magnificence of which in jewels and various ornaments, must have made it the pride of the land. It was enjoined as due to the pious man that "his body be honored here on earth, as his soul is glorified in heaven." Editha, his Queen, is interred on the south side of the shrine. In other places, in this chapel, are costly monuments to kings, queens and royal infancy. Thus the babe of nine months, and the child of three years sleep in innocence and beauty beside those who grew old and withered amid the cares of state and the vexations of life. The coronation chairs are objects of curiosity, making one think how brilliant must have been the pageant of those occasions; but that thought is soon expelled for another, the tablets, near by, telling that all that was mortal of the sovereigns, who came in splendid robes to receive their crowns, has been put out of sight and returned to dust.

In the cluster of distinguished names are those of Peel, Pitt, Palmerston, Canning, Wilberforce, Sir Isaac Newton, and poets too numerous to mention, who have illumined England with a light that will never grow dim. Very interesting to Americans, as appertaining to our country's struggles, are the monuments of General Wolfe, killed at Quebec, and Major André. General Washington's figure is introduced on the latter stone. He receives, at the hands of the bearer of the flag of truce, the letter penned by André the night before his execution, praying that the mode of his death might be adapted to the feelings of a man of honor,—that he might not die on a gibbet. Some of the naval tombs are stupendous, like the grief that wrapped the nation when those great heroes perished. The tributes, that read from pedestals and tablets, are the perfection of language; and, should we desire our virtues to be pleasingly chronicled, we might ask, at our death, that order of epitaph. A representation of conjugal love is marvellously and meritoriously given in sculpture,—the tomb erected by an only son to his parents, bearing the names of Joseph Gascoigne Nightingale—died 1752, aged fifty-six; and Lady Elizabeth, his wife—died 1734, aged twenty-seven. The young wife, the embodiment of perfect beauty, lies clasped in the arms of her husband. He sees the skeleton form of Death creeping out

from the dark vault below, to aim the deadly dart at
his cherished spouse; and the look of despair, mingled
with eagerness to shield her from the insidious shaft, is
most painfully depicted upon his features. Adjoining
this monument is one to Sarah, Duchess of Somerset,—a
name adorned with charity, and rendered as illustrious
as any within these walls, by the performance of good
deeds—clothing the poor, feeding the hungry, sheltering
the widow and orphan, educating youth, and endowing
the Church. All around, Fame speaks from the marbles of brilliant achievements, military, naval, etc.; but
at this one little spot we might say, with Byron—

> " The drying up a single tear has more
> Of honest fame, than shedding seas of gore."

June 13.—Last evening afforded us a pleasurable
treat in a visit to Madame Tussaud's Gallery of Wax-
works. In the brilliantly lighted rooms, not only is
the mind exercised, but the eye is charmed, for, as we
look upon the gorgeously grand costumes of courts, from
the time of William the Conqueror to that of Victoria,
so are we brought to think of the struggles, vanities,
glories and sorrows of all those eventful years set forth
in history. One need not go to court to see royalty and
it splendid regalia, when there exist such faithful representations as are here to be seen. The fabrics of these
costumes are made up of " purple and fine linen," bro-
cades, velvets, satins and ermine, and it is not a difficult
thing, in looking upon these figures—pointing back to
eras long since passed,—to imagine that we are living
in their various reigns, and standing in the presence of

the great sovereigns themselves. I do not propose to
touch on the Normans and Saxons, or the Houses of
Lancaster and York, interesting as the characters are;
but, upon the union of the white and red roses, it is impossible to pass by that disturber of the peace of the
nation, and of fair women,—Henry VIII. Divorce
and murder seem written on his brow, and hate for such
an object is so natural a feeling that one is glad to turn
to the unfortunate wives surrounding him, as pleading
for that gentle emotion, sympathy, and afterwards to the
children that reigned after him, Edward VI, Queens
Mary and Elizabeth. The figures of Louis XVI, and
Marie Antoinette are especially attractive. Resplendent
is the queen in a robe of pale blue satin, with diamonds
and other precious stones glistening in her hair! A
jeweled mirror hangs at her side, and from beneath her
robe a foot peers out, encased in a shoe with a diamond
buckle. If this costly slipper caused us to revert to the
bright days of her pride, wealth and fashion, so did it
evoke a thought of the dark hours, when there were no
shoes with which to cover her feet. The Dauphin and
the Duchess d'Angoulème are also represented in the
zenith of happiness at the side of their royal parents.
In one scene, that occupies considerable space, the present
Emperor of Austria appears in the uniform of a General,
with the star of Maria Theresa and the Golden Fleece,
and his beautiful spouse, seated near by, wears green
satin with garniture of point appliqué lace. Her pose
is admirably graceful and life-like as she looks up to
address a royal personage. The Empress of France,

CC*

also seated, is attired in white, embroidered in gold, but her beauty seems to pale before the bright, coquettish style of the Austrian Empress. This may be a deception in *wax*, and it would therefore be wrong to judge of their respective merits from models. The little prince stands at her feet, forming the picture of filial devotion of which he is so truly an exponent, and not far off is Napoleon III, wearing a Lieut. General's uniform, decorated with the Star of the Garter. Queen Isabella of Spain is arrayed in violet satin, embroidered in floss silk to represent the lily of the valley, with clusters of its dark green leaves. The ex-King of Greece and his consort; Victor Emmanuel of Italy, and other sovereigns; military heroes of the Russian war, and the French army form an array strikingly handsome. Another court scene presents the royal family of England; the late Duchess of Kent, mother of Victoria; Lord Palmerston, &c. But there is no end of personages, eminent as poets, philosophers, statesmen, generals and churchmen, and lack of time will only permit mention of the following: Joan of Arc; Mary, Queen of Scots, and her handsome second husband, Lord Darnley; Madame St. Amaranthe—the beautiful widow of a member of the body-guard of Louis XVI—who, at twenty-two years of age, suffered death at the hands of the vile Robespierre; the Duke of Wellington, lying in state upon a canopy of velvet and cloth of gold; several charming little children; the babe in the cradle, fair, rosy and innocent in type; and Mme. Tussaud, the keen, bright little woman among *crowned heads*, who, wearing only a *wax-diadem*, had a right to be very proud of it.

America is represented by Abraham Lincoln, Jefferson Davis, General Grant, John Slidell, and General McClellan. Some of these figures are not correct likenesses; but that of President Andrew Johnson is a success, except that it does not convey a true idea of his physique. There were some interesting relics of Napoleon I, that led us, in thought, to his coronation in Milan; to his disastrous Russian campaign; to the island of Elba, where, for a time, his power was shackled; and to the willow at St. Helena, where he lay down in the slumber of the grave. Now let us turn to the dark side of Madame Tussaud's picture,—a chamber of horrors, where about forty criminals appear, all of whom, however, do not wear the atrocious look of murder on their countenances; and to the guillotine, the identical instrument that hurled twenty-two thousand persons into eternity during the French Revolution. Near by are additional reminders of its bloody work, in the models of the severed heads of Robespierre, Louis XVI, and his Queen. A question was put to me by a woman who was gazing in wonder at the spots of blood on the features of Marie Antoinette: "Please, ma'am, tell me what those red spots are doing on the face;—and why did n't they put a body to it?" This verdant, yet happily ignorant creature, upon being enlightened, walked away, saying: "How awful it is for folks to do such things as that!" Next to the guillotine, and appealing deeply to the feelings, is a model of the Bastile, with the incarcerated Count de Lorge, who, it is recorded, lived there thirty years, and became so accustomed to the life of solitude, that, when given his freedom, he

asked to be carried back.   He died six weeks after his
liberation.   *   *   *   *   *   *

The attraction to-day was the Sydenham Palace.
Favored with fine weather and pleasant company, that
so happily influence time, the run of eight miles seemed
to us a mere span.   Thousands had already gathered
within the beautiful, fairy-like structure,—a palace by
name, but, in every sense of the word, different from
that which constitutes a dwelling for kings,—it being
more like an immense conservatory, especially under the
centre of the nave, where the super-sunniness of June
glows down on the crystal fountain, and warms the flowery space around.   The *Victoria Regia* spreads out its
broad leaves to receive the drippings, whilst over-hang-
ing baskets, various kinds of plants and shrubbery,
make up so charming a green place, that we might have
succumbed to a *dreamy languor* if we would.   The resting spell, however, came a few moments later, when,
sitting in the Pompeian Court, we fancied ourselves in
one of those very Italian villas—exhumed from the
scoria of lava—that sadly and brokenly point to their
former splendor, and to the human life that once animated them.   Alas! the rich pictured walls, the mosaics,
luxuries and ornaments, which those people made their
idols, forgetting, in their blind devotion, there was a
Power who could turn the fiery mount—the boast of the
land—into a swift, remorseless agent, to destroy their
fair abodes!   The Alhambra Court, recently burned, was
undergoing repairs; still did its charred wreck afford an
adequate idea of the decorative art of Spain.   Then we
started for another section of the building, feeling that

there was too much worthy of being seen, to admit of
any great delay. At every few yards, statuary arrested
our progress—copies of many of the most celebrated
marbles of Italy, among which were the Three Graces,
Venus in a variety of attitudes, and other goddesses,
gracefully supported by the company of Apollo, Mer-
cury, and such gods as are fit to mingle with the beau--
ties of the palace. Mythology is here charmingly realized, giving far more pleasure than did the book of ideal
pictures that once delighted our youth. Monstrous
figures of sculpture also rise up, associated with Baby-
lon, a name so antique that it should be defended from
criticism; yet, it is impossible for the mind not to com-
pare its rude, disgusting productions, with the more refined works of later days.

The grand concert, that took place at four o'clock,
brought together an immense crowd, computed at twenty
thousand, to listen to the soul-inspiring Titiens, and
other singers of her Majesty's opera—a medley of names,
some of which are not the most musical in sound—Mlle.
Bauermeister, Mme. de Meric Lablache, Signors Fe-
rensi, Fiorini, Casaboni, Herr Rokitansky, and Mongini.
When the charm of music passed away, the throng dis-
persed, affording one a good opportunity to see an English crowd in gala dress, the ladies being chiefly attired
in robes of delicate, frail organdie, that withstood, marvellously well, the "crush," and particularly so, consid-
ering they were made with sweeping trains. Why is
not the neat and cleanly short walking costume adopted?
Charming to look upon was the fresh, peach-like bloom

of these daughters of England!—whether the result of climate or exercise, it is very justly their boast; and other nations might be excused for envying them so beautiful a possession.

We repaired to one of the restaurants, in search of a repast, and there, hungry nature grew rebellious at the lack of system and attendance. Can we ever forget the taxed and tortured waiter, who vainly endeavored to evince partiality to our party? Answering to the calls of dozens, he went at the speed of lightning, misdelivering articles at every step, such as giving a fork for a vinegar-cruet, and a spoon for a napkin. Gentlemen rapped with their fists, and ladies plead, and double price would they have paid for even a morsel of bread. After twenty minutes of patient waiting, our beseeching tones melted the heart of that perplexed waiter, and lo! there came to us one-half of our order,—a fowl, some lively English ale, and a salad. We borrowed salt from the adjoining table, and returned the favor with pepper from ours; and so, at *cross-game*, the meal was made.

It was, indeed, a relief to get outside, to enjoy the open air. Some of the party sat down on the stone-steps that overlook the garden. The view therefrom was charming, the sun setting in gorgeous splendor, and tinging the landscape with colors that no artist has ever yet fully imitated; but Clara and I, having a fancy for the floral patches below, and the verdure-clad colonade, repaired thither, and devoted a half hour to inhaling the sweets from the flowers, and wandering about the walks admiring bright, beautiful nature. On a *fête* occasion, the hours at Sydenham are all taken up as closely as a school-girl's time, and, when six o'clock came, the company was regaled with some delicious *morceaux* of music on the great festival organ. Opposite the instrument is the box for the accommodation of the royal family, none of whom were present on the occasion; perhaps preferring their palatial abode, whilst we strangers on English soil were filling every crevice of our hearts with the notes of that dearly loved tune, which recalled our own dear homes, " 'Mid pleasures and palaces."

Towards nine o'clock, the lovely night being then as warm as if under the influence of the sun, the pyrotechnic display commenced. The heavens were fairly in a blaze with rockets, magnesium-lighted balloons and comets; and, the very stars—the lamps that God has set in beauty to illumine our earth—paled before the dazzling glare. Handel's fire-work music, in delightful strains, formed the prelude to a pyrotechnic artifice, in which the name of Handel appeared in fiery beauty, surrounded with an emerald wreath. Two other devices were especially attractive,—" God save the Queen," whereupon the band played the air that stirs to enthusiasm the Briton's heart; and " England hails her Sailor-Prince,"—a brilliant greeting to the Duke of Edinburgh. " The great Cascade," also, was rapturously received, falling from a height of seventy feet, in a golden spray that spread out over an area of seven thousand square feet. Afterwards, when various colored stars burst suddenly upon the sight, it seemed, indeed, as if heaven was pouring down precious jewels from her

casket, making all who stood under her bounty as rich
as Midas.   Finally, came the illumination of the park
and fountains, the vivid calcium lights, and a *girandole* of
two thousand rockets, that seemed sufficient to consume
all Sydenham.   The great Crystal Palace glittered as
diamonds do when they catch the brightest light, and to
it, in its beautiful, lustrous appearance, never *to* fade
from our minds, we said *good-night* and *farewell.*

The stampede for the cars was a repetition of several
scenes witnessed at railway depots in Paris.   Jostled
and bruised, we gained the station, and saw depart three
trains, heavily freighted with the most venturesome of
persons.   Our prudence would have dictated a stay over
night, but thanks to English courtesy, seats were cheerfully resigned to us by a party of gentlemen, and thus
were we carried back to the city.

June 14.—A sabbath in London, and where to attend
divine service!   A vote taken resulted in a decision in
favor of that bold and eloquent dissenter Spurgeon.
The tabernacle, as we drove up to it, bore testimony of
the great interest manifested in the preacher, as there
was a large crowd of strangers striving for admission,
and many pew-holders passing in by tickets.   Fortunate
were we in gaining immediate entrance, as some persons
who had arrived in advance of us were made to wait,
and feel the truth of the Biblical saying, " The first shall
be last, &c."   Within, the crowd was even greater, and
twenty minutes must have elapsed ere seats were tendered us, our party, by that *time, being considerably

scattered.   The edifice is plain and spacious, and looks like an amphitheatre.   It has three galleries, from the lowest one of which projects a platform for the preacher; and there, from that simple stand, devoid of ornament, does he, by his rare and impressive elocution, engross the attention of his hearers.   In this church no notes are heard from deep-toned organ, but one fervent sound of praise ascends to God in the mingling of five thousand voices; the congregation seeming to be worshipers in the true spirit.   Spurgeon is a man of robust appearance, with voice suited to his vast tabernacle, and his earnestness is tempered with gentleness and affection. In chiding his people for errors committed, he also greatly encourages the wayward sinner, and seems to gainsay whatever there is of reproach with an expression of love.   "Come into my fold with the taint of sin, and we will together strive for the good."   It is by such persuasion and proffered help that converts are made. Is it not true, that sermons carefully prepared, graceful, and oratorically attractive, often fail to produce the effect of a few extemporaneous words from a zealous heart?   *   *   *   *   *   *   *   *

This lovely afternoon enticed some of us to Westminster, where exquisite music floated through the solemn aisles, lending a tinge of sadness to our thoughts; creating a link of sympathy with a spot that has witnessed the anguish of countless human hearts, and that shelters so many melancholy tributes of affection.   May the goodly influences of the day last beyond the shadows now closing it, that slant athwart the paper as I write!

DD

CHAPTER XXII.

THE magnificent proportions of St. Paul's, the largest Protestant Cathedral in the world, can scarcely be appreciated, hemmed in, as it is, on all sides, by dingy buildings, and worthy is it to crown a nobler space—beautiful "Temple of the living God!" But for the monuments scattered about in the interior, one would hardly suppose it to be a sanctuary, its immense body, bare of seats, rather suggesting some great municipal hall—and a gloomy one at that. The only relief to the austere aspect comes from the frescoed dome and the gilded arches. Neither the inner gallery, of *whispering* fame, nor the outer *golden* one, that surrounds the summit of the dome, and presents to view the magnificent panorama of London could induce us to the herculean labor of mounting hundreds of steps, although, we were importuned to make the ascent about twenty times. Tickets are constantly thrust at the visitor, and a *six-pence* demanded for every sight. One of our party, more annoyed than the rest, exclaimed with some spirit and emphasis—" How importunate are these money-changers! Let us form a battalion, and drive them from the temple, as was done with *those* of old!" Yet, it is only by paying a fee that the tomb of the great architect Wren can be seen—but, why place over his remains a simple stone, when this grand edifice must ever commemorate his genius? The crypt, also, contains monuments to Nelson and Wellington, the former of granite, and the latter of porphyry, somewhat in imitation of Napoleon's, but lacking the surroundings of *Les Invalides*, that grand, bright temple, radiant under beautiful sunshine! All is funereal-like; the gloom of the vault; the dusky banners; the dark trappings, and the ponderous car that bore the remains of the "Iron Duke," and which is regarded as a great relic, having been cast out of the cannons captured by the hero. A sable wing seemed to hover there, and we did not regret leaving the darkness to ascend, even though we might again be greeted with the cry of "*six-pence, your Honors!*" Sure enough, with the first streak of light, we caught a glimpse of one of these vampires, who followed us to the portals with a very significant gesture, which certainly meant "another six-pence, if you please."

The next place of gloomy interest was the Tower of London. Upon approaching that ancient, hoary pile, it seemed entirely enwrapped with dark shadows, little conveying the idea that it had ever been a royal palace, the scene of splendid pageants, banquets, and bridal festivity; and that from its gates had gone forth sovereigns to be crowned at Westminster, and chivalric knights to the tournament. Any attempt to portray a gay picture is sure to fail, as sombre colors must ever predominate, —the sufferings of by-gone ages speaking from the dungeon-towers, where was sacrificed many a noble victim

to the caprices of bloodthirsty monarchs. Once within
its thick, grim walls, and led through all its intricacies,
the mind becomes so completely overswept by the storms
of the past, that it is not difficult to imagine oneself
contemporary with the poor, unhappy captives. We are
inclined to sympathize with the person, who, gazing
into Sir Walter Raleigh's cell, is said to have asked
the warder, "Where is he?" The abstraction came
from a commiserative feeling for his sorrowful situation,
and from an engrossed mind—it could not have been
ignorance. Passing up a narrow staircase, in the White
Tower, we saw the traditionary spot where the bodies of
the royal children were concealed; and, in the famous
Beauchamp Tower, various inscriptions and autographs
that prisoners had left upon the stone walls for future
generations to read with pitying eye. Among the most
conspicuous and interesting was that of Philip Howard,
who, in the consolation of his religion, faithful to the
last, left these words—which, although quoted and recorded by almost every tourist, can never, by repetition,
lose one jot of their truth and beauty.—"The more suffering with Christ in this world, the more glory with
Christ in the next world." At the age of thirty-nine,
in the year 1595, he expired during his imprisonment.
The name of Poole—the two brothers who languished
and died here, under the accusation of conspiring to
make Mary, Queen of Scots, Queen of England—is
coupled with the following triste memorials: "A perilous passage maketh a pleasant port," and "That which
is sown by God in tears is reaped in joy." Then, the
the simple name, IANE, pointing to the sorrow of the

youthful martyr, Lady Jane Grey, arrests the attention; it is believed that the hand of her husband, Lord Guilford Dudley, carved, in anguished and loving remembrance, these letters. A neat piece of sculpture, three wheat-sheaves—the arms of the Peverels—and a crucifix, a bleeding heart and a skeleton—joint emblems of torture, despair and death—were very appropriate to the place where so many captives had dwelt in the agony of suspense, and had been led forth to an ignominious end. Scores of names, not inscribed there, rose up in my mind, and none with more pity, blended with admiration, than that of Scotland's valiant chieftain, whose blood was shed to remove the yoke of his beloved land. After deciphering the sad tracings of wearied hands, we were conducted to a room where were several instruments of torture, such as the " thumb-screw," and the " scavenger's daughter;" the latter so constructed as to confine the neck, wrists and limbs. What suffering has not the poor human frame endured in the days of tyranny and iron rule! We saw also the axe, and the block upon which the brilliant Earl of Essex was beheaded. On it are marks of the fatal blow; and, not far removed, is the figure of Elizabeth, grand and imperious, seated on horseback. Who that steps from the hacked block to the effigy of the Queen does not think of her cruel resentment, and the sad doom of one of the most chivalric of her courtiers? St. John's chapel, entirely divested of furniture, with pillars and arches of Norman architecture, is solemn and stately in its antiquity, and seemed to-day more awe-striking in its death-like stillness and loneliness than any other part

DD*

of the Tower.   The Council Chamber, where state trials were held, and where Richard III sentenced Lord Hastings to immediate death, for sustaining Jane Shore, is an apartment unrivalled in the artistic arrangement of its weapons and fire-arms—even the railing that encircles an aperture in the floor being formed of swords and pistols. In the Banqueting Hall the devices are perfect, such as stars and passion-flowers of glittering brightness, whilst the ceiling partakes of the same character, being one mass of polished steel.   The Horse Armory, a very interesting exhibition of effigies in armor, and ancient arms, occupied us fully a half hour, during which time our guide proved not only patient, but quite entertaining. He remarked that for a number of years he had been engaged in conducting visitors through the Tower, but that our appreciative interest would be remembered by him with pleasure; and we ourselves will not soon forget his accurate knowledge of historical events and dates, his several quotations from the English poets, and the sprinkling of wit, which, whilst it brightened up his wrinkled face, seemed to lessen the years that had whitened his hair.   The armor on exhibition embraces the period beginning 1272 to 1683.   That of Edward I points to the days of Bruce and Wallace, in the contest between this country and Scotland.   The magnificent armor that clothes the figure of Henry VIII, and which is curiously wrought in devices and "saintly legends," elicits more marked attention, because the name of worthy Queen Catherine is associated therewith.   This armor was a gift from the Emperor Maximilian to Henry VIII, on his marriage with that lady. Everywhere around are stout cuirasses and weapons, and, in another room, military trophies, the recountal of which comes more within the province of a guidebook. Out again in the open air, we stood upon the spot known as " The Green," where the life-blood of woman had flowed under the headsman's axe, but this patch of verdure, with the sun's bright rays upon it, could not dispel the thought of the crimson stain, when beauty, virtue and innocence were there made to perish. Leaving this place of sad associations, and viewing, at the next moment, the gorgeous regalia of England, our minds were less impressed by the magnificence of the display, because we knew that crowns of precious worth, and sceptres waving in pride and greatness, were not always emblems of happiness. May the lustre now shed over England, in this reign of peace and love, continue to grow brighter, and be as enduring as the jewels of Victoria's costly diadem!

Several hours were disposed of at the British Museum. Among its vast collection of antique art are quaint monuments of Egypt, and beautiful sculptures of Greece—the model of the noble temple, the Parthenon, being the most attractive. In admiring the Elgin marbles, I could not help thinking that a flagrant theft had been committed, in order to enrich these galleries. Who would not rather view them on that classic ground, where famous sculptors conceived and executed their rare beauty! The National Gallery, with its pictures; the Library of 700,000 volumes, and the new Reading-room of 17,000; together with the celebrated Rosetta stone, that deciphered and explained the mystery of hieroglyphics, were all interesting; but, more particularly, the collection of autographs, which appeared to invest the precincts with a sacred spell. It seemed that some unseen hand had lifted the veil that separates the dead from the living; great men and honored women being once more on earth; that the throne, the pulpit, and the desks of the poet, philosopher and historian, were filled again with mighty spirits of the past;—"God's toiling thinkers," gathered to Himself, come back to thrill us with the grandeur of their thoughts. There were missives from Catherine of Arragon; Mary, Queen of Scots; Anna Boleyn; and the handwriting of Lady Jane Grey, in a book of prayers used by her on the scaffold. Following these, were *names*, brightened by the fame of battle, the rule of kingdoms, and that more enduring glory, intellect—which raises man to the brightest sphere of earthly happiness—Napoleon, Wellington, Frederick the Great, Richard III, Elizabeth, Catherine de Médicis, James I, Francis I, Michael Angelo, Sir Walter Scott, Addison, Dryden, Tasso, Martin Luther, Calvin, Cardinal Wolsey, Thomas Cranmer, Sir Isaac Newton, Sir Walter Raleigh, Byron, Ben. Franklin, and "last, but not least," George Washington. A lock of Nelson's hair, his sketch of the battle of the Nile; the original draft of the will of Mary Stuart; and Milton's original agreement for the sale of "Paradise Lost," were objects of great interest.

June 16.—This was the day, of all others—a balmy

breeze tempering the ardent sun—to quit thunderous, busy London, for the quiet sylvan beauty of Richmond and Hampton.

At noon we entered Hyde Park, to see it in its loveliest aspect, with foliage of brighest green, and lawns of velvety smoothness. It was not the hour for the fashionable world to congregate, when fine costumes and pretty faces absorb the praise that would otherwise go out to nature; yet, a few carriages were observed on the roads, and, now and then, appeared a graceful equestrienne, followed by her groom. A youthful, arch face, peered out from under a small, round hat—London knows how to furnish the becoming style—and the sparkling eyes were duplicates of a pair that will never be forgotten by me, although long since closed in death. The English women ride well, out-door exercise and sports coming naturally to them. For several miles, through the suburbs, flowers regaled the eye, almost every house having its garden; and even the windows displayed some bright-hued blossom. Up to this time, London had compared unfavorably with Paris, for the centre of this city seems entirely destitute of those natural adornments that grace almost every residence of the French capital. However, there is, unmistakably, some sentiment beyond the massive structures of this mighty metropolis. We all must acknowledge that a leaf or a flower can soften the asperities of a "world life" trameled with cares, and that it ushers peace and fragrant spring-time into the heart:—how much more, then, do the greater gifts of nature yield delight, nowhere so bounteously spread out as in the varied scenery stretch-

ing westward from Richmond Hill. Hampton blends
with its green charms and village simplicity, the stateli-
ness of a palace, pinnacled and turreted, and magnificent
with fretwork and paintings. It was in this costly
structure, built by Cardinal Wolsey, that Henry VIII
flourished; that his wife, Jane Seymour, died a *natural*
death, as if by Divine interposition; and that Catherine
Parr's nuptials were solemnized with great splendor.
Other monarchs made it an abode; Philip of Spain and
Queen Mary; Charles I, Charles II, William and
Mary; and George II, said to be the last of the royal
occupants. We saw portraits of the "Beauties of
Charles the Second's Court," and the Raphael cartoons,
the pride of the galleries. But why dwell on the productions of art, when, outside, in front of the palace, a
more lovely picture unfolds itself—avenues skirted with
foliage, flower-plots bright with the hues of scarlet geranium and fuchsia, and, farther on, a stream, along whose
margin are thickly clustered trees, with rustic benches
beneath their shade! There we stopped to enjoy the
tranquil beauty of the scene, and to listen to the sweetest kind of concert—birds warbling most joyously their
afternoon carols. Peeping up out of the grass, near our
seats, were some tiny blue flowers of wild growth—a
star with a gold centre—which, though perhaps unnoticed by many who roam here, possessed a peculiar
attractiveness and merit in our eyes. Beautiful, also,
were the white lilies, that nestled in their bed of green
leaves, so close to the surface of the brook; but, soon we
had to leave that lovely spot for a rare sight in the garden attached to Hampton Court,—the famous grape

vine, about a century old, yielding upwards of twenty-five hundred bunches of grapes a season. This fruit is exclusively reserved for the royal family, and as we stood under the rich purple clusters, silently yearning for a mouthful, we could but think that those favored people must be very selfish in appropriating all of the luscious supply, which is certainly more than they can eat.

On our route back to the city, we stopped to take dinner at the Star and Garter Hotel, Richmond; and such meals as are there furnished, are indeed worthy of the patronage of the nobility, and all *bons vivants*. Among the dishes temptingly served, was the famous one of White-bait—little fish so pitifully wee, that it took hundreds to make up a plate for one person,—and I hesitated ere indulging in the delicacy, believing that if I did so, it would be encouraging a monstrous cruelty. The view from the windows of the private dining-room was the finishing stroke of beauty to the charming panorama, that all through the day had flitted before our eyes. Nearest to the vision were star-shaped flower-beds, glowing with every variety of color, and next, the terrace, with its snow-white balustrade, where many persons were gathered—some strolling about, and others standing in groups, evidently fascinated with the scene. Far down in the vale ran the Thames river, winding in and out among trees of noble growth and a wealth of verdure. A slight haze, blending with the rays of the setting sun, beautified, if possible, what was "altogether lovely," and thus Richmond—a name very dear in my own land—created a mute friendship in my heart, and a life-long bond with memory.

CHAPTER XXIII.

WENT by rail, this morning, to Greenwich, noted for its Observatory and Hospital. After promenading through the little town, which makes a respectable display of merchandise, we undertook the ascent of the steep hill—a very mountain to our overtaxed feet—and half way up, in sight of the little building, where time, so valuable to us poor mortals, is computed, we grew heedless of the flying moments, and sat down to the enjoyment of a fine view and pleasant breeze. The entire day might have been passed agreeably in a lazy loll on the green slope, but for the desire to carry out the morning's programme in a visit to the Hospital, which accommodates upwards of 2600 old and disabled seamen. The large hall speaks to the praise of Wren, who nobly planned it, as he did every other edifice of which he was the architect. Portraits of naval celebrities adorn the walls; also, pictures of several brilliant engagements; Nelson's glory being the most conspicuously portrayed. Various articles known as his property are on exhibition, among which are the coat he wore when he received the fatal wound on the *Victory*, and a small piece of wood cut from the spot where he fell. An interesting model of the battle of the Nile is ingeniously carved out of

wood—upon the water, represented so faithful to nature,
the vessels lie grouped around, dealing out the deadly
shot.   Of the few statues belonging to this room, one of
courtly grace and splendid physique amply compensates
for the lack of numbers, and whatever may have been
the station of the man it honors, England has undoubt-
edly lost a noble son.   "Oh! that marble might be imbued with life!"   Such was the thought that filled my
mind as I gazed upon the faultless stone.

On the return trip, by way of variety, we took the
boat, stopping first at the Thames tunnel landing.   At
the dock, a number of ragged urchins met us and followed on our steps, piteously begging for pennies.   How
much might be said of the poverty of London, which
mingles its spectral faces with the ruddy complexions of
those who have never known want,—misery and starvation making up one side of the picture; prosperity and
wealth the other!   Some of this squalid wretchedness
appears in the midst of the most fashionable quarters—
the babe in the mother's arms, with its weird, famished
look, and tattered dress, affording a painful contrast with
the child of fortune, richly clad.   What a vast field for
the exercise of charity and pity is this great city!

The descent to the Tunnel, by seventy-five or more
steps, impresses the visitor with the stupendousness of
the undertaking, and the wonderful amount of skill and
energy expended in its construction.   Walking half the
length of the archway, I tried to work out the problem
of the marvellous mechanical achievement, but failed
entirely, and was glad to appeal to an officer on duty,

EE

an intelligent man, who kindly gave me the desired information. One can hardly believe that a river flows above, and that there is security under its depths. Surely, no great degree of cheerfulness can ever be felt by those who pass entire days here, engaged in traffic, as it is not only damp, but gloomy, the only light coming from a few scattered gas-jets. Some little stands, with paltry articles for sale, are attended by half-grown girls, pale and sickly in appearance, whose shrill voices are constantly appealing to passers-by, leaving an echo, in the stillness of the place, of the most unearthly character.

Leaving this subterranean passage, and taking another boat, we passed beneath the arches of some of the many noble bridges that span the Thames, and, on nearing the Tower, gained a good view of Traitor's Gate,—those gloomy portals that have been crossed by many dejected spirits, weeping over lost happiness and hope. *   *   *

The pleasure of the day, to me, has been in greeting a friend direct from home, who will soon glide into the footprints left by our party in the old world, and we tender a wish that those same paths may yield him pleasure and profit.

June 18.—As the child seeks frolicsome recreation after the studies of the day are over, so, last evening, felt I inclined, having of late kindled much of deep and stately thought in faithful bondage to the London sights —and where to go? Leaving the boundary of a world of intellect, art and grandeur, we found ourselves at Cremorne, just the spot to banish from the mind every

Stygian shadow that comes from association with things austere and gloomy. Perhaps the summer-night had much to do with attracting us to the picturesque gardens, and Hesper's rays shining out boldly, promised to appear far lovelier, stealing through covert nooks and flowery haunts. Not far from the entrance, ere the eye had time to rest on the encircling foliage and the lanterns that played down in various tints upon gay groups and isolated couples, my escort was lured to light the "fragrant Havana" he held in his hand. The proffer came so blandly sweet, from a pretty damsel presiding at a table, all garlanded in flowers, that to have passed indifferently by those cerulean eyes would have been a breach of politeness to England's fair charms. A few moments afterwards we joined the many hundreds who were wending their way to the dancing arena. Who that beholds the merry scene, does not think of those spirited lines of Schiller, that great poet, who sometimes left the radiant heights of spiritual verse to stray into trivial thought?

" See how the couples whirl along the Dance's buoyant tide ;
  And scarcely touch with winged feet the floor on which they glide,
  Oh ! are they flying shadows, from material forms set free ?
  Or elfin shapes, whose airy rings the summer moon-beams see ? "

When tired of the sound of music, and the buzz of voices, we wandered off a short distance, where our attention was attracted by a sign-board, bearing upon it the figure of an old Hermit, so venerable in appearance that it was impossible to refuse his invitation to adventure.   The path to his cave lay first through beds of exquisite flowers; and then, winding in and out, at some length, through green copses, led us to the desired goal. Other mortals, curious as ourselves, had ventured to this retired spot, and, having had their fortunes told, were coming away with beaming faces.   There sat the Abyssinian, in his dark cell, wise as Plato, thoughtful as Newton; his long white locks and beard telling of years of experience and midnight toil.   Before revealing to the visitor the bright or dark side of fate, he scans the features, asks the Christian name and age, and soon thereafter sends forth a missive, neatly folded and closely sealed.   The moment is an anxious one for the parties interested, as they are surmising whether destiny will cast into their hand a sweet flower,—*couleur de rose*— whispering love and happiness, or an ugly, rude thorn to wound the heart.   Thanks to the smiling star that answered to my name, and made this auspicious prophesy! " The Hermit of Central Africa tells thee, after a careful search in the constellation, that an unexpected fair fortune will be thine—health, wealth, happiness, and a future partner whose virtues the gods might envy.   A model of thy sex, thou shalt be blessed with every earthly joy!"   On the investment of two more shillings, there was promised to us a vision of lover and sweetheart, in a magical mirror.   We asked ourselves, will they be forms of matchless beauty, or of hideous ugliness?   Lo! I looked, and swift to my eye appeared a picture of Napoleon III, which dispelled the illusion with me, for I knew that I was not born for a crown—and besides,

Eugenie's health is *good*. The next magic view disclosed to my friend a fair beauty, glorious as Aurora,
with golden locks as treasure. Was it rash to hope that
she would prove constant, and not gladden other eyes
than his, at least until we had passed beyond the mysterious enclosure, where, in the quiet walk, we might laugh
at our folly, still trusting to the enchanted future?

June 18.—It being our last day in London, each
member of the party made a superhuman effort, and
managed to reach the breakfast-table at a reasonable
hour; and a beggarly meal it was, like all that have
been served since our sojourn at this house. One would
suppose that the sole aim of the proprietors was their
own emolument, and not the pleasure and comfort of
their guests; but, at this season of the year, when all
hotels are crowded, perhaps some allowance should be
made; and, therefore, we will drop the subject, and tell
of our brief visit to the South Kensington Museum,
where are to be found contributions of art of all ages
and of every country. To describe or even enumerate
these objects, ornamental and useful, ancient and modern, would require a swift pen, unwearied energy, and
more patience than we possess; however, it will not do
to pass in silence the beautiful statuary, the rare, antique
jewelry, and the many exquisite paintings in the gallery,
which is an inestimable treasure, because the splendid
works of Hogarth and Landseer are there. In this valuable collection are sketches of village life, merry and
blithe; scenes so solemn and pathetic that they might

EE*

start a fountain of tears; and portraits of rare finish—
woman wearing beauty on her brow like a jewel, with
love deep-mirrored in her eye; and little children, like
"roseate blossoms," bright and lovely in the morn of
life.

Next, we gave an hour's ramble to the Zoological
Gardens, so rural and attractive with meadow and
stream, flowers and cottage, and swarming with animal
life. In an enclosure filled with various species of birds
there was a very curious one, that stretched its neck to
an incredible length. It bore so striking and droll a
resemblance to an individual of our acquaintance, that
we laughed immoderately; and, indeed, for some moments after witnessing the sight, our spirits were made
as "buoyant as the wild-goose feather." The idea that
human beings can borrow something from the brute-
kind is not erroneous, for, in the monkey quarter, it would
be an easy matter to shake hands with a brother or sister. If the reader should have any doubt on the subject, a glimpse at these wonderfully intelligent faces and
cunning tricks would soon dispel it. These monkeys
are familiarly kind, too, and will almost talk, but are
inimical to spectacles; and, on one occasion, a poor man,
who was beguiled too near, had his glasses torn from his
eyes, his face terribly scratched, and scarcely a hair
left on his head. At these gardens everything is mirthful and active, except the wild beasts, who are remarka-
bly sluggish and sleepy until the *feeder* comes along.
The big, clumsy elephant, who is allowed some freedom,
and who tramped like a giant right into our path, mak-

ing us betake ourselves to the greensward, proved a serviceable animal, carrying a lively little party on his back. Their high seats were evidently very much liked, judging from the exulting manner in which they looked down upon us in our lowly condition. When Elephant & Co. were out of the path, we continued our walk, and soon caught sight of a little green canopy, displaying a huge sign, that said *Ginger-pop*—pray what is that?—ginger-bread, and pies in which there was no ginger, but some apple-sauce—a temptation which, although not promising the choicest kind of food, was not to be resisted in our hungry state. *   *   *   *   *

A quiet reverie brings the comforting reflection that we have seen nearly the whole of London, during a short sojourn. Besides the places already noted down, others might be added to adorn the picture,—the royal palaces, Buckingham and St. James; the splendid mansions of the aristocracy; the stately club-houses, those great centres of literary, political, military and social life; the monuments commemorative of great men and events: of the latter, the most notable is that telling of the fiery scourge of 1666, which swept over a large section of the city in wild fury; and Temple Bar, associated with those days when traitors' heads were suspended there as gory ornaments. This gateway is the boundary of the city *proper*, and is always open, except on the very rare occasion of a sovereign's passing through it—a formality that is time-honored. The approach of the sovereign is announced by a herald; the gate is then opened, and the Lord Mayor issues forth and delivers up his sword, which is immediately returned to the municipal head. If places and landmarks, in granite and stone, are stamped enduringly upon our minds, so, also, is there preserved a recollection of what is more perishable—the life which pulses this vast metropolis, seen in the bustling masses that fill the marts, intently pursuing those magnet-stars, riches and power; in the luxurious aristocracy, who whirl by in magnificent coaches, on the fashionable squares; and in the many thousands, boasting of wealth without rank, that thread the great thoroughfares, Regent street and Piccadilly.   *   *   *   *   *

Midnight.—Our party, that had been somewhat scattered during the day, met by agreement, at Blanchard's, to dine, and in that comfortable, well-managed restaurant, soon forgot the skeleton dealings of "Charing Cross Hotel." Afterwards, we went to Haymarket Theatre, to see Sothern, who was not only *"A Hero of Romance,"* but one of the most worthy of the stage. Forgetting the requirements of etiquette, as regards dress for the theatre at this season, we wore our walking costumes, which were plain, indeed, when contrasted with the rich toilettes all around; *decolleté* dresses, elaborate coiffures, feathers, flowers and diamonds. One of our ladies thoughtlessly took her parasol, and another had carelessly dropped her gloves. Horror of horrors! What was to be done? Fortunately, a gentleman friend, more provident than most of his sex, had an extra pair in his pocket, and he kindly loaned them. Being very much engrossed in the performance, she was for some time blissfully ignorant that her hands looked as if they belonged to a giantess, who had shrunk away unawares. Sothern obtained a large amount of praise; and every one seemed bewitched by the heroine of the play, a beautiful blonde with golden, wavy tresses. The song of the reapers, returning from the labors of the day, still sounds in my ears, answering the sweet strain of music in my heart, leading me across the ocean to a cherished home.

On our return to the hotel, three of us, resisting fatigue awhile longer, repaired to the supper-room, and drank a farewell-bumper to the old world. Sitting near the window, viewing for the last time the flickering lights of London, and glancing down upon our tiny withered bouquets, their fragrance quite departed, we felt the potency of these lines:

> "Thus may we, as hours are flying,
> To their flight, our pleasures suit,
> Nor regret the blossoms dying,
> While we still may taste the fruit."

—And this fruit is *memory*, that saves the broken threads of the web Pleasure has woven for us abroad!

LIVERPOOL, *June* 19.—Here we are, at the Washington House, after an unpleasant journey, owing to the extreme heat of the day! We came out of the cars looking much like coal-miners, just as black and disgusting, —those insidious enemies, dust and cinders, having done such serious damage to the complexions of several of our blondes, that they declare a week's scrubbing will not relieve them of the ugly coating. A bustling aspect the Liverpool hotels present on the eve of the departure of an ocean-steamer—maids rushing frantically up and down, assigning rooms to the newly arrived travelers, and herculean porters piling up the luggage many feet high in the lower hall! Should robbers make an invasion to-night, what a splendid booty these trunks would make, filled as they are with valuable jewels, silks, laces, satins and trinkets, gathered by the fair Americans that are to sail with us on the Scotia! All this excitement brings the event of departure very closely to our minds, yet we are endeavoring to look upon it as heroically as possible. It cannot be denied that regret creeps in sadly as our farewell to Europe is whispered, still we are counting the loving hearts that long for our return, and our thoughts, in advance of the morrow, impatiently begin the voyage.

ROYAL MAIL STEAMSHIP SCOTIA.

June 22.—Out upon the vast ocean, with memory and love as precious cables to link us to the land we have left, and the one we seek. We who launched forth in this pet ship of the line, trusting to the chance of a pleasant voyage, had a damper thrown upon our hopes before leaving Queenstown—a heavy rain destroying all prospect of shore perigrinations. Only one lady besides myself was brave enough to visit the deck, to take a last view of the Emerald Isle. Wrapped in our water-proof cloaks, and standing under a mammoth umbrella, we heard loud voices in command—the Captain and his officers, who were covered from head to foot in yellow oil-cloth garments. Curious objects were they, and their

preparations for rough weather, together with the sudden
appearance of a few storm-birds, unnerved us not a little, suggestive, as they were, of disaster. It is well,
however, to exchange a gloomy scene for a bright one,
which is to be found in the saloon, where cheerful faces
are everywhere visible. Our company embraces much
talent, wealth, beauty and distinction. Near Captain
Judkins, engaged in animated conversation, is the celebrated Charlotte Cushman, who has left a bright Italian
home for a visit to her own country, where she reigned
so long a brilliant star. Her great dramatic genius en-
wraps her with glory wherever she goes; and, to-day,
even as she stands among us in private life, I seem to
see the queenly character of Catherine, the proud and
remorseful Lady Macbeth, and the wild, weird Meg
Merriles. She is accompanied by her friend, Miss Steb-
bins, the sculpturess, whose face beams with intelligence
and amiability.   *   · *   *   *   *

June 30.—The worst phase of *mal de mer* has been
visited upon me; and oh! what should I have done
without the stewardess, a very *Nightingale,* in nursing
and attention; the lively, comforting presence of a Penn-
sylvania widow, as rich in kindly feeling as in worldly
treasure; and, that best diversion from ship-troubles, the
recountal of merry scenes and happy days abroad, by an
interesting lady, the wife of a United States naval officer. But thanks are now rife on all lips that we have
passed the dangers and discomforts of stormy weather,
icebergs and fogs; have steered up the bay, in splendid

rig, with the steady rays of sunshine in the blue sky and in our grateful hearts; and are safely anchored off Jersey City. Yet am I wrong in saying that all are equally happy, for, near me, stand several persons from my own city, who return with sad emotions. They have left dear ones sleeping in distant graves, under the soft Italian sky; and another grief still more poignant—the intelligence of which was received yesterday through the pilot, and held in close reserve by the passengers— is yet to be disclosed to a gentle wife and mother, who will look vainly for a meeting with her husband. His cup of misfortune was drunk to the dregs, and he passed from this world by a suicidal act. May such sorrow be tempered by heavenly comfort, and the severed ties be reunited on a brighter shore! For us who have nothing to mar our joy, there remains one precious thought, "Home again," and the expectancy of that sweet word, chanted by angels and sung by mortals—*Welcome!*

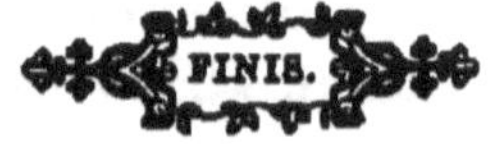

www.ingramcontent.com/pod-product-compliance
Lightning Source LLC
Chambersburg PA
CBHW051215120726
47905CB00004B/1135